*Her eyes skimmed down the length
of him…she couldn't help herself.*

"You're going to stop that, kitten," Damien murmured. "Because if you provoke me much more…"

Ariane knew he was going to catch her, but she was compelled to run anyway. She made it out of the bedroom, but he caught her from behind. She was spun and pressed up against the wall before she could make a sound.

He was raw sexuality, sheer physical power. Ariane knew she had no business allowing this. She didn't know him, she didn't like him…and gods, how she wanted him.

"Mmm, I love the way you smell," Damien murmured, his breath tickling her ear in the most delicious way. Only his hands, his fingers twined with hers as they held her captive against the wall, seemed capable of holding her up.

He drew back, brushing his nose against hers. "Now let's see how you taste."

D0974018

Praise for **KENDRA LEIGH CASTLE'S DARK DYNASTIES NOVELS**

Midnight Reckoning

"Castle demonstrates considerable skill in crafting a tale that offers readers a conflict-ridden forbidden love interlaced with political intrigue and betrayal...The author's world-building is intricate and cohesive...plenty of action...I like Castle's voice and look forward to reading more of her work." —USAToday.com

"4½ stars! Power acquisition and consolidation are driving the action in this exciting series as the vampires of the Cait-Sith bloodline strive to break free of their former masters. Intriguing characters add a well-rounded feel to this tale that is also packed with treachery and drama. Pick it up today!" —*RT Book Reviews*

"Absolutely a must read!...I love this new and exciting world that Kendra Leigh Castle has created...[She] is an extremely talented storyteller, and it is easy to fall into the world she creates and the characters she brings to life in her books...smooth, fast, and exciting...I can't wait to see what Castle has in store for us next!" —GoodReads.com

"Betrayal, forbidden desire, shattered dreams, and an unlikely romance come together to make this a not-to-be-missed read...I definitely want [to] visit Castle's Dark Dynasties world again soon...Paranormal romance, vampire, and shifter fans, even urban fantasy fans, will enjoy this one. Put it on your wish list today." —BittenByParanormalRomance.com

"The chemistry between Lyra and Jaden is absolutely sizzling, and when they finally give into their attraction, the sparks definitely fly...The blend of action, politics, and sensuality was completely breathtaking...Recommended for fans of forbidden romance, heartbreaking betrayal, and finding strength in the most unexpected places."

—Romanceaholic.com

"Twists and turns and plenty of action and drama...Ms. Castle once again wowed me with *Midnight Reckoning*, and I know I've found a new series to love." —SeducedByABook.com

Dark Awakening

"Kendra Leigh Castle has set the stage for a phenomenal new vampire series which will take the paranormal genre by storm. *Dark Awakening* has one of the most interesting and well-thought-out vampire hierarchies that I have encountered in a vampire novel. Vampire novels just don't get any better than this!" —FreshFiction.com

"Rising star Castle is sure to please with an exciting new series...Castle does a good job of laying out the bloodlines that distinguish her differing clans. Passion and loyalty collide as the hero is forced to reevaluate the choices that have driven his life." —*RT Book Reviews*

"5 stars! I'm so glad this is the beginning of a series... While the world-building is rich and layered, its complexities are seamlessly incorporated into the story and contribute to making it a satisfying read...Ty is everything I love in a hero...The secondary characters were fleshed-out and interesting. And frankly, I want more." —Red Hot Books

SHADOW
RISING

Also by Kendra Leigh Castle

Dark Awakening

Midnight Reckoning

SHADOW RISING

A Tale of the Dark Dynasties

KENDRA LEIGH CASTLE

FOREVER

NEW YORK   BOSTON

Dynasty illustrations by Franklin Daley III

Copyright © 2012 by Kendra Leigh Castle
Excerpt from *Immortal Craving* copyright © 2013 by Kendra Leigh Castle

Forever
Hachette Book Group
237 Park Avenue
New York, NY 10017

www.HachetteBookGroup.com

Printed in the United States of America

First Edition: July 2012
10 9 8 7 6 5 4 3 2 1

OPM

Forever is an imprint of Grand Central Publishing.
The Forever name and logo are trademarks of Hachette Book Group, Inc.

The Hachette Speakers Bureau provides a wide range of authors for speaking events. To find out more, go to www.hachettespeakersbureau.com or call (866) 376-6591.

The publisher is not responsible for websites (or their content) that are not owned by the publisher.

ATTENTION CORPORATIONS AND ORGANIZATIONS:
Most HACHETTE BOOK GROUP books are available at quantity discounts with bulk purchase for educational, business, or sales promotional use. For information, please call or write:

Special Markets Department, Hachette Book Group
237 Park Avenue, New York, NY 10017
Telephone: 1-800-222-6747 Fax: 1-800-477-5925

To my brother Kirk
It's been a joy watching you become
who you were always meant to be.
I'm so proud of you!

THE DARK DYNASTIES

Known Bloodlines of the United States

THE PTOLEMY

LEADER: Queen Arsinöe

ORIGIN: Ancient Egypt and the goddess Sekhmet

STRONGHOLDS: Cities of the Eastern US, concentrated in the Mid-Atlantic

ABILITIES: Lightning speed

THE CAIT SITH

LEADER: Lily-Quinn MacGillivray

ORIGIN: A Celtic line originating with the Fae

STRONGHOLDS: United with the reborn Lilim in the Northern United States

ABILITIES: Can take the form of a cat

THE DRACUL

LEADER: Vlad Dracul

ORIGIN: The goddess Nyx

STRONGHOLDS: Cities of the
Northern US and Chicago
(shared with the Empusae)

ABILITIES: Can take the form
of a bat

THE GRIGORI

LEADER: Sariel

ORIGIN: Unknown

STRONGHOLDS: The deserts of the
West

ABILITIES: Flight is rumored due to
their mark, but no proof

THE EMPUSAE

LEADER: Empusa

ORIGIN: The goddess Hecate

STRONGHOLDS: Southern United
States; Chicago (shared with the
Dracul)

ABILITIES: Can take the form of
smoke

THE REBORN LILIM

LEADER: Lily Quinn-MacGillivray

ORIGIN: Lilith, the first vampire, now merged with the blood of the Cait Sith

STRONGHOLDS: Northern United States

ABILITIES: Lethal bursts of psychic energy; can take the form of a cat

SHADOW
RISING

chapter ONE

A RIANE."

She stood at the floor-length window, staring out at the rolling ocean of sand that had been her home since before her memories began. Not a breath of wind moved the gossamer curtains that she'd drawn back, though she had opened the window wide in hopes that some air might clear her head.

No such luck. All she'd found was the crescent moon hanging above the same beautiful and barren landscape that she looked upon every night. Nothing changed here. Nothing except her. Not that the implications of what she was about to do didn't make her heart ache. But she had no choice.

Life eternal notwithstanding, this place would kill her, or at least the best part of her, if she stayed much longer.

"Ariane, please look at me."

With a soft sigh, Ariane turned away from the window and looked at the man who had entered the shadowed room. She had lit but a single candle, not wanting the harshness of the light, and it played over his concerned face, over features that were as hard and beautiful as chiseled stone.

Sariel. There was a time when she would have been honored by a visit from him. And to her chamber, no less. He had been the leader of her dynasty since it began, or so she understood, and his word among the Grigori was law. Ariane respected him, deeply. But Sariel was content with all the things that made her restless. He could accept that her dearest friend had vanished without a trace, where her every waking moment had become a nightmare of worry and dark imaginings. And she knew that while he cared, while some effort was being put into finding the missing Grigori, he didn't remotely understand what a loss Sam was to her.

"I appreciate your concern, Sariel. But I'm fine. I didn't expect to be chosen," Ariane said, hoping that she was concealing her bitterness well. To have been passed over was bad enough. But to have been pushed aside for Oren, to have seen the blaze of vicious triumph on her rival's face...it hurt in a way no wound ever had. And in her training, she'd been cut plenty.

Sariel approached, shutting the door behind him. To anyone else, even their own kind, Ariane knew he would have been incredibly intimidating. The men of the Grigori dynasty of vampires, particularly the ancient ones, all stood nearly seven feet tall, broad-chested and well muscled, with skin like pale marble. But in the dim light, he looked so like Sam that she could feel nothing but the same dull ache she had felt for a month now, ever since they'd all realized Sam was not simply traveling, but gone.

Sariel's face belonged on a statue carved by a Renaissance master, but his beauty, like all Grigoris' beauty, was cold. His white hair, the same shade as all ancient ones had, was an oddly attractive contrast to a youthful face. It fell to his shoulders with nary a wave to mar the gleam of it. His eyes glowed a deep and striking violet, a shade they all shared, in the dim light.

"I know you had your hopes up, Ariane," he said, his normally sonorous voice soft. "You don't have to pretend you didn't. If it helps, you were strongly considered. But the others felt that, ultimately, Oren was the better choice." He paused. "If Sammael can be found, he will be. I realize he is important to you, as he is to us all."

The better choice. Simply because she had not been handpicked by the elders, because the circumstances of her turning had been borne of emotion instead of reason. No matter how hard she worked, how lethal she became, she would be seen as a mistake. The weakest among them. And Oren, above all, had orchestrated her being shunned for it.

The Grigori were taught that hate was a wasted emotion. But for Oren, who excelled at the art of subtle humiliation, Ariane feared she felt something very close to it. And now he had bested her again, finally taking from her something she desperately wanted.

"Yes, Sam is important to all of us," Ariane said, trying to choose her words carefully as she turned back toward the window, the beckoning night. "But of everyone here, I am closest to him, Sariel. I think you know that. I don't understand why we're sending only one of our own to search for him when he could be hurt out there. He could be *dead*."

It was her greatest fear, and Sariel was as dismissive as

she'd expected him to be. He simply didn't give in to his emotions. She didn't really expect a vampire like Sariel to understand how much a simple friendship meant to her. He seemed above such things, beyond them. He was strong, unlike her; she was weakened by her attachments and her most private dreams. In those dreams, which she had never shared with a soul, she was happy, fulfilled, even loved—and far away from here.

A palace, however opulent, could still be a prison.

"Ariane," Sariel said, affecting the air of a parent lecturing a willful child, "your concern is admirable, but if Sammael is still alive, he shouldn't be difficult to find. We are adept at seeking as well as watching, as you know." He paused. "Tell me, little one, is this about my brother? Or is it about your desire to get beyond these walls?"

Anger roiled deep within her at his suggestion. Of course she wanted to get beyond these walls! But her own needs paled in comparison to Sam's... wherever he was.

Finally, she managed to speak, her voice steady only through the strongest effort.

"Sariel, I swear that I'm only concerned about Sam. But since you brought it up, you're obviously aware of how stifling my situation is. In all these hundreds of years, I've been out exactly once. *Once*, when I have worked harder than anyone to show my worth. Do you know how that feels?" She waved her hand before he could answer. "No, of course you don't. If you want to go out into the world, you go. But I..." She trailed off, wanting to make him understand how she felt about her life. "I can only sit here. Wander the grounds. Try to enjoy the little bits of life that the humans who are brought here carry with them before they're taken back."

"The palace is huge, as are the grounds," Sariel pointed out. "Everything you could want to do is here or could be brought here. We're not beholden to the same rules as the others. It's why this place is hidden, why we are hidden. You know that. The vampires accept us as their own, and it's important that they continue to do so. The less they know about us, the better."

"But we *are* vampires," Ariane snapped, exasperated by the same old conversation. "Aren't we? We don't walk in the day. We drink the blood of humans to survive. We are the *same*!"

"Yes and no," Sariel replied, his expression guarded. "We carry a responsibility the others do not. We are the oldest by far, though that, too, must stay hidden. Especially now, when things have begun to shift. We are watchers, *d'akara*. We do not interfere. Sammael understood this. The others understand this. But you..."

He trailed off, letting Ariane finish the thought herself. And how could she not? She'd heard the words enough times, even when she wasn't supposed to.

You're not ready. You'll never be ready. You're different.

"I may not have been chosen," Ariane said, trying to keep all anger from her voice, her face, "but that doesn't mean I'm incapable of carrying out our duties. The duties I have trained for alongside everyone else. I'm *ready*, Sariel."

She'd promised herself she wouldn't beg. And yet here she was again. Sariel's indulgent smile made her want to scream.

"Of course you are. One day soon, perhaps. Though, it isn't just up to me. Given the circumstances of your turning, there is concern about your ability to refrain from intervening."

"That was hundreds of years ago," Ariane interjected, a snap in her voice she couldn't cover. "I'm being punished because I was upset when I was turned?"

Sariel's eyes darkened. "*Upset* is the wrong word, as you well remember. A traumatic siring will linger, Ariane, sometimes forever. Do you really think you could stand by and watch what happened to you and your family? Even your sire could not and succumbed to weakness."

"My sire—"

Sariel held up a hand to stop her. "You already know I will not tell you who he is. He asked that the shame remain his own. It's best for both of you. For all of us."

Ariane stiffened, even as her stomach twisted into knots the way it always did when she had a conversation like this...and there had been many. She remembered so little of her siring, and only flashes of what had come before. Those brief glimpses of horror were bad enough. There had been blood, smoke, hideous laughter...beloved voices raised in tormented screams. Then strong arms, a hushed voice. Darkness.

Most of her mortal life remained a mystery to her. Her memories began in earnest at the weeks she'd spent confined to her chambers, weeping so long and hard that the tears had turned to blood. Weeping without truly knowing why. And there was no one to give her even a piece of her mortal past. Only the ancient ones knew who her sire was, and they kept their silence on the matter.

Sometimes she wondered if they'd killed him for what he'd done.

"We have all felt it, the desire to shape things to our

will instead of watching events unfold," Sariel lectured her, his tone soft and condescending in the way only an ancient one could manage. "But that is not our place. We must detach from instinct, leave our humanity behind us. Living as we do and trying to exist any other way is madness. Yet even now, Ariane, all these years later, I still see you struggle with what you were."

"But Sam said—"

"His name is Sammael, *d'akara*. Show his name the respect it deserves."

Ariane's mouth snapped shut at the steely command. It was worthless to argue with him, and she should have known better. He demanded respect, but he called her *d'akara*, "little one," as though she were a child. She was fast and strong. She could speak a multitude of languages, debate music and philosophy and art. She could fight more nimbly than most of her blood sisters and brothers. And she had learned these things for... what? To sit here and rot because she had *feelings*?

No. Not this time.

"Sammael, then," Ariane allowed, trying not to say it through gritted teeth. "He said it was important to remember how to feel for the mortals. To not just watch but to be able to understand. He's an ancient one too. Do you disagree?"

Sariel's expression shifted quickly from insincere warmth to genuine displeasure. "Sammael has an... unnatural affinity for the humans. Always has. I've indulged him, but humanity is like a troop of bellicose monkeys. Understanding them is simple enough. It was a defective design, I've always thought," he said with a small, cold smile.

Ariane never knew what to make of him when he said things like that. It was as if he had never been human, though more likely it had just been so long that he had no recollection of what it was like.

Sariel waved his hand dismissively. "In any case, Ariane, this is not an appropriate first mission for you. It's too delicate a situation, and time is of the essence. One day," he continued, stepping closer, his eyes glowing softly in a way that might almost be called warm, "I will make sure you get your chance to keep our watch. You have my word on this, *d'akara.*"

She stayed still, though his nearness had begun to make her uncomfortable. The visit itself was highly unusual. Sariel's interest in her well-being was even more so. She couldn't recall him ever paying much attention to her...though Sammael's disappearance, and her connection to him, seemed to have remedied that in spades. She should have enjoyed it. And yet somehow it provoked nothing but a faint revulsion.

Another sign she was finally ready to go.

As though he'd sensed the direction of her thoughts, Sariel murmured, "I have no idea why your beauty has escaped my notice for so long. All these centuries, and you and I have never truly spoken."

"That's true," Ariane agreed with a small nod, self-consciously tucking a lock of long, silvery blond hair behind her ear. Her hair was pale even for a Grigori, almost as silver as an ancient one's. She'd always thought it made her more of a spectacle than beautiful...but the way Sariel's eyes tracked the motion of her hand through her hair made her wonder if she'd been wrong about her appeal among her own kind.

She hoped he didn't reach for her. What would she do then? Running was always an option, but a very poor one when your pursuer was a seven-foot-tall vampire.

To her relief, Sariel seemed to realize that his sudden attentions had surprised her. He came no closer, but the keen interest in his gaze was unmistakable.

"I would like to see you, Ariane. To spend some time with you. Tomorrow night, perhaps? We should get to know one another, after all this time."

It was all she could do not to sob with relief. "Of course," she replied, and even managed a small, demure smile. "I would enjoy that."

It seemed to satisfy Sariel, and he nodded.

"Good. I'll send someone for you then." He turned and strode to the door, but stopped just before leaving, looking back at her. "Don't worry about Sammael, *d'akara*. If he lives, he'll be found, and he would not be so easily killed. Trust me . . . I've known him a great deal longer than you have."

Ariane nodded. "Then I'll just keep hoping for the best," she said.

When the door shut and Sariel was finally gone, she expelled a long, shaky breath, her legs going wobbly. She bent at the waist, placing her hands on her knees and breathing deeply, trying to regain her balance. The visit had rattled her, even more than she'd thought. Why had he really come? Was he worried that she might do exactly what she was planning? And if he was, had he seen that he was right?

She didn't think so. Whatever Sariel had come looking for, whatever he had seen, nothing had changed. For once she had a choice, and she chose to act. It was terrifying, yes.

But Ariane had faith it would also be freeing.

When she thought enough time had passed, Ariane moved to the bed and pulled a small beaded satchel from beneath the mattress. In it was the handful of things that held any importance for her. A sorry commentary on a life that had lasted so long and yet meant so little to anyone. She slung the long, thin strap of the satchel across her body, then moved to the window, her diaphanous skirt swirling gracefully about her legs.

She flipped a small latch, and the two panes of glass swung outward, revealing a gateway to the night. Ariane paused for only a moment, steeling herself. She had no desire to look back, to take in the pretty room that had been her safe haven for so long. It would be too easy to lose her nerve, and she would need all of that and more if she really wanted to find her friend. Not to mention evading her own capture. The Grigori did not take kindly to deserters. If she ever returned here, she doubted Sariel would be inviting her to his chambers again.

Not in the short space of time before she vanished forever.

No. That isn't going to happen. I can do this. And if finding Sam doesn't sway them, then I'll stay gone and stay on my own. Make a real life. Somehow.

Reassured, Ariane stepped onto the slim window ledge, glad that her room faced the desert and not the courtyard. Her only witness was the moon. She closed her eyes, breathed deeply, and summoned the gift that she had so rarely been able to use. She felt them rise from her back, sliding through her flesh as easily as water flowing from a stream. Her wings.

Ariane extended them, allowing herself only a moment

to turn her head and admire the way they shimmered in blues, lavenders, silvers—twilight colors. And gods but it felt good to free them, to free this part of herself. She lifted her hands to her sides, like a child balancing on a beam or a dancer poised to begin.

Then she leaped into the darkness and, in a flutter of wings, was gone.

chapter **TWO**

DAMIEN TREMAINE LEANED A HIP against the Master Shade's desk, made a show of examining the snifter of brandy in his hand for a moment longer, and then cocked an eyebrow at the man who'd been his employer for a good two hundred years now.

"A Grigori," he repeated, knowing he hadn't misheard his boss and wondering exactly how that could be.

Drake nodded, and the look on his face indicated he wasn't really in the mood for Damien's pithy commentary this evening. Which was a pity, since of all the things people said he was full of, pithy commentary was one of the few he could admit to and enjoy.

"Yes, a Grigori. And before you start bitching about how creepy they are, I'd like to reiterate that this is an opportunity I've been waiting for since I started this operation."

Damien snorted. "Mmm. A thousand years without a single request from their dynasty for spying, killing, or general dirty work. That's a hell of a snub. Why do you want to bother with them again? And for the record, yes, I do think they're creepy. Bloody big buggers too. The combination isn't one I fancy getting involved with. Can you imagine what their women look like? If they even have women. Or maybe some of the ones wandering around *are* women, and you just can't tell."

He grimaced at the thought, then downed half the brandy in a single swallow. It wasn't nearly as satisfying as a pint of O-negative would have been, but he did enjoy the taste, and the memories. Well, some of the memories.

"Why do you always feed me the shit brandy and think I won't notice, Drake?"

"You're wrong. I'm well aware you'll notice, Damien. And your reaction never ceases to amuse me. Now, to answer your question, new avenues of business are always good. And you, of all people, should appreciate that, since the fact that you opened one saved your ass not too long ago."

Damien gave Drake a humorless smirk and then tossed back the rest of the brandy, figuring he might as well enjoy the buzz if he couldn't enjoy the flavor. Gods knew the pleasure of his own little triumph had long since worn off, which was unfortunate as hell. But that was what happened when you lived on adrenaline. Each rush was somehow inferior to the last and became exponentially shorter.

The emotional numbness he had grown to feel between jobs was a strange blessing, but he had come to appreciate it.

Alistair Drake watched him from behind his monstrosity of a desk with eyes so midnight blue they were nearly black. His long fingers were folded in front of him, his sharp-featured face betraying no emotion other than the sort of low-level annoyance the man always seemed to exhibit. In his charcoal-gray suit, Drake could have passed for a young executive, with his eternal air of deadly seriousness indicating he held a position of some power.

One would never have guessed he was a master thief and assassin, and the head of a tightly run network of purveyors of exactly the same sort of work he himself had long plied as a trade. A powerful vampire indeed. A man to be feared.

Or he would have been, if Damien hadn't ceased to be afraid of anything. One had to care about the future to be afraid, and he'd learned long ago to live in the moment. There was little worth worrying over in the long term, especially now that he looked to be gainfully employed for whatever remained of his increasingly long life. Apparently there was a lot to be said for helping the heiress to a long-dead vampire dynasty...even if his aid hadn't been given entirely willingly. And to his surprise, he'd actually come to enjoy the vampires he'd met and reconnected with through Lily MacGillivray, ruler of the reborn Lilim.

Of course, it hadn't hurt his standing with Drake that these friends were all very powerful vampires—Vlad Dracul; Ty MacGillivray, Lily's husband; Jaden, who'd gotten himself involved with a bunch of werewolves and managed to work it to his and the Lilim's advantage. The wolves of the Thorn didn't seem a bad sort, if you could get past the doggy smell.

"So are you going to take the job or not, Damien?" Drake said, leaning back slightly, his entire affect one of cool disinterest. It was an act, Damien knew, and a good one. But they'd known one another too long. Drake needed the best for a delicate job like this. And despite the missteps that had led to his involvement with the Lilim, Damien was still considered such.

Damien sighed, put his glass down on one of the many stacks of paper covering the expansive desk, and gave a careless shrug.

"Might as well. It'll be interesting, if nothing else."

Drake's lips quirked. "Yes, when you find the mark, you can make him answer all your burning questions about Grigori women." He picked up a slim folder in front of him and handed it to Damien. Curious, Damien opened it and skimmed the single sheet of paper within. Clipped to it was a 4 x 5 photograph of three humans smiling in a crowd. Behind them, circled in white in case the person looking at the photo was blind, was a white-haired giant making his way through the sea of people. The Grigori in the shot was only in profile, but Damien figured he'd be easy enough to recognize—it wasn't as though one ran across these oddities of the vampire world all the time.

Damien looked up and met Drake's inscrutable gaze. "This isn't much to go on. The leadership wants this Sammael found, but they don't want it known they're looking for him. They don't want me to touch him, if possible. I'm to call them the instant he's discovered, and they suggest"—he paused, rechecking the instructions—"some very interesting methods of restraining him should I need to. This is going to take a little shopping to find these materials, but beyond that, this looks like average bounty hunter type work."

"Despite the odd customers, it is," Drake replied.

"Except that the information we'll get out of this is worth a great deal. Look, we already know what it takes to shut one of these giants down. And I have a feeling there's a lot more. This is only cut-and-dried on the surface."

Damien nodded. "Obviously. They wouldn't have come to us otherwise. I'll keep my eyes and ears open." He grinned. "And I'll hope like hell I don't have to go head-to-head with this Sammael. I'd rather not give him a chance to crush me—you know the stories about what they can do."

"After seeing the one who walked in here asking about the contract, I believe those stories," Drake said. "It's one thing to see a Grigori from a distance. But gods, they're big bastards close up. Never smile either. This one had eyes like a serial killer, except that they were purple."

"Oh, you'd hire one in a heartbeat if you could find one desperate enough to come to you," Damien scoffed, and Drake chuckled.

"Damn right I would. He wouldn't even have to sneak around to get the job done. Who's going to say no to a vamp who looks like he might rip your limbs off for fun?"

"So speaking of bounty hunting," Damien said, turning the subject to one of his favorite matters, "what *is* the bounty? And more importantly, what's my cut?"

Drake's eyes lit up. This was, Damien knew, one of his favorite subjects as well. It was one of the reasons the two of them got on fairly well, despite some glaring personality differences.

"Oh, you'll like this. If you succeed, you get something of your very own. And before you start gloating, I get one just like it, only a bit bigger. He left both here... for incentive." Drake leaned over to remove something from a desk drawer, and then deposited a diamond the size of a Grigori's fist in the middle of the desk.

Damien's eyes widened. "Holy hell. They do want this done right."

"Have a look," Drake said. "But drop it on the floor and I'll kick your head in."

Gingerly, Damien picked up the polished and cut diamond, feeling the weight of it. Every facet danced with light, as the stone was as clear as water. It was a moment before Damien realized that its light was coming from within it, and that it was casting rippling patterns on the walls and ceiling as though it were actually made of water.

"What is this thing?"

"This Titus tells me it's a piece of something called the Star of Atlantis."

Damien's eyebrows lifted. He'd heard and seen plenty of stranger things, but jewels from lost cities weren't an area of his expertise. "Oh? And you believe it?"

"A diamond's a diamond." Drake shrugged. "They can name it whatever they want. But as you can see, it's not exactly a regular diamond. You know what something like this is worth normally—hell of a lot more with that extra something thrown in."

Damien looked into the stone, watching the light dance. He felt a strange sense of calm steal over him, a soothing sensation of floating, drifting. For a moment, all the trappings of his life were revealed as meaningless and were replaced with the simple truth, the incredible beauty, of lights in the water.

He had to have it.

"Is there anything else I need to know? I'd like to get started."

Drake held out his hand, a knowing smile on his face, and Damien reluctantly parted with the stone. He watched it, feeling a tug of longing as it vanished back into its drawer. Peace, contentment—two things he had longed for in his heart of hearts for many years before giving up on ever finding them. And yet it seemed that they could come from something so simple, so extravagant, as an ancient bit of stone. Who knew?

Damien shifted uncomfortably, trying to push aside this new hunger. He didn't like to want things too much. Whenever he'd really wanted something, it had gone to shit in a hurry. It was how he'd ended up a vampire in the first place.

"You'll find a list of places to search on the sheet," Drake said, "as well as some potential contacts. Titus felt you would be more successful at getting information out of these individuals than any of them would."

Surprise flooded him, another emotion he wasn't used to feeling. "He actually *asked* for me?"

Drake nodded. "Specifically. I did warn him you were an awful pain in the ass, but he insisted. They do seem to keep their eyes on things."

"Watchers," Damien said, his lip curling even though his vanity was pleasantly flattered. "Some call them that. It's creepy, Drake. I mean it."

"Yeah, well, they're rich and creepy. We deal with plenty of that, and more. You'll manage. Now go on, I know it'll take you hours to pack."

Damien smirked, gave a little bow. "At your service, as always, my lord."

Drake rolled his eyes. "Spare me the noble rogue routine, Damien. I'll bet most of your ancestors were beheaded by the rabble, if they were anything like you."

"Maybe a few," Damien replied, then turned to go. Drake knew him too well. It really was going to take him hours to pack. He liked to be prepared for any eventuality, and a love of dressing well had always been one of his weaknesses. Hadn't his father railed at him for running up ridiculous debts at the tailor's? And at the club, of course. And at a number of other places around town. But when one was the "spare" bit of the old adage "heir and a spare," Damien had always figured one might as well be pretty and useless, rather than just useless. He had been utterly debauched, but in style.

And that was a long time ago, Damien thought, his smile fading as his hand closed around the doorknob. He was heir to as little now as he had been then. The Lord of Nothing. And he continued to behave accordingly. Damien grimaced at the sudden shift in mood. He really shouldn't drink; it always made him maudlin.

"Oh, one more thing," Drake said, prompting Damien to pause and look back at his employer. "I can't believe I nearly forgot, considering. There was something about a woman."

Damien did his best leer. "Oh? Do tell."

Drake laughed. "Nothing very promising, I'm afraid, but information you should have. Titus indicated that you may run across one of their women who has taken it upon herself to look for this Sammael personally."

"Huh. I didn't think the Grigori simply took it upon themselves to *do* anything."

"Yeah, well, he didn't sound happy about it. If you should meet her, he insists that you not help her, and that you let me know where you've sighted her. I'll relay the information."

"At which point things will end badly for the Grigori revolutionary," Damien said. "Got it. Hopefully I'll be able to tell her apart from a male Grigori. If I can, we're golden. I don't work well with others anyway."

"Don't I know it." Drake waved him off, his attention returning to the piles of work before him, folders full of jobs, dossiers on his own men and women. "Go on. Make nefarious plans. Agonize over wardrobe choices. Whatever you do to get ready. And keep me posted this time, damn it."

"Don't I always?"

"No."

Damien tossed an arrogant wave over one shoulder and let himself out, happy to leave Drake to the tedium of paperwork. The adrenaline had begun to flow again, provoked by the promise of a new adventure. For all that had happened in his life—in both of his lives—he'd never quite lost the simple joy of the hunt. And if there was the potential for feminine distraction? Even better, though he seriously doubted this Grigori interloper would interest him. Still, pure curiosity had him anticipating meeting her... and besting her.

Yes, Damien thought with a predatory smile, it was high time he got back to work.

chapter THREE

SHE HAD BEEN in the world a month.

It was hard to believe sometimes, Ariane thought as she scanned the dimly lit club, searching for a familiar face and sipping at her chocolate martini. There were nights when this all still seemed like a dream. And then there were other nights, like tonight, when it was her old life that was hard to believe in. Out here, everything was busy, bright, vibrant…*alive*. It made the Grigori compound seem dead and airless by comparison.

Pity, then, that this world she was so fascinated by continued to be so hard for her to live in. But she would keep trying. And at some point, hopefully soon, she would be able to stop second-guessing her every step, action, word. She would belong here. Because even if she found Sam, Ariane already knew she was never going back.

Conversation ebbed and flowed around her, and thankfully no one seemed very interested in the small, dark-haired woman perched on a stool at the bar. She reached up to surreptitiously adjust her wig, which was itchy and sweaty and completely uncomfortable. It was also necessary. Ariane had a fleeting and wonderful vision of taking it off later and giving her poor head a good scratch. She'd known her coloring and looks were unusual. What she hadn't realized was that in the human world, her idea of "unusual" was actually "unheard of." She didn't blend in. Not even among vampires, who she'd quickly realized didn't exactly welcome her presence. Was it because her bloodline kept so much to themselves? Were they considered snobs? Ariane had no idea, and no one else seemed inclined to tell her. They were too busy giving her a wide berth. It was just another reason to be appalled at how isolated she'd been. And after a month away from home, she had found plenty of reasons. She wanted to drink in everything, experience everything. But so far, most of what she'd done was simply watch. Even the vampires were full of a life and emotion that was far beyond anything she'd experienced in her long years in the desert.

Could she become like them? In time, maybe. If they could accept her. In time...

Ariane took another sip of her drink, enjoying both the chocolate flavor and the mild buzz she was getting. Actually, she was enjoying the city itself, as much as she could given the circumstances. Charlotte, North Carolina, was the last place Sam had been seen—that much she'd gleaned from Sariel before he'd turned her down for the mission to find him—so this was where she'd headed. Thus far, she hadn't found out anything to make her leave. Actually, she hadn't found out much of anything at all. And that was a problem. Hopefully tonight would change that, if the kind Empusa she'd met the other evening had been telling the truth. If so, there was a man who frequented this place who might be able to help her.

She certainly hoped so. The city might be lovely, but she wasn't here for a vacation. Sam was out there somewhere; she knew it. And she needed to catch a break, because the longer he stayed gone, the greater the chance that he wasn't coming back.

The lights in the cocktail lounge cast a dim blue glow over the expanse of mahogany bar. A jazz trio filled the space with a warm, down-tempo tune from a raised platform at the other end of the room, and people chatted at the bar, at high, skinny tables scattered about the space, and in large, comfortable booths lining the walls. Waitresses and waiters glided through every few minutes, dressed smartly in black. Ariane watched them all, seeing not a single vampire. But she was patient. And finally, about ten-thirty, one appeared.

Ariane had just ordered another drink to nurse when, from the corner of her eye, she saw movement by the door. She turned her head, curious, and at this point fairly certain that the man she sought wasn't going to show. But instead of another couple or a knot of young mortals just starting their evening, she saw ... him.

He strode in as though he owned the place, moving with predatory grace. Ariane took in the broad shoulders, the sandy hair spiked up a bit in the front, the pressed jeans and well-cut sport coat, worn over an open-collared white button-down shirt. Everything about him marked him as the type she was growing used to seeing, a young blueblood with old money—everything except for the subtle signs only another vampire would pick up on when recognizing one of their own. He was just a little too pale, a little too graceful...and more than a little too beautiful to be mortal. When he turned his head to look at the jazz trio, Ariane let her eyes skim over his profile, enjoying the view.

Of all the new pleasures she'd discovered outside the desert, watching the seemingly endless variety of male vampires was one of her favorites. As she'd so often been reminded, the Grigori wanted only warriors. She was used to big, muscular men who would have looked right at home swinging a sword or an axe. She'd never realized that it was only the Grigori who had such a narrow preference in type. This man was more how she might have envisioned the handsome princes in the fairy tales she sometimes read. Then his cool blue eyes, which had been scanning the room, settled on Ariane, and she realized something else about this particular vampire: he was dangerous.

In the instant their gazes met, she saw nothing but cold calculation. He was looking for something or someone, and it wasn't her. All the lovely warmth she'd experienced upon sighting him vanished...and yet she still couldn't look away.

Neither, it seemed, could he. His eyes darted away and then returned, catching and holding her gaze. Ariane didn't know why she kept staring back. She'd known right away that this wasn't the man she was looking for, who'd been described to her as slight and dark-haired. Another random vampire wasn't going to do her any good, especially not one who looked as though he'd just as soon shove a dagger through your neck as speak to you. But something compelled her. And as she watched one of his slim brows arch, giving him a quizzical look that did little to soften her initial impression of him, those frigid eyes seemed to warm just a little.

She felt her cheeks flush and, utterly disconcerted by her reaction, turned her head away. She frowned at her drink, taking in a deep breath. She might be sheltered, but she was smarter than this. Her body's needs had no place in what she was doing here. Gods knew she'd put them off for this long. What was a few months, even years more?

The thought was suddenly, painfully depressing.

She was about to down the rest of her martini to console herself when a warm, sensual voice sounded very close to her ear, accompanied by a faint tickle of breath that had every nerve ending in her body vibrating in anticipation of the lightest touch.

Dangerous. Oh yes, he was. And Ariane wondered just how hard his kind of danger was going to be to resist.

Damien walked into Shades of Blue with the intention of finding Thomas Manon, getting the man to buy him a drink, throttling some information out of him if necessary, and then finding a willing woman to blow off some steam with for whatever was left of the night.

Unfortunately, and in keeping with Damien's recent run of bad luck, Manon was nowhere to be seen. Instead, a quick scan of the room revealed a bunch of insipid mortals, a mediocre jazz trio, and a great set of legs on a vamp perched at the bar. He might have admired them in passing and then kept looking for Manon, except for the fact that the vamp they belonged to was staring at him.

Not just staring at him either. It was more like she was imagining what it would be like to lap him up like a bowl of cream.

Maybe, Damien thought as she blushed prettily and turned away, tonight wouldn't wind up being a total bust if Manon decided not to show after all. He made his way over and leaned in, catching a seductive whiff of flowers and moonlight before he murmured his introduction.

"Evening, kitten. Care for some company? I can't bear to see such a lovely thing sitting all alone."

When she turned her head to look at him, Damien noticed two things immediately: one, what had seemed beautiful from across the room was absolutely exquisite up close, and two, she had eyes the color of Scottish heather. The combination could mean only one thing.

"Fuck me," he blurted. "*You're* the Grigori woman?"

Those amazing eyes narrowed. When she spoke, her voice was faintly musical, with a hint of an accent he couldn't place.

"I have no idea who you are or what you're talking about," she said stiffly. "Now if you'll excuse me, I'm… waiting for someone."

Then Damien watched, incredulous, as she turned her back, dismissing him without another word. He was used to all manner of poor treatment (and quite a bit of good, as well, depending on the nature of the job), but being summarily dismissed by some slip of a woman, particularly one who he already knew planned to interfere with his work, was not something he intended to tolerate.

Besides… he wanted another look at that face of hers.

A hard glare, with a bit of a bellicose mental push, sent the man occupying the stool next to her bolting away. Damien slid easily onto the warm stool with a smile, signaled the bartender, and ordered a dirty martini. He knew she knew he was there. Her discomfort was palpable, and

Damien wasn't ashamed to enjoy it. He'd learned long ago that being noticed was far better than being overlooked, no matter how you got the attention.

Finally, just as the bartender set down the drink in front of Damien, she spoke again. Her tone was clipped.

"Why are you still here?" she asked. "I believe I told you I'm busy, and I'm not interested in your advances. Please leave me alone."

Her speech was a little awkward and formal, a bit like the couple of male Grigori he'd run into over the years. He hadn't found them nearly as charming, though. Intrigued, he decided to play with her to see what more he could discover. "Ah, you may not want my company, but you don't have much choice in the matter right now. Best to try and enjoy it. After all, it could be worse. I could just get up, walk away, and call in the cavalry. They want you back, and they're looking for you. I'm in a position to know, being a Shade." He tilted his head, saw her shoulders stiffen, and smiled. Being a cat-shifter had earned him no love in his long life, but becoming a Shade had at least gotten him some healthy respect.

"By the way," he continued conversationally when she said nothing, "is that a *wig* you're wearing? It's bloody horrible."

As a method of getting her to look at him again, the combination of a thinly veiled threat and an insult worked like a charm. As a way of endearing himself to her, not so much. Still, Damien felt another fascinating punch of desire as he got to take in the Grigori woman's face up close. She jerked her head to the side to glare at him, those brilliant amethyst eyes reflecting both anger and fear. Damien ignored both for the time being, allowing himself to peruse her delicate features: the aquiline nose with a stubborn little point at the tip, the pink rosebud lips, finely arched brows, and long, dark lashes. Her face was a perfect oval, set off by high cheekbones, and the emotions it reflected were as transparent as glass.

In some odd way, Damien found her reaction to him refreshing. In his line of work, honesty, in any form, was a novelty.

"I don't know what you're talking about, but if you won't leave, then I will." She started to rise, but Damien's hand shot out to catch her arm, squeezing just enough to make it uncomfortable.

He leaned in so that only she could hear him. "I don't think so, love. Fortunately for you, I'm in a giving mood this evening. Entertain me for a bit and I may decide to let you go . . . for now. What do you say?"

Damien watched her go through outrage, uncertainty, and finally a cautious sort of resignation. Such a face, he thought wonderingly. She must be a terrible liar. And that had to be a problem for her, since who could help but look at her all the time? What else had he ever seen that was quite so worth looking at?

It was an unbidden thought, and disturbing. Damien brushed it aside and concentrated on the matter at hand. He'd seen plenty worth looking at, he reminded himself firmly. Particularly in the female department. And women like this, obvious innocents, had never been his cup of tea. Too much damned work for too little payoff.

Slowly, the tension beneath his hand eased, and the woman sank back down onto her stool. Damien released her reluctantly. His hand tingled where he'd touched her. For a moment, her awkwardness vanished, and the woman looking back at him was every bit as cold and ancient as her dynasty mark proclaimed her to be.

He wondered fleetingly if playing with a Grigori this way was wise, then brushed it aside. He'd lived for centuries doing just as he liked, and it had served him well enough. Why stop now?

"I'll stay. For now. But I'm not going to entertain you...cat." Her gaze dropped to the concealed top of Damien's right collarbone. There, beneath his shirt, was the mark of his bloodline, a trio of entwined black cats fashioned into a Celtic circle. It branded him as Cait Sith, a cat-shifter.

And without looking at it, she shouldn't have been able to tell so quickly.

"How did you know?" Damien asked.

The woman shrugged, a dainty lift of shoulders exposed by the sleeveless little black dress she wore. The movement made him look below her neck, which he instantly knew he shouldn't have done. He could stay distracted for weeks by the wonders showcased by that dress. With some effort, he dragged his eyes back up to meet hers.

"I'm good at indentifying who's who," she said, her tone defensive. "I studied."

"Really. And what identified me?"

She turned her head to glare into her drink. "Does it matter? You're just going to make fun of me, whatever I say."

The accusation startled him...more because she was probably right. And for whatever reason, the knowledge bothered him.

"I won't. I'm genuinely curious."

She didn't even look at him. "I doubt that. You're just bored. Go away."

Damien watched her face, seeing the frustration likely borne of fumbling her way through modern vampire society without a lifeline for at least a couple of weeks, and something in him softened. He didn't bother to try and analyze it, but his voice sounded strange to his own ears as he sought to reassure her.

"I'm not leaving until you tell me. But I'm happy to drag this out if you'd rather."

She looked up at him through long, dark lashes with such world-weariness that he had to fight back the urge to pull her into his lap and nuzzle her. The idea had some merit, actually...but Damien was pretty sure that would just put them back at square one. The longer they looked at one another, the more Damien had the unnerving sensation that she was sizing him up, judging him by some measure he couldn't begin to guess at. The intensity of her focus on him was as pleasurable to Damien as a caress. To his shock, he had to swallow back an inadvertent purr. He didn't purr for anyone. *Anyone*. And certainly not for something as cheap as a little attention.

At last, she relented with a sigh. "It's your eyes, for one thing. The pupils do some interesting things in the light. They're very feline, if you look close enough. But mostly it was just the way you move. I'd read about it, but the words didn't really do you justice."

He lifted his brows, surprised by the simple honesty of her answer. "Oh?"

She nodded, obviously an eager student of a subject Damien was inclined to find ridiculously flattering. He didn't think any woman had ever remarked on the way he moved before...out of bed, that was.

"Yes," she said. "Very graceful, very sinuous. Very..."

She trailed off, and it seemed she'd been about to say a lot more than she'd intended. Damien watched her pale cheeks flush again.

"Well. It's unique anyway. So..." She looked a bit at a loss, grabbed the martini she'd been nursing, and took a large gulp. Then she looked at him over the rim of the glass, eyes glittering in the dim light, and Damien found himself momentarily lost again. All vampires were beautiful. It actually got boring after a while. But this one was damned near a work of art. Sculptors would have carved her likeness on temples; famed poets would have composed masterpieces extolling her beauty and then drank themselves to death over her. He could imagine it easily.

Except that she acted like she'd been locked in a closet for the last five hundred years.

The swig of alcohol seemed to bolster her a bit. Damien picked up the glass beside his elbow and sipped, intensely interested in what she might say next.

"Are you sure it's all right to talk about these things here?" she asked quietly. "Out in the open?"

Damien glanced around and smirked. "Relax, kitten. It's just us and the mortals, and mortals tend to be incredibly stupid as a general rule. They're not paying attention."

Her eyes swept the room, which was bustling with life. He was surprised by the regret he saw reflected in them.

"I don't know any mortals," she said.

"You're not missing anything, trust me," Damien said. "They're as wretched now as they ever were."

"I wouldn't know," she murmured, more to herself than to him, it seemed. Still, the comment was impossible to ignore, and raised even more questions about this woman when Damien thought he'd answered the only important one—whether Grigori women were anything like the men. Based on this one, he'd give that a resounding no.

"Let me guess," Damien said, playing with his glass. "You were raised in a convent, where your innocence was stolen by a vampire masquerading as a priest or monk or something."

She blinked and gave him a strange look. "No."

Damien slouched a little and frowned. That had been his best guess. Disheartened, he tried again. "Noblewoman in the Dark Ages tucked away by your father as leverage for an alliance? Kept from court to maintain your innocence, not to mention your maidenhead?"

Now she looked slightly scandalized. "*No*. Why does it—"

"Temple priestess?"

"No!" She said it sharply enough to turn a few heads in their direction. He watched her realize it, blow out an exasperated breath, and then lean in closer to speak so no one else could hear.

"Stop guessing. You're only getting more insulting and not any closer to being right. My past is none of your business."

"Damn it." Damien drummed his fingertips on the bar. "And you're *sure* you weren't a nun?"

She gave an irritated little growl that he found incredibly entertaining. Grigori or no, she was far easier to get a rise out of than any vamp he'd met. No wonder she'd taken off. Being the only interesting person in a sea of uptight and boring had to be crazy-making.

Though right now, he seemed to fall into that category for her as well.

"Why do you care? Why are you even still here?" she asked. "If you're not going to turn me in, I'd think a Shade would have better—well, maybe not better, but *other*—things to do."

His lips curved up into a smile. "I do, in fact. I'm looking for your missing blood brother, Sammael."

The news didn't go over well, if the angry flash of her fangs was any indication.

"You waste your time. We take care of our own. The Grigori don't need outside help."

Damien chuckled softly. "Don't you qualify too? You're not exactly authorized to be running around playing detective, are you?" He didn't wait for an answer. It was as plain as day on her lovely face. It surprised him. Grigori did not defect, they didn't disobey the leadership, and they didn't just get something in their heads and go act on it. It was hard to imagine this nervous and slightly awkward beauty being a "fight the power" type. Still, he was well aware that looks could be deceiving.

"No need to worry, kitten. If Sammael is out there to be found, I'll find him. The pay's too good to fail."

"Who's paying you to interfere? Another dynasty?"

Damien gave a short, sharp laugh. "Sariel, by way of some hulking lackey who was sent to work the deal."

Her mouth dropped open. "Impossible," she hissed when she'd collected herself enough to speak. "They sent Oren. Why would they need you?"

"That's easy. Because I'm the best," Damien replied, enjoying her outrage while he took another sip of his martini. "This Oren must be pretty worthless, since I haven't seen him. Oh, and before you accuse me of lying about all this"—he held up a finger when she opened her mouth to speak—"I've got a dossier of information provided by your leader, as well as some Atlantean diamond being dangled as a prize. Besides, how else would I have known about you?"

She didn't seem to have an answer for that. Her frown deepened, and her lips pursed ever so slightly. Damien was possessed of the sudden, intense urge to lean over, take her full bottom lip into his mouth, and suckle it. His body stirred in response. Damned if he wasn't getting hard for her already.

"A hired thug," she finally said. "I don't even know what to say. If the ancient ones needed more help, there were plenty of our own who would have answered the call." The disgust written so clearly across her face pricked at Damien's pride more sharply than it had any right to. It surprised him and, like most things that caught him off guard, sparked his temper.

"Like you?" Damien asked, letting his contempt show through. "Yes, I can see you've got it all under control. Your situational awareness is awe-inspiring. What *could* they have been thinking, leaving you behind?"

He knew the instant the words were out of his mouth that he shouldn't have said them. Years of working among thieves and killers had sharpened his tongue and short-ened his fuse, but none of his associates ever paid much attention. They were all like that. The Grigori woman, however, reacted as though he'd slapped her in the face. She inhaled sharply, sitting up straighter. And though she still wore her innocence like some invisible mantle, Damien saw he'd misjudged a bit about her spine.

There was more to this one than looking like some del-icate, ethereal flower. And he was busy royally screwing up any chance he might have had at getting his hands on her in any meaningful way. He was charming, damn it! She was supposed to notice!

Of course, she might have if his mouth hadn't gotten in the way.

She motioned to the bartender, who brought her a check that she glanced at quickly before slipping a few bills out of the slim black clutch resting on the bar. Damien watched, feeling an unfamiliar hunger when she managed a brilliant smile for the bartender, who all but melted in return. Damien's lips thinned. So she'd smile for a worthless mortal, but not for him...

She appeared to be collecting herself to say something, and when she finally turned her attention back to him, Damien saw he'd been right: There was absolutely nothing delicate about the wounded fury that blazed at him. There was plenty of power beneath the pretty trappings, too, easily seen now that her control had slipped just a little. The question was whether she really knew how to use it. He'd never met a vampire who'd seemed quite so innocent at first blush, so sheltered.

It was a puzzle he couldn't begin to figure out, and one he knew he'd be turning over in his mind long after she walked away from him...which she seemed in a hurry to do.

"You think you'll find Sam because they're paying you. But I know I'm going to find him, because I actually care." Her voice quivered slightly, but there was steel in her eyes.

Another first for him: strong emotion from a Grigori. Interesting.

"Kitten, I hate to tell you this, but caring doesn't

count for much. It tends to be more hindrance than help."
Damien heard the sound of regret in his own voice and
immediately tried to pull it back, lock that part of himself
back down. Sympathy, empathy…they had no place in
his life. In *any* vampire's life. He was telling her the truth,
even if she didn't want to hear it.

"Don't call me that. I'm not a kitten, and I'm not your
pet," she snapped. "It doesn't matter what you think about
it. I wouldn't expect a man like you to understand."

It stung him, another surprise, and an unpleasant
one. *A man like him?* What the hell was that supposed to
mean? Damien watched her rise, feeling a little like she'd
just slid a sharp blade between his shoulders. The pain
was just as sharp, and just as unexpected.

He caught her hand in his before he could think better of
it, rising to stand only inches from her. Her skin was cool
and silken, and Damien pulled her closer. She was surprised into compliance, and Damien used the momentary
advantage to move in, murmuring directly into her ear.

The desire that made him shiver at her nearness was
nonsensical. He knew it. But Damien could no more fight
the sudden attraction than he could just let her walk away.
And once again, he found himself using that gentle, unfamiliar tone.

"Wait," he said softly. "Don't go storming off. You…
surprise me. Grigori aren't exactly known for their deep
emotional attachment to one another, you know."

He could feel the tension thrumming through her, but
she made no move to break away from him. She turned
her head slightly to respond, and Damien knew that to an
outsider, the two of them looked like lovers, about to go
home and do unspeakable things to one another.

I wish, he thought. Instead, he now had the very sharp point of a small dagger biting insistently into his abdomen.

"You know nothing about my kind," she said, "and you underestimate me. Try and turn me in if you want, Mr...."

"Damien," he said, amused again at her formality. "Damien Tremaine. It's not 'Mr.' anything. And if you make me bleed on my new shirt, I'm going to be very put out."

"Damien, then," she continued. "You can try to turn me in, but they won't catch me. This is too important. I don't know what's going on, but I intend to find out... whether or not you try to get in my way."

"I believe you can count on that... *kitten*. And next time we meet, I'll be stealing that terrible wig."

She pulled back just enough for him to see her eyes flash angrily as she yanked her hand out of his. He caught just a glimpse of silver as she slipped the dagger back into... gods above and below, was that a *garter*?

"My name is Ariane, not *kitten*," she hissed. "You won't find me so amusing if our paths cross again. Good night."

With that warning, she spun on one sexy, spindly high heel and clipped away on those long legs of hers. Damien watched her go, hungrily taking in every tight little swish of her ass as she headed out the door. He wasn't alone either. There wasn't a man in the place who wasn't drooling into his lap over her.

Bemused and frustrated, Damien settled back onto the bar stool to finish his martini. Her scent lingered around him like a ghost. *Ariane*, he thought. A pretty little kitten with intriguingly sharp claws. He looked forward to "getting in her way," as she put it. She might want to avoid him, but he planned to show her just how tenacious he could be when he wanted something.

He wanted to win.

And right now, he wanted her.

chapter FOUR

SHE'D HOPED to sleep him off.

Two nights after her initial encounter with Damien Tremaine, Ariane finally had to admit it wasn't working. Between her fruitless search for Thomas Manon, who seemed to have dropped off the face of the earth, and restless dreams full of a slim, sandy-haired devil whose mouth she had an unholy fixation on, nothing was going the way it was supposed to. And she'd thought she'd planned for setbacks.

With a frustrated sigh, Ariane adjusted the wig on her head, then stepped back to take a good look at the picture she presented. A little severe, she decided, looking critically at the violet-eyed wraith staring back at her. She'd really prefer another dress like the one she'd borrowed the other night. The black leggings, black V-neck tunic, and black boots were supposedly stylish, but with her coloring and the wig from hell—and damn that obnoxious vamp for being right about it—she looked a little...pale. Still, the dark color kept her less noticeable. She needed to be able to blend in.

As though that was going to happen.

With an angry little huff of breath, Ariane dragged the hated wig off her head and threw it across the room. She felt an unexpected surge of pleasure. Sure, throwing things was childish, and she'd probably messed up the stupid thing beyond what she could repair, but...

Just getting angry and expressing it had felt *good*. It was a luxury she'd never before had.

"Enough," she muttered, deciding the wig was staying on the floor. Either she'd find a better one, or she'd just walk around *au naturel*. It wasn't like she'd been so successful at going incognito anyway.

A quiet knock at the door sounded just as she'd dug her fingers into her hair, freeing it from the tight coil she'd flattened against her head and sending the platinum locks tumbling around her shoulders.

"Ari? You in there?"

The husky voice was both familiar and welcome, spurring Ariane into action. She moved quickly across the small room to answer it. She opened the door a crack and peered out, her face brightening as soon as she saw the petite brunette waiting at the threshold.

"Elena! Come in!"

Elena Santiago, the vampire who ran this safe house for some other vampire called Strickland, one of the more successful lowblood power brokers in the city, lounged against the door frame. Her exotic beauty—waist-length waves of rich chocolate hair, café au lait skin, and curves that could stop traffic—was a convenient cover for a woman who was as tough as the claws she could extend

without warning. Ariane undid the heavy chain that provided a small—very small—barrier to anyone trying to
barge in uninvited. Even as inexperienced as she was, she
understood that the chain was more of a psychological
reassurance than anything. It wouldn't do a thing to slow
a determined vampire. Elena's eyes, a striking pale green
and decidedly feline, widened as the door opened the rest
of the way.

"Something wrong?"

Elena blinked and shook herself slightly. "No. No,
it's just…the hair. It caught me off guard. I guess I sort
of forgot that the wig was a wig…" She trailed off for
a moment, her eyes skimming over every pale wave.
"Damn. For a bloodline that's so big on keeping to itself,
the Grigori have an awful lot of 'look at me' going on."

Ariane shrugged, uncomfortable with the scrutiny. "It's
not on purpose. Believe me." She stepped aside to allow
Elena entrance.

Elena sauntered in, and Ariane watched her with a
mixture of pleasure and trepidation. The Cait Sith with
the sultry smile and the ferocious temper was already as
close a female friend as she'd had in her life…not that
that was saying much. Within days, she'd been simply
"Ari" to Elena, who shared random tidbits of gossip gathered from the ever-changing residents of the safe house
and was a veritable encyclopedia of tips to help Ariane
avoid getting killed whenever she walked out the door.

Ariane had a bad feeling this visit was going to involve
more lecture than gossip. Sure enough, as soon as she'd
shut the door, Elena spun on one heel to look at her with a
stern expression.

"Doesn't matter what you look like anyway. You

shouldn't be so friendly, Ari," Elena said. "I told you not to unlock anything until *after* you'd gotten a look at who's on the other side of the door. This building is full of sketchy vamps in hiding for one reason or another. See that window?" she asked, jerking her head in the direction of a single, small rectangle letting in the light and sound of the city beyond.

Ariane nodded.

"If one of them knocks on your door, use it."

Ariane fought back a smile despite her frustration. Gods, she must look helpless. It was something she could probably turn to her advantage, provided she could stop being so irritated by it.

"I can take care of myself, Elena," Ariane said.

Elena raised an eyebrow. "If you say so. You don't seem to know much about modern society. Or other vampires."

That rankled. "I know plenty about the other blood-lines! My not having been out much is a...separate issue."

To her surprise, Elena chuckled. "Touchy, touchy. Hey, look, I hope you *are* tougher than you look, Ari. The Grigori men are intimidating, but I've never seen one of their women before you. As for whatever knowledge you've got, what's written down is great to know, yeah. But dealing with vamps in person is a different story. You'll pick it up quickly enough...provided you stay alive."

That blunt assessment stunned Ariane into momentary silence as Elena surveyed the small, shabby room with those fabulous eyes of hers. Ariane looked around, unsure of what Elena was seeing or looking for. There was a single bed with threadbare linens, a battered dresser, and a nightstand that didn't remotely match it. The wood floors were scarred and bare. The window was a small relief from the dreariness of the room, but it looked out on nothing particularly inspiring. Ariane had learned that these safe houses were never in a good part of town. It made it easier to hide... and easier to feed.

Elena turned her attention back to Ariane with a light frown. "I get traveling light, but this is insane. You've been here two weeks, and it's like you're not even here. How long are you planning on staying? I've seen a lot since I've worked here, but this whole deal with you is weird."

Ariane stiffened at what felt like a rebuke. She liked Elena, as much as one could like a woman who held so much of herself back. That reserve was the product of harsh lessons learned early, Ariane expected. And she was under the impression that Elena liked her well enough. Enough to be treating her like a slightly slow younger sister, at least. But this was no friendly visit... that was rapidly becoming clear.

"I travel light because I need to. What's the problem, Elena?" She paused, watching the shadow of an emotion she was quickly becoming used to shimmer briefly across the other woman's fine features. Suddenly she knew. "You're throwing me out." It wasn't a question, just a flat statement of fact.

Elena's face was all the confirmation she needed.

"And am I allowed to ask why?"

A desolate sigh. "You're making the other vamps nervous, Ari. Truth? Having a Grigori here is lousy for business. You can't stay. I just got off the phone with Strickland. He won't turn you in... but he wants you gone before the sun rises." She sounded faintly pleading, her cool and confident mask slipping just enough to reveal the regret and guilt beneath. "It's not you specifically, babe. But it's hard to miss what you are. And that's the problem."

"I see," Ariane said stiffly. "I'll get my things. I thought you, of all people, would be immune to this fear people seem to have of my bloodline. I'm sorry to have been wrong."

She really was. Fascinating though the world was, finding an ally in it was proving to be an almost impossible task. It seemed the most genuine person she'd met was Damien. Not that he earned any points for being genuinely crass and intolerable.

Ariane frowned and turned away to get the few personal items she'd put in the dresser. The last thing she wanted to think about was the obnoxious cat-shifter. Especially because she couldn't seem to keep her mind off him for any length of time.

She heard Elena's heavy sigh. "Damn it. Just hang on a minute and hear me out, okay? It's not like that."

"Oh?" Ariane opened the top drawer but turned to look back at Elena standing there, distinctly uncomfortable, in the middle of the room. That, at least, gave her some small amount of satisfaction.

Elena expelled a long breath. "Ari. This is a safe house. The vamps here, mostly lowbloods, I might add, don't want to get noticed. And you . . . Jesus, babe, I know you're not from around here, but have you taken a good look in a mirror lately? And that's *before* you strap on that big ass sword you walked in here with."

Ariane cast a quick glance in the mirror that hung from a single nail above the dresser and saw nothing unusual. Her hair was messy. Her cheeks were slightly pink from embarrassment and anger. And the black tunic was getting burned at the first opportunity, wasted money be damned. She looked like a ghoul.

"I see only myself. Should I see more?"

Elena rolled her eyes. "You should see what everyone else does—a highblood! The hair, the eyes—"

"I'll put the wig back on." She paused. "And...I'll try to hide the sword on my way out." She disliked having to rely on the dagger, but it would have to suffice. These vampires all seemed disturbingly unarmed. Hadn't any of them trained in swordplay?

Elena winced. "Forget the wig, please. It's awful. I thought it was a dead animal in the corner when I first walked in."

Ariane's jaw tightened. "Fine. Since I've failed so miserably at blending in, I'll go stick out like a sore thumb elsewhere. You can go, Elena. I understand."

And on some level, beneath the hurt, she really did. Ariane was fairly sure Elena had enough problems just protecting *herself* in the night-to-night running of this place. Even if she was as capable a fighter as Ariane knew she must be, the woman had her hands full enough without harboring a Grigori. A *wanted* Grigori, if what Damien had said was true. Though she couldn't imagine they would focus on bringing her back so quickly.

Elena shifted her weight restlessly from one foot to the other. "Look, this isn't what I want, okay? I'm not used to tossing out vamps who mind their own business. But it's not my call."

"Mmm," Ariane murmured, neither agreeing nor disagreeing. She didn't trust herself to speak, didn't want to get into an argument she didn't stand a chance of winning. Instead, she focused on placing on the bed the scant articles of clothing she'd acquired, along with her satchel, and then removing a carefully folded black duffel bag from the single drawer of the nightstand. She quickly put everything in the bag, just managing to stuff her scimitar and sheath in, though it strained the fabric to its limits even with the hilt sticking out. She noted with a small, humorless smile that there was still plenty of room to spare. She missed her things... just as she missed the luxury of taking them for granted. Cash was precious now, and she didn't want to sell anything else she cared for.

Elena was still talking, the words coming out in a guilty rush. "I mean, I appreciate that you've tried to lie low. Maybe another safe house in Charlotte will take you. Strickland doesn't own them all. You're quiet. You don't make trouble. You even tried to cover that *hair.* But..."

"But I'm Grigori. Hated. Feared."

Elena's expression turned to shock. "No! No, Ari, it's not hate. Fear, yeah, but not hate. Not to mention envy, which can be dangerous. You are *beyond* slumming it here. Don't you get that?"

The packing was done, and Ariane turned, bag in hand, ready to go. She felt a sick twist of her own fear in the pit of her stomach. Where would she go now? Another city, maybe, if she could find information that indicated Sam had left here before he'd vanished. Another safe house, like Elena said, if they would have her. But not for long. She could see already that it would never be for long. Her hunt for Sam seemed suddenly impossible. She'd been so naive...

But then, she could lay the blame for that squarely at

Sariel's feet. He and the other ancients who kept them all so isolated for reasons they refused to say. How could she have known?

"What do I need to do?" Ariane asked quietly. "How can I stop them from fearing me wherever else I go?"

Elena seemed surprised by the question. "I'm not sure you can. It's not just being a highblood, Ari. When a Grigori turns up, trouble—big trouble—is never far behind. I don't know if your people bring it, or if you just sense it and are drawn to it, but it doesn't make much difference. The end result is the same. A Grigori's presence always bodes ill."

Her denial was reflexive. "The Grigori do no harm."

But we watch it. And are forbidden to make it stop.

The rules that had decreed her an outcast from her first breath as a vampire had never seemed so ludicrous. And becoming aware of the general perception of her kind made her question what the ancients' true purpose was in the missions they devised. Ariane had always assumed the Grigori observed many facets of life when sent into the world. Did they really only bother with tragedy?

"Well, they might not *cause* harm, but they sure like staring at carnage," Elena replied. "It's creepy. You not knowing any of this is also creepy. What did they do, keep you locked in a closet for hundreds of years?"

Elena would never know how close to home those words hit.

"No. Though I'm beginning to think they might as well have." Ariane shook her head, pushing back against the resentment that wanted to bubble up more and more since she'd begun to discover all she'd been kept from those many centuries in the desert. "I know it doesn't matter, but I'm not here as a Watcher. I'm only looking for my friend. You believe what you like."

She felt deflated, and so incredibly tired as she started across the room toward the door. She would run into this again. Maybe hiding among humans would be easier, though it would pose plenty of its own problems. Things to consider...

Elena's hand shot out to catch her arm as she brushed past.

"Wait," she said as Ariane whipped her head to the side to glare at her.

It was a struggle to tamp down the flash of fury at being grabbed, restrained. *If she thinks to fight me, she's a fool...*

But Elena simply blew out an exasperated breath, and the hard set of her mouth softened. "Damn it. I had instructions to come in here and toss you out tonight, but you're making it tough." She rolled her dark eyes heavenward for a moment, then sighed again. "Okay. You need a place to stay. I've got one. Come on."

Ariane stared for a moment, not sure she'd heard right. "You're...offering me a place to stay? Away from here?"

An edge of annoyance crept into Elena's voice. "Yes, away from here. I may slum it for the job, but I've learned a few things from Strickland. I've got my fingers in more than one pie, and one of those pies is income property. *Nice* income property in vamp-safe areas. One tenant just vacated and headed for Borneo, so I've got an opening."

Ariane quickly ran through a mental inventory of what little she had left to bargain with. The reality deflated her considerably.

"I don't know how much I can pay," she began, but Elena cut her off with a curt wave of her hand.

"No. This is gratis. Throwing you out would feel like kicking a damned puppy, which isn't something I make a habit of doing. Anyway, I could stand to earn a little good karma once in a while. So come with me. Strickland's holed up in his office. He can get his ass out of it for a while and do something useful while we're busy. You'll either get lost or mugged if I don't take you there, no matter how well you think you can handle yourself."

Ariane hesitated for only the barest of instants. Going with Elena was a risk, yes. But staying here was a bigger one.

"All right. And th—"

"Don't," Elena interrupted, holding up a hand to fend off the gratitude. "Do not thank me. I may toss you out of the place before the week is out. Don't think I won't. You make a mess, you attract a news crew, you become a pain in my ass in any way, and out you go. Also, don't make the mistake of thinking this is permanent. It isn't. If you're staying in Charlotte, you have to get your feet under you sooner rather than later and find your own place here. Got it?"

Ariane fought back a smile at all the bluster and nodded. The words didn't matter. What mattered was what was beneath them. And so far, all she saw was a good-hearted vampiress who really, *really* didn't want anyone to know it. She could live with that.

Elena eyed the duffel bag. "That's it?"

"That's it."

"Only the one piece of freaky-ass medieval weaponry?"

Ariane hesitated. "The daggers are in my satchel. But they're small."

"Oh. Great."

"I'm wearing the larger ones."

Elena paused. "That's...scary."

"I do appreciate this, Elena."

Elena made a face, but it seemed more for show. "Don't let anyone else hear that. I'm supposed to be a hard-ass. That's why Strickland pays me to keep this place in order." Then she paused, looked intently at Ariane for a moment, and shook her head with a rueful smile. "Come on, Ari," she said. "I guess you need a friend. It might as well be me."

chapter FIVE

DAMIEN STOOD OVER the headless corpse of his only lead and cursed.

"Is he really dead?"

Damien whipped his head around at the sound of the voice, spoiling for a fight. It would help let off this head of steam that had been building for days with no outlet. His first look at the vampire who'd slunk into the waiting area, probably from a hiding place beneath his desk, left Damien completely unsurprised. Just another pretty, pampered highblood wannabe. A *pet*.

Damien gave a disgusted sniff and recognized the scent of fear he'd picked up on the moment he'd stepped into the office. Possibly a witness. Probably more trouble than he was worth. The latter impression was reinforced when the vamp gave a loud gulp.

"No," Damien said flatly. "No, no, do not puke here, no." He closed his eyes, threw his head back, and groaned at the first dry heave. "Have some self-respect, man!

You'll sick up a bunch of blood and make everything worse!"

"Is Mr. Manon really d-dead?" The newcomer tried again, sucking in far more air than he should have, evidence of the unabated nausea. His eyes darted quickly from the corpse to Damien to a series of hideous landscapes some tasteless idiot had hung on the wall and around again. It was as though he was afraid to let his eyes linger too long in one place, for fear of what they might see.

The weakness made Damien want to put a fist through the man's head, but that would have been counterproductive. For now, at least. What mattered was that his one possible link to Sammael the Grigori was now permanently incommunicado.

"Unless I'm missing something important, yes, the man is dead," Damien finally replied. "I think his head is over there behind the desk, if you need further proof. Are you finished being overly dramatic yet?"

"His *head*?" The vampire gave a pitiful moan, his eyes rolling.

"Ah, apparently not. Lovely." Damien turned away from the fledgling before he became responsible for ruining the rest of his evening and began to pace the waiting room, fists balled, claws already starting to extend. His appointment was shot. The only one who might have heard anything useful was a blithering, burping wreck, and now he was even further away from getting his hands on that diamond.

He might have had more patience if he'd been sleeping better. Who ever heard of a vampire having fucking sleeping problems?

There was the sound of stumbling, a whimper, and he saw a tottering figure out of the corner of his eye. Damien was on him in a flash, long years of assassin's instinct kicking in. He needed to get it together, now, before everything else went to hell. He could waste time brooding later.

Even though he did *not* brood, as a general rule. He knew enough angsty cat-shifters.

"Don't you dare pass out on me, you pathetic piece of shit. I'd do us all a favor and kill you now, but I need answers." Damien grabbed the wavering vampire by the collar, lifted him off the ground a few inches, and hissed into his face. "You heard something. You must have. I suggest you tell me what before I lose what small amount of patience I still have."

That stopped the moaning, but the vampire's eyes, when they locked with Damien's, were half wild with shock and fear. *Very* young, Damien decided. And whoever had made him ought to be ashamed for choosing one with such a weak constitution. He felt no pity.

"Please," the man said, his voice choked and quavering as his feet dangled above the floor. "Please don't hurt me. I didn't kill him. I didn't—"

Damien's fists tightened. "No, you didn't. You probably pass out from the sight of your own victims. Who met with Manon before me? What did you hear? I ... want ... *answers.*"

Absorbed in controlling his rapidly rising temper, Damien didn't hear the door open. All he knew was that one moment he could smell nothing but blood and sweat and fear, and the next, his senses were flooded with the scent of a rose garden in full bloom. An outraged voice, light and musical despite the fury, filled the room.

"Put him down!"

He knew that voice. Damien shuddered, a wave of intense and utterly unexpected pleasure rippling through him. The physical reaction stunned him. Stunned...and then disgusted. Damien let go of the vampire in his fists, letting him crumple into a heap on the ground. He hit the floor with a pitiful grunt.

It helped. A little.

"There. As you wished," Damien said smoothly. *Cold*, he reminded himself as he turned. *Get it together. She's unimportant, just a tasty little bit of trouble sticking her nose where it doesn't belong. If this is going to be a problem, just turn her in instead of screwing her; it hardly matters...*

He was full of advice for himself in the seconds before he turned to glare at her, the Grigori who'd been slinking through his dreams, bad wig and all, and leaving him hard and restless when he awoke. The advice, and the glare, died as soon as he got a look at the woman standing in the doorway.

He finally understood the wig, the dark clothes. She'd been hiding herself, and he couldn't help but think that was a good thing, at least for the sanity of the male population of Charlotte. More of Ariane walking around, and the men of the world would be reduced to groveling simpletons, besotted twits trotting along behind her and her ilk like dim-witted puppies.

He had the urge to do just that himself. Though if he had, he would have been in trouble. She was furious, if the violet fire in her eyes was any indication.

Ariane's eyes moved quickly from Damien to the vampire whimpering on the floor to the headless corpse. He could see the conclusion she jumped to almost immediately. It was hard to blame her, since this sort of job would normally have been very much in his wheelhouse, minus what he felt was incredible sloppiness. Still, he found himself launching a defense immediately.

"This isn't what you think."

"How do you know what I think, you...you miserable piece of shit?"

"I see you've learned some naughty words since we last met," Damien said smoothly, all the while darting quick glances around to see where he might dive to avoid whatever a Grigori might be able to do to him. He was sure Drake would be interested to know what that turned out to be, but he had no desire to be a guinea pig.

"I know a few more, if you'd like to hear them while I kill you," Ariane snapped. "How could you? I knew you were going to make trouble for me, but did you really have to kill the man after you got the information out of him? He was all I had to go on!"

There was a note of despair in her voice that tugged at him and brought on a wave of guilt, even though he hadn't done a thing. It was disconcerting.

"No, look...," he began, then hesitated. What was he going to do, *comfort* her? What did he care if a dead body hurt some Grigori busybody's feelings? Damien curled his lip.

Ariane reached behind her and drew her blade.

And not just any blade. It was the sort of sword no vampire had any business carrying. The kind of sword that said, "I am ancient and terrible and I don't have time to let those who annoy me live."

Ariane looked decidedly more than annoyed.

"Bloody hell, woman! I didn't do—"

Damien leaped out of the way just as the sharp and glowing edge of the ornate scimitar sliced mere centimeters from his head. He got an up-close look at the engraved blade and decided that was quite enough.

"*I* didn't kill him! Aren't you Grigori supposed to be analytical? Patient?" He gave another shout as the blade whizzed by his ear. Damien jumped and landed on one of the waiting room couches. "Hang *on*, will you?"

Ariane advanced on him, wielding her sword as though it were an extension of herself. Even in the way she held it, her skill was obvious.

"I don't believe you," she said. "You already threatened to turn me in. I'm being hunted. And now I have nothing left to lose. Do you have any idea what I risked coming here? What I gave up? What's going to happen to me now? Or worse, to Sam?"

Another slice, far too close before he leaped to a chair. It looked like his initial impression of her as a guileless, untried innocent had been a bit off base. Ariane certainly *looked* like a goddess of vengeance. Her hair tumbled in platinum waves around her shoulders, the light reflecting off of it so that it seemed to glow. The cupid's bow of her mouth was open, her lips pulled back over fangs that glittered in the light she gave off.

She swung the blade up and around her head, ready to bring it down in a final blow. Damien froze, his heart caught in his throat, arrested by the sight of her. In that moment, he wasn't sure whether he was desperately attracted to her or terrified out of his wits.

Coherent thought returned just in time for him to leap onto the desk that dominated one corner of the room.

Behind it, Manon's head gazed placidly up at him from dead, dull eyes. Damien glared at it before focusing again on Ariane, who sliced the scimitar through the air, once, twice, in graceful, dancing, deadly motions as she approached.

Damien put his hands up in front of him, knowing he had nowhere left to go. "Damn it, woman, calm down and hear me out before you decapitate me! Manon was dead when I got here! That's why What's-His-Face is sitting over there in a puddle of vampire vomit wetting himself!"

He heard a soft wail and just caught sight of the fledgling vampire crawling across the floor and trying to wedge himself into a corner, hands thrown over his head.

Ariane didn't even glance in the fledgling's direction. The force of her fury surprised him, but what surprised him even more was the pain and hopelessness in her eyes. Just that glimpse of her emotions resonated all the way through him, awakening feelings and memories long— and better—buried.

It made Damien wonder what had happened to her, that she was so different from her fellows.

Then the blade was at his throat, and he couldn't move. Only one thought was left: *Oh, hell.*

Damien swallowed hard, and the movement of his Adam's apple caused the blade to nick his skin. He felt a thin rivulet of blood snake its way down his neck. She'd caught him, and he'd never been caught. Not like this. The woman was nearly as fast as a Ptolemy, and far more skilled than he'd given her credit for. Her beauty, so delicate, was deceptive. It looked as though he'd made his final mistake in the "don't judge a book by its cover" department.

And yet . . . she hesitated.

The suspense didn't settle well with Damien. Not when he was bleeding, slowly but steadily, all over one of his favorite shirts.

"If you're going to kill me, just do it. I'm not going to beg. I'm hardly worth it."

Damien didn't realize what he'd said until he saw the surprise on Ariane's face. He clenched his jaw, his anger now directed fully at himself. He'd sounded like a typical, self-loathing lowblood. And he wasn't. He just didn't care all that much about staying alive. In his mind, that was an entirely different issue.

Of course, he also didn't much care for pain, so if the woman was going to do him in, Damien wished she'd just get it over with instead of staring at him with that odd look of . . . understanding.

"I don't believe you," she repeated, more softly now. The question Damien found himself asking, however, was which thing she didn't believe. That he hadn't killed Manon? Or more disturbingly, that he wasn't worth her time?

"It's a free country, last I checked," Damien replied with a shrug, making an effort to keep his own tone low and even. Ariane made him feel off balance. Uncertain. He needed to find some solid ground on which to deal with her, and soon.

"If you didn't kill Manon, who did?" she asked. The vicious, curved blade didn't move from his throat, where the sting of it slicing into his skin was rapidly becoming torment.

"Are you saying you believe me, after all that?"

Ariane didn't reply, and she didn't have to. Damien could see that she would stand there forever, if necessary, waiting for an answer. Of course, he'd be out of his mind by then from the slow-dripping blood, the insistent sting of the blade's edge.

"This is interesting," Damien said, wanting her to do something, anything to break the impasse. "I didn't figure you at all for the sadistic type, and yet here you are, watching me bleed. Does my blood turn you on, love?"

Violet eyes narrowed. "Don't call me that. It's very obvious you're only in love with yourself. Nothing about you interests me."

It stung, which was ridiculous. Her petty verbal slaps at him were the least of his worries. And yet everything about Ariane smacked of a challenge. Her rejection of him most of all.

Not interested? We'll see about that.

"Deadly *and* astute," Damien said, his voice a bored drawl. "Look, are you going to separate my head from my body, or are you going to lecture me? I had a governess growing up, you know. I don't need another. And you're even duller than she was."

He lashed out from habit, accustomed to being as cutting as he pleased without anyone thinking much of it. Ariane's flinch was barely noticeable, but Damien caught it . . . and immediately felt like a cad, something he thought himself incapable of feeling even before he'd been turned.

"I may be dull to you," Ariane said evenly, her chin tipping up just a little in defiance, "but I'm the one holding the sword. I'll decide what to do with it after you tell me what happened here."

"I discovered a headless corpse and a simpering moron moments before being attacked by a crazy vampiress with a ridiculously large sword."

The slight curve of her lips was cool. "Funny."

"I was being deadly serious," Damien snapped. "Though it's nice to know Grigori have a sense of humor."

"We don't."

"Well... shit." He bared his fangs at his own reflection in the gleaming blade. It wasn't supposed to end like this for him, done in by a beautiful woman immune to his charms over something he hadn't even done. For once.

Still she watched him silently, until he wanted to scream. Instead of that, however, he did something unthinkable: he told the truth.

"I arrived only a few minutes before you did," Damien said, his voice clipped as his accent thickened the way it always did when he was angry. "I'm sure you're aware that Thomas Manon is—*was*—a wealthy broker with a lot of high-profile accounts among the dynasties. My information was that your friend Sammael supposedly saw him before he fell off the face of the earth. I had an appointment." He glared balefully at her. "I don't usually kill my appointments."

Something flickered in her eyes. "Usually?"

"Look, everything's got its occasional exception." He hated the way his voice sounded, strained and petulant, like a child facing his inevitable punishment after being found out. What was the point in defending himself to her?

Damn it, stop reacting and do what you're good at, he told himself. *Quit whining and start saving your own ass!*

It seemed an odd time to try and appeal to the better angels of Ariane's nature—whatever those were—but charm, normally his first line of defense rather than his last resort, was all he had left. She'd been immune the last time. He'd just have to try harder.

Or maybe not. He caught her eyes drifting down to the blood still trickling slowly from his neck, staining his clothes. Damien could see her anger had faded considerably. And discomfort had come to replace it. She might be a skilled fighter, but it looked like she wasn't in the habit of killing after all. It would explain why he was still alive.

"Ariane," he said gently. "I think you know I'm telling the truth. Our purpose is the same."

"I doubt that," she replied, her expression wary. "Men like you aren't usually chosen for simple reconnaissance work."

Well. She was no fool, no matter how naive she was. Damien tried for his most innocent expression.

"I can handle myself in dangerous situations. I'd say anyone capable of taking down a Grigori qualifies as quite dangerous."

"You're a killer," she protested.

He tilted his head at her. "As are we all. You realize that if you kill *me*," he said slowly, lifting a hand to touch hers where it was wrapped around the scimitar's hilt, "it would simply be more senseless bloodshed."

Skin brushed skin, and he sucked in a breath. Touching Ariane was like touching a live wire...and yet, there was a pleasure in it, enough that he let his fingers wrap gently around her wrist.

He saw her startled blink, the sudden rise of her chest, and knew she enjoyed his touch as well. And that she hadn't expected to.

"You're a Shade," she said. "You lie for a living."

"In fairness, that's only one part of what I do for a living. And not nearly as lucrative as others. Ariane, love... you're hurting me."

"How else am I supposed to get you to talk?" she asked, sounding unnervingly like someone from an old gangster movie. Hopefully she hadn't gotten many ideas from any of those.

Damien immediately thought of several ways he'd enjoy being coerced, and just as quickly had to shove them aside. This was so far from the time and place...

"Even in my line of work, cutting is toward the more extreme end of coercion." He shifted purposely, then sucked in a breath and winced when the blade cut just a little deeper. Just as he'd expected. The sensation wasn't pleasant, but the look on Ariane's face made the momentary pain worth it.

The hand on the hilt of the blade finally quivered.

"I—"

She didn't get another word out. In a series of motions Damien could execute as easily as breathing, he twisted her wrist so she dropped the sword. As it fell to the floor with a muffled thump, he lunged for her, pulling her against him and dropping both of them to the ground before she could pull out any other sharp objects she might have on her person. He pinned Ariane beneath him, gripping her wrists at either side of her head. She was completely at his mercy now.

That was, if he could get over how it felt to have every inch of her pressed against him. His eyes wanted to roll back in his head as every nerve ending began to sing something suspiciously like the "Hallelujah Chorus." He distracted himself the only way he knew how.

"Ariane," he scolded her. "Pity is charming, but in my case, ill advised. You should never trust a Shade."

Her fangs flashed at him. "Bastard!"

Damien chuckled. "Ooh, another naughty word. Are you being tutored?"

Ariane gave a sharp, infuriated yelp. But though he felt her muscles tense, he knew she couldn't move. She might be powerful—hell, what he'd seen left him thinking she was uncomfortably close to Lily in that department—but size and weight had their advantages.

"Let me go!" she demanded.

Damien barked out a laugh. "Are you joking? You just had a sword at my throat! I'd like to keep my head tonight, thanks. And you deserve to suffer a bit. My shirt is ruined."

"I hate you." She hissed the words, words he'd heard thousands of times before, including from his own brothers on numerous occasions. They'd ceased to bother him centuries ago—both the words and the brothers, who were long ago dust and bones—but from Ariane's lips, they sounded harsh, wrong. She didn't seem a creature made for hate, even with a deadly weapon in her hand.

"No," he said quietly, hardly knowing why he spoke. "You don't hate me."

Despite the frustration still pouring from Ariane in waves, Damien quickly became aware of the way her curves fitted perfectly against him, the way her heart pulsed against his chest. Her skin warmed beneath his hands, and her breath fanned his face, cool and sweet.

His cock hardened immediately. Damien knew she would be able to feel it, rigid and unmistakable along her thigh. He didn't give a damn about that. All he was going to get was a raging case of blue balls that he deserved anyway for doing such a piss-poor job handling things tonight.

He didn't expect to feel her hips shift beneath him as she tried, one last time, to throw him off. In an instant, he found himself nestled directly, and very firmly, between her thighs. Damien's breath left him in a stunned rush as Ariane's cheeks flushed a deep, embarrassed pink.

"Maybe you do hate me," he gritted out.

"Let me up," she said, sounding more than a little breathless. "I've decided not to kill you."

He lifted an eyebrow. "Lucky me."

Ariane frowned up at him. "You're wasting time with this! I want to know what the other man might have heard. Don't you? I think we can at least agree on that, unless you're going to try and find a way to keep me from talking to him too. Where is he?"

Damien sighed. "For the last time, I did *not* take Manon's head off. And the fledgling can't have gone far. I can still hear him blubbering back in the offices somewhere. Can't you?"

She was still for a moment, listening, and then nodded slowly. He should have let her up then. Damien knew she was right, that they both had a vested interest in cornering Manon's unfortunate associate and gleaning what information they could before the man went completely off the deep end. But something kept him in place, whether it was the surprisingly *right* feeling of her body nestled against him, or the look in her eyes as they stayed locked with his, anger slowly shifting to confusion and . . . something very like desire, tentative, but there just the same.

That was all it took to send every rational thought from his mind.

Damien felt the purr welling up in his throat again, just as it had the night he'd met her. It was already clear he would have to be very careful where she was concerned. He really ought to turn her in and get her out of the way.

And yet...

"You're going to make trouble for me, aren't you, kitten?" he murmured.

"No more than you've already made for me," she replied.

He felt a rare, genuine grin curve his mouth. "Ah, but you're interfering with my livelihood, whereas you're just on an altruistic little adventure. And, as you've already mentioned a few times, I'm a Shade. My scruples run from questionable to nonexistent. If our paths keep crossing, I'm going to start taking liberties to punish you for getting in my way." His grin widened as her flush grew deeper.

"Get in *my* way again and more than just your shirt will get ruined."

Damien chuckled, amused that she thought she could intimidate him when she looked and sounded so charmingly disgruntled. "Really, kitten. Give me a little credit. I believe I'm going to take a liberty just for the insult to my considerable skill."

"*Don't.*" She wiggled a little in protest, which did nothing but create delicious friction between the two of them. He saw the bright shock of it stamped clearly on her face as she abruptly stilled. Oh, she would be an adventure to educate, if he had the time.

When he had time. He'd make some, just as soon as he figured out where she was staying so he could drop in. Preferably through a window, directly onto her bed.

It was a struggle to talk around that damned vibration that wanted to rumble up from the depths of his throat, but he just managed.

Don't purr, don't purr, do not purr...

"Don't what?" he asked, his eyes growing heavy-lidded in anticipation. "Something like this?" Damien lowered his head to Ariane's neck, barely letting his nose graze her skin as he inhaled, deeply, breathing in the scent of an English rose garden. Longing, far more powerful than he'd anticipated, rushed over him in a wave.

He heard Ariane's shuddering breath, could smell the wild, sweet scent of her arousal mingling with the roses. It provoked him, more than he could contain.

"Or perhaps I shouldn't do this," he said, lowering his head farther. As he did, the purr finally rumbled up, the sound rippling from his throat while he licked a long, hot trail up the side of Ariane's neck, ending at her earlobe, which he gave a flick with his tongue, then a nip.

The sound she made as she rose up against him was like music, and Damien forgot where they were, forgot himself, forgot everything but the promise of what Ariane could, and would, give him as they lay here...

Glass shattered, viciously tearing him away from the warm cocoon of fantasy. Ariane went rigid. Damien's blood ran ice cold. He whipped his head up and cursed. He could still taste Ariane like honey on his lips, and yet once again, some stupid vamp had decided to suck all the pleasure out of his evening.

He was on his feet in a heartbeat, pointedly ignoring the sight of Ariane sprawled invitingly on the plush Oriental rug. He had the sick feeling that he always got in the pit of his stomach when things began to go horribly wrong. And as they hadn't really gone right yet, it could only be the harbinger of nothing good.

Passing darkened offices, Damien sprinted down the

hallway toward the single light. The pitiful moaning of the terrified young vampire had stopped, a bad sign. And when he arrived at the doorway of the lit office, it got much worse. Glass littered the floor, letting in the sultry heat of this late summer night. There was a great deal of blood.

And no sign of the fledgling.

He felt Ariane at his side, staring at the scene. Damien couldn't decide whether he was angrier at her for being so obstinate about pursuing a job he was being paid to do, or at himself for not being able to concentrate properly when she was around. In the end, it was easier to choose both.

"I told you I didn't kill Manon," Damien snapped, crunching through the glass on the floor to look out into the night. As high as they were, fifteen floors up, he wasn't sure how the other vampire had been taken—but where supernatural powers were concerned, he knew that where there was a will, there tended to be a way. A look into the night revealed nothing, neither in the sky nor on the ground below. The fledgling vampire and the attacker who had come back to finish what he or she had started were gone.

As was his sole lead.

He rounded on Ariane, who was looking out with a strange expression on her face.

"I hope you're happy," Damien growled. The anger was a welcome change from the confusion that seemed to descend over him every time he got too close to the woman. "Now I've got nothing to go on. If you hadn't wasted so much time chasing me around with that ridiculous sword, I'd have gotten what I needed."

It took a moment, but Ariane finally turned to him.

Still, he felt like he had only half of her attention at best. She seemed troubled. And not at all intimidated by his snap of temper.

"We've both made a mistake, I think. It isn't safe here."

Damien snorted. "What gave you that impression?"

Again, she ignored his sharp tongue, frowning as she turned to look at the spray of blood that screamed "slit throat" to Damien. Wherever the fledgling had gone, he doubted that the vampire's weak constitution was a problem any longer. And unfortunately, tonight confirmed that tracking down this Grigori was going to be a lot stickier than he'd hoped. Really, he should have figured. Why else would he have been hired if the work wasn't going to be difficult and dirty?

"I don't understand why anyone would go to these lengths over a single Grigori. We don't get involved in dynasty politics, apart from our seat on the Council," Ariane said, more to herself than to him. Still, he was compelled to answer her.

"In my experience, highbloods never need much of a reason to be complete bastards to one another. It's like sport. Maybe somebody's got your friend locked up tight until they can get all of his secrets out of him. Maybe some idiot killed him for fun and is covering it up so he doesn't get dragged off to whatever desert hellhole you came from. Or, and I think this is quite likely, your Sam has decided to cast off the shackles of white-haired oddity and get a life, and just really doesn't want to be found. I've seen plenty of vamps kill because they want to disappear. It's about time one of your kind tried it."

Ariane shook her head. "No. He's one of our ancients. He takes his responsibilities very seriously."

"So maybe he cracked. It happens," Damien replied with a shrug. Being a giant white-haired vampire with all the personality of a rock would make anyone miserable eventually. If he wasn't being paid to do otherwise, he'd be inclined to let the man go and try to enjoy himself. The more he thought about it, the more this seemed the likeliest scenario. This had all the hallmarks of a vampire purposely trying to vanish.

A stubborn little crease had appeared in Ariane's forehead. She didn't appear to agree . . . not that it surprised him.

"You don't know him. I do. And Sam wouldn't do that. Someone's taken him, or killed him. And whoever that is has been following one of us. There's no way that this happening tonight is a coincidence."

She looked so upset about her theory that Damien had a momentary urge to indulge her little fantasy and comfort her. But he didn't have any more time to waste on playing with Ariane tonight. Besides, the very real possibility that he would find himself purring again was too humiliating to think about.

Now it was time to try and track, before all the scents grew cold. The blood of the newest victim would help. Sloppy work on the part of the killer, and Damien was grateful for it.

He gave a small, mocking bow to Ariane. "Well, I wish you luck with your theories. I'm afraid this is where I take my leave, my lady, and I'd suggest running along yourself. Manon was a powerful man. You don't want to be involved with this. Not if you want to stay free a while longer, at least. I can't believe I'm saying this, but you ought to pull that hideous wig out of the trash too. That hair is a beacon."

Ariane stood there amid the bloody wreckage and crossed her arms over her chest.

Damien had to force himself to step away. It didn't help that she was back to looking lost again. She truly didn't seem to have any connection to the vampires Damien was used to. Nor did she seem to want to.

"You think we should just leave?" she asked. "A man is dead. Probably two men."

"Someone will be along. They weren't technically open tonight, but obviously I got an appointment, and I'm sure he would have had one or two of his higher-profile clients stopping in on a night they wouldn't have to deal with the rabble."

"But...won't anyone care? Isn't there someone who should be notified?"

Damien watched her, surprised by the sincerity that was just about pouring off of her. It really was amazing she'd survived this long in Charlotte.

"Kitten," he chided her, "you're in the real world now. Vampires die all the time. I would prefer to stay alive. You really need to learn to deal with it. Do yourself a favor and enjoy your time in the city. Make friends, go shopping, and ditch the sword from hell. I'll find your friend, if there's anything left of him to find."

"You can't just pat me on the head and send me away, as much as you'd like to." She paused, then slowly said, "Maybe we should think about sharing information—"

Damien cut her off immediately. "Absolutely not. I work alone. And I never work with amateurs."

She stiffened, her eyes turning to violet ice. "I think you'd be surprised at the things I can do."

Oh, I'll bet I would be ...

Damien gritted his teeth and shoved from his mind the X-rated thoughts that immediately tried to surface.

"You don't want to be a part of my world, Ariane, trust me," he said softly, and meant it.

"Now run along and hide. Don't forget your blade, if you don't want to be found. And...stay out of my way. If you interfere again, I'll find a few more places to lick, and you won't be getting up until I'm good and through with you."

Before Ariane could do more than make a strangled, outraged sound, he shifted into the form that had carried him through centuries of successful criminal activity. As a large black cat, sleek, powerful, and silent, Damien leaped through the window.

And was gone.

chapter SIX

FINDING A CAT who didn't want to be found, especially in the dark of night, was like looking for a needle in a haystack. But Ariane could smell blood as well as any Cait Sith, so rather than waste precious minutes trying to track Damien, she set off immediately in pursuit of the scent that wound like a ribbon through the darkness.

Fresh blood and death.

The city streets were full of humanity, chattering, walking, blissfully unaware of the other things that stalked their summer nights. Ariane walked quickly through the mortals, feeling hunger stir and then awaken with unexpected strength at their warmth, their intoxicating, pulsing lifeblood. She frowned as she skirted a young couple holding hands and laughing.

She'd been eating, but not enough. Nerves had kept her meals light. She needed to be careful...even the Grigori cautioned their members of how quickly things could get out of hand.

Soon, she decided. But not yet. She'd be damned if Damien would always stay a step ahead of her.

The ribbon of scent took her through the heart of the city, beneath the glittering crown of the Bank of America building, and then farther, to where the shine began to fade and the cracks in the veneer of civilization began to show. Wary eyes peered at Ariane from shadow as she kept moving, her pace never faltering. She knew she was scarier than anything remotely human here, even if they didn't.

The scent grew strong enough to taste just as she walked past a seedy-looking nightclub. Music pumped out into the street, and a line of twentysomethings stretched along the sidewalk in front of it, talking and complaining while waiting to get in. Next door was a crumbling, empty building with boarded up windows.

It was also redolent with the smell of both her witness and, Ariane realized with a wrinkle of her nose, Damien. He was fast. But then, she supposed that if Sariel really had hired him, there had been reasons. It certainly hadn't been his personality.

"Hey, you don't wanna go in there," a voice called to her as she walked past the line and far enough up the walk to see the padlock and chains effectively barring the front door of the abandoned building. Ariane gave the helpful human the barest glance.

"Of course I do," she murmured. She heard a few cat-calls and some interesting commentary on why a woman like her might be sniffing around an abandoned building. The thoughts and emotions of the crowd threatened to swamp her, swirling around her in a cacophonous jumble that made it almost impossible to pluck out individual threads or make any sense of it at all. Keeping her thoughts private from the other Grigori was second nature, and vice versa, but vampires' sensitivity to human thought was a new experience for her. It took effort to quiet the din and focus.

Slowly, her mind went quiet. Ariane breathed a sigh of relief, then turned her attention back to finding what she was now sure would ultimately be a very dead end. Just as importantly, she wanted to show Damien Tremaine that he wasn't the only one with some hunting ability.

She slipped into the narrow alley between the two buildings, vanishing into shadow as though she'd never been there. The thudding of the bass next door was surprisingly muffled here, and she had the sudden, unshakable certainty she was being watched.

Damien. Of course it was. He was probably sitting just out of sight watching her approach and laughing.

She frowned at the thought and kept moving, the world seeming to fall away a little more with every step she took. There really was something eerie about this place, whether or not Damien was having fun at her expense somewhere close by. Her senses sharpened; her breathing slowed. Everything she'd been taught about battle over her long years, every scrap of information she had feared would always be useless came flooding back.

And still, she felt those eyes on her.

Ariane's feet made no sound as she headed for her entry point, a window halfway up the building that was open and missing a board. She could see the tattered curtains moving gently with breeze from either within or without. Damien would have jumped in. In his cat form, panther-like in looks, size, and grace, he could easily have cleared it if he could leap from a fifteen-story window and land without a scratch.

For her, it would take a little more doing.

Ariane glanced around again, hating that she was in the worst position—she couldn't see anyone, but there were plenty of hidden places from which others could observe her. Still, if she wanted up and in...

Her wings unfurled from her back, slipping through her skin and clothes like water and then becoming solid. Ariane couldn't hold back a relieved sigh. At least in the desert she could let them show, spread and stretch them even if she was forbidden to fly anywhere. Here, hiding them was sometimes just added strain. And even now, she couldn't bring herself to violate that law of the Grigori: no outsider, mortal or immortal, must ever know about her wings.

Newly invigorated, Ariane leaped lightly up and kept going, lifting herself vertically with the strength of the batlike wings that shimmered the deep purple of twilight. She alighted easily on the windowsill, paused to fold her wings back against herself until they vanished once again, and then slipped inside.

Damien stood slouched against the far wall of a room that at one time must have been a family room, but that now featured nothing but peeling wallpaper and scarred wood flooring covered in dirt and grime. A few wrappers and empty syringes littered the corners.

At the sight of him, all of her trepidation vanished in favor of annoyance. He'd obviously been waiting just to taunt her. She stepped away from the window and strode forward.

"Before you say a word," she threatened, "remember

I've brought along that sword you like so much. Now where is he?"

She knew even before she finished speaking that something was really wrong. The posture she'd initially taken for casual disregard was unnatural, like something was holding him by the—

Ariane's eyes widened as his body swung, ever so slightly, as he tried to move. A soft, muffled gag reached her ears at the same time. And behind her, the window slid shut.

"So many sent for the hunt," a voice said softly behind her. "The Shade matters little . . . but I will be sorry about you, sister of my blood."

She spun, catching just a glimpse of violet eyes very much like her own before a blow to the side of her head knocked her off her feet and sent her crashing into the wall. Ariane thought she might have cried out. She wasn't sure. Her ears rang, and in the precious seconds before she struggled to her feet again, there was the insidious feeling of something warm and sticky leaking from the ear on which she'd been hit.

It will heal, she told herself, even though the pain was excruciating right this second. *It doesn't matter. No matter how much it hurts.*

Here was the familiar sound of wings, a *whoosh* of air as her adversary landed in front of her. Ariane couldn't get her legs to work properly, even though she heard the scrape of metal that meant he was drawing his sword. He was a Grigori. She was going to be killed by one of her own, and she didn't know why. Her people were not killers, they were not—

When the blade came down, she just managed to get her feet under her and push as hard as she could. She felt the rush of air pass less than an inch from her head as she lunged to the side, saving herself... for the moment.

"Stop this!" she cried. "I'm Grigori too!"

The voice, deep and sorrowful, spoke again. "I know. I regret I must do this. But I will not be hunted any longer. Not when the real danger waits to rise."

The words chilled her, especially spoken in the emotionless tones she'd grown so accustomed to over the centuries. There was no reasoning with such a voice.

"I only want to find Sammael," Ariane said, hoping she had enough time to draw her own sword. She had a better view of her assailant now, and seeing him knocked the wind out of her.

He looked like one of their ancients. Incredibly tall, broad, muscular, with braided white hair that fell down his back. He was as much cold perfection as Sam. But this one had steel in his eyes, and she knew he would kill her, kill Damien... and feel nothing.

The question was, why?

When the sword came down again, she wasn't as ready. Pain ripped through Ariane's upper arm as she fumbled to get her own sword out of its sheath on her back. This time she knew she cried out, but it didn't stop her from rolling to one side and finally, finally getting up with her blade in her hand.

"We don't kill! Especially not one another!" she shouted, the blade of her scimitar flashing as she swung it.

"I am honor bound. We do what we must, *d'akara*."

The old endearment in the language of her people, so casually and callously used, hurt worse than her head. She staggered a little on her feet, both hands on the hilt of her sword.

"No. I'm honor bound to find my friend, whatever you've done with him! Sariel couldn't stop me, and neither will you!"

Her words seemed to set him back. She saw some understanding dawn in those cold eyes, saw that she had startled him. Ariane summoned her strength, dredging it up from the depths, and used the moment to her advantage. She swung the scimitar over her head and brought it down. The other Grigori moved at the last second, but not quickly enough. She cleaved a long, deep gash in his chest, forcing him back. His wings flared out to the sides as he moved to balance himself.

Ariane spun and sliced into him again, a battle cry tearing from her lips that she barely recognized as her own voice. Once more, but this time her sword sang as it clashed against his. Blood poured down his chest, then slowed as his body began to knit together again.

"Tell me where he is!"

"No." Still so calm when there should have been pain, but the Grigori's breathing was uneven. It wasn't enough.

"You will tell me." Emotion, dammed up behind a wall she'd been constructing for centuries, found a crack and began to pour through. "He was all I had in that place. You *will* tell me."

Her own strength surprised her as she pushed back against the bigger vampire's blade. But at her words, there was another flicker of something in his expression. Uncertainty, she thought, or maybe just disgust that she would admit to having actual feelings. But his words indicated neither.

"No. Not tonight . . . Ariane."

He pushed away without warning, exploding upward

in a burst of power that propelled him through the rotting wood of the ceiling and roof and out into the night. Ariane stared upward, gripping the hilt of her sword so tightly that her hand shook. He had known her name. And he had made the decision to back down despite having killed two vampires who would likely have done little more than point her in a direction.

For the wisdom of all the gods, *why*?

All of her fury and despair erupted in a single, primal scream that echoed up into the night sky. She was about to leap and follow, her back tingling where her wings lay furled, ready to burst forth and lift her after him, when she remembered that she was not alone.

She was torn, but only for a moment. If the Grigori was as old as she suspected, she would never catch him in the air. His liftoff alone guaranteed it. Damien, on the other hand, was suffering. And as conflicted as she was about him, there was no way she could leave him as he was.

Collecting herself as best she could, Ariane hurried to Damien on legs that felt dangerously close to giving out on her. All her life, she'd only ever trained for battle, never really fought in one. But tonight she'd drawn blood with intent to kill... and she already knew it wouldn't be the last time. The image of the Grigori's chest splitting open flickered in her memory, and Ariane felt nausea uncoil like a snake in her stomach.

No, she commanded herself. This was her reality now, and she was going to have to get it together.

"Damien," she said when she reached him. "Can you hear me?"

He'd been used as bait, and that was exactly how he'd been arranged, hung by the neck with wire designed to cut deeply without actually severing his head…unless enough pressure was applied. His hands were bound to his sides with the same wire, blood seeping around the edges where it had sliced into his skin. His hair, once so perfect, was sweaty and mussed, and his skin had gone a sickly, corpselike shade of white. Dazed blue eyes rolled up to look at her, pleading wordlessly.

He looked helpless and wounded. And against her better judgment, Ariane felt herself softening toward him. He was an insufferable jackass…but he needed her. It was a role she was far more comfortable with than killer.

She freed his hands first, disturbed by how they dangled limply at his sides. Then she slipped an arm around him, bracing him while she cut the wire that ran from his neck to the ceiling. Damien slumped against her, weak from losing so much blood and being unable to heal around the wire. He made some sound, a pathetic gurgle that attempted to be a word.

Whatever it was meant to be, Ariane had a feeling it would spoil the tender moment, so she chose to ignore it. She needed to bank a little goodwill toward the mouthy Shade, because whether either of them liked it or not, they were now in this together.

"Come on," she said, bearing most of his weight as she tried to get him upright. "I saved your life. You can at least try to help me get you out of here."

She was unsurprised when instead he blacked out, slumping into her arms. She had to move fast to catch him. Then Ariane stood for a moment, holding his cool but thankfully alive body against her own, and wondered whether this had been inevitable from the moment he'd unwittingly tried to pick her up at the bar. One thing the

Grigori believed firmly in was destiny, and Damien's seemed to be intertwined with hers, at least for now. Part of her wished she could fight it—as attracted as she was to him, she didn't actually like him much, and she wasn't foolish enough to think Damien would be capable of thinking beyond his own wants and needs. Theirs would be a short, and likely contentious, allegiance.

Still, he needed her. And the way he'd purred...she would never forget it.

It was a start.

"And you think I'm difficult," she told his still, accursedly perfect face. Then she wrapped her arms around him, lifted the wings that emerged from her back with the barest thought, and carried Damien up and out into the night.

chapter SEVEN

ARIANE'S RENTAL WAS in a beautiful complex in South Park that featured high-rise apartments above an open-air, cobblestoned center of shopping and dining. It took its name, the Falls, from an ornate sculpture that functioned as the centerpiece for the public area. Strickland, cheap though Elena insisted he was, seemed to pay well for running herd on the rotating residents of his safe houses. Even with her limited experience, Ariane knew this was a pricey home... and Elena had indicated that this was one of her smaller properties.

It was a convenient, and high-class, hunting ground.

It was also the last place Ariane thought she should be taking a wounded vampire who was highly ranked in the most notorious guild of thieves and assassins, but she didn't have much choice. For now, this place was what she had. She just hoped Elena didn't decide to stop in... as she had every night this week since she'd moved Ariane in.

Ariane groaned softly. Well, she'd enjoyed the posh accommodations while they'd lasted.

She kept as high as she could on the way, frustrated by how bright the city lights kept things. Before they had gotten far, she realized that Damien had come around and was clinging to her so tightly that she doubted he could still feel his fingers.

"How are you feeling?" she asked. Her arms were wrapped around his chest, high up beneath his arms, and he faced away from her, legs dangling down and making him more unwieldy than he might have been. Not that she expected anything involving Damien to be easy.

His voice was as tight as his knuckles. "Don't. Drop. Me."

It was stupid to be relieved that he was alert, but Ariane couldn't help it. Nor could she help enjoying his soft groan when she dipped and rose on the warm currents of night air.

She smiled to herself. Payback, as Elena was fond of saying, was a bitch.

It was a short trip, but arrival posed a problem. It was late, but it was also a Friday. At midnight, people still milled about the common area, sipping wine at outdoor tables and sitting at the edge of the waterfall sculpture. Ariane's only choice was up, so she landed lightly on her small, wrought-iron patio. There was just enough room for a woven wicker chair, a pepper plant, a tomato plant . . . and two vampires. One of whom didn't seem interested in standing on his own.

"Wings," Damien muttered in a thin voice. "Bloody *wings*!" He was slightly hoarse but didn't sound much worse for wear. His entire body felt rigid enough to simply shatter into pieces as Ariane folded her wings against her back to have them vanish again.

She had no idea what his problem was.

"Let... let me go, damn it, I—" He shoved away from her, turned, and then proceeded to fall forward. Ariane caught him and dragged him back up.

"Your color is terrible," she said. "You've lost too much blood, Damien. Stop struggling. I'll get you inside."

He glared at her out of eyes that seemed fever bright compared to his complexion, which was still just shy of death itself. His wounds had stopped bleeding, but they also weren't healing nearly quickly enough for Ariane's liking. The Grigori, whoever he was, had managed to nearly bleed Damien dry. That alone wouldn't have killed him, but it would have turned him into a ravenous monster that wouldn't even be able to converse intelligently right now. It was small comfort. Still, seeing his wretched condition was a far cry from reading about such things.

"Bugger off," he growled, his face just a breath away from hers.

She glared up at him, her brows drawing slowly together. "No. I don't care what you are or what you do, Damien Tremaine, but you're in no position to be ordering me around. You need my help."

"I don't need anyone."

She ignored his comment and kept pressing. "You're going to stop acting like a spoiled child, shut up, and do what you're told for once."

She could feel the slow, steady beat of his heart against her chest, the chill of his blood-deprived body in her arms. Damien stared into her eyes, trying to intimidate her. But as their gazes stayed locked, neither one interested in backing down, she saw the wild look in his fade, the pupils going from feline slits back to something more human, and for the briefest instant, Ariane could see how afraid he actually was before the emotion was covered by his usual indifferent sarcasm.

"Very well, Mother. Are you going to feed me a bottle when we get inside?" His eyes dropped to her chest. "Or maybe—"

"Oh, shut up," Ariane snapped. Damien appeared to have two default settings: jerk and letch. She was in no mood for either.

Ariane quickly considered her limited choices and decided there was only one real option. She'd pay her friend back somehow. A quick kick to the handle of the French door broke a hole right through it, and the door swung inward. She helped Damien stagger in, taking most of his weight on herself, and was grateful that vampires were gifted with far more strength than the average human—he was a lot more solid than he looked.

She paused, looked at the narrow, stylish couch, then turned Damien in the direction of her bedroom. He managed a faint chuckle but offered no commentary, which she would have felt better about had it not been a testament to just how weak he was.

Ariane didn't bother to hit the light switch, her eyes perfectly adjusted to the dim light coming in from the windows. She steered him toward the queen bed piled with pillows, yet another bit of the apartment that bore the stamp of Elena's surprisingly frothy decorating taste.

"It looks like the entire baroque period threw up in here," Damien muttered.

"On the bed," Ariane replied. "And . . . we need to get you out of these clothes. They're ruined. I don't want them to ruin anything else in here. These things aren't mine."

"I'm glad to hear it," he said.

They made it to the side of the bed, and Ariane eased him away from her enough to try and allow him to fumble with his shirt, which was covered in a mixture of dried and still-tacky blood. A quick look told her his pants were probably decent enough to leave on; because of the angle at which he'd been hung and propped, they'd escaped all but a few spatters. The jury was out on the shoes. Likely dry, probably messed up anyway, she decided. And he'd be more comfortable without them.

Damien frowned down at his shirt and attempted to undo the buttons. Ariane watched and didn't interfere, knowing he'd probably just push her away if she tried to help. He was intently focused, working with fingers that didn't seem to want to cooperate. Finally, he got the top one unfastened, but it took enough out of him that he swayed on his feet when he looked up at her.

He looked so defeated, and so utterly exhausted, that Ariane had a sudden urge to gather him to her and wrap her arms around him. The need to comfort him, to be close to him, surprised her, especially in how strong the feeling was. She kept her hands to herself, though. Somehow, she didn't think Damien was accustomed to simple acts of affection.

"Don't," he said quietly, letting his hand fall back to his side. "You're as transparent as glass, Ariane. Don't even think about pitying me. I'm awful, and I'm comfortable with that. This is just an occupational hazard. I'll recover, and then continue to be awful. That's the way it goes."

"You're not...*that* awful," Ariane protested. Then she sighed. "Would you please let me help you do this? You need to lie down."

"Far be it from me to protest if you want to undress me," he said, trying for a lecherous grin, then grimacing. "I can't feel my damned fingers. And I'm...getting very hungry, Ariane. You may want to hurry. Believe it or not, I don't want to hurt you."

She could see the light in his eyes intensifying and noted the reddish cast they were beginning to take on. His body was trying to heal, but it needed fuel. And when it came down to it, she knew the hunger would take over and he would drain every drop from her without a thought as to what he was doing. She gave a curt nod.

"Okay." She quickly unbuttoned the shirt, her fingers working nimbly down the front of him before she pushed back the stiff fabric over his shoulders. The first sight of the sculpted contours of Damien's chest and stomach had her swallowing hard, fighting off a wave of hunger of her own. His body was perfect, with a physique well honed by and for his chosen occupation. His mark, the Celtic trio of snarling cats, stood out against his pale skin high on his collarbone. Beneath and just to the right was the small but unmistakable crescent moon of the House of Shadows. When her fingers accidentally brushed his bare skin, smooth and tight, he shivered.

"Kitten, my inhibitions are low enough as it is. Careful, please."

"I'm trying," she replied with a frown. It was unfair that the gods had created a vampire who was at once so impossible and so incredibly appealing. She slid behind him to pull the shirt off and sucked in a breath as she pulled the fabric away. Damien had worked very hard thus far to be unsurprising, but this...

She knew that some vampires liked to enhance their manifested dynasty marks with ink tattoos. In the case of the House of Shadows, they inked the small crescent moon as an identifier. But she hadn't expected Damien, so buttoned up and aristocratic in his impropriety, to have added anything to what he already had. And yet covering his muscular back was a celebration of his status as a Cait Sith, a beautiful copy of the three cats, snarling and stretching in a tribal circle. It told her that he didn't just accept his status as an outcast, but also he reveled in it.

What kind of man did that? Not one she could trust. But then, trust had nothing to do with what she was feeling right now.

"It isn't nice to stare," he chided her gently.

"I... it's... I was admiring your tattoo. It's beautiful," she stammered.

"My little secret. I'm sure even you have a few. Secrets, that is. I'll be happy to examine you for extra tattoos later."

Her mouth went dry. The mere thought of his eyes on her bare skin was wickedly appealing. And there was no way she was letting him know that.

"That's... not necessary. Here, get settled. I'll be right back," she said, helping him get onto the bed and situate himself against the pillows, pulling off his shoes and socks and arranging them neatly on the floor beside the bed. Ariane then rushed into the kitchen, pulling open the refrigerator door to get Elena's supply of "emergency pick-me-ups." There were two bags labeled O-positive in the door, yet another benefit of working for someone who had ties to the vampire black market, Ariane supposed. A couple of minutes later, she had two of the largest mugs she could find full of one bag's contents. Taking care not to spill, she carried them quickly back into the bedroom, where Damien regarded her with eyes that were even redder than they had been.

She stopped short, just out of reach, seeing that he was no longer quite himself.

"If you want this," she said, indicating one of the mugs, "behave yourself."

"Why would I want a glass of cold and dead when I've got you standing right in front of me?" he asked, his voice a harsh rasp. He blinked, then shook his head as his eyes cleared. "Just give me the damned mug, Ariane, before I have my teeth in you."

She kept as much distance as she could while handing one over. Damien lifted it to his lips, took a sip, and made a face while he gagged.

"There is a thing," he managed, "called a microwave."

"There is also a thing," Ariane replied flatly, "called gratitude. Drink it before I pin you to the bed with my sword and force it down you."

He looked at her curiously for a moment. "I think I like this side of you, kitten," he said, then drank deeply, draining the glass in seconds without coming up for air. He pulled it away from his lips with a gasp, his expression leaving no doubt as to his thoughts about what he'd just drunk.

"Disgusting. Absolutely cold, lifeless, and disgusting."

Ariane pulled the mug out of his hands, then leaned down to get a better look at him. "It might be disgusting," she said, "but it worked. You already look better."

His eyes were cool blue again without a hint of red,

and even as she watched, his neck finished knitting itself together. In seconds, his color was back to normal. The only reminders of what he'd been through were the red-dish stains on his skin from the blood and his disheveled hair.

"Yes, well, I think I'm going to pass on round two, if it's all the same to you," he said, looking pointedly at the other mug. "I prefer fresh and warm, myself."

"It's for me," Ariane said, annoyed at his attitude even though she knew she shouldn't have expected anything different. "I realize everything is about you, but other people actually get hungry while you're busy expecting the world to meet your needs."

"Now my feelings are hurt," Damien said.

"What feelings?" Ariane snapped, realizing that she was the one whose feelings were hurt. All these years of wanting to build a real life on the ashes of her forgotten one, of wanting to go out and make a difference to *someone*...and when she finally saved a life, all she got was insults and complaints. It wasn't what she'd hoped or imagined. At all.

"Good point," Damien said, relaxing into the pillows. "Drink your medicine, Ariane. I'm going to enjoy this."

Ariane perched at the foot of the bed, still leery of being within reach, and lifted the mug to her lips. It was far from ideal—she would much rather have gone down to the wine bar and found someone drunk and easy to lure off for a bite, but her own clothes were spattered and smeared with crimson, and taking them off anywhere near Damien seemed like a really bad idea. Besides, the hunger was beginning to really bother her, and she had no intention of letting Damien see her weak. He was obnoxious enough already, and her temper, always so long, was short and rapidly fraying.

The first sip triggered her gag reflex. Damien had been right. This blood was cold, dead, lifeless. It had a strangely overripe taste that was just this side of rotten too. She heard a quiet chuckle, grimaced, and muscled her way through the rest of the glass all at once, just the way Damien had.

It was a minute before she was sure if it was actually going to stay down, but it did.

She very quickly felt her energy levels rise. The beast within quieted, for now. Ariane breathed a sigh of relief.

Damien was watching with obvious amusement. "That was the best part of my night, by far. Verdict, kitten?"

"Vile, but probably worth it," Ariane admitted. She toyed with the empty mug in her lap. "And once again, I'm *not* your kitten." She took a deep breath. "Tonight sealed it. From here on out, we search together."

His look hardened instantly. "No. We went over this before."

"Yes," Ariane agreed. "And that was before I saved your life."

Damien's eyes narrowed. "You seem to think I have a working code of honor. That's very sweet, but I don't. You chose to save me, which is your problem. I'm not interested in working with anyone else on this. I want my diamond."

Ariane got up to set the mug on the nightstand beside the small electric alarm clock, then pulled Damien's out of his hands and set that down too. She took a moment to collect her thoughts before answering, trying to decide the best plan of attack for getting what she wanted out of him. It was tough. She didn't think she had anything he wanted, apart from the obvious. And even if she was inclined to give in and sleep with him, she doubted it would mean anything to Damien. He'd just put another notch in his bedpost and move along.

"Well, I *don't* want your diamond, so that's a bonus for you," Ariane finally said as she got resituated at the end of the bed. "In fact, I don't want anything from you except your expertise."

He gave a short, sharp laugh. "In what arena, Ariane? I'm a man of many talents."

"You also have a one-track mind," she said with a sigh. "Look, it's obvious we're going to keep running into one another. We want the same thing. Pooling our resources makes sense."

"You *have* no resources. I'm holding all the cards here, Ariane, and I say no."

She fought the urge to punch him. "Hear me out. I'm not stupid, Damien. I'm well aware that you have better contacts and that you'll find the next step easier than I will. Manon was the only lead I had, and that was an accident. But I have more to offer than you think. This is all just… more difficult than I'd expected." She frowned at the floor and muttered, "And now it's even more complicated."

"You mean the Grigori who strung me up," Damien said, shifting slightly on the bed. "I *told* you this didn't seem like a normal abduction. Who was he? Another friend of yours?"

"No," she said, shaking her head as the strangeness of the encounter hit her anew. "That's what I mean. He's one of ours, but I don't think I've ever seen him before. It makes no sense. There aren't really that many of us."

"Well, I'll agree with you," Damien replied. "That *is* odd, and bears looking into. But you not knowing him doesn't exactly make you more useful as a traveling companion. I'm still not understanding what I get out of this partnership you're proposing."

Ariane looked at him, at his impassive, politely curious expression, and knew he wouldn't take her on out of compassion, or even pity. He was a creature who worked on the basis of what and how much he could get, a system utterly divorced from emotion. Maybe Sariel had been right—she relied too much on her own emotion. She needed to come at this logically. It was the only way she would get anywhere with Damien.

"I'm an extra set of hands, and I can hold my own in a fight," she said. "I've got enough money to pay my way; that's nothing you'd need to worry about. And I know Sammael. I understand him, just as I understand the Grigori in a way you don't. Considering what happened earlier, I think that would be very useful to you."

Damien tipped his head at her. "Persuasive. I think Drake would find you fascinating."

"Drake?"

"The Master Shade. My employer. Collecting information has been a very lucrative hobby of his...but he knows next to nothing about your dynasty. It annoys him to no end. I suppose spending time with you might reveal a few things he'd be interested in. And if he's interested, I get things I like." His gaze was shrewd. "Your wings, for instance. Useful and pretty and very, very strange. No wonder your kind hides in the desert. That would be hard to conceal otherwise."

She felt slightly ill. It figured that she would pay for

saving him. Still, this changed nothing. She needed Damien to find Sam. And regardless of what secrets she revealed or not, she could not go home.

"I guess it wouldn't do any good to ask you to keep that information to yourself," she said quietly.

"No. But if it makes you feel any better, it likely won't go far. The knowledge is much more valuable if almost no one has it." He sat up and leaned forward, and she saw much more of the cat in him than she ever had before.

"You need to realize up front, Ariane, that this is just another job for me. I'm not going to coddle you or keep your secrets out of some misguided sense of fair play. If we work together, it's a business arrangement, nothing more, and one that is going to end up working to my advantage. Is that really what you want?"

Ariane took a deep breath. In his own way, Damien had been perfectly honest with her from the beginning, and he was being so now. She shouldn't want any part of him. He certainly had no intentions of changing to accommodate her. But he knew this world, knew the underbelly of it where she could barely skim the surface. His goal was the same as hers, though his payoff was very different. And though she knew it was probably monumentally stupid, she couldn't shake the memory of that lovely, throaty purr or the feel of that hot tongue laving the side of her neck.

She had no intention of returning to the desert. But if she ended up caught, or worse, then she wanted to at least have tasted something of desire.

"If that's how it is, then yes. I'll handle it."

"All this just for a friend?" he asked, looking puzzled again. "He may not want to be found, Ariane, if he's still alive. In which case you will have sacrificed everything just to piss someone off."

She shook her head gently, knowing this was one thing Damien wouldn't understand. "We are Watchers, Damien. All my life, I've never been allowed to make a difference. This time, this one time, it's worth it to me to try."

"Is that why you saved me?" Damien asked. "Wanting to make a difference?"

She shrugged, uncomfortable with his shift from sarcasm to genuine interest. "I guess. And also . . ."

"Yes?"

"I . . . may have liked the idea of having you in my debt." She couldn't help the smile that rose to her lips, and it broadened when Damien's slow, Cheshire cat grin appeared. She doubted he smiled like that often, when it reached his eyes and warmed them. Ariane felt a little like melting into a puddle right there on the comforter. The art of teasing was still foreign to her, but Damien seemed to have appreciated the effort.

"Nicely done, kitten. You may learn after all. I'll tell you what . . . since I am, in fact, glad to still be in possession of my sorry hide, I'll give you something for your trouble."

She looked at him warily. "You can keep *that* to yourself."

This time he laughed, a full, rich sound that seemed to roll up from deep in his chest. Ariane found herself laughing with him despite herself. He had a way about him when his guard went down, and she found herself wishing he did it more often. It was probably just the shock of the evening that had altered him, but she would enjoy this side of him while it lasted. Even when Damien's laughter subsided, his eyes stayed warm.

"You've already got me pegged, Ariane. I'll have to work harder at shocking you."

She laughed again. "No, don't, please!"

"Music to my ears. You're doomed, I'm afraid." He swung his legs over the edge of the bed, paused as though checking to see if everything was still in working order, and then rose to his feet. Her eyes skimmed down the length of him again; she couldn't help herself. Nor could she stop her mouth from watering. Streaks of crimson had dried on his chest where the blood had seeped through his shirt. Ariane wondered what it would be like to lick them off...slowly.

The tightness between her legs was enough of a warning that she needed to save that particular line of thought for another time. But when she met Damien's eyes again, they'd gone so dark they were almost black, and she could see he knew exactly what she'd been thinking about.

She rose from the bed and took a quick step backward, an instinctive response to the predatory gaze now fixed on her.

"Oh no, you don't," he said softly. "Bloody innocent. You're going to learn to stop that, kitten...because if you provoke me much more, I won't."

She knew he was going to catch her, but Ariane was compelled to run anyway. She made it out of the bedroom, but only steps before Damien caught her from behind. He spun her and pressed her up against the wall before she could make a sound, and once she was face-to-face with him, she couldn't quite manage to exhale.

His eyes glowed brightly in the dark, and his breath was uneven when he drew it in. She closed her eyes when he lowered his head, expecting to feel his mouth on hers . . . and was shocked when instead he pressed his nose into her hair, inhaling deeply while he rubbed his cheek against hers.

He was raw sexuality, sheer physical power. Ariane knew she had no business allowing this. She didn't know him, she didn't like him . . . and gods, how she wanted him.

She made a soft whimpering sound. It was all she could manage when her body seemed to have ignited in flames. Her breasts rubbed against his chest, turning her nipples to hard little pebbles beneath her shirt. And though none of the rest of him touched her, she could feel how close he was, knew that if she arched her back, she'd have him pressed rock solid between her legs.

Now that she knew how it felt, it was a struggle not to want it again. Why did he have to be so *compelling*?

"Mmm, I love the way you smell," Damien murmured, his breath tickling her ear in the most delicious way. When the purr began to vibrate through him, Ariane's knees went liquid. Only Damien's hands, his fingers twined with hers as they held her captive against the wall, seemed capable of holding her up.

He drew back, brushing his nose against hers. "Now let's see how you taste," he breathed.

He took his time with it, tormenting her with small, soft kisses and suckling gently at her lower lip. When she moaned, he was ready, sweeping his tongue inside to mate with hers in a hot, openmouthed kiss. Ariane clung to him, digging her nails into his shoulders. It was only then she realized that he'd released her hands. He'd found far better things to do with his own, slipping one hand up beneath her shirt to cup and knead her breast.

And he purred for her, the sound rippling through her

and pooling with the moisture at the apex of her thighs. When he tweaked her nipple, she gasped, the sensation only serving to make her tighter, hotter. She slid one hand down to grip his hip and pull him against her. He thrust against her hard, growling.

"Is this what you want?" he asked.

Her head was spinning too fast for her to lie.

"Yes," she said, and his mouth was on hers again, more demanding now. Ariane's hands skimmed over his back, his broad shoulders, sliding into thick, soft hair. He leaned into her touch, letting her know without words how much he liked what she was doing. The pleasure of it, the unexpected give and take as they tangled up in one another, was a bright shock to her system. All of the sensual education she'd been deprived of in the long years she'd lived among the Grigori seemed to have been concentrated into this one heated exchange.

She ran her nails lightly down his chest, making him shudder; then, before she could begin to think better of it, she began to fumble with his belt buckle. She was so tired of thinking; it was so much better just to feel.

Damien moaned into her mouth as she wrapped her fingers around his cock and gave it a tentative stroke. The skin was like hot silk, and the power she felt as he shivered beneath her touch was heady stuff. His hand snaked around her wrist and jerked it away before she could do more.

"No, kitten, don't," he panted. "I'm already too—"

But his words were lost on her. Uncertainty had quickly given way to delight, and then to something hotter, wilder that threatened to consume Ariane unless she had more...all...*now.* She bared her teeth and scraped them over the sensitive skin of his throat, reveling in the feel of Damien's hands tangling in her hair as he drew her closer. She wanted to ride him until she dropped, to bite, to feed while they joined...

When the key rattled in the lock, he tore away from her so quickly that she nearly fell to the floor. Her hands slammed against the wall behind her, the only thing propping her up. Damien had backed up several steps, very pointedly not meeting her eyes while he hurriedly tried to fix his pants. Ariane watched him, her breathing harsh and uneven. She wasn't at all sure what had just happened, but she was quite sure she hadn't wanted it to end. Damien, on the other hand, seemed flustered in a way she hadn't believed him capable of.

Her eyes moved to the door, which opened as she leaned against the wall, trying not to let her legs just crumple beneath her.

Elena stepped in, flipped on the light, and then stopped short. Her eyes went from Ariane to Damien, who was fumbling with his belt. Ariane watched Elena's eyebrows shoot up to somewhere around her hairline and wanted to groan.

"If I'm interrupting something," she said slowly, "I can leave until you're...ah...finished."

"No. It's not...no...," Damien stammered.

Ariane turned her attention back to him. He looked disheveled, deliciously rumpled—and panicked half out of his mind. Ariane had to wonder what she'd done. Granted, her experience with kissing was close to nil, but she doubted her inexperience was what was making Damien look perilously close to a full-blown panic attack. Instinctively, she sought to soothe him.

"Damien's had a long night, Elena," she said, her eyes darting anxiously between the two of them. "He was nearly killed. I brought him back here to help him until he could heal himself." She moved away from the wall on weak legs, toward where Damien now stood looking like he wanted to bolt. She couldn't help touching him, just a quick brush of her fingers over his back. She thought she heard the faintest beginning of a purr before he began to cough.

Elena frowned. "You sound terrible. I'm no healer, but I can call someone who—"

"No, no, that's not necessary. I'll be fine," Damien said, his voice huskier than usual. "I'll grab a bite on my way back to the hotel and be none the worse for wear."

"You're leaving?" Ariane asked, surprised, and more than a little wary. His eyes returned to her, and she could see he understood.

His expression was faintly mocking. "So little faith I'll honor my word already, kitten? I'm hurt."

She hated that he'd reverted so quickly to cool, detached sarcasm. There was more to Damien than that. She'd seen it, *felt* it. But then, maybe it took a life-threatening experience to bring the other side of him out. The thought was depressing.

"You've already bragged about your word not meaning much," Ariane said. "I want to know where I can find you."

He raised his eyebrows. "Even if I told you the hotel, what's to say I'll be there tomorrow night if I don't want to be found?"

She glared at him, and he rolled his eyes, relenting. "Fine. I'm at the Ashby. But don't be banging on my door at sundown. I'll come fetch you here."

Ariane crossed her arms over her chest and tipped up her chin. The defiance was an excellent way to cover up her fear. She didn't want him to vanish on her... not now. "And how do I know you won't just decide to leave me hanging here?"

He gave her a faint smile. "You don't. But I won't." His smile faded as their eyes stayed locked. Ariane felt caught, unable to look away and even less interested in doing so. She saw the heat flicker in his gaze, and it curled through her, warming her to her toes. Then just as quickly, it was gone as he turned his head away from her to look at Elena.

"You'll need to keep a close eye on her for the rest of the night," he said. "She's prone to getting into trouble."

"I'm not her keeper," Elena replied, her expression hardening when her eyes dropped to his mark. Ariane cursed inwardly. Despite Elena's associations, Ariane was pretty sure she wouldn't want a Shade in her apartment.

"I don't *need* a keeper," Ariane added, irritation blooming quickly to replace desire. Damien only glanced at her, moving toward the door.

"Yes," he said with so much assurance she suddenly wanted to punch him, "you do. You'll also need a hat or a wig." He paused. "A *good* wig, if that's what you decide. We'll go over the rest tomorrow. For now, I have a few calls to make. I'll be here at nine tomorrow. I expect you will be as well."

Elena was watching him with a mixture of curiosity and hostility. "Careful with the orders, cat. You're lucky I'm letting you stand there, considering what you are."

His smile was faint. "Hypocrisy. Charming." He looked pointedly at Ariane. "You really do have terrible taste in people. That can't end well for you, you know."

With that cryptic and solemn statement, he crossed to the door, turned, and executed a small, aristocratic bow. His eyes, however, never left Ariane.

"Ladies," he said. Then he was gone, vanishing out the door so quickly and silently that it took Ariane a moment to realize he'd gone.

"He wasn't wearing a shirt," Elena said. "Or shoes. And the pants looked questionable when I first walked in. Must have been some doctoring."

Ariane thought about the shoes he'd neglected to pick up from the floor of her room and groaned inwardly. She'd been so preoccupied that she hadn't even noticed his bare feet.

"It's a long story," she said wearily. And she discovered she wasn't really in the mood to tell it. Still, she was compelled to add, "It's not quite what you think."

"Mmm," Elena replied, tossing her keys onto the counter. "You do realize he's one of the bad guys, right, Ari? He's hot, I'll give you that, but you hang around with Shades and you're going to find a whole lot of trouble."

"Do you know him?" Ariane asked, lifting a hand to rub at her temple.

Elena's mouth thinned as she leaned against the breakfast bar. "Not really. I've seen him around once in a while. Kind of an asshole, isn't he?"

The blunt assessment struck Ariane as funny, and she burst out laughing. "Yes. He is, mostly. But he has his moments."

Elena smiled, but it held more than a hint of reproach. "Moments don't make the whole package any better for you. I'd steer clear, Ari." She shook her head. "You want to make yourself scarce tomorrow night, I'll run him off."

Ariane had no doubt Elena would. But it wasn't what she wanted. "No, he's helping me look for Sam," she admitted. "Though I guess he thinks he's letting me tag along while he looks for Sam."

Elena snorted. "Typical male. You'll have to show him up."

"I already tried to cut off his head. It didn't seem to make much of an impression."

Then it was Elena's turn to laugh. "With guys like him, it takes a lot more than trying to kill them to impress them. He's got the arrogance thing down pat." She wrinkled her nose. "He was probably some worthless aristocrat. Probably still bitter that he got bitten by a Cait Sith instead of a Ptolemy."

Ariane frowned and looked away, giving voice to one of the biggest things that bothered her about Damien. "He doesn't seem bitter. Actually, he doesn't seem to care at all. About anything."

"That's a Shade, Ari. Being one requires having a healthy disregard for life, including your own." She angled her head. "You sure you want to get involved with him?"

"I'm not... *involved*," Ariane protested. "I need the help. I'm failing miserably on my own."

Elena looked dubious as she moved to the couch, sat down, and took off her boots. "You could have asked me."

Ariane stilled, surprised at the hint of hurt in Elena's voice. "But you've done so much already," she said. "How could I ask for more?"

Elena rolled her eyes, then smirked. "Only you would have an issue with asking for help from a friend, Ari. I have a job that comes with a lot of connections, remember? And in case you hadn't noticed, I like you. I worry a good amount about you getting your ass kicked, so obviously I like you. You remind me of my little sister."

Ariane settled herself in the chair opposite Elena, smiling. She was touched. If she'd had siblings, she didn't remember them. Just like she didn't remember any of her human life, whenever that had been. To be considered a sister to someone was new, and very sweet.

"You have a sister?" she asked.

"Had," Elena said. "I don't know many siblings who get eternity together. Not that it would have helped Maria. She was gone by the time I was turned."

Her expression changed subtly, and Ariane saw that there was an ocean of pain beneath that single statement.

"I'm sorry." It was all Ariane could think to say.

Elena shrugged uncomfortably. "Thanks. She was... innocent. Naive. Maria trusted everyone and died at the hands of a man who was supposed to protect her."

"I truly am sorry," Ariane offered quietly. It was inadequate, but all she had.

"I knew he wanted her. I just didn't know how far he would go." Elena's eyes were dry but full of old sadness. "I couldn't protect her then... but I can help to protect you now. Let me help, Ari. I'm no Shade, and I've got to stick around Charlotte for obvious reasons, but there are things I can do."

"I'm not sure what more there is..." There would be no putting her off, though. Elena had collected herself quickly, and Ariane already knew that her friend was like a dog with an old bone when she got an idea.

"I'll sniff around for you," Elena said, leaning back. "I can at least find out if and where there have been Grigori around here in the last, what, six months or so?"

Ariane nodded, surprised again that Elena's help was

so easily offered, so easily given. Though now she had a much better idea about why.

"I can also get you some new, sharp, shiny goodies," Elena said, casting a critical eye at the scimitar resting on the coffee table. "You're not the only vamp who likes to roll with a sword, but I think we can get you hooked up with weapons that are a little less obvious. Weaponry is one of my specialties."

Ariane stared at her in mute gratitude, reaching for something appropriate to say. As it happened, she could really think of only one, simple thing.

"Thank you," she said. "Really."

Elena deflected the sentiment with a casual wave of her hand, though her smile was genuine, making her eyes glow with pleasure.

"*De nada*. I had a feeling you'd liven things up around here if I kept an eye on you. Didn't even take that long."

"I don't want you to put yourself in any danger for me," Ariane said, voicing her one fear about Elena getting involved in any way, no matter how small. "I mean it. Because it looks like there's going to be some. The Grigori are looking for me, and it seems Sam may have been taken, somehow, by one of our deserters."

She briefly explained the situation, surprised at how good it felt to have a friend with whom to get things off her chest. Only now did she understand how sterile and detached her life had been among her own dynasty. There were cordial acquaintances, but few true friends. And yet in just a month out of the desert, she'd managed to find both a real friend and a man who saw her as desirable. She doubted Damien was capable of feeling much more than that for anyone, but still, it was real, hot desire.

She planned to savor every taste of this life she could, desire included. Particularly because she was now fully aware it could end at any moment, one way or another.

Elena listened quietly, seeming to process all the information, then nodded and rose, heading for the kitchen.

"Sounds like things are going to get interesting, then. But I've seen worse, Ari... I promise you that. This calls for a bottle of wine, I think. I'll tell you about my shitty night cleaning up after two vamps who decided to go after one another's arteries, and you can tell me all about this half-naked Shade I'm going to have to keep away from you."

Ariane let out a shaky laugh as Elena poured each of them a glass of Pinot Grigio. Her body was still humming faintly from Damien's touch, and the taste of him, dark and decadent, lingered on her lips.

She felt a little like a disaster. But Ariane also felt a surprising amount of relief.

"Sounds perfect," she said, and decided that, just for tonight, she could enjoy the fact that she wasn't alone.

Not anymore.

chapter EIGHT

H<small>E NEEDED</small> to get his head on straight.

Damien sat on the edge of the hotel's roof, looking out over the city. He'd showered and changed into a fresh set of clothes, and his hair was still damp, slicked back against his head. Impossibly, Ariane's scent still clung to him, wrapped around him as surely as the woman herself had been. She was night in an English garden. She was poetry in darkness, a winged vision of—

"Oh, for God's sake, this is pathetic," he muttered, swinging one leg absently and shifting his gaze to watch a plane coming in, the lights twinkling in the distance. He needed to work, not to get caught up in some pointless infatuation. Even as a youth, he hadn't succumbed to things like this. He'd simply bedded every passably attractive maid in his father's house and then moved on.

But Ariane was different. And it wasn't just because of those freakish, yet rather lovely wings of hers. Gods, he couldn't wait to hear what Drake had to say about that.

Later. He wasn't quite ready to share Ariane with anyone just yet.

The phone in his pocket began buzzing, as though Drake had sensed Damien thinking of him. He wasn't much in the mood to talk, but the conversation had to happen sometime. It was, at least, better than sitting here composing terrible poetry about Ariane's virtues. He pulled out the phone and put it to his ear.

"Tremaine."

"Did you plan on calling to let me know about Thomas Manon?" Drake's voice was tired, irritable.

That, Damien thought, was what being all work and no play did to you.

"I was indisposed this evening. And I knew you'd hear about it anyway."

A snort. "I hope whoever indisposed you was worth the ass-chewing you're about to get. I also hope you got something out of the man before he left us to sing in the choir eternal."

Damien looked up, wishing absently that the lights didn't block out the stars. Nights at his family's country manor had been pitch dark, the sky scattered with stars like diamonds thrown across velvet. Sometimes he would lie out in the garden, breathing in the scent of roses, and stare at them…

He frowned. He hadn't thought of these things in years and hadn't particularly wanted the memories back. So little good was in them. Though what little there was, Ariane had caused to surface. He didn't understand why. It was deeply troubling.

"I was there, Drake. I was the one who found him. But since I was plagued with Grigori trying to kill me all evening, it didn't really cross my mind to pick up the phone."

He knew he sounded peevish, but Drake ignored it. Instead, the weariness vanished from the Shade Master's voice, cold fury taking its place.

"Trying to kill you? Tell me who it was, and I'll have Shades crawling right up Sariel's ass. I don't care who he thinks he is—we have a contract!"

"I don't think you need to do that quite yet," Damien said, and explained, piece by piece, the events of the evening. He embellished a little where he felt it was necessary and omitted where his vanity dictated, but overall Drake got the whole picture. After Damien finished, there was a long silence on the other end of the line.

"Figure out how to take advantage of this yet, Drake?" he asked blandly, smoothing a wrinkle out of his khakis. If anyone could turn a liability into an advantage, it was the vampire he was speaking to.

"Actually, I'm just trying to figure out why you haven't called the Grigori in over this little...what's her name again? Ariel?"

"Ariane," Damien said.

"Whatever. If they find out you're running around with her, Damien, it isn't going to look good. You know they want her back."

"They're not paying me to bring her back," Damien replied, surprised to find himself irritated with Drake. The nature of the work had never been a point of contention between them. Not even when he'd decided to enjoy a mark's favors before turning her in, a thing that had happened occasionally in the past.

"A little goodwill never hurt," Drake shot back. "What do you care? You hate people in general. Turn her in and get over it. You're shallow; it shouldn't be hard."

"Lovely. Look, she's going to help me find him, Drake."

The response was quick and cutting. "You ass. I'm not paying some fugitive to do your work for you."

Damien sighed, knowing what was coming. "She's going to *help* me find him. Ariane doesn't want anything, just wants to know her friend is safe. With another Grigori involved, she could be very useful. We know nothing about them, Drake."

"You're sleeping with her."

"No," Damien spat. "I'm not."

"You must be," Drake said. "Because I have never, in over two hundred years, heard you willingly partner up with someone else on a job."

"Yes, well, she's not so much a partner as she is simply a means to an end. A useful tool." The words were unusually bitter on his tongue. How many had he said such things about? Hundreds. And he'd meant them. So why did the words sound so ugly this time?

"Anyway, things change."

"Not with you, Damien, no, they don't. It's one of the things I like about you. You're predictable."

"Ah. I love being damned with faint praise," Damien replied. "Look, Drake, Ariane is useful and wants nothing in return. I can't see how that's a problem."

"Oh? Tell me something, Damien. Is she beautiful?" Drake asked, his voice deceptively calm. "And don't bullshit me, because I can find out easily enough. She probably sticks out like a sore thumb."

"She's...yes. She's quite beautiful," Damien replied grudgingly. He hated being treated like this, lectured as though he were a willful child. But since Drake paid the bills and signed his paychecks, he had to take it. To an extent.

"White hair? Purple eyes?"

"Platinum blond. And her eyes are more of a light violet," Damien replied, not thinking about how his quibble would sound until it was already out of his mouth. Drake's beleaguered sigh came through loud and clear.

"You listen to me. I need this job. I want this job. This is a connection I've waited hundreds of years for. How the hell do you plan to get anything done running around with a Grigori fugitive?"

Damien stared into the distance and considered how to answer this. He didn't rightly know the answer. In all his long years, among all the women whose skirts he'd gotten under, no one had ever made him quiver the way Ariane had with just a simple touch. None had made him purr like a spoiled house cat. And when she'd gotten her hands on his cock, he'd nearly embarrassed himself and gone off right then, a thing that hadn't been a problem even when he was an untried youth.

For some reason, Ariane threatened his control. For that reason, she was almost certainly bad news. But slinking away from her would do no good now, and in any case, his pride wouldn't let him. No woman had ever bested him, and it would stay that way. Besides, Ariane was right about one thing: They were on the same path. From a realistic standpoint, pooling their knowledge and resources made sense. At least, it would if he could detach himself the way he'd always been able to before.

Finally, he gave Drake the only answer he had. "I'll make it work. You'll just have to trust me."

Drake groaned. "Do I need to remind you how many

Shades we've lost over the years who've said the same thing to me? Famous last words, Damien. Women and work don't mix. I'm just surprised I have to tell you that."

"She's nothing to me," Damien said flatly. "I'm surprised you're taking issue with my decision to use the sort of resource that rarely comes along."

Drake was silent again. Finally he said, "All right, Damien. You've never broken my trust in the past. But let me make one thing very clear: She screws this up, and I will teach you a lesson for the ages. You like to play, but this isn't a game. This is my business, and that crescent moon you wear means I own you. Forget where your loyalties are, what your job is, and you will be reminded in the strongest way possible. Is that understood?"

Drake's voice had roughened, deepened, and Damien shifted uneasily on his perch. He rarely heard the man like this, but it was never a sign of anything good. It was also a reminder that for all the years Alistair Drake had had to pile on a veneer of civility, he'd sprung from a dark and blood-soaked time where his personal body count had been incredibly high even before he'd been made immortal. The barbarian still lurked beneath…and Damien knew he'd do well to avoid provoking it further.

"Understood."

"Good. Update me when you have something."

Then he was gone. Damien pulled the phone away from his ear, looked at it, and then set it back down beside him. He breathed in deeply, taking in the scents of the city below him, the night sky above, keeping his mind carefully blank and open. But before long, her face surfaced in his mind again.

Drake was right—he'd never wanted to bring another

vampire on board and had never complained about betraying someone if the money was good enough. But that had been before. Before the Lilim, before he'd somehow won back Ty's friendship and forged another with Vlad Dracul.

He was changing. This strange infatuation with Ariane was just another symptom. And he needed to make it stop, because as little as he liked it, what Drake had said was true. His unchanging nature was what made him so good at his job.

"Doesn't matter," he told himself softly. "None of it. Just the job."

The problem was, he could say it all he liked. What he needed to do was start believing it again.

Oren waited until the still, small hours of night to emerge from the shadows outside the abandoned building. The pulsing and pounding from the music next door had just ceased, and he'd busied himself watching drunken humans, in ones and twos, in small groups, stagger into cabs and cars. He could smell their blood. He wanted it, badly.

And he took great pleasure in crushing the need inside himself.

Discipline was key. Denial was strength. These were things that vampires like Ariane would never understand. She had been born of weakness, carrying it still, infecting the bloodline by her very presence. She was a symbol of all that the Grigori stood against . . . and yet somehow, she had been allowed to live.

It was her fault he was so poisoned with rage, threatening his control.

Shaking off the dark thoughts that he wore more and more like a shroud, Oren spread his massive wings and, with barely a flicker, was at window level and letting himself in.

The smell hit him like a fist when his feet hit the floor. The scent of the Shade's blood was everywhere, dark and insidious, tempting. Oren's fangs lengthened instinctively, and it took him a moment to lock the hunger down again. He inhaled deeply, forcing himself to deal with the smell, the need. Then he walked to where a pool of blood was still drying on the bare floor, his eyes moving over the cut wires.

So. His tracker had been used as bait. But for who? At this point, it didn't really matter. Whether wittingly or unwittingly, Lucan had drawn out Ariane—and revealed himself. Sariel's suspicions had been confirmed. But it remained to be seen whether Sammael was a part of this against his will or by choice.

Oren hoped very much it was the former. Killing one of his brethren was enough. He would not have the pleasure of destroying their other deserter. Pacing the room, he looked for clues that were, to his annoyance, not there. Every breath carried with it the scent of roses.

Ariane.

He wished Sariel had not been so adamant that she be returned alive.

At least now she would be easy to track. How she had involved herself with the Shade he neither knew nor cared. It was a useful coincidence. And the cat, clever and foolish in equal measure, had no doubt been blinded by her beauty, drawn to the very weakness that made her unfit to wear her mark.

Disappointing, in a way. But useful. She would be out of the way soon, and then the important work could resume. The cat had been an excellent choice, like the hounds that human hunters used to flush out the fox, though he doubted the Shade would care for the analogy.

A strange night. But he was one step closer to Lucan, and to Sammael. Sariel would be pleased.

Oren sprang up, his wings unfurling in that single, graceful leap to carry him up through the opening that Lucan had left in the roof. The traitor was close. Ariane was closer.

"Sleep well, sister," Oren murmured as he soared above the lights of the city. "Soon, you return home."

chapter **NINE**

ONE THING ARIANE had picked up quickly was how easy it was to find humans to feed on. She'd never needed to hunt in the desert, but she'd quickly learned once she'd left. There was a pleasure in it that she'd been reluctant to allow herself to feel at first. The Grigori regarded feeding as a function of biology, nothing more. But the thrill of pursuit, the taste of warm life on her tongue as a human melted into her arms...

There was plenty appealing about all of it. And from what she'd seen, the Grigori were the only ones who didn't admit to enjoying the process.

She looked up into the eyes of the human she'd lured into a dark corner of the bar, her body pressed against his. He smiled at her, his gaze a little hazy both from the beer he'd been drinking and the light thrall she'd put on him so that he would behave himself. His arms were loosely wrapped around her, his hands resting at the small of her back.

"You're so gorgeous," he murmured. She rose up on her toes, a smile curving her lips.

"So sweet," she said. "Let me give you a kiss."

He moved to meet her lips, but she tilted her head to avoid the kiss, instead pressing her mouth against the warm skin of his neck. She heard the shuddering sigh and knew it was time. Ariane nuzzled into his neck, knowing her hair hid what she was doing from whoever might pass by, and sank her teeth in. The man didn't even flinch, instead gathering her even closer with a soft groan as she began to feed, drawing deeply from him.

"That's a pretty picture," a voice murmured in her ear. "And flattering. Do you always bite men who look like me, kitten?"

Startled but sated, Ariane licked the bite wound to seal it and then pulled away from this evening's blood donor. She could feel Damien hovering inches away from her, knew that if she leaned back, she'd be pressed against him. The thought was tempting, but she had other things to attend to first—and no matter how much she wanted him, she sensed that to actively pursue him would only end in unhappiness. Damien struck her as a man who tired of his toys easily.

"I have to go. Run along back to your friends now," she told the man—Matt, she remembered—staring into his eyes again. He blinked, looking confused, and nodded.

"Okay...wish you didn't have to...later..." He wandered away, bumping into a bar stool a few feet away before continuing on. He didn't look back, and Ariane knew that by the time he returned to his friends, he would have forgotten almost everything about her, save for the fact that she'd slipped away.

And damn it, he did bear a resemblance to Damien. She hadn't done it purposely, but there was no question she'd had the Shade on her mind.

Ariane turned to look at her company. The smug expression on Damien's face told her that he'd gotten over whatever had rattled him so much about their encounter last night. His usual snarky, disaffected façade was firmly back in place.

"I would have let you bite *me*, if I'd realized you were so keen on it," Damien said. "No need for a poor imitation like that."

"And what then? When this is all over, you'd run off and I'd be left with a mark that looks like a flying cat, probably," she said. Taking enough blood from another vampire would permanently alter one's dynasty mark. For a highblood, sullying that mark generally resulted in expulsion from the dynasty, so the change most often signified either a great love or a terrible punishment.

This would be neither, and Ariane didn't think she wanted to carry a reminder of her first great lust on her body forevermore.

"There's nothing wrong with a flying cat," Damien replied with a shrug. "It would be unique." He didn't deny that he would vanish after this. She needed to remember that.

His eyes darkened as he leaned close. "Not to mention, I think both of us would enjoy it."

She could smell his cologne, something earthy and woodsy, and beneath that the musk that was his alone. It wound around her in the semidark, threatening to break her resolve.

"Oh?" she asked, arching a brow and trying to seem

as casual as he always did. "Maybe you'd rather bite *me*, then, so *you* could have the flying cat."

She knew she'd called his bluff when his eyes dropped from hers. Which was, unfortunately, an opportunity to notice his incredibly long, thick lashes. She'd bet he was the picture of innocence when he was asleep.

"I've got two marks already, though," he said. "Three seems a bit like overkill." When he looked at her again, his expression was more guarded than teasing. "Well, if you're going to be anti-fun this evening, then I suppose we should get going. I've already wasted time having to come look for you. Didn't I tell you to wait at the apartment for me?" His eyes raised just a bit, and he reached out to finger a lock of hair that had escaped from the loose bun she'd fashioned.

"This does not look like a wig or a hat. Are you trying to advertise your bloodline to every vampire in the area?"

"I haven't had time to find anything yet. It's less noticeable up, I think," she said. Ariane knew she sounded testy, but at least half of it was from the way he was toying with the single loose strand of hair. Damien had graceful, strong, elegant hands. And they felt even better when he—

"It will be even less noticeable once I find you a baseball cap," Damien said, tucking the strand behind her ear and then removing his hand.

Ariane gave him a dirty look and started for the door. The crowd had grown thicker, and she could feel the barest touch at the small of her back as Damien squired her through the room. It was another unexpected touch of chivalry, and it made her wonder if Elena was right about his past.

Once they were out of the crush of people and noise, the hand vanished, but Ariane could still feel the warmth where it had been. Funny how such a light touch could make her feel so much more than the embrace of the man she'd drunk from.

She turned her head to look at Damien, impeccably put together as always in a crisp pair of khakis and a fitted black T-shirt. His hair was spiked up in the front. It looked meticulously done. He was beautifully, annoyingly perfect.

"I did wait for you," she said, now that it was quiet enough to adequately defend herself. "You took forever, and I was hungry. Elena said she would tell you where I was. Wasn't she up there?"

She didn't tell him how worried she'd been that he simply wouldn't show. Or what Elena had said she would do to him if he bailed on them.

Damien slid a disgruntled look at her as they walked, passing the waterfall sculpture. She wasn't sure where they were going, but her assumption was the parking lot, so she allowed herself to be led in that general direction.

"Yes, she was there. May I ask why?"

"She wanted to see me off." *And make sure I had a few new blades and a functioning cell phone*, Ariane nearly added, but decided that Damien didn't need to know everything she would be bringing with her. She still wasn't sure quite how far she could trust him, and having a spring-loaded knife strapped to her forearm would be excellent insurance if things went bad. The thin straps of tonight's sundress wouldn't have hidden that particular toy, but she was anxious to try it out.

"She's got an overabundance of unhealthy curiosity,

that one," Damien grumbled. "Lucky we're heading out now. She was probably still trying to figure out a way to profit from you."

The casual insult put Ariane's back up. "Don't say that. She's responsible, and she cares about me. That's more than I can say for most vampires I've met, so you can keep your opinions about Elena to yourself."

Damien looked mildly surprised. "Sensitive, are we? How sad, kitten. You're going to make me think you've never had any friends."

"I haven't. Just Sam. And now Elena. That's . . . that's it." She felt herself blushing and looked straight ahead, not wanting to see the mockery on Damien's face. She really needed to learn to watch her words more carefully. At home, honesty was valued, expected. Here, nothing was what it seemed.

She waited for the cutting reply, but Damien's words, spoken softly, surprised her.

"Well. If it makes you feel any better, I haven't had many either. It isn't everything, you know. The friend thing."

She turned her head to look at him, waiting for the punch line . . . but none came. Instead Damien looked at the ground, seeming deep in thought before straightening up and changing the subject completely.

"I think we should direct our attention to the Empusae next, mainly because I can't think of any better place to start over. Their numbers aren't what they were, but this is, at least technically, the seat of what remains of their power. I'm working on getting a meeting with one of the Empusa's higher-ups, but it could take until tomorrow. None of the Shades in the area have seen or heard of a rogue Grigori, so he's either kept himself very well hidden or he hasn't been on his own long enough to garner any notice. But the Empusae keep very close track of their territory, even though they're quiet about it, so"—he shrugged—"we ask there. *The* Empusa—it can get confusing when you're in a bunch of Empusae, since they take their dynasty's name from their ruler—owes me a favor, though she won't like me collecting on it."

"I know why they're called Empusae," Ariane shot back. "Just like I know that Empusa herself is sometimes called Mormo to differentiate."

Damien snorted. "I wouldn't try calling her that, if you enjoy having your head attached to your body. The lot of them are awfully prickly about treating her as anything less than a revered oracle. Mormo is a name reserved for those closest to her." He smirked. "Or those she needs too much to destroy."

"Hmm." Ariane filed the information away, glad she hadn't had to find it out the hard way. "Anyway, I'm glad we're going to the seat of the Empusae," Ariane said. "It was one of their dynasty who told me about Thomas Manon. Diana. She was very kind, and I'm sure she'd tell me if this Grigori has been seen around."

"Ariane," Damien said, reproach in his voice, "I'm not sure that announcing your presence to every highblood in the area is going to help you in the end. You know your people are looking for you."

"I didn't *then*," she replied, thoroughly exasperated. "And besides, Diana approached *me*. She wondered if I'd heard anything about Sam. I guess they were friendly enough that he kept in touch, to an extent. She mentioned that Sam had had a lot of contact with Manon. Sam apparently handled most of the dynasty's business with him."

They paused at the edge of the complex, beneath a stylized arch that served as an entrance to the parking lot.

Damien was frowning. "You know, your knowledge of your friend's activities outside of... well, wherever you came here from... seem to involve an awful lot of guesswork. I thought this was your closest friend?"

She opened her mouth, hoping some kind of reasonable answer would come out. When nothing happened, she closed it again. Why did she always end up embarrassed when he asked questions about her life? It was true—what she'd regarded as friendship back at the compound had turned out to be just a pale shadow of what it seemed to mean here. But there was no question that her kind was far from normal, even among vampires.

Damien picked up on her consternation almost immediately. "You know, you blush more than any vampire I've ever known. Believe it or not, kitten, that was an honest question."

She blew out a breath and looked up at the sky. "*Why* do you keep calling me that? I'm not your kitten. I'm not a pet or a small, fuzzy animal!"

When she looked at him again, he had tilted his head slightly, regarding her with plenty of interest, but without, thankfully, any malice.

"It seems to fit," he said. "Beautiful. Touchable. Very sharp claws. I'd promise to stop calling you that, but I'd be lying."

She laughed. She couldn't help it. And the burst of affection she felt for him in that moment set off warning bells immediately. *No*, she told herself. *No no no. Lust is one thing. Liking him is quite another.* But gods, it was hard when he was grinning at her like a naughty little boy.

"You're awfully blunt for someone who claims to be an expert in subterfuge," Ariane said. "Are you so honest with everyone?"

"No," he replied, and she laughed again. His eyes glowed faintly with pleasure as he watched her, and for a moment, Ariane completely forgot they weren't the only two people in the area. He had a way of doing that, she'd noticed. Wicked or not, he was certainly a compelling presence.

"I'm glad you find me so entertaining. Even though it's only going to puff up my already inflated ego," he said. "Come on, then. It's possible we'll run into Diana at the Empusae compound. If nothing else, she's an avenue to explore if Mormo—and I *can* call her that—decides to be difficult."

They turned down one of the aisles of cars. Ariane looked at the light reflecting dully off the metal and wondered what sort of car Damien drove. Something fast, she guessed. Sleek but not overly flashy. She was curious to see whether she was right.

They passed car after car in silence. Damien didn't give any of them more than a passing glance. Finally, however, he headed for a new red BMW convertible at the very edge of the lot sitting all by itself. Ariane smiled as he pulled the key fob out of his pocket and unlocked it. She'd been right.

"Why do you think she'll help us if she's inclined to be difficult?" she asked. "And don't tell me it's your good looks and charm."

He looked disgruntled, but far from ashamed. "I'm a Shade, Ariane. This may offend your delicate sensibilities, but what exactly do you *think* my kind does to curry favor with people? Bake them cakes?"

"You've killed for her," Ariane said slowly. The reminder that she was going to be traveling with—and was actively considering sleeping with—a cold-blooded killer was like a hard slap across the face. Maybe she needed the reminder. It was far too easy to forget.

"Her enemies are clever," Damien said with an unmistakable note of pride. "Not only does Mormo pay well, she always provides a challenge. Or she did. A shame that—" He caught himself from finishing the sentence and simply shook his head. "Never mind. Let's be off."

Ariane hesitated when he opened the car door for her.

"So you've...killed a lot of people, then?" Ariane asked, suddenly unsure of what, exactly, she was doing getting into a car with a man like him. It was one thing to know he was a Shade. It was quite another to hear him talk about the specifics...and leave the impression he really enjoyed the work.

Damien sighed loudly and looked at his watch. "Yes, Ariane. Look, it's past ten already, and the estate is outside of the city. Could you just get in?"

He seemed to realize then that something was wrong and looked at her closely. Ariane had to struggle to stay still beneath the sudden intensity of his gaze. She'd folded her hands in front of her and realized he'd probably noted that one hand had the other in a death grip.

"You look afraid of me all of a sudden, kitten," Damien said, stepping closer, his eyes turning feline in the dark. His voice was soft, but there was an undercurrent that made Ariane want to run. It took everything she had to stand her ground, but she refused to back away. It would only encourage him.

"Not afraid," Ariane said, though it wasn't quite the

truth. "I just…Does life mean so little to you? All the people you've killed, all the things you've destroyed…you never regret living this way?"

He arched a brow. "That's quite a question, coming from a pampered highblood who's never had to lift a finger for anything in her life."

"But weren't you pampered once too? You seem so—"

He laughed, cutting her off, and it had a cruel edge to it she didn't like.

"Well mannered? Yes, Ariane, my governesses made certain I had lovely manners. And the fact that my father looked at them as pretty toys to be taken in and then discarded when he was through with them ensured that I had plenty of teachers. Are you so interested in my pedigree, sweet? Looking for the prince in the heart of the killer?"

The bitterness in his voice, so strong, caught her off guard. If she'd wondered whether he felt real emotion, she now had her answer, for better or worse.

"I'm trying to understand you," she admitted quietly.

"There's nothing to understand. I was an aristocrat once. Now I'm not. I do what I like, when I like, just as I did then. Nothing has changed, except that people now pay me to behave badly." He moved even closer as he spoke, his voice dropping to a dangerous growl, until he was only a breath away from her. Desire unfurled, hot and unexpected, deep in Ariane's belly. She didn't have time to question why she should want such a broken creature. All she could do was react to him.

"Stop trying to run me off," she said softly. His eyes glowed like blue fire so close to hers. Her entire body sizzled with his nearness, with the prospect of his touch.

Damien's expression twisted into something pained.

"You should be running, Ariane. You're so damned innocent. You'll end up ruined."

She managed a small smile. "I don't think worrying about being ruined really has a place for a woman in the twenty-first century. Even I know times have changed."

He shook his head gently. "No, kitten. I'm not talking about your reputation. I'm talking about your heart and soul. There are still lots of ways to destroy those. And that is what I worry about with you."

The admission, simple and sweet, left Ariane momentarily speechless. It was the look in his eyes, so haunted and impossibly sad, that moved her to slide her arms around him and press her mouth against his. He turned his face away, his breathing heavy, though he didn't try to disentangle himself from her.

"Don't you dare feel sorry for me, Ariane. I neither need nor want your pity. So don't you dare." His voice was rough with whatever emotions had finally slipped through the wall he'd built. She knew better than to engage him like this, even knowing him so little. He seemed to be looking for a fight because it was easier.

She wouldn't give it to him.

"It isn't pity," she murmured, and pressed her lips to his cheek. Willing him to heal whatever wounds had made him this way would do no good, but the urge to hold him was far too strong to resist.

She felt Damien shudder, and his arms came around her, squeezing her to him tightly. His hands fisted in the fabric of her dress. In that instant, she could feel the tension that made him thrum like a live wire.

She melted into him, willing him silently to let go.

Then there were footsteps and a burst of laughter that

shattered the moment into pieces. One of the humans, cheerfully drunk as they made their way to their car, called out with a suggestion that she and Damien get a room.

He pulled away, though at least not as abruptly as he had last night. This time she saw the regret on his face. With his indifferent mask having slipped, he looked tired and vulnerable.

He needs me, she thought wistfully, then cursed herself for letting an idea like that into her head at all. She knew Elena was right. That way lay heartache.

For once, Damien had no pithy comment, no cutting aside. "Let's go," he said. "Night's wasting."

And with nothing to say, as confused about these odd feelings for him as she had ever been about anything in her long life, Ariane got in the car.

chapter TEN

T HE SEAT OF the Empusae was an old mansion set back behind a field of tall, sweet-scented grass and a thick wood beyond. The mansion was hidden from view of the road, visible only to boaters where it looked out over Lake Wylie, and the long drive was lined with cherry trees that burst into clouds of baby pink each spring.

Now, in the heat of July, the trees wore only deep green leaves, but the effect was still one of an entrance into another time. Damien tried to concentrate on the road, but he couldn't help noticing Ariane's reaction to the place, her nose pressed against the window.

He had to find a way to distance himself from her. He'd always enjoyed expressing himself physically ... as long as that meant giving some willing wench a tumble before getting back to his own business. But he'd thought he was long past needing something so simple, so pure, as someone's arms around him.

And yet he'd felt something inside shift and begin to crumble away at Ariane's touch.

Though he would never admit it to another soul, it scared the hell out of him. He liked things fine the way they were. He was perfectly comfortable not giving a damn about anyone but himself, with some small space reserved around the periphery for those he found interesting enough to call friends.

Innocence had always disgusted him. So what the hell was different this time?

"Oh," she sighed as they drove through the trees and the house appeared in front of them.

It had been done in the Greek Revival style, a massive white structure with graceful columns. Soft candlelight flickered through the windows, giving the place an unexpectedly welcoming effect. Damien found himself smiling a little. Vampires did love their candlelight. More flattering, more mysterious...and also more comforting to the many who had been born long before the age of electric lights.

The grounds stretched out along either side of the house, with a beautiful little domed building that Damien knew to be a temple off to the left. It was a beautiful place, well suited to the women who called it home.

He pulled up to the tall wrought-iron gate that blocked them from the house. A comm box was mounted just before it, and Damien knew full well there were cameras in the trees. The Empusae might revel in the past, but some bits of modern technology were too useful to pass up.

He pushed the button, and after a moment, a light female voice said, "State your business, please."

Damien slid a glance at Ariane, who looked good enough to eat tonight. Her jaw was tight, the only sign of her nerves apart from the hands clasped tightly in her lap. She seemed to be worried they would reject her coming. He knew the truth, however. Mormo was desperate to remain relevant. A Grigori visiting her court would be more than welcomed.

He, on the other hand, might not be. He had not been summoned. Fortunately, what Ariane had shared with him gave them an excellent cover.

"Ariane of the Grigori to see the lady Diana," he said into the comm. Here, he was comfortable using Ariane's real identity. According to all the sources he'd tapped, word hadn't gotten out about Ariane. The Grigori appeared to be rather invested in keeping word of defections quiet.

There was barely a pause. "Drive in, please, and welcome."

The doors of the gate swung slowly, silently open in front of them, and Damien cruised slowly into the large circle of stamped concrete.

"You can breathe now, kitten," he said without looking at her. There was a loud exhalation beside him, and he had to struggle to keep his amusement to himself. Ariane's honesty, in both word and action, would be a problem in some places. Here, however, it would be a boon. The Empusa herself, it was said, could see into a person's very soul. He doubted that, but the Empusae as a whole were uncanny judges of character.

Damien pulled the car off to one side and killed the engine. Though he didn't see a soul, he knew they were being watched. Dynasty courts never wanted to look paranoid, but they all were underneath. So afraid of losing power, he thought disgustedly. Though he supposed that if they weren't, he'd be out of a job.

Damien got out, walked around the back of the car, and opened Ariane's door for her. Part of it was old—very old—habit. The other part was simple enjoyment of her obvious puzzlement at being attended to. He got the sense that she had often been overlooked among her own kind. How, he had no idea, but it marked the Grigori as being every inch the useless fools that their highblood counterparts generally were.

Ariane was sweet, and kind, and beautiful. Like one of those bloody fairy-tale princesses who were always accompanied by singing wild animals.

He looked down and noted that this particular fairy princess looked rather ill and was making no attempt to get out of the car.

"I'm not sure about this," she said, lifting her bright violet eyes to his. Damn her, he thought, for having a face that kept knocking him on his ass every time he looked at it. He would *not* coddle her.

"I am," he said. "You wanted to team up, so here we are. I don't know what you're worried about. I have every intention of doing all the work."

"They're going to know," Ariane blurted. "What if they've been told to look for me? Who's to say Sariel hasn't put out word among the dynasties? I don't want to go back, Damien. I can't go back."

The sudden shift in her demeanor surprised him. He leaned down for a closer look and quickly saw what he hadn't noticed on the trip over. Ariane wasn't just worrying. She was rapidly moving into a full-blown panic.

"Darling," he said without thinking, then bit his own tongue in silent reprimand. "Ariane, they won't know. The other Shades don't even know. Sariel isn't concentrating on you at present. Be thankful."

"They told you," she replied. "And your boss."

Damien shrugged. "It was pertinent to my job. You rarely hear of a Grigori leaving the flock, Ariane, and then only long after the fact. I don't think they want it known. When Sammael is found, one way or another, I imagine they'll start hunting you in earnest. Save your fears for then, all right?" He paused. "Was it really that bad?"

She took a moment to collect herself, and Damien watched her as she squared her shoulders, breathed deeply, and slid out of the car.

"It wasn't bad," she said, finally answering him. "But it was barely like living at all."

"Hmm. Don't want to return to boring same-old. I understand," he said.

But Ariane shook her head. "No, it's more that I don't want to disappear. That's what happens to our deserters. They're brought back, and they vanish."

He wasn't surprised—he'd seen every manner of harsh punishment inflicted on a vampire for lesser transgressions, so why not? But the thought of those big, white-haired bastards dragging Ariane off and making her vanish filled him with a dark, ugly rage. Even as he sought to tamp it down, he was reassuring her, something he'd sworn he would not do.

"You won't vanish, Ariane. I'll make sure of that. Now let's go in—we look ridiculous standing out here."

She seemed to take his words to heart. Ariane nodded, her expression relaxing. His eyes dropped to her mark, so

clearly seen with her hair swept up. Wings, done in a style
that was very formal, classic...strong. It was apt. He'd
seen Ariane fight, and she was much stronger than she
looked. It was hard to forget how all that tightly coiled
strength had felt against him.

"I'm going to hold you to that, and I don't care how
much of a liar you are," she said. He knew she meant
keeping her safe...but she just *had* to say it while he was
thinking of undressing her.

"Feel free to hold me to anything you like," he murmured, and something in his face made her blush prettily,
though she didn't look away.

"Maybe I will," she said.

If only.

"You have a dirty mind, kitten," Damien said. "I told
you I'm a bad influence. Now let's go see what we can
discover."

Ariane stayed close to Damien as the double doors to the
house swung open without assistance from any visible
beings. Beyond was an enormous entry hall, with two
staircases curving away from one another before meeting at the top. Everything was marble, from columns to
the floors, and an enormous medallion with the flame of
the Empusae as its center was carved into the center of the
floor. Candles flickered from sconces on the walls, and
beyond the columns on either side, gauzy curtains framed
floor-to-ceiling windows. The entire effect was dreamlike,
and reminded her in some ways of the Hall of the Grigori.

She stepped over the threshold, barely noticing the
wispy column of smoke that rose before them until it
solidified into a familiar shape.

"Diana!" Ariane said, surprised into a grin that eased her tension considerably. Hearing about the unique abilities of each bloodline was one thing, but seeing them was quite another.

Diana, a slim blonde with pointed features and eyes that shifted between green and gold, reached out to clasp Ariane's forearm in greeting. Power sizzled up Ariane's arm at the contact, but there was no threat in it.

"Ariane. A lovely surprise. I hoped I would see you again." Her smile was warm, though it cooled considerably when her gaze turned to Damien. "I see you brought a...friend."

Damien smirked. "Hello, Diana. You're looking quite lovely, as always."

Ariane watched Diana level a cool stare at him and wondered whether there were any vampires who actually liked the man beside her.

"And I see you still have a knack for latching on to your betters so you can freeload," she said. "Shall I have you frisked for flammables, I wonder?"

Damien shifted position, his smile lazy, his eyes hard as stone. "Not at all. I'm only an arsonist on Wednesdays. I like to keep to my schedule."

"Damien is helping me," Ariane interjected, sensing that the verbal warfare was about to escalate quickly. When Diana turned her attention back to Ariane and raised her eyebrows, Ariane nodded.

"Please tell me you're kidding."

Ariane blew out a breath. It wasn't exactly how she'd hoped to start, but she supposed she ought to get used to it. "We're both looking for Sam...which is what I've come to talk to you about, if you have some time."

Diana sighed, her face falling. "He's still missing, then. I heard about what happened to Manon last night." Her eyes flicked to Damien. "I hope *you* weren't involved."

"Not this time," Damien replied. "I was there shortly afterward. His missing head put a damper on my appointment to talk with him."

"How very sad for you," Diana replied flatly, then turned her attention back to Ariane. "I would help if I could, but it's been months since I've seen or heard from him. And honestly, we're friends, but on his terms. He's very reserved. I only found out he was handling a lot of the finances with Manon because he slipped and said something about going there as he was leaving me one night. Beyond our chess games, I knew little of him."

"Chess?" Damien asked. "Is that a euphemism, I hope?"

Diana bared her fangs.

"We need to see M—the Empusa," Ariane said, only barely catching herself. That certainly stopped Damien and Diana from arguing, but from their expressions, it might not have been the best thing to blurt out.

"Subtle, kitten," Damien muttered, looking away.

Diana's eyebrows lifted as she looked between them. "Oh? I see. I've been used as a pretense."

"No, not at all!" Ariane said quickly. "I wanted to see you too. You were so helpful before that I thought you might have seen or heard something else. But things have gotten a little more…complicated…since I last saw you. This is your dynasty's territory. I think your leader should know what's going on. And maybe…I was hoping…she could help."

She held her breath as Diana mulled this over. Damien was silent, and Ariane was grateful for it. She guessed that even he knew nothing he said would be anything but a hindrance.

Finally, Diana relented with a soft, irritated sigh. "Well. I can't say you were wrong to come. Even though I must tell you that whatever Damien has promised you where my mistress is concerned is at least half lie, likely more." She shot Damien a hard look. "You know she doesn't involve herself much in worldly affairs anymore. Especially not at the request of a Shade."

Ariane's hopes deflated considerably, though Damien seemed only more determined.

"We'll see what she says when I actually make the request, then."

Diana's composure wavered. "Damn it, Damien," she hissed, her voice dropping. "She's not well, and you know it! And she's in no shape to see you, or anyone tonight!"

The look on Diana's face, contorted for the briefest instant into a mask of fury and despair, told Ariane that the rumblings she'd heard since coming to Charlotte were true. Somehow, the ancient leader of the Empusae, the child of Hecate, was dying.

Diana rounded on Ariane. "Not a word of this to anyone," she said, her tone slightly softened but no less urgent. "Please. We all know there are rumors. If they were confirmed..."

She trailed off, but Ariane understood. She nodded. "Of course," she said gently, knowing that the reality had to be worse than the rumors. And if the leaders of the other dynasties knew for certain how weak the center of the Empusae had become, there would be no mercy in seeking to claim what remained of the dynasty for their own.

"It's only a matter of time," Damien said quietly, his voice devoid of any compassion. "You'd do better to be searching for a replacement, rather than pinning your hopes on a miracle."

Diana collected herself then, straightening, schooling her features back into simple, unreadable beauty.

"The Empusae's affairs are not your concern, Damien." Her lips thinned. "You will, of course, continue to be paid well for your work on our behalf and for your...discretion." She inclined her head toward Ariane again, and for the first time Ariane could see the weariness shadowing Diana's eyes.

"Why don't you come in for a drink? You came all the way out here, and while I'm not as skilled as my mistress, if you tell me what's going on, I may be able to offer something. Besides," she continued with a soft smile, "I'd like to show you our court, Ariane. It's not often I get to show off for a Grigori. Sam refused to come inside without an invite from the Empusa, and I never wanted to trouble her for the invitation. Good thing we have a chess table outside."

"I'd love that," Ariane said.

"Wonderful," Diana said, and sounded as though she meant it. "We can join my other guest in the conservatory. It seems the gods decided I needed company tonight. Come on."

She beckoned as she glided forward, leading them into the west wing of the house. Damien walked beside her as they followed, uncharacteristically silent. Finally, he spoke just loudly enough for her to hear.

"I don't like this."

Ariane turned her head to look at him, curious. He was frowning at the floor, his brow furrowed.

"Like what?" she whispered. They passed rooms where beautiful women played music, or painted, or were simply engaged in conversation. It occurred to Ariane that she had never been in a place so utterly feminine. But then, that made sense. The Empusae were the only dynasty that was comprised of only one sex, female to the very core.

"This. We should be out there working, not sitting inside clinking our glasses together and celebrating how wonderful we are. That's such a bunch of highblood bullshit."

Ariane gave a soft huff of laughter, as intrigued as she was insulted. "Oh? It seems classier than, say, blackmailing an entire dynasty."

He snorted softly. "I'm not blackmailing them. Mormo—or whoever is actually running things right now—pays the House of Shadows well for our silence. You can take it up with Drake if it bothers you that much. I guarantee you'll get nowhere." He looked around, seeming to take in the serenity of the surroundings, then shook his head. "Pity. I didn't know it had gotten that bad. If she's really incapacitated this time, it won't be long before they fall."

"Don't say that," Ariane murmured.

Damien looked bemused. "Why not, kitten? It's the truth. I thought you appreciated my honesty."

She didn't answer him, couldn't look at him. Instead she watched Diana, following her lead. He would only laugh at her if he knew what the problem really was. She didn't mind his honesty. What bothered her was his complete lack of empathy. Ariane had read about what happened when dynasties fell. It was an ugly process, usually fraught with some vampires fighting and dying in a futile attempt to preserve their bloodline and the rest being assimilated into the conquering dynasty through what was known to be a painful and very humiliating process.

No doubt he knew that, had possibly seen things like it. And he felt... nothing.

Remember that when you're imagining his hands on you, Ariane told herself. *All you seem to do is feel, and he can't feel anything anymore, if he ever could.*

A sudden wave of sound came crashing through the hallway, scattering her dark thoughts to pieces. Ariane stopped in her tracks, eyes widening. She didn't think she'd ever heard music like this, wild and impassioned as someone's fingers danced over the keys of a piano. It required the kind of emotion that the Grigori were so good at containing. Some of her blood brothers and sisters could sing so sweetly it made humans weep, but that was borne of skill.

This was passion, something her kind had forgotten... something she wanted desperately to experience.

Diana paused in front of a pair of large glass doors to look in, and a soft smile touched her lips. She looked back over her shoulder, and whatever she saw on Ariane's face had her beckoning.

"I knew if I left him here, he wouldn't be able to resist. Come, you haven't lived until you've heard Vlad play."

"The Dracul is here?" Damien asked.

Ariane barely heard him, enchanted by what she was hearing. She walked to the doors, which were open just a crack, and looked in. In the center of the room sat an enormous black grand piano, gleaming in the candlelight. What transfixed her, though, was the man seated at it.

He was beautiful. There was no other way to describe him, though "beautiful" was probably too feminine a word. His hair was pale gold and swept away from his brow. His features were both strong and sensual, with a sharp nose and a mouth that looked like it would be just as capable of cruelty as seduction. She could tell he was tall even though he was seated, and his broad shoulders were showcased perfectly in a severe black suit.

All of that was arresting enough. But there was something about the way he looked as his fingers drew the music from the instrument, a hot intensity that would likely melt any human who attracted it, that stilled Ariane's breath.

Lucifer himself seemed to have stepped from the pages of *Paradise Lost* to sit down and play a song.

As the final chord reverberated out into the hall, she heard Damien's chuckle right before he slid by her and walked into the room.

"For God's sake, Vlad. All you need is a sparkly jacket and a gaudy candelabra."

Ariane looked to Diana, who was watching the scene unfold with a wry half smile.

"Is he trying to get killed?" Ariane asked.

"I wonder that sometimes," Diana replied as the gorgeous pianist rose, grinning, to greet Damien. "But not tonight. For whatever reason, Vlad likes him." She shook her head and rolled her eyes.

"If nothing else, you and Vlad have now reminded me that there's no accounting for taste. Come on, and let me introduce you to Vlad Dracul."

chapter ELEVEN

DAMIEN RELAXED into the plump leather chair and swirled the mixture of fresh blood and an excellent red wine in his glass. For the first time in weeks, he felt relaxed. He wouldn't have thought it could happen here, sitting in the temple of a dying queen while a winged homicidal maniac lurked gods-knew-where out in the night. But he had learned to take his pleasure where he could and not question it.

The four of them—he, Ariane, Diana, and Vlad—sat comfortably in the oversized furniture in front of a darkened fireplace that he was sure was the picture of coziness in winter. As it was, it was still incredibly pleasant. The translucent curtains moved gently in the night breeze while the cicadas sang outside to accompany the rumble of the occasional passing motorboat. The piano now sat silent, though not forgotten, at least by Damien.

He had once been quite proficient. But never like Vlad. Some bastards really did manage to get it all.

"And that," Vlad was saying, "is why Bram Stoker was and always will be a flaming, lying asshole."

Ariane laughed, the lilting music of it making it impossible for Damien to focus on anyone but her. She seemed to have relaxed, too, with her feet tucked up beneath her on the couch, having slipped out of her shoes when she'd thought no one was paying attention. But he had.

Thank the gods the woman seemed to have no clue just how much he watched her. Or how long he'd been trying to catch a glimpse of the dagger he was certain she had tucked into some frothy bit of lace around her thigh. Except it wasn't the dagger he was interested in.

She rested one elbow on the arm of the couch, curled up and happy like the kitten he liked comparing her to. Her hair was beginning to come loose, shining pale strands of it framing her face, making his fingers itch to pull out the pins and send the rest of it tumbling around her shoulders.

He was far too enamored of her hair. Much like every other part of her.

And it hadn't escaped his notice that the Dracul seemed equally fascinated.

"So he wrote an entire book about killing you off just because you wouldn't give him an interview?" she asked. "That's taking spiteful to an entirely new level."

Vlad chuckled. "Well, it was the lack of an interview, and then my instructions to all of my people that they were *not* to turn him, no matter how he begged. I've found that the ones who want it that badly are almost always complete disasters as vampires."

"I'll take your word for it," Ariane said, her smile as warm as the summer night. "I've never known a human to ask to become a Grigori."

"It could be because you have so little contact with humans," Vlad said. "Is it true that your people bring in rotating groups of blood donors, rather than leave the desert and hunt?"

Damien made a disgusted noise. "Careful, Ariane, he's slipping into professor mode. If he starts this, you'll be asleep long before sunrise out of self-defense."

"Oh, I don't mind," Ariane replied. "I think the differences in all our bloodlines, in the traditions of our houses, are fascinating." She returned her attention to Vlad. "How on earth did you know about the Chosen? No one knows about them!"

As Ariane, with Vlad's gentle prodding, began to talk about the humans who came to stay for months on end, pampered beyond their wildest dreams in exchange for regular donations of their blood, Damien glanced at Diana. She sat on the opposite side of the couch from Ariane and had lapsed into being surprisingly pleasant, apart from a few barbs. But now, when she felt Damien's eyes on her, she met his gaze, lifted one corner of her mouth in a knowing smirk, then returned her attention to Vlad and Ariane.

Damn her, she sensed Vlad's interest, too, and she knew full well it was bothering him.

Damien considered saying something wildly inappropriate just to turn Ariane's attention back to him, but he knew it would backfire. Vlad was too used to him for it to really work. He looked around the room, hoping for inspiration to hit him as Vlad launched into one of his many pet theories on everything that was utterly boring in the world.

"You know," Vlad said, his faint Eastern European accent more pronounced now, as it always was when he let his guard down a little, "I've never gotten a good look at the Grigori mark until tonight."

Diana laughed. "I'm glad you never tried. I don't think you'd be sitting here with us now if you had."

He looked mildly chagrined. "I could take down a Grigori if I had to."

"No," Ariane said. "You couldn't."

"You should see the swords they train them with," Damien muttered, irritated when no one even looked at him. This had turned into the Vlad Dracul show, complete with two rapt women and an utterly extraneous wingman: him. Vlad was one of the few people Damien could actually say he liked, but the animal magnetism thing with the opposite sex could be very annoying. Especially because Damien knew that a big part of the man would be perfectly content wrapped in a bathrobe, locked in his library poring over a bunch of dusty old books.

"Now, if only your men wore such fetching dresses, I might have seen the dynasty mark long before now. I would have been traumatized, but I would have seen it." He paused, and with a flash of white-hot anger, Damien knew what was coming.

"Do you mind," Vlad asked, leaning forward, "if I take a closer look at yours?"

Damien gritted his teeth. The man had to be stopped. The only solution that popped into his head wasn't a particularly good one, but it would at least save him from having to watch Ariane be lured into some kind of threesome right there on the couch.

The very thought of it had him shooting to his feet so quickly that the other three froze, staring at him as though he'd lost his mind.

He probably had, Damien decided. Not that it changed anything.

"I have an idea," he announced, feeling a hundred kinds of foolish. "Not that your proposed game of I'll-show-you-mine-if-you-show-me-yours doesn't sound engaging, but your little performance earlier got me thinking, Vlad."

"Oh?" Looking decidedly amused, Vlad sat back in his chair.

Damien had a sudden, terrible flash of clarity: The man had been baiting him all along. Which meant he'd been incredibly obvious. Which meant he'd walked right into this sick little trap...

"Do tell," Diana purred, looking like the cat that got the canary.

Ariane simply waited, quiet and composed, utterly unaware of what he'd just been forced to reveal. He let his eyes linger on her for just a moment, still struggling with the wave of hunger even that brought on. Not hunger for blood but hunger for her attention, her interest, and some nameless *more* he could neither define nor deny.

"I've heard, though this was never confirmed, that the Grigori are often possessed of beautiful voices. I thought you might sing for us, Ariane."

She blushed, as he'd known she would. He wondered how quickly he could make her flush if he had her under him... on top of him...

"How did you know that?" she asked.

"I've picked up a few things from the professor's dissertations," Damien replied, jerking his head at Vlad. "I tried not to, but it's such a bloody flood of useless information that a few things stuck." He saw her uncertainty, and right then knew that he had to hear her sing. Not because of Vlad, but because it was another facet of the woman to uncover. It was madness, that such a beautiful creature could be so self-conscious.

Drawing her out of her shell, unlocking more of her secrets, was suddenly the most important mission in Damien's universe.

"I'm not really used to singing for an audience," she hedged.

"Look, I'll accompany you," Damien pressed. "I was passable at it once. But I'm bound to be rusty enough that I'll be the one making noticeable mistakes. Humor me, Ariane."

"Do," Vlad agreed. "I've heard him play. We'll need your voice to cover it up."

Ariane laughed a little nervously, but Damien had to fight back the satisfied smirk when she stayed focused on him and not Vlad. Mission accomplished.

She stood, smoothing her simple sundress down over curves that made his mouth water every time he paid them too much attention—which was a lot. Damien held out his hand, torn between guilt and pleasure when just the feel of her hand sent heat curling down his arm and through his body.

"Just like old times," Diana commented, lifting her glass to her lips and not bothering to mask her curiosity. "Really, really old times."

"Not as old as you, darling," Damien said with a sharp grin in her direction before returning his focus to Ariane. He led her to the piano, settled himself on the bench, and looked up at her. The blush had faded, and she was now several shades paler than usual.

"You're going to pay for this," she said under her breath. "I'm not a performer."

"That," Damien said, "is refreshing. What shall we torment them with, kitten?"

She surprised him by selecting something he knew right off the bat, a piece he'd often enjoyed at the gatherings and parties he'd attended as a mortal, and after. His fingers were rusty, but they remembered the motions well enough, and Damien got through the introduction with a minimum of clinkers. For just an instant, sitting at the piano with company and candlelight, he was back home, surrounded by people he enjoyed, his life, his *real* life, ahead of him. Before he'd really understood what darkness was.

Then she began to sing, and that first high, sweet note cut him to the quick.

Damien barely felt his fingers on the keys. Vlad's dusty research had not done the Grigori's gift of song justice. But then, he doubted the source of the knowledge had ever heard Ariane. She sang words, but all Damien could hear was her emotion. Her voice was full of more longing than he'd ever heard expressed, the sort of longing he'd foolishly thought did not exist outside himself. The song rose and fell, rose and then built toward a note that arrowed right through him.

Memory, so long suppressed, flooded him. Sunshine in the gardens, the kind voices of the many women who'd had a part in trying to raise him. The elusive ghost of the woman who'd birthed him, laughing as she danced with him in her arms. Music. Friends. Warmth. Light.

But with the good came the rest. And as Ariane's voice slipped into a minor key, all Damien could see was his father, red-faced and corpulent behind his massive desk, calling him a disgrace to the Tremaines. Decrying Damien's lack of shame when the old man had none himself. Comparing him to the brothers who were never bothered with him.

And finally, on the last night he'd ever set foot in Hawkesridge, recoiling in horror from what his youngest son had become.

That was the night Damien had looked into the darkness and discovered what he was really looking into: himself.

The final note was struck, Ariane's song complete. There was utter silence for a moment as Damien struggled to compose himself. He hadn't thought of those last months at home in years, perhaps even a century. What did it matter that he was lost? He always had been.

Except that wasn't true. And he hated remembering the days before he'd understood he would never have anyone to rely on but himself. His innocence had died a hard and early death . . . but it had existed once.

The rush of memory left him shaken.

"Beautiful," Vlad said.

Then Ariane's hand was on Damien's shoulder, bringing him back to the present, a small but important anchor.

"Are you all right?" The words were soft, breathed into his ear. He wished he could turn his head and bury his face in that glorious hair, could lose himself in her. But Damien knew that if he got too close, he would ruin her, and risk breaking the part of himself that had allowed him to survive this long.

"I'm fine, kitten," he murmured, turning his head and

finding her face just inches from his own. He breathed her in before he could stop himself, his head full of her scent. Her eyes glowed faintly, the color of storm light.

"You play very well," she murmured, her eyes dropping to his mouth. He swallowed hard, flexing fingers that wanted to pull her against him. He'd warned her she was playing with fire.

"Your voice covered the considerable flaws," he said, hoping his voice didn't waver. "I've never heard anything quite so beautiful."

When she realized he was being serious, she beamed. The simple pleasure he got from that blocked out everything else...except the scent of ancient spice carried on a breath of night air that might have drifted, hot and dry, from the desert itself.

His instincts, honed to a fine point over many years, were too strong to ignore, though when he broke the moment, it was with the sort of regret he thought he'd long since left behind.

"We're being watched," he said, his voice so soft and smooth he might have been baring a bit of his heart. Instead, he watched Ariane's smile fade at the warning.

"Don't look at the windows. Don't say a word," Damien said. "Leave the room and shut the door behind you."

He watched her inhale, saw her draw in the scent of her kinsman. He expected to see the recognition on her face. What he didn't expect was the sick fear that accompanied it.

"Oren," she whispered, her eyes going blank for one horrific instant. Then she looked directly into Damien's eyes, and he saw something that shook him even more than her voice had. Something that he had been well acquainted with, that he had learned to blithely ignore even when it came to himself.

Slowly, she shook her head.

"This fight is mine. He'll kill you all to get to me. It's his right. You have to go."

And in her eyes, he saw death.

chapter TWELVE

ARIANE BARELY NOTICED Vlad and Diana rising from the couch, nor did she truly feel Damien taking her wrist with a grip that suggested he had no intention of leaving the room without her. All she could think, repeating on an endless loop inside her head, was:

It's over. He's found me.

Part of her had known he would. And still she was surprised, unprepared. It was so much sooner than she'd expected. She wanted to believe that simple bad luck had put her and Oren in the same place at the same time.

But she knew it wasn't true. Was her final humiliation truly so important to him that it overshadowed even the needs of the ancient ones? It made no sense...and it didn't matter. He was here.

"Come," Diana said brightly. "There's something I want to show all of you."

When Damien dragged her out the door, all she could do was follow numbly. Of course, he wasn't doing what she wanted and leaving her here to fight, to die. And part of her was absurdly grateful that he never did as he was told, even though her confrontation with Oren was now inevitable. He'd been waiting centuries to finish this.

Diana shut the doors to the conservatory, but Ariane could still smell him, the scent now seeming to pour into the hallway from other rooms, other windows. He would know she sensed him, would be taking pleasure in it.

"I think," Damien said flatly, "that you'd better explain why a bunch of Watchers feel perfectly justified in trying to kill us. Because this is a hell of a time for them to decide to stop standing around staring at wreckage and doing nothing useful."

Ariane sighed, rubbing her hands over her arms and thinking about the small dagger sheathed against her thigh. It should have been reassuring. Instead, it only made her think that no amount of weaponry would be enough to stop Oren.

"It's very simple," she said, her voice surprisingly even. "I left without permission. That changes the rules. It's me they want, but that won't matter if you get in the way."

Vlad made a soft noise of understanding, and Ariane looked at him, unsurprised. He was a dynasty head. Of course he would know.

"A friend of mine has gone missing," she explained to him. "I felt I had more to contribute than just sitting in the desert. So here I am."

"Ah. Sammael. Diana mentioned someone was looking for him. I hadn't realized it was you. And that you were here without permission," Vlad said.

"Neither had I," Diana added, sounding less than pleased.

Guilt coiled into a knot in the pit of Ariane's stomach. She had put these people in danger.

"*I* knew," Damien said, sounding as though he thought the others were a little slow for not having caught on. "But between last night and now this, I'm beginning to think that someone forgot to mention we were operating under an entirely different set of rules." His eyes narrowed. "So why don't you explain just what it is this Oren will do to get you back where he thinks you belong? The look on your face tells me he won't just be lecturing you."

His eyes, so warm only minutes ago, had gone arctic. He thought she had lied to him. He was no doubt used to being lied to. But he was giving up on her awfully easily.

She pushed her frustration at that aside and tried to make him understand. "We are Watchers when it comes to others. But we're all trained fighters, Damien. The Grigori take care of our own." She looked away. "At any cost."

"If any of us stand in the way of this Oren retrieving her, which I'm sure he was ordered to do at the behest of Sariel, he's within his rights to kill us. The Council would agree. This is a dynasty matter, and in the eyes of our law, none of our affair," Vlad said. "He could knock on the door and demand her . . . but my guess is he'll bide his time outside to avoid a larger scene, if possible."

"He knows I'll face him," Ariane said. "Whatever else he thinks I am, he knows I'm no coward."

Damien looked at her sharply, but she couldn't hold his gaze. Instead, she slid the small dagger from the sheath on her thigh. It wasn't much, but it would have to do. She should never have left her sword in the car.

Likely it would make no difference anyway.

"Why haven't I heard about this rule?" Damien snapped. "I've never heard of a Grigori killing anything!"

"Because no one is stupid enough to fight them, and none of them ever flee the compound. The Grigori are very disciplined," Diana said, looking at Ariane thoughtfully. "It speaks well of you that you'd risk so much for your friend."

"That's debatable," Ariane said, looking around. "Look, I've put you in enough danger. I didn't think he'd make finding me a priority, and that's my fault. I should have known. Oren has a...a problem with me." She looked at Diana. "I'm sorry."

Diana shook her head, her smile troubled. "No apologies. He's no danger to me or mine, Ariane, unless we fight for you. And I know you understand why I can't do that."

Ariane nodded. Provoking a conflict with the Grigori would be a huge mistake with the Empusae so weakened.

Vlad frowned. "You mean to fight him, then."

"I won't go back with him," Ariane said. "I would rather die."

She hadn't realized how true the words were until she said them. She would die anyway if Oren brought her back. And she would much rather lose her life here than in the arid silence of the desert, among people who cared nothing for her.

Damien cursed softly beside her. "Hell with that. Nobody's dying except that nosy winged bastard outside."

She'd gotten used to Damien's acid tongue and quick temper, but it didn't occur to Ariane until too late that she'd seen almost nothing of his skill as a fighter...and as he kept telling her, he was one of the best.

He hadn't been lying.

Damien moved like lightning, throwing the doors to the conservatory open and crossing the room at a run so fast that he barely seemed to touch the ground. He leaped through a window and out into the darkness before Ariane could make a sound.

"No," she breathed as a feline snarl echoed into the night beyond. She looked down at the small dagger in her hand, then looked at Vlad.

"Please," she said, the blood beginning to pound in her head. Oren would kill Damien. Of that she had no doubt. And while the thought of being responsible for anyone's death was unconscionable to her, the thought of Damien's broken and battered body was somehow worse.

Wordlessly, Vlad pulled a long, elegant dagger with a simple silver hilt from a sheath on his belt and presented it to her. She took it and barely managed a "thank you" as she spun and set off after Damien, jumping the window ledge. But instead of taking the ground route after her would-be savior, she unfurled her wings and rose like a shot into the inky sky.

Vlad and Diana watched her go, catching a glimpse of shimmering wing as Ariane vanished.

"There's more here," Vlad murmured.

"Stay out of it, Vlad," Diana said, her voice quiet but urgent. "Whatever stirs in the desert, we must wait for Mormo's guidance. Right now all that stands between the Empusae and the abyss is the support of the Dracul." Her hand gripped his arm. "She will wake. She always does."

He turned pale blue eyes on her, the doubt in them evident. "Until the day she doesn't, Diana. You and your sisters need to begin preparing for that. And I have obligations of my own."

She drew in a breath and seemed about to rail at him. After a moment, though, she simply inclined her head. "Do as you will," she said stiffly.

And in a swirl of pale silks, she was gone.

Ariane saw them as soon as she cleared the trees.

Damien faced Oren at the water's edge, and his taunts cut like a knife through the sultry air.

"Your interference is going to cost you and your bloody dynasty," Damien said, his voice icy.

Oren's voice was calm, eternally, infuriatingly calm. But Ariane knew him well enough to hear the dark promise beneath the surface.

"I interfere in nothing. My mission is my own. You seal your fate by standing in the way of it."

Damien's laugh echoed through the night. "What an unoriginal threat. You know I'm not going to let you have her. She's valuable to *my* mission. One your master is paying me for, lest you've forgotten. I doubt he'll take kindly to you destroying a lead."

"Ariane is not a *lead*. She is a disgrace. A blight on our blood. She will be returned, and judged. And there is nothing you can do to stop that, little cat. Best you not try, if you value your sorry life."

Oren's words surprised her, but they were far less painful to hear than she'd imagined they would be. She'd known how he felt all this time, and he was far from alone in his assessment. This was not news to her. Damien, however, looked disgusted. The outrage on her behalf warmed her, even as her heart sank.

This was the part where he would get himself killed with that mouth of his.

She opened her mouth to shout down to them, but the words died in her throat when, with the barest flicker of movement, Damien opened up the side of Oren's face with his claws. She saw Oren's head snap sideways, saw the streaks of black blood well in long lines from temple to chin.

Gods, he was fast. And insane.

Oren closed his eyes, flexed his fists. It was only then that Ariane saw how much fury he had inside of him, all rushing to the surface. If he got his hands on Damien, he would tear him apart before continuing his hunt.

"Oren!" she shouted, even as Damien prepared to strike again. Both of their heads snapped up, and she would swear that Oren's eyes flashed red in the dark.

"Damn it, Ariane, no!" Damien shouted, but it was too late. Without even looking, the male Grigori sent Damien hurtling backward with a simple swing of his arm. And then he was coming for her, massive wings snapping outward, his lips peeled back in some obscene parody of a smile.

She hesitated for only the briefest of moments, stupidly wishing she'd been able to say good-bye to Damien. Her chances of getting out of this were slim, and she knew it. But she had to reach for that slim chance for as long as she could.

Ariane watched him flying at her, then turned in mid-air and dove, hurtling toward the ground before soaring once again. The wind rushed over her as she lured Oren away from Damien, whom she'd glimpsed moving where he'd been thrown. It mattered that he lived. She didn't know why, but she didn't question it.

She dipped and turned, rose and spun, leading Oren on a chase out over the water. In her hand she clutched Vlad's dagger, her knuckles white. Winning this last contest between them would mean driving it into his heart. He had always managed to best her, had always made a point of it in every lesson, every contest. Small, painful victories in his war of attrition.

This last time, it was winner take all.

Oren was close behind her but couldn't quite seem to catch up. In strength, he had always been her superior, but never in speed. In races he had always cheated or enlisted others to take her out by hurting her. Robbed of his usual tricks, Oren was struggling to close the distance, and Ariane used her advantage the way she'd always wanted to. She pushed herself, her muscles protesting the speed, the rapid pumping of her wings. She banked quickly, taking them over more woods and darkened houses far below.

"I'll catch you, Ariane. When will you learn you can't beat me?"

His voice was behind, but far too close. She answered him, her voice strained from exertion.

"Why is this so important? You should be working this hard to find Sam, not to drag me back!" She had to force herself to say the next words, even though she knew they were true. "I'm nothing to the Grigori!"

"Weak little fool," he snapped, his voice echoing through air that was rapidly cooling the higher they flew. "*You* became the priority as soon as you left the compound! You endanger us all with your stupidity! You should have been left to die on the ground, instead of being given the blood of an ancient!"

He was almost upon her, and she had to force herself

not to waver at his words. The blood of an ancient? Had she been sired by one of the ancient ones? It would explain a great deal...including the force of Oren's hatred. Only the worthiest were sired by the ancient ones. And she... she was...

Oren's roar of triumphant fury slammed into her as his hand caught her ankle, clamping down like a vise and yanking her backward. Ariane's breath escaped in a single rush. She acted on instinct, snapping her wings shut and wrenching herself around. Her ankle snapped like a twig, the pain so bright and hot that she started to gray out. Strong hands caught her by the waist as she fell.

And yet, despite the haze, she knew what she had to do. She grabbed Oren's shoulder and drove the dagger deep into his chest, straight through whatever passed for his heart.

She extended her wings again, catching her in the instant that Oren's blazing eyes widened. The strike through the heart wouldn't kill him, but the shock of it gave Ariane the opening she needed. She tore the dagger free, and as Oren began to flop gracelessly in the air, blood streaming from his chest, Ariane sliced neatly through one of his wings.

The sight of that beautiful appendage falling uselessly to the ground sent a sharp, stabbing pain through her own wings, twin bolts of hot agony that radiated from her back to the tips. Ariane arched in a silent scream, the pain too great to allow even a whisper. Her entire chest seemed to have seized. There was no air.

And then it was simply gone, vanished. Ariane drew in deep, convulsive breaths while she pumped her wings, reassuring herself that she was still whole. Below her, Oren was falling silently toward the ground. She dove after him, wishing she could feel nothing, that she could feel as bloodthirsty as he seemed. But just as she'd never been able to push aside her emotions, she'd never been able to hold on to her fury. She had never killed, never really wanted to.

Yet here she was, with only one option if she wanted to live long enough to save Sammael.

Ariane landed lightly on the ground a few feet away from where Oren had fallen at the edge of a field. He was writing in pain in a pool of blood, his one good wing curling and uncurling. Nausea coiled deep in her stomach. She had done that. *She.*

He must have caught her scent, because he spoke to her without even looking at her.

"Treacherous bitch. More will come after me. You deserve a worse death than you'll get for dishonoring the blood in your veins." He ground out the words, his pain evident in every syllable.

She forced herself to walk slowly toward him, slightly favoring the ankle that was already nearly healed, a death grip on the blood-covered dagger in her hand. She wasn't sure whether he had the strength to leap up and continue the fight, but she was taking no chances.

"I don't...I don't want to kill you Oren," she said, hearing the tremor in her own voice. "But I will if you don't stop. I am not the enemy."

He laughed, a pained, hollow sound, and turned his head to watch her approach. "You've already killed me," he said. "So many secrets you don't know. Secrets in the sand...in your blood."

She stopped short as he tried to lift himself up on one shoulder, gave a pained cry, and slammed back to the ground. There was nothing but the sound of him breathing heavily. She took a step closer, then another.

"Why are you hunting me?" she asked. "Just because I have the...the blood of one of the ancients? It shouldn't matter. None of them will ever claim me. I'm nothing, no one. I don't know any secrets, like you said."

"Because," Oren said, black blood leaking from one corner of his mouth, "every one of us is a living secret, Ariane. And you are a pathetic Grigori, but the ancient blood brightens your soul. You...you are perfect to stop the Rising...for another hundred..."

His words were interrupted by a spate of deep, painful coughing. When he stopped, his eyes were brighter but his breathing shallower. Oren seemed to be fading away while she watched. And she had so many questions...

"He stirs and hungers beneath the sand," Oren rasped, his gaze going far off. "Go home before you destroy us all."

Then, to Ariane's horror, he burst into flames.

"No!" she shouted, rushing forward. The dagger fell to the ground, unnoticed, as she ran to Oren's side, as she began to beat at the flames with her bare hands. She had wanted to get away—from him, from all of them. She'd wanted him to leave her alone. But the reality of Oren's death shook her to the core, where something seemed to break.

As he burned to nothing but cinders and ash, Ariane staggered away and was wretchedly sick. She had killed one of her own.

The screams of barely remembered loved ones on a night soaked in blood echoed in her memory, mingling with Ariane's broken cry beneath the same indifferent stars.

chapter THIRTEEN

H E'D THOUGHT she would die.

Damien had thought that he would find Ariane's battered and lifeless body on the ground or that he would see Oren carrying her limp form off to a delayed, but inevitable, death. Instead, he'd found her kneeling by the ashes of her attacker, improbably alive, but so grief-stricken that she'd been little more than a glassy-eyed wraith at first.

The relief he'd felt at the sight of her had nearly taken him to his knees.

It was the first instance of real terror he'd experienced in over a hundred years. That was why he hadn't allowed himself to touch her, instead hanging back and waiting for her to collect herself.

"You should have let me handle it," he'd finally said to her when she'd come to him, silent and haunted. "He doesn't deserve your grief. He wouldn't have gotten mine."

Though he was serious, he'd hoped to provoke her.

Something, anything to snap her out of her hollow-eyed misery. Instead, she'd just given a small shake of her head.

"I can fight my own battles," was all she said as they'd walked toward the road.

Yes, she sure as hell could, Damien thought. Why it bothered him so much that she *did* was a question that was going to plague him.

Which it did as he sat ensconced in the comfort of Vlad Dracul's private jet.

Damien and Vlad sat across from one another, each sipping a cocktail. Damien wasn't a huge fan of vodka, but with luck it would steady his frayed nerves. Ariane had taken up residence on the small leather couch behind Vlad, where she stared out at the night. She'd washed up as best she could in the small bathroom, but her blood-spattered dress was an ugly reminder of what had come before.

"Are you sure you want us staying right there at your house?" Damien asked, still rankling a little at what he couldn't help but perceive as Vlad's particular brand of high-handed charity. "There are plenty of bolt-holes in Chicago I can take Ariane to where no one will bat an eye at either of us. And it would cause you less trouble."

Vlad waved his hand. "If I didn't want you with me, I wouldn't have come looking for you." There was a knowing glint in his eye. "You don't need to get your back up, Damien. I'm not trying to babysit you. But what you're doing...interests me."

"Of course it does," Damien muttered, swirling the vodka in his glass. "You're interested in everything you shouldn't be."

"A problem we share," Vlad replied with a faint smile, inclining his head in Ariane's direction. She was paying no attention, but it annoyed Damien anyway. So he was attracted to her. So he'd allowed her to come along when he hated working with people. So he'd risked dismemberment by a huge winged vampire for her.

So bloody what?

He downed the vodka, put it on the small table with an angry little *smack*, and leveled a cool stare at Vlad.

"I'll need the use of your library. A car. Any contacts you have who might be useful, particularly those who've had dealings with the Grigori. As I told you, this Oren wasn't the only encounter we've had in the last couple of days. And I owe the one who's still alive a garroting."

"Mmm, the one who knows where Sammael is," Vlad replied, frowning.

"And killed Thomas Manon. Drake's mad as hell. Some people are saying the House of Shadows is responsible." Damien shook his head. "Sloppy, pathetic work. He doesn't want to own that. None of us do."

Vlad chuckled, and Ariane's voice, soft but perfectly clear, drifted from the couch.

"He's protecting Sam."

Both men turned to look at her. Ariane had pulled her gaze away from the window, and she looked exhausted, Damien noted. He started to tell her she'd be going to bed immediately after getting to Vlad's, but then bit his tongue. She could do as she liked. It was no affair of his, as long as she wasn't risking *his* life.

And yet he found himself studying the shadows that had appeared beneath her eyes, silently clucking over her like an old hen.

"Of course he is," Damien said. "I told you this didn't seem like an abduction. Manon knew something, or he thought he did and was poking around in places he shouldn't have. That big bastard took care of the problem. And if you and I had looked a little closer, I would guess we would have found a file or two missing." Damien rolled his shoulders, wishing the tension would go away. "Unfortunately, the question of why a Grigori ancient would go to ground and kill to stay there, along with what looked like *another* Grigori ancient who you say you've never even seen, remains to be answered."

"It truly is a pity Mormo isn't well," Vlad murmured. "She can see things none of us can."

Ariane looked as though she wanted to say more but seemed suddenly uncertain. He wasn't surprised. It had been a hell of a night, and she didn't know Dracul from Adam.

"Go ahead and ask him whatever you like, kitten. Vlad's trustworthy enough. Mostly because he'd rather be locked in his library than interact with people he could betray you to."

Vlad's brow arched, and Damien gritted his teeth. It wasn't the casual endearment, he was sure, so much as the gentle tone he'd used with her. To say it wasn't a tone he used often would be a massive understatement. It seemed to work, though, as Ariane spoke.

"In your research...have you ever heard of something called the Rising?" she asked.

It was a question Damien didn't quite understand, and Vlad looked to be in the same boat. He shook his head slowly, thoughtfully.

"No. I don't believe so. But that doesn't mean there's no mention of it in some book or other I have. Why? Is this something the Grigori speak of?"

Ariane looked troubled. "No. Just something Oren mentioned. Before." She closed her eyes for a moment, as though steeling herself against the memory, and then looked at them again.

"I'll have a look in your library, too, if you don't mind. Even if it turns out to be nothing."

But she clearly didn't think so, Damien thought, watching her relief as Vlad graciously invited her to make good use of whatever he owned that might help. He mulled the term over. Rising? It sounded like another mess waiting to happen. He would do some checking himself. On his own. While Ariane was firmly, and safely, ensconced in Vlad's library. The mansion was as solid as a fortress, and just as well guarded.

He wasn't cutting her out, he reasoned. But some things were better done solo. And if that had the added benefit of keeping the woman from the sort of bodily harm she seemed to attract like a magnet, well...

It was all for the better. She could get some rest. And he could get some air, some space...something.

At the pretty thought of Ariane poring over some dusty tome, warm and cozy in Vlad's library, Damien found his mouth curving. The tension in his shoulders finally began to ease.

If I'd lived, I'd have wanted someone like her as my mistress, Damien thought, thinking of how empty he'd often found his town house in London after returning from a night at the gaming hells. *I'd have tucked her away, given her everything, a bit of sunshine for when I most needed it...*

More memories, Damien thought, shoving them away the instant he realized he'd lapsed into some stupid fantasy again. He'd had no mistress, only whores. His town house had been taken apart and sold by his disgruntled creditors once his father had announced Damien's "death."

There had been no bit of sunlight. And now there never would be. He had only moonlight, as silver as Ariane's hair.

His plan to work solo the following night went off more smoothly than he could have hoped.

Though he had never been an early riser, Damien managed to be up right at sundown, dressed and groomed in record time and then quickly fed by a pretty mortal employee who was also in Vlad's stable of willing blood donors. It only bothered him for a moment when he realized that he felt no interest in her beyond a meal, where under normal circumstances she was the sort he would have lured off into a corner and dallied with.

He was preoccupied, after all. But nothing could dampen his enthusiasm for the night, and all that he would accomplish now that he was free to do as he pleased. Ariane might be irritated at being cut out, but she wasn't the one with the contract. And besides, once he discovered something truly useful, she'd be thrilled, impressed, and everything she ought to have been the first time she'd met him, instead of just barely escaping death.

It was a grand plan.

It was also, as of four hours later, a near-total bust.

At the stroke of midnight, Damien stood in the library of the Dracul mansion. A library that, he noted with annoyance, did not bear any trace of Ariane curled up like a bookish miss. He crossed his arms over his chest and stared at the wall of books in front of him without truly seeing a single title. He replayed every dead-end conversation in his head, trying to think of something he'd missed. Even his calls to his contacts back in Charlotte had yielded nothing. Both that city and Chicago were as debauched and undead as usual. His experience with the murderous Grigori seemed to have occurred in a vacuum.

No one else seemed to know such a creature existed.

"You're back early."

Damien didn't bother turning at Vlad's voice. "Yes, I suppose I am. I decided to come back when my abysmal luck was topped off with a phone call from my employer who is, shall we say, not happy. Not with the dead Grigori, not with my having been chased by the dead Grigori, not with the head Grigori responsible for the recent jackassery, and not with the female Grigori who Drake has agreed, very grudgingly, not to mention to the head Grigori. Because unless he gets an apology from Sariel, some assurances, and most importantly, compensation for my near-death experience, the contract between the House of Shadows and the Grigori is broken and done. Yet I must continue to work, most likely without pay." He inhaled deeply, then tipped his head back. "So this is how it ends for me. Afflicted with a plague of Grigori. If anyone else around here grows wings, I'm going to stab them in the head and light them on fire. I've had it."

Vlad chuckled softly, and Damien finally turned to look at him.

"That didn't drive you off? Well, hell, I'm losing my touch." Curious, he glanced at the leather-bound volume in Vlad's hand. "Doing my work for me, are you? I certainly hope so."

Vlad's mouth curved in a small smile, but there was a hint of frustration in it.

"No. I can't find any mention of anything called the Rising. I've gone through a couple of my oldest volumes already, but the term doesn't even ring a bell."

Damien shrugged off the disappointment. The Dracul was normally like a bloodhound with obscure bits of vampire history. "Maybe she misheard him. Maybe he was just having her on before he, you know, burst into flame."

"I don't know. It's odd for me to feel young as a vampire, but this is one of the times I wish I had the years that Mormo and Arsinöe do." Vlad shook his head. "And asking either of them about this is impossible, for different reasons."

Damien watched as Vlad moved to the wall and slipped the book back onto one of the many shelves lined with priceless volumes on everything from vampire history to modern literature. His friend seemed tired and preoccupied, both of which were unusual. But then, it was nice to know he wasn't the only one.

Restless, Damien shifted on his feet and then leaned against the back of one of the chairs scattered about the room. Some of it was undoubtedly the unsuccessful evening thus far—the one faintly promising bit of information would have to wait until tomorrow to be checked out, and he *loathed* waiting—but there was more to his mood that he didn't really want to examine closely. He didn't know quite what was happening to him, but he suspected that this was what Drake had always meant when he said a Shade was "losing the edge." After which Drake generally had that Shade quietly disposed of.

"So your contract has been broken without explanation or apology from the Grigori. Interesting. Even Sariel would normally try to make amends for one of his men attempting to kill the hired help," Vlad said. "The House of Shadows is nothing to be trifled with."

"Yes, well, maybe he would have tried to make amends if I were something other than a cutthroat gutter cat. But as I am, most highbloods would tend to see me as... disposable. Except you, of course," Damien said with a smirk. "You're *terribly* progressive."

Vlad gave him a baleful look as he moved to settle himself in an oversized, well-worn leather chair. "No, in your case, I just seem to be a glutton for punishment." He crossed his legs, resting an ankle on the opposite knee, and considered Damien for a moment. "Speaking of progressive attitudes, I'm surprised you didn't head straight in to check on your new partner."

Damien's eyes narrowed. He'd been waiting for the barbs to start. "Touché. She's lying in wait for me somewhere, I suppose? You wouldn't be looking so amused if she wasn't."

Vlad smirked. "I suppose you'll find out, won't you?"

Damien blew out a breath and studied an oil painting of some castle or other on the far wall, waiting for the subject to change. When Vlad just continued to stare at him, Damien fixed him with a glare.

What?

"You're awfully touchy about Ariane, you know," Vlad said, tilting his head and regarding Damien with interest. "Why is that, do you suppose?"

Damien groaned. "Don't look at me like that, Vlad. I'm not interested in being studied. You make me feel like one of those bugs that's been run through with a pin and mounted on cardboard."

Vlad smiled faintly. "I'm interested," he said, "because sneaking off like a naughty schoolboy is usually beneath even you. It's almost as though you *want* her to become disgusted with you."

"Oh, honestly. That," Damien replied, "is easily enough done without any effort on my part."

Vlad shook his head and made a disapproving noise. "You know, I've noticed that you tend to expect the worst of people, and even less of yourself. It's an interesting strategy for living."

"It's also an excellent way of avoiding disappointment."

"Hmm." Vlad's voice was mild as he changed the subject, as smoothly as any psychiatrist. Damien had to fight off a sudden wave of panic. The hell he wasn't being studied.

"Why didn't you take Ariane with you tonight anyway? You seem to have found her unusually useful thus far, considering I've never seen you willingly work with someone before."

Damien rolled his eyes. "What *is* this poking at me? Maybe I'm just on Grigori overload. Leave me be, Vlad."

"You're not the only one who's had a rough week, Damien. If you thought about it at all, you might realize that I was *not* visiting the Empusae for pleasure. You'll forgive me if I'm not in the mood for your usual line of bullshit," Vlad said, impatience creeping into his voice along with a more pronounced Eastern European accent.

It was a warning, Damien knew. He'd been told that the Dracul only went full Transylvanian when he was very pissed off, out of patience, or both. He'd never actually seen the normally cool vampire go off, but he'd heard enough stories to know he never wanted to.

"All right," Damien grumbled. "A simple answer, then.

I thought Ariane might be useful, yes. But hell if I know what to do with her now."

Vlad snorted. "She seems lovely. A trusting soul. Beautiful, of course. And far too good for you. No wonder you're terrified of her."

"Oh, indeed. You know what a fearful creature I am. It's the curse of having such a wounded inner child," Damien replied blandly.

When that earned him nothing more than a long, hard stare from eyes that had gone the pale, gleaming blue of arctic ice, Damien heaved a sigh, walked to where Vlad was sitting, and flung himself onto a comfortable velvet couch the color of cabernet.

"I thought you'd be tired of psychoanalyzing me by now," he said. "And the matchmaking bit is just tiresome. Come on, let's drink. I'm in a mood."

"You usually are."

Between Vlad's cool stare and the stiff aristocratic bearing, Damien had an uncomfortable flashback to some of the less pleasant heart-to-hearts he and his father had had long ago. Somewhere, up on the next floor and not at all far away, he heard the warm sound of Ariane's laughter. He picked his head up, would have pricked his ears in that direction if he'd been in his other form. Every sense immediately shifted toward her, hungry for more of her. The hours he'd spent away from her might have been months.

Too late, he remembered how closely Vlad was watching him. He couldn't have been more obvious if he'd tried. And still he couldn't keep himself from asking the question.

"She's feeling better, then?"

"You'll have to ask her if you want to know," Vlad said, his voice giving away nothing of what he was thinking.

Damien shifted uncomfortably. "Did I say I *wanted* to know? I'm just wondering how quickly she'll be nipping at my heels again. Though truly, I doubt she could worsen my luck at this point." He shook his head, letting his frustration show. "No one has seen that creature who tried to string me up. *No one*. He's a massive bloody winged vampire! How is that possible?"

"You're so used to finding them strange that you fail to appreciate their stealth," Vlad replied. "I've often thought they are only seen when they want to be. Consider: They're an ancient bloodline, and yet Ariane is the first confirmation of the fact that they have wings. Even living in the desert as they do, that's a difficult fact to conceal for so long. The Grigori are frighteningly disciplined."

"More like just frightening," Damien muttered. "Ariane is the only marginally normal one I've ever met, and it sounds like she was an outcast. Bloody fools."

Oh hell, had he just said that out loud?

Vlad's mouth curved up into a razor-sharp smile, and it wasn't exactly unfriendly, though it put Damien a little in mind of a great white shark. "Damien. For someone who professes to be so self-aware, you're being awfully stupid. Anyone with eyes can see you want this woman."

Damien fought back a grimace. He hated being told how he felt. Especially when the other person was right. So he forced nonchalance. "I'm not so old I've lost my appreciation for the sight of a beautiful woman, it's true," Damien said blandly. "But that's hardly newsworthy. You seemed quite enamored of her yourself last night." The mere memory of it had Damien's jaw tightening.

Vlad stiffened. "She is not for me. I would know if she was."

Damien raised an eyebrow. "Oh? Don't tell me the movies about you are right and you're going to spend eternity looking for some tart who threw herself out a window because she thought you were dead. I mean, it's been *done*, you know?"

Vlad stared at Damien for a long moment. "You know," he finally said, "a lot of times I'm not quite sure whether to laugh or punch you."

Damien shrugged. "Since you continue to speak to me, I guess it works for you."

Vlad just shook his head, though he didn't look particularly amused at the moment. "Yes, I suppose it must. And, no, the traditional story about me is...wrong. In some ways."

Damien looked up sharply from plucking at the fabric on the arm of the couch, his interest piqued. He knew little of Vlad's past, and the man certainly wasn't one to volunteer much about it. But he saw immediately that Vlad wasn't interested in continuing down this particular path.

He surprised himself by taking pity on the man and rising. Who was he kidding? He'd prolonged the agony long enough. He needed to see Ariane. Not that admitting it to himself made him feel any better.

"Well, I'll leave you to your books. Thanks for trying anyway, Vlad. I'll come up with something. I always do."

"You certainly do," Vlad agreed, the hard lines of his mouth softening into a smile. "I'll say that for you."

Damien headed for the door, then stopped and turned at the sudden memory of something Vlad had said in passing. It might or might not be pertinent, but he'd be damned if he missed something just because he was mooning over his would-be partner.

"What made your week so terrible, by the way? More fallout from the actions of our favorite demon queen?"

Vlad's smile turned rueful. He ran a hand through his hair. "Oh, I suppose this is just the new normal. I hadn't realized quite what a powder keg the Vampiric Council was until Lily started shaking things up. I knew that the Lilim's rise would create issues. But she is moving more quickly—and in different directions—than I would have expected." He sighed and shook his head. "Mormo said it long ago, that there would come a time when we would all have to come together, or shatter. But I always thought the change would come over time."

Damien raised his eyebrows. "Ah. So you went to seek Mormo's counsel."

Vlad sighed, a hollow sound. "For as much good as it did me. So much is shifting. Change doesn't even come easily to me, and I was the youngest of the leaders before Lily came. I'm proud to call myself her ally. But sides are being chosen very quickly, and I hear rumblings that Arsinöe is calling on some of her traditional allies overseas. The quiet right now is deceptive. There's a lot of movement beneath the surface."

"Arsinöe," Damien muttered. "That name has begun to turn my stomach. Her gambit to enslave the werewolves was half-assed but destructive enough."

"She plays with other bloodlines, other races, like toys," Vlad replied, suddenly sounding weary. "She takes her petty swipes at the Lilim, picking off the weak or the unlucky when she can. Her game with the pack of the Thorn was an experiment. She lost the battle but gained plenty of information, and it wouldn't surprise me to find that she's taken what she learned and has targeted a different pack. I can't say for certain yet. The Ptolemy have become very hostile to any outsiders in their territories. I've advised my people to steer clear...though, of course, I have eyes everywhere. Lyra is keeping her ear to the ground for me as well, though the Thorn have made enough of their own waves lately that the other packs are avoiding them."

"A mistake," Damien said, leaning one hip against a chair. "A wolf pack allied with a vampire dynasty would be valuable."

Vlad waved his hand dismissively. "They're as set in their ways as we are, Damien. But you're right—it's a mistake. There's trouble coming. The Empusae are weak. The Lilim are young and still organizing. And now this strangeness from the desert...some nights I wonder whether everything will simply shatter."

"You're right," Damien said. "You have plenty to worry about. All of this just confirms I made the right decision when I went into the thieving and stabbing business."

He expected Vlad to be amused. The Dracul usually was when it came to Damien's flippant jokes about his job. But this time, Vlad didn't even crack a smile. The look in his eyes chilled Damien to the bone.

"Even the Shades will have to choose eventually," Vlad said. "Likely sooner rather than later. You are not an island, Damien, no matter how much you would like to be."

Damien had no response for that. The certainty in his friend's voice shook him, and he wanted nothing more than to go bask in the bit of light—not sunlight, as he had fancifully imagined, but moonlight—that Ariane might provide him. The desire to see her tucked away, kept safe from all that Vlad seemed so certain was coming, rushed over him so quickly he was nearly drowning in it.

He turned away, thinking back to that stale-smelling town house of his memory, luxurious and yet shabby because he hadn't really given a damn about any of it. Full of things, and yet full of nothing. He had never had a true treasure to guard, to protect... not even now. If he found one, perchance, how might he go about holding on to it?

Would he even be able to?

Questions to ponder another time, Damien decided, hating the mood he was in.

"She could be good for you, you know," Vlad called to him.

When Damien turned his head to look back, Vlad had an unopened book on his lap and a glass of brandy in his hand. His gaze was still touched by that unmistakable sadness.

Damien forced a chuckle. "Oh, I'm a lost cause, Dracul. You know that."

Vlad lifted the glass of brandy and turned it in the candlelight, examining it, though his mind seemed somewhere else.

"It's amazing," he murmured, "how certain women are drawn to even the most lost among us... and find beauty in what shredded tatters of goodness we possess."

Damien considered hurling some pithy remark back at him on his way out, but Vlad's haunted look decided him against it. Instead, he left his friend there, alone among his books, lost in the sort of memory that Damien hoped never to create for himself.

chapter FOURTEEN

H E'S A COMPLETE ASS."

"Uh-huh."

"He's already trying to cut me out."

"Of course he is."

Ariane paused in her pacing of the bedroom, gave a couple of irritated swipes with the dagger in her hand, and frowned at her reflection in the mirror.

"Elena. If I didn't know better, I'd think you were trying to humor me," she said into the phone she had wedged against her ear.

Elena's burst of laughter provoked Ariane's own. It felt good. Better than good, after last night, to know she could still laugh with a friend. It was good to know she still *had* a friend, that it hadn't been just a figment of her imagination.

"Ari," Elena said, "you're the one who wanted to team up with a Shade. I did warn you. Waking up in another state with no stuff and no guy is pretty standard."

Ariane sighed, walking closer to the mirror and ruffling a hand through her hair. "Well, he's not exactly gone. But he certainly didn't invite me along to wherever he wandered off to."

"Again, standard. I've never met one who wasn't a loner, though they're that way for a reason—Shades don't tend to live as long when they work in pairs. At least he ditched you someplace a lot classier than some rat-infested safe house. Not that I'd have any experience with that. Hey, if you're going to be there a few days, I'll send along the weapons you left, and the clothes. You didn't leave much, and Strickland has a runner headed in your direction—he does a little business in the city."

"That would be great," Ariane breathed, cheered at the thought of having her things back.

Tonight she was in faded jeans and a tank top, both borrowed from one of Vlad's employees here at the mansion. She was comfortable, but she didn't want to leave behind what little she had brought into this world. At least Vlad had stopped to collect her sword from Damien's car before heading for the airport. She didn't care how outlandish Damien thought it looked; it was still *hers*.

"No problem," Elena replied. "I'll have Matt bring your stuff. And to the Dracul mansion, no less. You've moved up in the world—it doesn't get much safer than that."

"I care less about safety than I do about the fact that I'm sitting in Chicago, useless," Ariane replied, beginning to pace again. "I don't know this place. I don't know why Damien thought it was a good idea to come here. It feels like everything I *need* to be doing is back in Charlotte."

Her frustration bubbled back up quickly. Last night

she'd been in shock, reeling from what she'd done, and had allowed Damien to decide what was best. She'd given in to her only instinct, which was to get far, far away. Tonight was one of the first times she wished she'd been a little more, well, Grigori about it all.

"I doubt it," Elena said, sounding so sure of herself that Ariane wanted very much to believe her.

"Oh?"

"The weirdo Grigori who tried to kill Damien has almost definitely blown town. It seems pretty clear you got close quicker than he was expecting. No reason to stay in this city when there are so many other places to hide. So in the Shade's defense, Chicago is as good a base of operations as any while you try to figure out your next move. Especially with a dynasty leader who wants to put you up."

"True," Ariane muttered, holding the dagger up so that the candlelight glinted off the blade. She wasn't sure she wanted to admit to herself that what Damien had done was best. It was easier just being irritated with him.

"He still cut me out."

Elena chuckled. "Ari. Men like Damien pretty much have 'Does not play well with others' stamped across their foreheads. The only thing that surprises me is that he took you to Chicago with him. I would have guessed he'd just drop you here and vanish."

Another good point. It would have been easy to do. But what struck her about how Damien had been last night wasn't that he'd wanted to get away from her, but that he'd seemed to want to be *near* her. Granted, he hadn't patted or soothed. But he'd stayed close, watching her carefully on the entire trip here. And he'd looked worried. At loose ends, but worried.

And then there was the whole bit about how he'd been prepared to fight Oren for her when he really had no good reason not to let her have at it while he saved his own skin...

"Damn it," Ariane grumbled. "I can't be mad at him."

Elena sighed. "Had a feeling. Well, look, Ari, I'm probably not the best person to be doling out romantic advice, but here's what I've got. Shades can be fun, and dangerous, and wild, and that one is definitely sexy. Just...be careful with your expectations."

Ariane blew out a breath. Expectations? She'd given up on those a long time ago. Whatever her eventual fate was, it wouldn't have anything to do with her desperately trying to shape it.

"Don't worry, Elena. Right now, I'm just happy to have more life choices than which part of the compound to spend the night in. I didn't even really want to like Damien, but here we are."

Another throaty laugh. "Yeah. You have a point. Well, just remember, we Cait Sith make great lovers but lousy projects. Not so good at changing. Must be the cat in us."

Ariane grinned. "I wouldn't want to change you. I don't even want to change him." Her eyes narrowed as she imagined him out in the city, tracking down information without her. "I'd just like him to make a few small accommodations, is all."

"Now *that* you might get. Slowly, painfully, but possibly. Crap, Strickland's calling. I knew I was going to get called in on my night off. I'll get your stuff together and out. Call soon."

"I will," Ariane said, and hung up the phone. She set it on the bombe chest, her mind a million miles away.

Talking about Damien had helped her sort a few things out, but there was plenty she was still in the dark about. For a woman who'd never had a real romantic relationship, an emotionally unavailable assassin probably wasn't a great place to start. But she'd always been good at working with the cards she'd been dealt.

She wanted Damien. She was almost positive he wanted her, at least on a physical level. So...she'd figure something out.

There was a soft knock at her door, and she knew exactly who it was. He hadn't been out all night after all. Ariane tried to tamp down the satisfaction she felt at that as she crossed to the door. He'd come back for her. A small thing...but then, she had a feeling that even going *slightly* out of his way was different for Damien. It only reinforced her sense that there was something between them, some odd connection.

Maybe it was fate, the thing her dynasty was so often preoccupied with. Or maybe it was something far more ordinary.

Ariane opened the door, wishing she were experienced enough to know for certain.

He leaned against the door frame, looking every inch the dashing rogue. The way his eyes drank in every inch of her had Ariane's cheeks heating immediately. *This* was why she needed to step carefully. It was easy to deal with him in her head—but Damien in the flesh was a different animal altogether.

He glanced down at the dagger still in her hand. "You have exactly three minutes to shout at me," he said. "After that, I thought we'd see a movie or something. This house is stifling."

She stared at him, momentarily at a loss for words. Finally, she managed to process a statement that, even if she had been furious with him, would have gone a long way toward defusing her anger. Obviously he was an expert at this. He was impossible. And she wondered how many women he'd had screaming and throwing sharp objects at him.

It seemed there had been a few.

"Why would I want to shout at you?" Ariane asked.

He blinked, looking slightly taken aback. "Well...I assumed you'd be angry at me for leaving you here." He narrowed his eyes slightly. "Unless you just mean you're not interested in shouting. I'll put up with the silent treatment for about three minutes, too, I suppose, but that's all I can stand."

Ariane shrugged, hoping the motion looked as casual as when he did it. "I got up a little later than usual. And you weren't gone all night, so I'm not sure what you think the problem is. I'm fine."

Damien looked at her closely, and his confusion was well worth letting go of any lingering annoyance with him.

"Fine being code for you want to stab me, right?"

She swallowed a laugh. "No. I'll get my purse. A movie sounds good." She stepped away from the door and felt him walk in behind her.

"Aren't you going to interrogate me? Ask me if I found out anything useful while I was out searching for information without you?"

Ariane picked up her purse, opened it to make sure her smallest dagger was still inside. "No, Damien. I would assume that you'd tell me if you found anything important."

He stepped in front of her when she turned and glared down at her. She watched him, fascinated. His reaction to losing control over a situation was...interesting.

"Why would you assume a ridiculous thing like that? I lie for a living, kitten. I think I mentioned that."

"You agreed to work with me. Why wouldn't you tell me? Withholding something important would be stupid, and you're not stupid."

That seemed to give him pause. "Well. That's logical."

"Yes. And Grigori are nothing if not logical," she agreed with a small smile. She tried to step around him, but he moved into her path, as quick and graceful as a cat.

"You weren't being logical when you tried to take my head off with that big bloody sword the other night," Damien said. He was inches away from her, and his voice had gone silken the way it always seemed to when he got this close. She could smell him, the faint spice of expensive cologne mixed with something indefinable, irresistible.

"I was too," Ariane replied, though arousal took most of the bite out of her retort. "It made perfect sense to try and kill you if you were going to murder the only lead I had."

He chuckled, a low, warm sound. "Now you sound like a Shade."

Ariane raised her eyebrows at him. "A compliment? Yes, I do know how to handle myself, thank you."

"Not exactly a compliment...more a commentary on you having a bad influence." Something softened in Damien's gaze, and when he lifted his hand, he hesitated for the barest instant before grazing Ariane's cheek with the backs of his knuckles. The touch was far more tender than she would have expected. Still, he looked puzzled.

"Most women would have thrown that dagger at me," he said.

"I was locked in a closet for years, remember? I'm strange." She meant it to tease, but the moment the words were out of her mouth, she blushed, embarrassed. From what she'd seen of the world, she *was* strange. Maybe she should have simply thrown the dagger at his head to make him feel better.

"You're beautiful," Damien replied, tucking a lock of hair behind her ear. Ariane drew in a soft breath, surprised. It wasn't the words. It was the way he said them. Even Damien looked nonplused, but he made no move to step away.

"Gods, Ariane, don't look at me that way."

She tilted her head, leaning into the light stroke of his fingers. "What way? I like looking at you."

He laughed, flustered, as he let his hand fall away. "You look like you think there's something honorable in here. There isn't. You're going to end up disappointed."

There was something in the way he said it, some echo of the past that made Ariane think Damien was well acquainted with being called a disappointment. Whether it had been deserved or not, her heart ached a little for him. From the little he'd revealed to her, it didn't sound as though anyone had ever cared much for him. He would have been a beautiful child, she thought...and yet he'd been left alone.

No wonder he'd built up such excellent defenses.

"I won't be disappointed," she told him. When he only looked silently down at her, the oddest expression on his beautiful face, Ariane added, "I'm capable of enjoying you for what you are, you know.

Damien nodded. "A killer and a thief with a nonexistent moral compass."

She studied him for a moment, at the deadly serious expression on his face. He was such an odd combination of vanity and insecurity. She doubted many people even saw the latter. Damien didn't seem like the kind of man who generally let people get that close. It wasn't until this moment that Ariane realized Damien was just as lost about how to forge a real relationship as she was.

It was strangely comforting, to know they were fumbling together, even if their approaches were entirely different.

"If you would rather I get mad at you," Ariane said, "you'll have to try a lot harder than disappearing for a few hours. Most of the time I have a very long fuse."

"And I have a rather short one." Damien blew out a breath. "It would be better for you if you'd just decide to hate me, you know, even if you stuck around for a convenient business relationship. This...this *thing* we're doing, it's an incredibly bad idea."

"You keep saying things like that. If this is how you go about picking up women, no wonder you're single," Ariane said with a smile. She hesitated a moment, then gave in to the urge and reached up to run her fingers through his hair. It was incredibly soft, and at her touch, Damien's eye rolled back in his head as a deep, rolling purr began in his throat.

"I only pick up women I can easily discard. You're making it hard as hell to stay away from you," he said.

It was one of the more backhanded compliments she'd ever received, but it pleased her nonetheless.

He turned his head into her touch, feline in the way

he rubbed his cheek against her wrist. The purring was incredibly arousing.

"That's . . . lovely," he said, his voice growing strained. "You're so soft. And you smell so sweet . . . like roses." His eyes slipped shut as she let her fingers play through his hair, over the light stubble on his jaw.

"I must be going mad," Damien murmured, his eyes opening just enough for her to see slits of cool blue. "I have nothing to give you, kitten. If you knew me better—"

She pressed a finger to his lips, amused. He would stand here all night trying to talk both of them out of this, and the result would be the same.

"Stop trying to argue with me," she said. "My requirements are very simple. Here, let me show you."

She closed the distance between them, sliding her arms around Damien and rising up on her toes. And when she turned her face up to his, she felt him finally relent, lowering his mouth to hers.

chapter FIFTEEN

HIS MOUTH WAS ALWAYS BETTER than any daydream, soft as sin.

At first the kiss was gentle, with a tenderness that surprised her. Before it had always been about heat and need. This time was...different. More.

Maybe because this time he sensed, just as Ariane did, that there would be no interruption, no excuse to end it. They were finally alone, and alone they would stay.

Damien coaxed Ariane with his tongue to open her mouth for him, and the kiss quickly turned from sweet to hot.

She heard his sigh, a sound imbued with so much pure pleasure that Ariane found herself trying to get even closer, winding herself fully in his arms and still finding that it wasn't close enough. The purring thrummed against her chest, making her nipples tight and hard, leaving her breathless. She arched against him restlessly, needing the friction, needing more of him.

"Beautiful creature," Damien murmured, teasing her

lips with his as he slid his hands into her hair, letting it glide through his fingers as though he found it precious. "Why do you continue to have anything to do with me?"

"Because I want you," Ariane sighed, letting her head fall back as he kissed a trail down her neck.

Her answer seemed to please him. She gasped as he nipped the sensitive spot where her neck met her shoulder, very near her mark. Shimmering pleasure spread like wildfire through her, pooling into molten heat right at her very core. He laved her mark with his tongue, and Ariane gripped his shoulders, digging in her nails. She had wondered, on so many nights, what it would be like to join with another vampire.

She'd never imagined how hungry she could be for a man's touch, his teeth.

Of course, she'd never imagined a man like Damien.

He looked flushed, hot, and hungry when he raised his head to look at her, the feral gleam of his eyes reflecting so much longing that it took Ariane's breath away. The need she saw there was as deep as the ocean, and just as endless. It frightened her, even as it drew her.

For reasons impossible to fathom, he was all she wanted. And she was quickly learning that out here, a vampire's life could be as easily and quickly and senselessly taken as any mortal's. She would deny herself no longer.

Ariane pressed a soft kiss to Damien's mouth, and pushing aside a sudden flutter of nerves, she slid her hands up underneath his shirt, feeling the hard muscles of his stomach contract beneath her fingertips. He sucked in a breath but didn't push her away, instead pulling her closer as he teased her mouth with hot, deep kisses. Ariane let her hands explore his chest, his back, as his skin warmed to her touch.

Damien pulled back abruptly and pulled the shirt over his head before tossing it aside. Ariane drank in the sight of him, thinking he looked just as good as he felt. His eyes never left her.

"Now you," he said, reaching for her, lifting the thin fabric of the tank top over her head. She had no time to let embarrassment get the better of her, no time to worry that Damien would be the first man to have seen her this way. The shirt was gone in an instant, and the way Damien looked at the simple black bra that remained was enough to scatter her thoughts to the wind.

He wanted her. That was all that mattered.

Damien ran his hands down her torso, then reached behind her to unclasp her bra with a simple flick of his wrist. She stepped away, forcing herself to keep her eyes locked with Damien's as she let the bra slide off her shoulders and fall to the floor. Her skin felt hot where Damien's eyes touched her, and her heart began to pound more quickly.

"Ariane..." He trailed off, swallowed hard. "You're perfect."

Her laugh was soft, wondering. "That's not something I'm used to hearing."

"Then we shall have to work on that."

The look in his eyes nearly had her melting at his feet. All the wicked things she'd ever dreamed of were written there, a thousand seductive promises. All for her.

His eyes glowed, predatory and beautiful. "Let me worship you, Ariane. You're long overdue."

He didn't wait for her answer, and when his hands touched her bare skin, almost reverently, Ariane could no longer formulate a coherent response. All she could think was, *Yes. Finally, yes.*

Damien's hands skimmed deftly over sensitized skin, brushing against nipples that had become tight little nubs, then dropping to cup her backside and cradle it against him as he dipped his head for another deep, lingering kiss. The light dusting of hair on his chest abraded her breasts in a way that was exquisite agony, making them feel full and heavy as moisture pooled quickly between her legs. She rose against him, wanting to feel him hard between her legs. His breath caught in his throat.

"Slowly, kitten," he said gruffly. "You have no idea how badly I want to be inside you."

"Then do it," Ariane breathed, sliding one leg up to hook around his hip. "It's what I want too." A tiny moan of pleasure escaped her as the pressure made her throb.

"Mmm," Damien said, touching his forehead to hers. "I'm going to show you all sorts of other things to want first. I want your thoughts dirty and full of me at all times." He unbuttoned her jeans and slid a hand between her legs, fingers slipping through the little thatch of curls to toy with the sensitive bud concealed beneath.

Ariane jerked against him, giving a soft, startled cry.

"Shhh," Damien soothed, sounding slightly breathless as he moved his mouth to her ear, nibbling and licking at the lobe. He held her still with one hand and continued to play her with the other, his clever fingers parting her slick folds and swirling the moisture around her swollen sex. Ariane had to struggle to stay upright—her knees felt weak, and her hips began to move in time to Damien's expert strokes. Everything within her seemed to tighten, pulsing in hot little bursts of pleasure.

She had wanted this, imagined this in fevered dreams. And nothing, nothing held a candle to what Damien was doing to her. Her fingernails dug into his shoulders, and he gave her tender earlobe a final flick of his tongue before shifting so he could lock eyes with her.

"I'm going to make you come, darling," he said hoarsely. "Look at me when you come. I want to watch..."

Her orgasm hit her like a bolt of lightning. She surged against Damien's hand with a sharp cry, her womb clenching in waves as he continued to stroke her until she shook from the sensation. And the entire time, she saw only Damien and those burning eyes that promised so much more pleasure if she dared to let him give it to her.

"So sweet," he rasped, removing his hand. "Come to bed, Ariane. I want to see how you taste."

Somehow she managed to make her legs carry her into the other room, though they threatened to give out on her more than once. She turned when she reached the bed to find Damien stripping off his pants. Words were lost to her as she got her first look at him. His body was lean and firmly muscled, his fair skin dusted only lightly with dark brown hair. Ariane's eyes drifted over his narrow waist, down the taut muscles of his stomach, to settle on the rigid thrust of his cock. She felt no fear of the unknown, no trepidation. Only gladness that after all this time, it would be him.

"What are you thinking, Ariane?" he asked.

"That you aren't the only one who sees someone beautiful," she replied.

He looked slightly taken aback, but pleased. "You are a wonder," was all he said.

She slid quickly out of her jeans and underwear, savoring the way he looked at her as she shed the last of her clothes. He was all tightly controlled hunger, dangerous, lethal beauty. But there was something in his eyes, that fathomless need she'd sensed in him before, that pulled at her heart. She didn't know if anyone could be capable of filling up the empty spaces inside of him…but she could try.

She wanted to try.

It was at that moment she knew that she was falling, right or wrong, and that after tonight, there would be no going back.

So she slid back onto the bed and held her arms out to him.

He came to her, drinking her in with his eyes as though she were the loveliest thing he had ever seen, crawling onto the bed like the cat that always lurked just beneath the surface of his skin. Ariane met him halfway, the two of them tangling together in the center of the bed, connecting skin to skin.

He lowered her to the soft bedding beneath them, his mouth leaving hers again to kiss a path down her neck, her chest, lavishing first one breast and then the other with attention. When he suckled her, Ariane sucked in a breath and then forgot to let it go. Every deep pull echoed inside of her, making her tighter, wetter. When his tongue teased her taut nipples, she threaded her fingers through his hair, gasping at each decadent flicker.

His mouth blazed lower, tickling sensitive skin, making the muscles of her belly jump as he neared the very heat of her. She waited, barely breathing, as he paused. The sight of him there, his head between her thighs and looking like he wanted to lap her up, had her trembling again very near the edge of another climax.

"Lay back, sweet," he said. "I think we're both going to enjoy this."

He parted her platinum curls with his fingers and began to savor her with his tongue, licking and tasting and teasing while Ariane writhed beneath him. He kept varying the rhythm, pushing her toward a shattering peak and then pulling her back, until her hands were fisted in the sheets, her back arched, and her soft gasps had become insistent moans.

"Please," she begged, dizzy from being strung as taut as a bow for so long. "Damien, please!"

Then she felt it, a deep, throaty purr vibrating against hot, sensitized skin as he used his mouth on her. She broke apart in seconds, a wild cry tearing from her lips as she reared up against him, the orgasm slamming through her even harder than the last. Before she had finished riding out the waves of it, Damien slid on top of her, his face flushed, eyes gleaming, his purring still rippling through him and into her.

Ariane lifted arms that she could barely feel, stroking up his sides and back. She saw his mark, the cats, the crescent moon, and did what she'd wanted to the first time she saw it. She rose up and licked it, licked the salt from his skin, then kissed him on the symbols that had made Damien who and what he was. His breath left him in a single, startled rush that caught on a groan.

He entered her in a single hard thrust, driving into her all the way to the hilt. There was a brief, stinging pain as the final barrier between them tore. Then there was only the two of them, joined in the most intimate way possible. She could feel him throbbing deep inside of her when he stilled, looking down at her.

"I'm your first," he said, his voice a reverent whisper.

"You're my first," she replied, reaching up to stroke

his hair, his face. Then she rose to brush his lips with her own, trying to tell him without words that she wouldn't have chosen anyone but him, that she gave him this small part of herself without regret.

He made a soft, broken sound and deepened the kiss, baring his emotions in the only way he seemed able to express them to her. Deep inside of her, he shifted with the kiss, and there was no pain, only pleasure. She lifted her legs, bending her knees to slide them up Damien's back and biting her lip as the angle intensified the sensations rippling though her.

His eyes went blurry when he raised his head. "Gods. Yes. Like that, darling."

Then he began to move in her, slowly at first, but more and more strongly as he lost control, until the bed rocked with every wild thrust. Ariane clung to him as he rode her, the sight of him coming undone intensifying her own pleasure until she felt everything in her gathering, coiling ever more tightly, begging for release.

The urge to sink her teeth into him rose, hot and strong as lifeblood. She had to struggle to fight it back, knowing that binding herself to him that way was a step she couldn't take. But she wanted it, wanted her teeth in him, his in her. Joined. Eternally.

Then Damien reached between them to stroke her, and the need in his eyes, his voice, eclipsed everything.

"Come with me," he rasped breathlessly. "Now, love."

Then she shattered, seeing nothing but beautiful darkness, clenching around him as he cried her name.

chapter SIXTEEN

CRAWLING AROUND in a dusty old shop full of moldy books and charming things like shrunken heads wasn't normally Damien's idea of a good time. Strangely enough, doing it with Ariane made it almost enjoyable.

Oh, hell, who was he kidding? It *was* enjoyable.

"I keep thinking that something's going to crawl out from between the pages and bite me," Damien grumbled, peering over the edge of a slim tome that had seen better days at Ariane, who appeared engrossed in a much larger volume. The owner of the shop, a squat troll of a man named Perkins, walked by them as he had done every few minutes since their arrival.

"I'm not a library," he snarled, revealing yellowed teeth. "If you want something, buy it."

Damien waved him off. "I've got plenty of coin to spend in here, Mr. Perkins. Leave us be, or you won't see a dime of it."

Perkins glared back at him in such a way that Damien

wondered what, exactly, the man was. He was pretty sure he wasn't a vampire, and the Shade who'd recommended this place, a Ptolemy half-breed named Yvaine, had been very adamant that Damien not ask. He found it was fairly easy to resist opening his mouth on that count.

Perkins looked like the kind of thing that, when biting, did not have a simple drink of blood in mind.

"I think we need this book," Ariane said, walking over to him and pressing against his side to show him the pages she was interested in. It took him a moment to focus. Even after a week of sleeping—and doing a great deal more than sleeping—together, his physical reaction to her had, if anything, intensified. And the more he tried to warn her off, the more comfortable with him she seemed to get.

It was incredibly twisted.

He couldn't seem to get enough of her.

"What do you see, kitten?" he asked. "This one's got as little about your kind in it as all the others. I'm beginning to wonder why anyone ever bothered to write anything about the Grigori, if all they had was a paragraph's worth of information."

With Oren dead, no sign of the Grigori who had killed Manon anywhere, and complete silence from Sariel—according to Drake—he had decided to focus on Oren's cryptic reference to Ariane about the Rising, whatever that was. It was a better focus than nothing, and he could tell it had been on Ariane's mind. Tonight's trip to this miserable little basement shop, a hidden place that Yvaine had informed him was only for the most serious collector of . . . whatever one termed these sorts of things . . . had pleased Ariane. She was as restless as he was in some ways. The discovery had surprised him.

And still, he wondered what she could possibly want with him. There was always an angle, always a catch. Everyone, he had discovered, wanted something. Everyone had a price. But she professed to want nothing.

A puzzle. And one that increasingly plagued him the more time he spent with her.

"Here, look," Ariane said, pointing at a page of age-softened paper and an illustration. "I've never seen anything like this, not even in the Grigori libraries. But…he looks like us."

Damien frowned down at the picture, a massive winged being that certainly looked like a Grigori. There was something even more ominous about this one, though. The wings had been blackened, and the face, though drawn in a fairly rudimentary fashion, was obviously contorted to reveal a great many more sharp teeth than the average vampire. Each finger ended in a claw. Scrawled beneath the drawing was a short description.

> *The demon Chaos, fallen from on high*
> *Eater of souls, cursed angel*
> *He sleeps in chains,*
> *But when he wakes, comes the Rising*
> *And the claiming of the world of night*

He looked sharply up at Ariane, who was still staring at the picture, a slight frown creasing her brow.

"You really think this is what Oren was talking about? Some chained up soul-eating demon?"

Ariane shrugged, looking up at him. "Maybe. The 'claiming of the world of night' sounds like something you'd want to prevent, right? Oren made it sound like putting off the Rising was something he'd been involved with. And he mentioned my soul being the thing that would put it off."

Damien made a soft, strangled sound. "Highbloods keeping a chained demon and feeding it souls. I wouldn't put it past most of them, but, kitten, don't you think you might have noticed in the last—"

"Nine hundred years." She looked away. "And no, not necessarily. You'd be amazed by how quiet the ancients can be about things they don't want you to know."

Damien stared at her, momentarily startled into silence. "You're nine hundred years old?" He had assumed she was younger, far younger.

Her cheeks flushed lightly. "Give or take. I don't really remember anything from before I was sired. It...took me a while to adjust. It doesn't matter."

It didn't really, Damien thought. But the fact that she'd been kept isolated for so long startled him. And she'd remained innocent of so much, whereas he'd been hopelessly corrupted well before his siring. Maybe it would have been different if he'd forgotten everything, too, started fresh.

Though he rather doubted it. And that Ariane's memories were gone indicated a very traumatic transition. He looked at her a moment longer, finally beginning to understand the strength that lurked beneath the angelic façade. Fledglings born in the sort of violence that wiped memories clean often went mad. She hadn't.

He found little in his world worthy of respect...until now.

Unsettled, Damien returned his attention to the book, studying a picture that seemed to grow more hideous the longer he looked at it.

"On the one hand, I want to say that even though we're rather odd creatures ourselves, a massive winged demon chained in someone's basement being fed souls seems like a stretch. But on the other hand..."

"On the other hand, this is the only mention we've seen of a Rising. And you have to admit, the thing in the picture does look kind of... similar," Ariane asked. "Even if this isn't exact, you have to admit that it's a possibility."

They looked at the book together in silence for a moment, and Damien thought back to the night at the Empusae compound, when he watched Ariane streak across the sky chased by her blood brother. He tried to imagine this particular fate awaiting her, becoming demon food. The thought filled him with sick dread. He'd known something was off about this entire deal. But this?

Damien kept his thumb in the page and flipped over the cover to look at it. "What's the title, anyway?"

"*Demons of the Ancient World*," Perkins's gravelly voice answered.

Damien looked up, irritated that the man had been eavesdropping.

Perkins simply looked smug, shuffling over to slip the book from Damien's hands. "This is a rare one," Perkins said, looking curiously at Ariane. Even with her hair piled on top of her head in a loose bun and dressed simply in a flowing summer skirt and tank top, she was an otherworldly beauty. There could be no mistaking her for anything but what she was.

He'd enjoyed looking at her so much that he'd stopped poking at her to find another wig. Stupid, he told himself. Careless. Things being quiet didn't mean they were safe, and now they were in this godforsaken basement with whatever Perkins was.

"I've never even heard of this book, or the things in it," Ariane was saying to Perkins. "There's no author. Who wrote it?"

"One of your kind, of course," Perkins replied with a lopsided yellow grin. His teeth were jagged, and Damien once again found himself wondering what the man ate.

"My kind?"

"Grigori. Watchers," Perkins grunted. "You can see this is handwritten, hand bound. It's the only copy, and word is the one who wrote it got in plenty of trouble when they found out what he was up to."

Damien lifted an eyebrow, skeptical. "Ah. A Grigori got in trouble for writing an academic book on demon myths. Right. And then he, what, gave you the book to make a little extra money?"

Perkins narrowed beady eyes that glinted strangely in the dim light. "The story is he handed it off to a friend before he disappeared. Or got disappeared. You have a smart mouth, cat. Careful. I'm sure the lady here can tell you that the Grigori are greedy with their secrets. That drawing you were looking at resembles a Grigori, yeah?" He chuckled, an unpleasant sound that had the hair on the back of Damien's neck standing up. "If Grigori had wings, that is. Just a rumor, though."

He slid a glance at Ariane that was full of unpleasant speculation.

"Bull," Damien snapped. "All of it. I've never seen a demon, and I've seen damn near everything."

Perkins looked amused. "Well, I guess you've got nothing to worry about, then. Good thing too. Demon's way more powerful than a vamp. Theoretically speaking, of course." He tapped the book. "All kinds of interesting theories in here."

"You still didn't tell us how you got this," Ariane said, looking as though she wanted to rip the book out of Perkins's stubby hands.

Perkins shrugged. "I have my channels. You buying, or what?"

Damien knew it was going to cost a fortune. He also knew he had to have it, even if the theory was a little strange. It was more to go on than they'd had. And it wasn't outside the realm of possibility. After all, he'd seen a hungry, flesh-eating gypsy curse tear a path through a bunch of Ptolemy when his bloodline had been freed. All sorts of things were possible.

Even if he didn't want them to be.

"How much?" he asked, and watched Perkins smile.

Fifteen minutes later, they were out in the night, back among reasonably normal mortals and drinking in fresh air. In one hand, Ariane had the book, wrapped in tissue and stuffed in a handled paper bag. Her eyes had a far-off look as she walked, the loose tendrils of her hair blowing gently in the warm night breeze.

Out here, it was easier to think of some winged monster as nothing more than a fairy tale. Easier to focus on the present instead of on dark things buried out in the desert.

Damien smiled as he watched several mortals, male and female, nearly fall on their faces when Ariane passed. She was utterly oblivious to her effect on people, which he had decided was part of her charm.

He seemed to spend a lot of time lately dwelling on that charm, and all the myriad parts of it. He'd never imagined he'd like working with someone. But then, Damien reminded himself, technically this *wasn't* work any longer. He wasn't getting paid, and Drake was allowing him to continue sniffing around for a short time only on the off chance the Grigori decided to come back to the table.

Damien's smile faded.

That grace period would no doubt soon be over. Plenty of other jobs awaited, one of which would be thrown in Damien's lap. He knew Drake. As soon as something lucrative enough came up, he'd set Damien on it. And Damien would go, because that's what he had signed on for when the crescent moon had been inked beneath his mark so long ago.

He'd traded a good bit of freedom for profit and adventure. And it had never bothered him a whit...until now.

"I'll find some way to pay you back," Ariane said, pulling him out of his thoughts. He looked at her, surprised.

"Perish the thought, kitten. It was nothing."

Her eyes rounded, the violet glowing faintly. "It cost a fortune!"

He chuckled ruefully. "Well. Yes. One of a kind, as that charming shopkeeper kept repeating. But you'll have to believe me when I tell you that in my case, money is not an issue."

Ariane looked dubious. "You're that rich?"

"I'm that rich." He thought, briefly, of the beautiful apartment he had in Seattle. It was full of ridiculously expensive odds and ends, with a horde of treasure a dragon would envy. He set foot in the place a handful of times a year. It was, in essence, a stylish storage facility.

The London town house redux, he thought with a touch of pure misery. Had he really changed so little in all this time?

"Still, you didn't get hired to deal with this part of things," Ariane said, shaking her head. "Winged demons that eat souls...I'm not even sure I want to know if it's true, except now I'm worried it may have had something to do with why Sam disappeared. Or went into hiding."

Of course it did, Damien thought. Both of them knew it.

Part of him, a lot of him, actually, had begun to hope the trail stayed cold. There would be no winning against a thing like what was drawn in that book. He knew his limits...though he feared Ariane wasn't nearly as certain of hers.

"Let's hope not," Damien said, dismissing the subject for now. "Look, consider the book an extremely disturbing present, if it helps. Not exactly light reading, but that's the sort of thing that's probably better out of circulation anyway. We've done the world a favor snapping it up. I only wish it got us closer to actually finding Sammael. Your Elena hasn't had a hint of anything, has she?"

Ariane shook her head. "No. She's busy, but nothing unusual. And she's definitely been keeping an ear to the ground."

The two spoke often, Damien knew. Somehow, it no longer surprised him that Ariane would choose for a best friend a Cait Sith who appeared to make a living doing odd jobs as a bodyguard/smuggler/mercenary.

"Well. We'll have a look at that thing when we get h—er, back to Vlad's," Damien said. Good Lord, had he almost called Vlad's place *home*? Had he called anywhere home in the last three hundred years?

He sensed Ariane's eyes on him, but he didn't dare meet them. Gods knew what she would see.

Her question, which he'd been expecting for days now, was tentative. "Damien…where *do* you live anyway? You never talk about it, but you have to live somewhere, right?"

It was, perhaps, the only subject he wanted to discuss *less* than a soul-eating demon.

"Not exactly. I mean, I have a place. Seattle, where the House of Shadows is based. I'm just hardly ever there." He glanced at her, saw her intense interest.

"My things are there, but it's not like a *home*, kitten. I'm usually traveling."

"Hmm," Ariane said, a soft noise of surprise he didn't quite understand.

"*Hmm* what?"

"Oh, I knew you probably traveled a lot. I just pictured you with a little oasis tucked away somewhere for your downtime." She smiled, and it made her eyes sparkle. "Somewhere stuffed with things you've picked up on your travels. A cross between a magpie's nest and an armory."

He laughed, genuinely amused that she'd thought this out. "A cozy assassin's den. I like the idea of it. I may have to set one up just because you said so."

"It's really just a boring apartment you never see?" she asked. "That doesn't sound like you at all."

"Ah, well," he began, surprised to find himself at a loss for words. How did he explain the way he lived? Nothing in that apartment held his interest; nothing he dumped in it mattered any longer than the time it took him to walk away from it. Even the Star of Atlantis, the diamond he'd taken this job for, would have sat on a pillow on a shelf not long after he'd brought home his new toy.

He pressed his lips together in disgust. This was why he despised self-reflection. Shallowness was far less depressing than the truth.

"Maybe you'll come see the magpie nest sometime. You may find it more interesting than I do," Damien finally said when they reached the car. He opened the passenger door for Ariane, and she slid in.

It was only when he saw the surprised pleasure on her beautiful face that he realized he actually meant the invitation.

With a sinking feeling, Damien realized he knew exactly what his sterile apartment lacked. But the treasure he wanted to add would never consent to sitting on a shelf and waiting for his infrequent visits.

And he couldn't drag her into the sordid work of his life, risking her more than she was already risking herself. He understood enough about Ariane to know that she was happy to fight for a purpose, but that violent intrigue for the sake of coin wouldn't be her thing. Hell, maybe it wasn't his thing either, anymore. He'd gone too numb to really examine it or care. He had obligations, and that was enough.

Or it had been.

Damien stalked around to his side of the car and got in, trying to convince himself to do what he had always done. Enjoy the moment, and hell with the rest. But the truth kept smacking him in the face. For the first time in three hundred years, he'd found something he wanted to keep…

…and it was something he would never be able to have.

chapter SEVENTEEN

TWO NIGHTS LATER, Sammael surfaced.

Vlad was just finishing up on the phone when Ariane rushed into his office. The summons his assistant had given her was brief, but it had been enough to bring her running. Damien was already there waiting for her, standing beside one of the empty chairs facing the massive mahogany wood desk.

The grim set of his jaw wasn't reassuring.

"What is it? What's happened?" she asked, trying to keep the fear out of her voice.

"Easy, kitten," Damien said. "He's on the phone with Lily, the new Lilim queen. Sam's alive. Focus on that."

"Ariane. Good," Vlad said as he hung up the phone. "Please, sit. We've some things to discuss."

She sank stiffly into a chair, comforted when Damien perched on the arm of it, staying close. Everything about him, his scent, his solid presence beside her, gave her an anchor just as everything around her felt as though it were beginning to shift in dangerous and unpredictable ways.

"Just tell me he's all right, and I'll calm down."

Vlad's arctic eyes were far away and troubled, but he managed a smile. "They were found near Tipton, Massachusetts, late last night. He'd been beaten and bled, but he was conscious. A good sign. He's being given time to heal. One of his wings was nearly severed, but it seems to be healing as well. Your Sammael is lucky to be alive, but he *is* alive."

"His wing," Ariane murmured, feeling slightly nauseous at the memory of what had happened when she'd severed Oren's wing. It had killed him.

"Only another Grigori would have been able to hurt him like that," Ariane said. "Sariel must have sent another to look for him."

And for me. She was suddenly glad to be ensconced in the relative safety of the Dracul mansion. She'd defeated Oren, barely. But she wasn't sure she'd be able to repeat such a feat so soon. Especially not when the Grigori would have been sure to send someone even more skilled.

Vlad nodded. "Sariel seems to have sent more than one, in fact. Both Sammael and the blood brother he was traveling with are in bad shape. The other has a wing that's more shredded than severed, but the healing seems to be slow."

Damien leaned forward. "So he *is* traveling with the one who slit my throat. He was massive, that one, and he looked like an ancient."

Vlad's mouth thinned. "Possibly. That one, Lucan, is damaged enough that he isn't exactly talking yet. According to Sammael, it was two ancients who came after them." He looked pointedly at Ariane. "Whatever caused your friend to run, it's a secret the ancients are desperate to keep."

She thought of the picture in her book, of the fierce winged demon called Chaos, and shuddered.

"I didn't think there was anything they would kill for," she said quietly.

"I'm afraid there's something for most everyone," Damien replied. "We'll want to get to Tipton immediately, of course," he continued, looking at Vlad.

Ariane nodded. "Please. I want to see Sam."

And despite the condition he was in, she felt a surge of joy at knowing he was alive. Once that simple fact began to sink in, she couldn't hold back her smile. "He's really alive," she said, her breath catching. It wasn't until that moment that she realized she'd stopped expecting to find him at all. She'd begun to believe he was gone.

Vlad inclined his head. "Of course. Once he found out you were with me, he immediately began asking for you. I've already arranged for the jet. You leave in an hour."

Relief flooded her, so much that Damien's voice sounded far away when he spoke. All she could see in her mind's eye was Sam's face. Since she'd left the compound, she'd begun to realize the value of the gift he'd given her in refusing to ostracize her the way so many of the others had. Sam was the only reason she understood friendship. The only reason she hadn't gone as cold as so many of her kind.

"You're not coming?" Damien was asking Vlad, sounding surprised. "You'll usually use any excuse to get up there. I know you like to supervise."

Vlad's smile was thin and strained. "I would prefer it,

but I can't. Lily's call about Sammael and Lucan was not the only news I've had today. Mormo has awakened and is insisting on a Council meeting. Since she may well want to announce her successor, I can't deny her. Her lucid periods have grown few and far between."

Damien gave a soft humph. "For all the good it'll do her to pick someone. No one has been groomed, and I can tell you that the sharks are circling. When Mormo dies, someone is going to eat what remains of the Empusae. My money's on the Ptolemy, but there are a couple out-of-country dynasties interested in getting a foothold. It's going to be ugly. No one she's got is strong enough to hold them."

"Be that as it may," Vlad replied, "in three nights, on Friday, I will be hosting the leaders of the North American dynasties." He looked at Ariane. "Sariel will be among them. You can see why it's more prudent for you to be elsewhere."

Damien bared his teeth. "You're still going to host him? What if we get to Tipton and Sammael tells us that what's in that book is true? And even if it isn't, there's something really bloody wrong with him if he's having his own people murdered simply for leaving. He was ready to have Ariane dragged back home, and Oren made no bones about the fact that they were going to kill her, whether it was to have something suck out her soul or just to perform your standard decapitation! You're going to sit and smile and make nice with *him*?" He threw back his head. "Of all the *ridiculous* highblood bullshit..."

Damien had stood during his tirade, and Ariane watched with amazement as he finished shouting at one of the more powerful vampires in the world. It was true—

he'd opened up more with her than she'd imagined he might in the short time they'd been together. But she'd never expected him to become publicly outraged on her behalf.

It seemed to be a night for welcome surprises.

Vlad didn't seem at all perturbed by the shouting. But then, he was friends with Damien. He had to be used to it.

"If you're finished, Damien. Think about this. Rationally."

Damien exhaled loudly, shoved a hand through his hair, and shifted his weight from one foot to the other. Finally, he glared at Vlad. "I suppose you want him here so you don't have to go off to the desert to destroy him if he turns out to be guilty as sin. Which he is."

Ariane arched a brow. "You can do that? I wasn't aware the Council could do much in this case, short of war. He's only hunting his own people."

Vlad shook his head. "If this Rising is really something the Grigori are involved with—even if they're feeding some monstrosity souls to prevent it—then it's something that affects us all. It's no longer just a matter for the Grigori. And with Mormo here, gods willing, she can perform a divination for final proof. Then there can be no question."

Damien's voice was sharp. "She has agreed to this?"

Vlad nodded. "She has."

"Well. Holy hell," Damien said wonderingly. "You really do think they've got a demon chained in the basement."

"I think there's something very wrong. At the moment, that's enough," Vlad replied.

Ariane looked between them, confused. "What is a

divination? I don't remember ever running across that term when I read about the Empusae."

It was Vlad who answered her, his deep, rough voice quickly regaining her full attention.

"Empusa, or Mormo, was a powerful witch even before she was a vampire. She retained some of her powers in the change, one of which was the ability, under certain circumstances, to reveal past, present, and future. It's extremely difficult for her, now more than ever, and she is frail. Several powerful vampires are required for the ceremony. But to be perfectly honest, she and I have both been waiting for something like this ever since the Lilim's awakening."

The description sent a chill down Ariane's spine. "Something like what?"

"I don't know," Vlad growled, his frustration showing through. His long, elegant fingers curled into his fists on the desk. "There are so many old legends, old stories. All point to great upheaval wherein old dynasties reawaken, where the night races will have to come together or be torn apart. But torn apart by what is never clear. Your book is just another piece of the puzzle. But it's the clearest piece I've seen, especially if the story this Perkins gave you about how it came to be is true."

"I admit, the Chaos thing is...disturbing. But don't you think you're overreacting, Vlad? There have always been times that were rougher than others among us. And yet we go on, as we always have. There doesn't have to be some boogeyman behind it all, some chained beast lurking in the closet just waiting to be unleashed."

Damien, Ariane noted, sounded more like he was trying to convince himself. She didn't blame him. Thinking of their entire world being ripped apart was nothing she wanted to dwell on either.

"Hopefully you're right," Vlad said, and then smiled, appearing to relax a little. "This is why I like you, Damien. Feet always on the ground. You're a realist."

"No. I just tell you what you want to hear. But for now, I'll take it," Damien replied.

He held out his hand to help Ariane up, a casual, chivalrous gesture that he barely seemed to notice, but one that made her smile. She slipped her hand into his and rose, enjoying the warmth that spread from her fingers up her arm.

Ariane turned to Vlad before leaving, trying to keep all her worries from marring her joy at the simple fact that Sam was alive, that she would see him tonight, and that she might, at least, get peace of mind where he was concerned. The rest was for the dynasty leaders to sort out. And for right now, though she was deeply unnerved by Vlad's talk of dark legends, she was happy to leave the larger problems to others. Hopefully the divination would reveal something that could be sorted out among the leaders.

She doubted it, but for tonight, she would let her relief overrule everything else. The thought of facing down a flesh-and-blood version of the illustration in her book was more than she could handle right now.

"There is one thing," she said. "Why were Sam and this Lucan up in Massachusetts?"

"Ah," Vlad said. "It was actually a fortunate accident. They'd decided to get as far north as possible, hoping to find somewhere remote in Maine to hide. Concealing themselves in a city of the Empusae had provided them no protection, and they thought they might have better luck going to a part of the country that has more werewolves than vampires. They had expected that the small area the Lilim currently controls would be the safest place to stop and feed. Unfortunately, they were wrong."

"Maybe it's for the best," Ariane replied. "If they'd made it up into wolf country, they would have been on their own."

Damien chuckled. "Only you could find a silver lining in that, kitten."

Vlad inclined his head. "She's right. If nothing else, it was the right place to be able to survive an attack."

It suddenly occurred to her that her part in all of this was ending. She had no reason to return here. It might well be the last time she saw the Dracul, at least for a long time. She would have to find a safe place to conceal herself after this, of course, but Vlad wasn't obligated to do any more for her than he already had.

"Thank you for helping us," Ariane said. "I don't know what we would have done without you."

"You're more than welcome, Ariane," Vlad said, his eyes warming a little. "You are the only Grigori I've spent much time with, and it has been a pleasure. I realize you have a lot to think about, but once you've made certain that your friend will be all right, I'd like to help you make a place for yourself, wherever you decide you want to be. I have some ideas that might suit you, in fact, within my own ranks. You may not be Dracul, but I think that time is past that the dynasties can afford to rely on such small distinctions. You will always be welcome here. And protected."

Ariane smiled and thanked him, the offer a balm to

her ragged nerves. It was good to feel accepted somewhere, even if she wasn't sure this would ultimately be
her place. She would have a lot of decisions to make...
after. Her eyes drifted to Damien, who had stiffened ever
so slightly and looked away.

He didn't need to find a place, she thought. Damien
seemed utterly comfortable with his life.

It wasn't as though he'd lied about the fact that he was
the only one who fit in it.

Enjoy him now, she told herself. Damien seemed to live
only for the present. For him, there was no past and only
a murky sense of the future. He seemed to like pleasing
her and had surprised her with his obvious affection. He
had given her what he could, and she treasured it. But she
was under no illusions. Damien had spent his life walking
away from things. He would walk away from her too.

Ariane pushed aside her worry and tried to focus on
the good things, on the simple pleasure of Damien's hand
at the small of her back as they walked from the room. He
was here now. When she finally saw Sam again, Damien
would be with her. He had helped her see this through,
and that was a gift.

She tried to tell herself it would be worth the piece of
her heart that Damien would take when he had gone.

chapter EIGHTEEN

WHEN SHE STEPPED onto the tarmac at the Bonner County Regional Airport in the wee hours of the morning, Ariane had to remind herself that she was not, in fact, dreaming. She really had come this far, from the barren desert to teeming cities and finally to this tucked-away place that smelled of earth and trees. The temperature was comfortable, and a light breeze lifted her hair, toying with it and then vanishing in a single, sultry breath.

She loved this place instantly, without reservation. It felt natural to her in a way that nowhere else had. And for the first time, there was a whisper of memory from her mortal life—the briefest flicker of smiling faces that vanished before she could catch them to examine. She froze, willing that small shred of the past back to her, but nothing came. It was tantalizing...and frustrating.

Had her home been like this place?

"Jesus, Damien, could you have found a bigger suitcase?"

Ariane turned her head to see a slim, dark-haired man approaching the jet. He wore black jeans, a black T-shirt stamped with the logo of some band, and a welcoming grin. His hair was chin-length and tucked behind his ears, and as he got closer, the brilliant blue of his eyes was apparent. A vampire...and yet there was something different about him. His scent, faintly musky but not unpleasant, still had her instincts stirring in the oddest way.

It was only when Damien addressed him by name that she understood. This was the vampire who was mated to the wolf. Damien had only mentioned him in passing, and without much commentary, but she'd heard some of the Dracul muttering about the union using terms that were far less kind.

"Piss off, Jaden. It's not like you have to carry it," Damien said with an answering smile.

"What are you doing here? Don't tell me Lyra's thrown you out."

Ariane was glad to see him relax a little. He'd been unusually quiet on the plane. She kept catching him watching her, too, looking lost in thought. Maybe he was trying to decide exactly how to say good-bye to her.

The thought made her sick to her stomach.

"Nope," Jaden replied. "Ty and Lily have already left. Lyra and I had come up for a visit, and once everything went down it got...extended. We're keeping an eye on things while they're gone."

"Already gone?" Damien asked. "That's early, especially considering the situation."

Jaden Harrison, husband to the first female Alpha werewolf of the Pack of the Thorn, closed in on Damien and Ariane while the sole flight attendant closed the luggage compartment beneath the jet. She had to smirk when she realized that her small duffel really did stand in marked contrast to Damien's substantial suitcase. He'd mentioned that he kept some things at Vlad's, as he often used the mansion as a stopping point on his travels.

"Some" apparently had a different definition for Damien than most people.

"The situation is the problem," Jaden said. "Lily and Arsinöe haven't been in the same room since...everything. And some of those damned Ptolemy who've been hanging around our borders picking off cats got caught up in the Grigori fight. Lots of bodies. Guess who she's blaming?"

"I wonder. Don't blame Lily for trying to head off the mess pre-meeting, but it won't work."

Jaden grinned. "She's still an optimist."

Damien and Jaden exchanged a couple of quick, hard claps on the shoulder. Curious, Ariane watched them greet one another. Damien might not have many friends, but he didn't seem to put up his usual icy shield with the two she'd now met.

She wondered how he chose who to let in. He probably had some sort of convoluted test for them to pass. He'd warmed up fairly quickly with her, but their circumstances—fighting murderous Grigori and sleeping together—were a little unusual.

Jaden turned his bright blue gaze to her, his eyes widening. "Wow. Hi. You must be Ariane."

She took his proffered hand with a smile. "That's me. It's nice to meet you. Damien's talked about you."

He chuckled as he squeezed her hand in a firm grip and then let it go. "Whatever he said, only believe half of it. Maybe less." He paused, though the smile didn't fade. "Sammael made you sound…bigger."

She winced. "Gods, does everyone think female Grigori look like him?"

Jaden laughed, a soft, low sound that vibrated up from his chest almost like a purr. He was beautiful, Ariane thought, in an entirely different way than Damien was. Not aristocratic, but edgy. And those *eyes*…

"Short answer? Yes. I'm glad that the reality is a lot less disturbing. Hang on, I need to have a word with the crew. We're putting them up for the day. There's a car here for them, but they need the keys."

When Jaden walked away, Damien drew closer, dropping his head to speak directly in her ear. The feel of his breath made her shiver. It shouldn't be possible to want someone this much every moment of the day and night.

"You look happy, kitten. I insist you take it out on me later," he murmured, brushing his hand lightly down her arm, just barely grazing her breast.

She turned her head to answer him, her nose almost touching his, when she realized they were being watched, very closely. Embarrassed, she took a step back, while Damien looked irritably at Jaden.

"It isn't nice to stare."

"Whatever, Mr. Manners," Jaden said, though he gave them another lingering, curious look before shaking his head and moving to pick up Ariane's bag. "Car's right out front."

"Will I be able to speak with Sam as soon as we get to where we're going?" she asked, forcing her thoughts back to the present. She was anxious to see her friend, though worried about what she might find when she spoke to him. Jaden's expression softened with understanding.

"Sure. He's tired, and beat up, but he knows you're coming. No sense of humor, but I'm guessing that came in the original packaging."

"That sounds like Sam," Ariane replied, flooded with affection at just the description of her friend. No matter what had happened to him, he would be the same beacon of strength and sanity he had always been.

And she...well, what would he think of what she had become?

"Come on," Jaden said. "Let's head back to the house, and we'll get everyone settled in."

The ride into Tipton was uneventful, cruising along in a large, comfortable SUV. Ariane watched the lights of the town come into view, watched houses and shops as they passed them. It was a pretty New England town, with lots of comfortably worn old homes, enormous trees, and a downtown that looked to have survived mostly intact from another age.

All of it fascinated her. The cities would never fully be hers...too many people, too much noise and activity without any peace. But this...this spoke to a part of her she hadn't even been aware of.

A child's high-pitched laughter. The song of a bird. "Annie, catch me if you can!"

Ariane jerked up straighter in her seat, drawing in a sharp breath. For the briefest instant, she had been... somewhere else. But the moment it left her, she could do nothing but snatch at empty air.

All that lingered was the inescapable sense, real and bittersweet, that she had just touched something dear. Something long gone.

They turned off the main street, then again onto a drive that stopped short at a tall, spiked wrought-iron fence. Beyond, through the trees, Ariane could see the lights of a large Victorian mansion twinkling. The glow was homey despite the estate's obvious size.

There was a call box set up just before the gate, but Jaden didn't bother to press the button. All he did was look up at a camera mounted in the branches of a tree that overhung the drive and give a small wave, and the gates began to swing open.

"Have you gotten the place buttoned up pretty well now?" Damien asked. He sat beside her in the back, and though there was plenty of space, he'd sprawled out with his foot touching hers on the floor.

"Pretty well," Jaden agreed, glancing at him in the rearview mirror. "The property is fully fenced now, and we've got lots of security out here. Cameras, sensors, and the guard, of course. The humans in town have decided that Lily's gotten a little paranoid since her, ah, abduction, so she's supposedly bought all of these highly trained guard dogs. Which I guess the wolves might pass for, as long as it's dark and you don't get too close. That being the point, of course." He grinned back at them. "It's genius, really. People already think she's running some kind of weird Goth-y B and B. It's not like having huge creepy dogs roaming the grounds at night is a big stretch past that. So between the fact that Lily is still very well liked despite being the town eccentric and, well, the public's fear of being eaten by slavering beasts, we're keeping most curious mortals at bay. Except, of course, *the* Bay. Did I tell you she got a dog?"

Damien groaned. "No. Not that I'm surprised. I'm

going to stop coming here, Jaden. I swear it. I'm sure she brings the bloody thing over." He looked at Ariane balefully. "Bay is Bailey Harper, Lily's friend. She is fixated on creatures that slobber. Though there are more of those around here than there used to be. I'm a little amazed the new Lilim deal with it as well as they have."

Jaden's look grew guarded. "Well...it was a little rough at first, but it really is getting better. The few scraps we've had have led to some new respect on *both* sides."

"And probably a lot of torn flesh," Damien said. "Still, once you get past the immediate instinct to hunt and kill one another, I expect having werewolves working for you does have some benefits."

"They work alongside us, not *for* us," Jaden said pointedly. "And, Damien, Eric is in this month's rotation of guards. I'm asking you now, nicely, to stay out of his face. He and Lyra have come a long way with each other, and he's finally started to loosen up a little since all the shit that went down. Leave him alone, okay?"

"Oh, the Puritan is here?" Damien's eyes lit up. "How...interesting."

"I mean it," Jaden said, his voice hardening.

Damien looked unperturbed. "I'll take it under consideration," he said smoothly. "Jaden, I'll never understand how a woman like Lyra could be so closely related to a humorless hardass like him."

"Just because he didn't appreciate the singing Strip-O-Gram..."

"Bloody prude," Damien snorted. "I'll bet you a thousand dollars he's a virgin."

Jaden looked in the mirror again, his eyes pleading. "Don't ask him. Seriously. For me, this once, don't."

They pulled into a small parking lot beside a beautiful brick Victorian as Jaden and Damien bickered amiably about a man who Ariane gathered was some cousin of Lyra Black's. Ariane craned her neck to get a look at the grounds while Jaden parked. Despite being so near the town square, the property seemed extensive and the house was set back quite a way from the main road. Old trees bordered the property, giving it added privacy, and even from here she could see that there was a lush garden behind the house.

He's here. Sam is here.

As she thought it, her heartbeat picked up and nerves twisted knots in her lower belly.

She could even smell him faintly, the same familiar, comforting scent that had surrounded her as she'd awakened for the first time in the desert. Even then, she had thought he smelled of incense and ancient secrets.

Out of instinct, Ariane reached for him with her mind and sensed him, even though he was, as always, closed off. But he knew she was here. He was indeed waiting.

She slid out of the car silently when Damien came around to open the door. He studied her closely, offering a small half smile that was full of the same inscrutable emotion she'd seen on the plane.

"Last stop, kitten. Come on."

Jaden carried most of the bags to the house, with Damien still dragging his own suitcase. The four of them headed up the steps, and out of the corner of her eye, Ariane could see dark shapes loping across the grounds, eyes gleaming with curiosity as they watched the newcomers. She found herself just as curious—she'd never seen a werewolf.

When they reached the top step, one of the gleaming wood doors flew open and a tall, gorgeous woman with bright gold eyes launched herself at Jaden with a husky growl. He dropped the luggage at once, laughing as he caught her. Ariane watched in wonder as the woman wrapped her legs around Jaden's waist, gave him a big, noisy kiss, and then leapt nimbly to her feet.

"Missed you, hot stuff," she said to him. Jaden simply stood there wearing a silly grin.

"I'm going to assume this is your wife," Ariane said, unable to help her smile at two people so obviously crazy about each other.

"Yeah. Anyone else does that, they meet a slow, painful death," the woman said with a grin, and stuck her hand out. "I'm Lyra Black." Her eyes, shrewd but friendly, gave Ariane a thorough once-over as they shook hands.

"Your friend has been waiting," Lyra said. "Damien knows how to get himself situated. Come on with me and I'll take you to Sam. He'll need to sleep again soon. He doesn't complain, but…the healer can only do so much for the pain."

Ariane nodded, swallowing hard. Any warmth she'd felt quickly evaporated at the look Jaden and Lyra shared and at the tense, unspoken emotion that passed between them.

She followed Lyra without another word, cold crawling over her skin. She'd wanted answers. Come what may, she had a feeling she was about to get them.

chapter NINETEEN

T HE BEDROOM WAS SHROUDED in shadow.

Ariane barely heard the door shutting quietly behind her. At first, in a darkness broken only by the flickering light of a single candle, she noticed just the basic setup of the room. A single nightstand. A washbasin. A massive four-poster bed.

Then she saw the wings.

They were beautiful, smoke gray tipped with jet black and covered with feathers that looked as though they would be as soft as silk to touch. They spread out across the snow-white linens of the bed, a display of such perfection that for a moment Ariane could think of nothing else. Huge, majestic, inspiring wings. She had never seen their like.

But then a flash of violet caught her eye and she saw him, her Sam, propped against the pillows watching her progress into the room. He was bare chested, covered from the waist down so that the wings could be accommodated.

His wings. She had never seen them. Now she understood why.

Her own wings, all other wings, were pale shadows compared to his.

"Will you be afraid of me now that you can see me as I am, *d'akara*?"

His tone was gentle, but there was a hint of vulnerability she had never heard in him before. And looking closer, she could see that the alabaster luster of his skin had dimmed. His face, always such cold perfection, now showed strain.

It was a shock to realize he wasn't as invincible as she'd always thought him.

Her nerves vanished, and she crossed the room quickly to climb onto the bed and throw her arms around him, pressing her cheek into the cool comfort of his skin. Her eyes stung, surprising her. She didn't cry, rarely even thought of crying... but then, things had changed since she'd left the desert.

"I missed you," she breathed. "I thought you were dead... and then... I didn't know."

Sam's voice was gruff when he spoke, rumbling through his chest against her ear. "And I thought you would be safer at the compound until Lucan and I had finished what we set out to do. I should have known you wouldn't sit idle."

Ariane shifted to a sitting position, staying close. She looked him over and finally saw the reason for Sam's weakened state. There was an ugly, jagged band of crusted blood carved into his left wing, marring the gray. It curved from the top of the wing to very near the bottom.

It was one thing to hear he'd almost had his wing

severed. Seeing it, though, drove the point home in a way nothing else could have.

"Sariel has gone insane to do this. It's healing, isn't it? Please tell me it can heal."

"It will take some time yet, but yes, *d'akara*. The wing will be whole. By the time the Council meets, we will be ready."

Ariane frowned, not understanding. "We?"

Sam gave a small shake of his head. "In time. There are some things we must speak of first, Ariane. Some things I need you to understand."

"Like why you vanished without a word?"

Sam sighed softly, the candlelight creating deep shadows beneath his eyes. "As I said, I assumed you would be safer at the compound. And far safer not knowing," he said. "I still believe you might have been."

Ariane's hand bunched and unbunched the coverlet as she remembered the odd way Sariel had acted that last night. It hadn't made sense at the time, but it did now.

"But Sariel thought I knew something. He wanted to get me alone. Spend time with me. I thought it was strange." She shook her head. "One more reason they would never have let me come after you, I guess. I was so furious they chose Oren."

The corners of Sammael's mouth turned down, and weakened though he was, he still looked incredibly dangerous.

"Oren. A waste. Sariel considered him a perfect example of what our dynasty should be. Loyal. Cold. So ironic, that a 'perfect' Grigori should be so jealous of the most mortal among us..." He trailed off at that cryptic statement, then shook his head. "Well. I am glad you escaped, then. Sariel has grown paranoid in recent years." Sam's eyes darkened to an indigo burn. "He should be."

"And yet you left me there," Ariane said, all her hurt and anger rising to the surface. It had been different when she'd thought Sam had been taken, somehow. But knowing he'd left her in the lion's den purposely, because he had just as little faith in her as everyone else, was a dagger in the heart.

Sam gave a small shrug, his face tightening just for an instant, as though the motion had hurt him. "I left knowing that I would eventually be hunted by the strongest among us, *d'akara*. It's only chance now that I'm still alive. The risk to you was unacceptable."

Her eyes widened. "You, the only one I had in that place, let me think you were out here hurt or dead. I've been hunted by my own. I had to take Oren's life. And the other Grigori here with you? I'm almost positive that he's the one who nearly killed me and the Shade who's been helping me! How is *any* of that more acceptable than just telling me the truth?" She saw something flicker in the depths of his eyes, then acknowledgment, at least, and maybe even a little guilt.

Sam's head drooped slightly. "Even the ancients often fall short of perfection, Ariane. Rail at me if you wish, but take pity on Lucan. We did not expect you. And he has seen horrors that make him quick to turn on our own kind."

The words gave her a chill. "But he killed innocents. Manon... and that poor clerk..."

The hard lines of Sam's face softened just a bit. "Ah, *d'akara*, there are few innocents in our world. Manon's rot went as deep as any other. His reach was longer in the city than even I knew. One of his men had sighted Lucan with me. That alone would have been enough to bring Sariel down upon us, and we were not ready. Manon was demanding payment from me for his silence, and still I knew that he would sell the knowledge elsewhere… ancients leaving the fold, conspiring. Sariel could not be sure I had disappeared voluntarily. But Lucan has been gone a year, and there could be no doubt that he had run—and why. For the others to know we were together would have raised the alarm sooner than I wished." His eyes glowed softly in the near-dark.

"Leaving the fold? I had never even seen Lucan before!" Ariane said, her volume rising. None of this made sense.

"He was there. Unseen. Like many things."

And she knew, all at once, that there was indeed something nightmarish beneath the sand of what had been her home.

"Chaos. The soul eater," she murmured, all of her anger leaving her at once, turning deadly cold.

Sam studied her a long time, his face unreadable in the shadows. "Clever child. I underestimated you. How did you learn of the demon?"

"I had some help from the Shade your friend tried to kill," Ariane said. Her joy at seeing Sam had tangled into a jumble of darker emotions. Only now, after she had been among other vampires, did she realize just how alien he was in some ways.

Sam's distaste was obvious.

"Ah, yes. The Shade. You surprise me with your choice of company."

The rebuke didn't sting the way it once might have.

"His name is Damien. Apart, neither of us would have found you," Ariane said. "I can see what you think of that, but it's true. Not everything in the world is black or white."

"And not everything is gray. He kills and steals for prestige and coin. Occasional moments of goodness don't make him worthwhile."

"He's more than you think he is!"

"And far less than *you* seem to think he is," Sam replied, turning his head to stare at the small, dancing flame of the candle. "He is not worthy of you. You will not change my mind."

Ariane flushed with anger and embarrassment. Sam knew. Of course he did. She had always been as transparent as glass. But now, after everything, for him to treat her like a child...she refused to listen to it. As much as she had looked up to him, there were some things about her, about people, that he was never going to understand.

"At least he's stuck by me," she said quietly. Sam said nothing, continuing to watch the flame. His silence, and the distance in his expression, brought her deepest fear, the thing that had plagued her every night since he'd vanished, to her lips at last. "You were all I had there, all those years. And you still left me there without saying a word. Do you...do you not care about me at all?"

Sam returned his gaze to her, his eyes full of some strong, unfathomable emotion, then said, "Ariane. *D'akara*. How can you even ask? I value you more than my duty. More than my own life." He reached out, the gesture strangely tentative for him, and brushed a lock of hair away from her face. "The others considered you my failing. The one instance I could not allow fate to take its course. But I have never been sorry for my actions that night. You are the only one of my blood. A strange turn of fate that I should look at you not as a warrior, but as my child."

Everything inside of her went still. She could only manage a single word, but it was the only important one.

"You?"

He nodded. "I sired you, Ariane. The others let you live, thinking to have you be a constant reminder of what weakness can bring. To be my shame. But instead, you brought me the only light I have known in ages. I have guarded you as best I could."

To hear the words, to know at last, brought her a kind of peace Ariane hadn't thought she would ever experience. All the years of doubt, all the petty cruelties she had endured, ceased to matter. Whatever lies had been told, one thing, the thing she had counted on, had been real.

Sam had loved her. And she knew for certain that his love had kept her from the emptiness that would have consumed her long ago had he turned away. She slid her hand on top of his, finally understanding the bond between them. He was the closest thing to a father she had. And she knew there was one more thing he could give her.

"Who am I?" she asked softly. "Who was I?"

At first, she wasn't sure he would answer. But after a moment, he began to speak, his sonorous voice seeming to fill the room despite how quietly he spoke.

"Your village was burning, sacked by a band of Normans who wanted to take what and who they could before moving on. My brothers and I had been in the country often, watching the upheaval, the transition. Looking for signs of... well, that hardly matters now. *He* was not there. But you were."

After centuries of nothing but blackness in the place where her human memory should have been, Sam's words stirred up voices and visions that began to whisper to her, as though she had needed nothing more than his admission to revive her past. She shivered, her skin going ice cold. It was like being whispered to from the grave.

"Are you sure you want to know? Sometimes the forgetting is a blessing, Ariane."

She nodded, though she wrapped her arms around herself to ward off the chill. "I need to know."

"Very well," he said, his voice laced with regret. "Here. I should have given this to you long ago."

Sam's fingertips were warm when they pressed against her forehead. Immediately, her eyes slipped shut as some sort of force passed through Sam and into her. It rippled through her body, lighting her up inside. Colors and sounds rose and swirled. And beneath all of it, she heard Sam's voice.

"You should have been dead. Your family, your siblings already were. Your home was aflame, and the soldiers had dragged you outside..."

At his words, images, terrible images sparked to life. And she remembered it all, in a series of hideous flashes that hit her like punches. From the silent dark of her memory came the screams, the terror on her younger brothers' and sisters' faces when the men had come. It had happened so quickly she'd had no time to get them away, and her father, standing for them, was cut down so quickly. They had pulled her outside before she had seen what happened to them, but she'd heard their cries, wailing her name.

And then there had been fists and rough hands... tearing and grabbing...

She curled over in pain as the memories slammed into her one after the other, each more nauseating than the last. Her family. They had killed her family, even the little ones.

"I was called Anne," she gasped out. "I remember their voices, calling for me."

"I came upon you as you ran a man through with his own dagger," Sam said, his voice sounding far away. "Such a will to live, though you were so badly beaten. The others would have savaged you worse for his death, though they never had any intention of leaving you alive. You looked at me." He stopped, and there was a faint wonder in his voice when he began again. "You looked at me where I stood in the shadows, and for the first time, I could not walk away. So much fight in you, but so much pain. So much love. Everything we were forbidden, everything I had held in contempt... and yet it drew me as nothing had before. So I took you. And the blood took your memories, because I willed it so."

She could see nothing but the faces of her family, so long hidden. Her father, his weathered face smiling in the sun. Braiding her sisters' hair while they giggled and told each other stories. Holding her youngest brother in her arms when he'd awakened from a nightmare about their mother, who had already passed in the birthing of a stillborn child. It had been a hard life. But it had been full of love.

Was it any wonder that she had so keenly felt its absence ever since, even without knowing what it was she'd missed?

Slowly, she opened her eyes. The past vanished, and there was nothing but Sam, just as he had always been. Strong. Solid. Real. He lifted his hand to her face again, this time to wipe away the tears she hadn't realized were streaming down her cheeks. There was pain in Sam's eyes, the first she had ever seen there.

"I am sorry, Ariane."

"For saving me?" she asked as her tears flowed freely for the first time in this life.

"No," Sam said. "For all your loss. I gave you new life, a new name, but I could give back nothing you really needed. I think...I had grown lonely. I'm so very much older than you know. To be in the world and never of it wears on a soul, even one as endless as mine."

She smiled despite the tears, gave his hand a small squeeze. Finally, she thought she understood.

"No," she said. "No apologies. You did the best you could with what you had, Sam. It was more than enough. I'm glad you found me. I'm glad it was you."

His smile was warm and full of the love she knew was there even if he might never be able to use the word.

And now she realized why he had called for her. He needed her help.

"Tell me what I need to do," Ariane said. "Whatever you need, I want to help set things right."

Sam's relief was palpable. "Thank you, Ariane. Lucan sleeps too deeply. I don't know if he will wake again. If he does, it won't be in time. I don't want to risk you, but you have the strength, and I have no choice. The longer our kind hides Chaos, the deeper the rot he creates. It took me too long to see it. What we have done—all the souls we have given him to keep him just sated enough, sleeping— it poisons us, until we are not his keepers but his agents. Unless things change, the Grigori will not prevent the Rising. We will enable it."

"So we start with Sariel," Ariane said. She thought of the big, unyielding warrior and hoped Sam had a very, very good plan.

"You will expose him to the others. And I will try to sway the rest of the ancients in his absence. This Council meeting provides an opportunity I had barely hoped to have."

She stared at him. "You want me to tell the leaders what he's done? Why would they listen? I'm no dynasty leader. And he'll be right there!"

"You are far safer in the midst of the strength of the dynasty heads. I won't pretend there is no danger, Ariane. But if there is any way to destroy Chaos—and even now, I don't know if it's possible—it will take the combined strength of the dynasties. Sariel will never allow even an attempt at that. Chaos whispers to him, as he does to all of us when we are near him. I don't know how long Sariel has been listening. All I know is that Chaos's hunger has grown, and there has been no attempt to check it. Sariel is not himself." He sighed. "But then, he was closest to Chaos before he fell. When he was one of us. Perhaps he mocked my weakness because he feared his own."

"One of us?" Ariane asked.

"Chaos was an ancient once. He was Grigori. He is our brother."

Stunned into silence, Ariane watched Sam sink back into the pillows, weakening before her eyes. They had been talking for some time, she realized...longer, probably, than he should have. She now knew that a wounded wing was a graver injury than it appeared. And if he—if *they*—were going to have any chance at pulling the Grigori's dark secret out into the light without Sariel stopping them first, she needed to let him sleep. There were some things that only the deepest sleep could heal.

"Rest now," Ariane said gently. "We've talked enough. Everything else can wait for tomorrow."

She had a great deal to think about, to plan. And, she realized with a sudden pang, she would have to find a way to tell Damien.

He inclined his head faintly. "Yes. I believe...that is best." His eyes began to slip shut. "We'll have to make preparations...tomorrow night..."

His voice faded away as his eyes closed completely. Ariane sat on the bed beside him, watching each slow breath. For so long, every day had been the same. And then she'd left, and it had been one change after another. Finding a place. Friends. Damien...

And now this. She'd spent centuries waiting for a chance to prove herself, to *matter*. It didn't get much more important than removing her dynasty's leader in order to take on a chained up, soul-eating demon that he happened to be related to.

With Sam behind her, she felt almost no hesitation. Except...

Ariane sighed and rose from the bed, walking toward one of the tall windows. There was no moon tonight, but the dark sky drew her nonetheless.

Even with everything Sam had revealed, her thoughts kept returning to Damien. What he would think? How he would feel? Maybe he would be relieved that she'd found something to do with herself that didn't involve him. Maybe he would be happy to get back to his life, to be free.

Or maybe...he would care enough to stay?

By the darkened window, Ariane finally let herself wish it, finally accepted that the one thing she really wanted, even when presented with a world full of wondrous options, was simply to have Damien by her side. He was ridiculously imperfect and would probably never behave himself. He might never want a home beyond his rarely visited apartment. He might not even want her.

None of it mattered to her but the last.

Because she loved him.

The truth, so simple, shook her to the core. And it terrified her as nothing ever had, not even that final leap into the desert sky. Damien was damaged and difficult and scarred. But he had brought a color and life to her existence unlike anything she'd known before. He professed to be a liar, but with her, he had been brutally honest about his strengths and his flaws. More, he accepted her own.

Behind the shield he carried, Damien was warm, funny, surprisingly loyal...and lonely.

She understood what loneliness could do.

Ariane wrapped her arms around herself and shivered, though the night was warm. So much to think about, and so little time. She needed to find the right words before she went to Damien.

But right now, words failed.

All she had was the truth: *Come with me. Don't leave me. I love you.*

And the lingering fear, in the deepest part of her soul, that no matter how much she'd gained, nothing she could offer would ever be quite enough.

chapter TWENTY

HE WASN'T GOING to look for her.

She'd gotten what she was after. Her large and frightening friend was safe, she was in a place where further attacks by Grigori hunters were unlikely, and from the look of things, she would soon have plenty more problems to contend with to keep her busy. Grigori problems, high-blood problems... not his.

And yet as the night drew closer to morning and the vampires of the manor retired to their respective quarters to relax, Damien couldn't seem to settle himself. Finally, rising from a comfortable chair in an uncomfortably empty room with a muttered curse, he set off to find Ariane.

He refused to let himself be disturbed by the fact that he knew, almost at once, that she wasn't in the house at all. So what if he'd gotten used to her scent, the very feel of her presence? They'd been together a lot. And besides, it wasn't unusual to want to think out in the open air. He did it often himself.

Within moments of stepping outside and shifting into a large, sleek cat, he'd nosed her out. She hadn't gone far. Damien reached her quickly, moving fast and silent on four feet until she came into view, hidden in the peaceful silence of the local graveyard.

He hadn't intended to lurk, but when he saw her, Damien had to stop, just for a moment, to drink in the picture she presented.

Ariane was perched atop a massive old marble headstone, her knees drawn into her chest, wings draping down behind her. To human eyes, she would have appeared just a part of the stone. But Damien could smell her, could see the shimmer of her pale hair in the darkness. He crouched beneath a tree nearby, blending with shadow as he watched her.

She looked incredibly beautiful...and so lost. As he thought it, Damien felt an unfamiliar ache somewhere in the vicinity of the place his heart should be. Whatever had passed between her and Sammael, it hadn't been the happy reunion she'd wanted. She'd gotten what she thought she wanted...and it hadn't been what she hoped.

He knew the feeling so very well. Had been the cause of that feeling more times than he could fathom.

But not tonight. She'd had quite enough disappointment for one evening.

Damien slunk from beneath the tree, padding over to stand before the stone and look up at her.

Ariane's eyes gave off a faint violet glow in the darkness as she stared into the distance. She had her arms wrapped around her knees, making her look both young and vulnerable. It gave him a jolt to realize she had been crying.

It was only then that Damien hesitated, suddenly uncertain. He'd never seen Ariane cry. He bloody hated crying. Normally he would have turned tail and run in the other direction, but something held him in place: the strange but undeniable impulse to soothe her. She was being so quiet about it, almost a part of the stone except for the silent tears that slipped down her cheeks.

Instead of disgust, he felt something far more unsettling. Doubt.

What if he was intruding? What if she didn't want him here? She hadn't come to him, after all... not that he blamed her, and gods knew he wasn't a nursemaid, but *still* ...

"Oh!"

He pinned his ears back, surprised at the sudden sound that escaped her. He had a flash of worry that she wouldn't know it was him—he'd showed off his skill in passing one night in Chicago, but it hadn't been for any length of time—but he saw Ariane recognized him immediately. She wiped at her eyes, and even in the dark he could see her blush.

"Sorry. I was just, um... yeah." She laughed, but it was a sad sound. "So much for Grigori not being able to feel things, I guess. Now you know the truth. We can cry and everything."

He tilted his head at her, then stood on his hind legs to put his paws on the top of the tombstone beside her. She looked down at him, gave him a curious half smile, and then slid her hand into the fur at the top of his head, beginning to stroke his cheeks, his ears. Damien's eyes slipped to half-mast as he purred throatily. Touch was the best comfort he could give her... and he rather enjoyed giving it. There were times he wished his feline form wasn't so big. At present, he could see the benefits of being lap-sized.

"Don't feel like being human tonight?" she asked. "Careful. I might decide to like you better this way. Kitten."

In the blink of an eye, he was a man again, and her fingers slid though hair instead of fur. For once, he didn't mind having it mussed. This time her smile was genuine. The sight did strange things to him. It made him feel obnoxiously good.

He realized he hadn't stopped purring. He also knew better at this point than to even try to make it stop.

"Ah," she said. "I thought that would do it."

He stood, and with a surprising lack of protest from Ariane, he gathered her, wings and all, into his arms. Her small form was light, insubstantial, and he sank to the ground to arrange her in his lap. For being in such an unfamiliar position, Damien found the arrangement surprisingly comfortable. It felt right, to have her here. Especially when she slid her arms around him and tucked her head into his chest.

Damien said nothing, only stroked her hair and rested his cheek on top of her head. As much as he'd always dreaded even the thought of having to give comfort, with Ariane, it was no effort. And inside himself, he felt something he had thought withered and dead stir to life. This was more than wanting her, more than needing her. Damien felt himself teetering on a precipice he had never even gotten near in his long life, and wondered at it even as he tried to back away from the edge.

"He's upset you," Damien said quietly.

"Sam is my sire," she said, her voice slightly muffled against his shirt.

"Ah," he replied. "That...actually explains a lot."

She lifted her head to look at him, and he felt that odd pain in his heart again as he got another look at her face, and the eyes that still shone with unshed tears.

"Were you close to your sire?" she asked.

"Um. No," Damien said slowly. "I killed him, actually."

She studied him a moment, and then, to his amazement, her mouth twitched. "Oh."

"It wasn't as though he was a great loss to society or anything," Damien said. "He was the sort of vamp who gets us called gutterbloods. And I...I...oh, hell with it, it's not like I killed him for the greater good or anything. You're actually amused by this?"

She continued to surprise him. Every time he thought that Ariane couldn't possibly continue to want him after some new revelation, she simply accepted it and moved along. As though she was willing to take the bad, of which there was plenty, along with the good. There being any good at all still surprised him, but she brought out things in him he'd forgotten he possessed. Empathy, for one. Honor, for another.

The scraps of these things appeared to be enough for her.

It made him wonder whether those long-forgotten qualities might emerge further the longer he stayed near her. Whether the empty spaces inside himself might shrink—or even vanish—if he filled them with her.

Mad thoughts, but perhaps not as mad as he had considered them when he'd first begun having them...shortly after they'd first met.

"I'm not *amused*, really," Ariane said, her eyes never leaving his face. "Sometimes I think you must stab everything that bothers you. Which is funny in theory, at least. And then sometimes I think that's sad. I told you once I was trying to understand you, remember?"

He arched an eyebrow. "No luck, I suppose. Though I did tell you I'm shallow. There isn't much to understand."

She shook her head, searching his face. "I think we both know that isn't true. Why *did* you kill your sire?"

He blew out a breath, looking out over the rolling grounds dotted with stones. "I was angry. For a very long time. I had everything before I was turned, you know. Son of an earl. Youngest son, so no title for me, but I was making the most of my time before Father finally bought me a commission in the army and got rid of me for good. I had money, fine things, women…"

"So you were happy," Ariane said. "Happy as a mortal."

"No. Not at all, actually. I was miserable, and a royal shit besides." It was the first time he'd ever admitted that to another living soul, and he waited for Ariane to shut down on him, to recoil from the sort of man he was, had always been. But she simply watched him, her arms around him.

"Why?" It was her only question, and a fair one.

"I… haven't really examined that in great depth," he replied, fighting the urge to squirm. "Not much on navel-gazing. If I had to guess, it's probably got something to do with being left to my own rather depraved devices for my entire life. Mother died when I was very young. I don't remember her. Father was disinterested; my brothers were older and busy with other things. Didn't ever keep the same governess long as father liked to, shall we say, sample the help and was easily bored." He shrugged. "So there you have it. It's not very interesting."

He'd never shared any of that, not in an honest way, at least, with anyone but her. He'd never wanted to. And now that it was out, he felt ridiculous, exactly like so many of the moaning, ridiculous lowbloods he'd met lamenting their place in society and blaming it on the fact that Mummy didn't love them. He knew he'd made his own bed. He'd accepted the consequences of his decisions.

He'd gone so numb that he hadn't even bothered to regret any of it. What for? It changed nothing. But Ariane, with her innocence and her wonder and her surprising strength, made him wonder, just a bit, if he could have more than what he did. If perhaps he could become... not good, really—that ship had sailed—but better.

Damien chanced a look at her face, wondering if he might finally see disgust, or pity, neither of which he wanted. But there was only interest, and her gentle warmth, which he craved the way he had once craved the light of a sun he would never again see.

"Actually, I think you're fascinating," she said.

"Indeed, kitten," he said, running his thumb down her cheek. "Your inexplicable interest in me is why I keep you around."

She laughed softly. "Did you feel better? I mean, after you killed your sire?"

He smiled. "No, darling. Why, are you thinking of trying for Sammael's head? I wouldn't advise it, fierce though you are."

"No," she replied, and her eyes went far off. "Do you know I'm the only vampire he's ever sired? He saved me,

for whatever reason. My entire family was killed in a
Norman raid, and he saved me from the men who were
trying to rape and kill me."

Her words hit him like a fist, a sucker punch in the
gut followed by a wave of shock and fury stronger than
anything he'd felt in a long time. This beautiful, innocent
woman in his arms, brutalized that way... *his* woman...
even the idea of it had him shaking with rage.

It was only her voice that brought him back to the present.

"Damien? Are you all right?"

"No," he said. "I hope he tore them to pieces. Did he at
least do that?"

Her lashes lowered. "I believe... they ran. And I was
in bad shape. I did kill one of them while he was... he was
trying to..."

Damien pulled her to him in a fierce embrace, holding her tightly against him, and pressed his lips to her
head. "Good Lord. I would have destroyed them, Ariane.
I would have inflicted the sort of pain on them that stains
the energy in a place forever. I'm so sorry, darling. I'm
so sorry that happened." His anger quickly refocused on
Sammael. "What, did he tell you all that just now? You
came all this way, nearly got yourself killed for him, and
he decided *that's* what he wanted to talk about?"

She hesitated. "No. Not exactly. He had a lot of things
he wanted to talk about. Once he told me he'd sired me, I
asked where I'd come from, and he gave me the memories
back."

Damien frowned, wondering if he'd heard her wrong.
"Gave them back?"

He felt her shake her head against him. "Don't ask. I
don't know how he did it. Sam said he'd taken them when

I was sired...or maybe just locked them up somewhere in my head. I'm not sure. Maybe forgetting was better, for a long time. I had a hard enough time adjusting. Now, though...I'm glad to finally remember. My family's faces, their voices. They didn't have much, but they were good people. I was loved. It's worth remembering."

"Yes," Damien agreed. "I suppose some things are."

"He told me...he thinks of me as his child." Her laugh was soft, wondering. "He was trying to protect me by leaving the way he did. And all this time I worried that he was only feeling sorry for me. Poor, pathetic Ariane, who was only allowed to live so she could be an example of why Grigori must be chosen very, very carefully."

He felt a stab of jealousy, though he knew he had no right to it. But he'd gotten rather used to being the only man in her life. Before this, Sammael had just been some faceless concept. Now, he was a flesh-and-blood man vying for her attention. He didn't like to share. Even with father figures.

Of course, at least she'd be in good hands once he left her...*if* he left her...

Which he was no longer quite sure how to do.

Flustered by his train of thought, Damien muttered, "Well, I know quite a lot about being a disappointment, Ariane. You aren't one. The Grigori have their heads up their asses, obviously, and good riddance to them."

She drew back to smile at him, and he let the simple pleasure of it sink in, soothe him. Funny how she did that, manage to make him feel better when he hadn't even known he needed to feel better.

Another point in her favor. What *was* he going to do with her?

"You're incredibly rude. I have no idea why you make me feel better."

"I was waiting for you, you know," he admitted. "You could have moped at me, instead of sitting out here alone."

"I guess I needed some time. And...I'm not really used to anyone listening to me when I feel like this. But I'm glad you came looking for me."

She snuggled into him again, and Damien curved his body into hers, surprised at the simple pleasure of holding her. The night was silent around them, the air soft and fragrant. It felt like they were the only two people in the world, and Damien found himself wishing that might be true, if only for a few more days. Or forever.

Oh, blast.

"Damien?"

"Hmm?"

"Thanks. For being here. I'm glad I'm not alone anymore."

Her words resonated somewhere deep inside of him, in the empty spaces he had long ago come to accept were just a part of him. And he realized, for the first time in a long time, he wasn't alone either. The need to be with her, to forge something beyond this fragile bond that had been created between them, was impossible to turn away from.

Fighting it as hard as he had been was more trouble than it was worth. He accepted it without much fuss from what passed for his conscience, and with a relief that surprised him. He still thought she was daft for wanting him, but it was past time to be trying to run her off. It wasn't going to work, and he was still going to spend most of his waking moments consumed with her in some capacity.

Beneath the stylish trappings, he was a practical man.

That, and a healthy self-interest, made him good at his job and good at getting what he wanted. Whether the impulse was a bad idea or not, he wanted Ariane. That wasn't going to change.

It was time to take steps to keep her.

Damien searched Ariane's beautiful face, the violet eyes completely focused on him, waiting for any prickle of warning, any sign that he was about to make a big mistake. But there was nothing, only comfort, pleasure. A sense of exquisite peace.

So he slipped his hand beneath her chin, rubbing a thumb over lips as soft as a flower petal, and told her with his kiss what he didn't know how to say in words. Her response to him was immediate, so honest and open that he still wondered how he had merited affection from such a woman. Time was past for questioning it, though.

The kiss deepened, and Ariane slipped her arms over his shoulders, sliding her fingers into the hair at the sensitive nape of his neck. Everything within him went loose and fluid at her touch, flooding him with warmth. She moaned softly, the sound a plea for more. It stoked the hunger in him, seemingly endless, and always for her. Her hands, as light as a butterfly's wings, stroked his neck, his face, his shoulders.

When he slid his hand up to cup her breast, she arched into his touch while he teased her tongue with his own. She sighed into his mouth.

"Let's go back to the house," she said. "I need you."

He shuddered, those words as pleasurable as a caress. But he had no intention of taking her back to the house, full of people. He wanted her here, alone...his. What was to be done would happen here, just the two of them in the dark.

"I've got you all to myself right now," he murmured. "Do you really think I'm going to give that up?"

He toyed with the hard little bud of her nipple when she pulled back to look at him. "But... we're in a graveyard."

He chuckled and dropped a kiss on her cheek, then on her jaw. "It's just grass and stone, kitten. Pretend we're in a park."

"A park," she sighed as his mouth played against sensitive skin, tilting her head back to allow him better access. "I could try that."

He nibbled at the soft skin of her neck. "Mmm. No one watching but the squirrels."

She laughed, and the sound rippled through him, making him smile.

"That's... creepy."

"You're right," he murmured. "Forget the creepy squirrels. Just focus on me."

"With pleasure."

There were so many things he wanted to teach her, show her. If there was one thing he understood, it was pleasure. Funny how he had never cared much about anyone else's until he had found her.

Damien kissed her again, allowing the feel of her, the taste of her to become everything. Every care and worry faded until there was nothing but the two of them, entangled in the grass.

Her need was so raw, so unguarded, that it fueled his own. Every small gasp she made, every moan was music to him. He took one of her hands in his own and guided it down, pressing it against the rigid bulge between his legs.

"See what you do to me, Ariane," he breathed, his

breath catching when she stroked him, pressing firmly against him with the palm of her hand.

"I know," she breathed. "I like making you hot."

He gasped as she changed her rhythm just slightly, making the muscles in his stomach tighten. "I've corrupted you. Utterly."

"Yes. Thank you," she said, flicking her tongue over his earlobe, then biting just hard enough to hurt. He surged against her hand, suddenly more aroused than he'd ever been in his life.

"Enough," he ground out, pulling her hand away. "I want to take my time with you. I want to make you burn like I do."

"I want you," she confessed, rising to her knees in front of him. "All the time."

He thought that he had never heard sweeter words.

"Then you shall have me, kitten. Turn around and hang on to the stone."

She obliged him without question, though there was a moment's hesitation when he realized she was reading the name of whatever poor sod was buried somewhere beneath them.

"He doesn't care," Damien said. "And if there are any ghosts here, they're cheering us on. Close your eyes, darling." He positioned himself behind her, sliding his hands up her thighs and gathering up fabric beneath them as he went. He drew the material up over the silky little pair of underpants she wore and stopped breathing for a moment at the sight of her firm, rounded little ass.

"Hmm. These are lovely, but they're going to get in my way." He extended his claws, and with quick precision sliced the fabric at her hips so that the two pieces fell to the ground beneath her. Then he reached beneath her to stroke and tease, finding her already deliciously wet. She shivered at his touch, and he saw her hands reflexively grip the top of the stone harder. He played her expertly, flicking a teasing finger over the tight little bud of her sex, then slipping it inside of her and back again. Her hips began to rock back against him, pressing hard into his hand. His own breath began to come in short, sharp little pants.

When he slipped his finger inside of her again, she came with a broken cry, arching back into him. Damien withdrew quickly when her climax began to ebb, shaking with need of his own. Her reactions to him were so open, holding nothing back, and here, in this, he would do no less for her.

"Don't move," he instructed her. She seemed to melt against the stone as he stood.

"Don't worry, I can't," she told him, her voice thick with pleasure.

He smiled and removed his clothes as quickly as he could. Kneeling behind her, he pulled her back against him, sliding his cock between her legs. She tensed reflexively, and his eyes nearly crossed with the pleasure. All this, and he wasn't even inside of her yet. He unzipped the dress. Wordlessly, she straightened and lifted her arms, allowing him to lift it over her head. Both that and her bra were quickly tossed to the side.

"So beautiful. I can't bloody think with you naked and on your knees," he growled. Then he pulled her hips back into him and thrust inside of her, burying himself all the way to the hilt. Ariane gasped, and her muscles clenched around him. Damien's mouth opened in a silent shout, and he only barely clung to what little control he had left. She was so hot, so very tight.

Slowly, he began to move in her, his every thrust and withdrawal provoking the sweetest sounds from Ariane. He kept his rhythm measured, contained, not wanting to overwhelm her by pinning her against the headstone and slamming into her until he was spent.

Then she reached back to squeeze one of the hands gripping her hips, looking over her shoulder with an expression that was pure heat.

"More," was all she said.

He couldn't have disobeyed her even if he'd wanted to. As soon as she turned her head away, Damien tipped his head back, dug his fingers into her hips, and began to move in hard, deep thrusts that rocked her body. He felt his chest beginning to vibrate with the purr that was always close to the surface when Ariane was near, losing himself in waves of increasingly intense pleasure. He took her harder, harder, until her hands had slid to the ground and she was on all fours in front of him, allowing him to drive deeply inside of her.

He faintly heard Ariane gasp his name as she tightened around him. The thread of his control, already gossamer thin, snapped completely. He withdrew, grabbed Ariane, and dragged her to the ground beneath him, driving into her with such force that she cried out.

He couldn't think, couldn't breathe. All that mattered was Ariane, taking her, keeping her, making her his in a way no one would ever be able to question.

Every inch of her body was pressed against his, tensed at the edge of a climax he knew would shatter them both. Beneath him, her eyes were heavy-lidded, fire bright with need, and her pale skin was flushed with exertion. Her mark, her wings, stood out in stark relief near her neck. The sight of them stirred the beast inside of him that he had always kept at bay. Until now.

He began to thrust into her again, his hips moving quickly as he pushed them both toward climax. Pure animal instinct had him lowering his head, putting his teeth to the soft skin of her throat. Her felt her press a hand to the back of his neck, urging him on.

"Yes," she whispered.

For once in his long, sorry life, there was no hesitation. He knew exactly what he wanted. Her.

Damien sank his teeth into her, tasting blood that was bright, pure power. There was a flash of white light before his eyes. Then he felt the prick of Ariane's fangs, and he was being bitten for the first time since his mortal life had been taken from him. His orgasm slammed through him, and he felt Ariane clamp tight around him as her body responded in kind. They rode each intense wave together, drinking deeply from one another as they joined with the sort of deep intimacy that only the night races were capable of.

It was bliss. It was everything. It was *right*. He felt it with every fiber of his being.

When the pleasure had ebbed and he could think again, when his mouth brushed hers as he gathered her against him, the two of them lay curled like a pair of kittens that had spent all their energy and needed a nap. Damien could feel the change Ariane's blood had wrought in him as it worked through his system and knew he had fundamentally altered his existence.

He didn't care.

Whatever happened next, Ariane would never be able to just walk away from him, something people had been doing with great regularity for both his mortal and his vampire lives.

Ariane was his. And he protected what was his.

Damien's fingers brushed the single black cat now curling around the edge of Ariane's Grigori wings, as though guarding them, and he was full of a single, satisfied thought.

Mine.

chapter TWENTY-ONE

DAMIEN HAD NEVER BEEN AN EARLY RISER, so he was surprised when his eyes opened to find the clock on the nightstand reading 8:34. Outside, in the world beyond the heavily lined curtains, he knew the sky was still beautiful and bruised as the sun vanished below the horizon.

Inside, he appeared to have spent the day curled around Ariane's lithe form, his nose buried in the silken cascade of her hair. Tentatively, he raised his head just enough to see her mark. It stood out dark against her skin, his cat guarding her wings.

He hadn't dreamed it. He'd joined with her. She was his.

Damien ruminated on this as he nuzzled her hair again, breathing in Ariane's scent. She stirred slightly, making a pleasant little noise in the back of her throat. He felt the purring start up in his own throat and didn't bother to fight it this time. It was no use.

Besides, he knew very well that he'd spent most of the previous night making the same sound.

Mind-bending sex would do that to a man.

Damien rested his hand on Ariane's hip, stroking it absently, and mulled where to go from here. She would need things. The *best* things. A lovely home, clothes, baubles, whatever struck her fancy. He protected his treasures, and Ariane was the greatest treasure he now possessed. He hadn't been a fool for imagining what it might have been like to have a woman like her after all, pampered, guarded, tucked away so that he could enjoy her light during every spare moment he had.

Somehow, he'd actually made it happen.

Damien smiled lazily, satisfied. They were well suited, really. He adored everything about her, and she seemed willing to put up with him even though he'd made no secret of his limits. He had little to offer a woman, or anyone, really. Not even his heart—he'd given up on the nebulous idea of "love" ages ago. He didn't believe in it. Love was just a word, a cudgel used to bludgeon someone into submission with until they got sick of it, or you.

But he wanted her. He needed her. He could provide for her. *That* was all real enough. So here they were.

Damien looked down at Ariane as she began to waken. Her hair fanned out on the sheets in a pale semicircle, draped over the arm he rested on and feeling like rare silk. Her long, inky lashes were still twined together, though he could tell she was no longer truly asleep by the way she rubbed her feet together where they rested against his legs. Her skin was luminous, as though the night they'd spent exploring one another had left a glow.

A pretty thought. She'd spoiled him for all other women. Nothing, he knew, would ever top last night... though he intended to spend centuries trying.

On the nightstand, his cell phone buzzed into life, the fact that it was vibrating instead of ringing making it no less annoying.

Ariane gave a soft groan. "It's *early*."

"I know, darling. I'll make it go away."

Damien lifted up on his elbow and looked at the number.

Drake. Of course it was. The man had a knack. Damien bared his teeth at the phone, then slid out of bed and fumbled around for a pair of pants to put on. Ariane barely stirred, opening one bleary eye to watch him.

"I have to take this, sweet. Just business. Close your eyes, and I'll be back in no time."

"Mmm," she murmured. "It's cold in here without you. Don't be gone long."

He left the room thinking that he would gladly spend the rest of his days lounging in bed with her. He always seemed to be hungry for her—her voice, her touch, her smiles. Her body. And though Damien knew it was archaic, knowing he had been her only lover had ignited the sort of possessiveness in him that even his rarest treasures could not inspire. She had given herself to him. Only him.

Now he would make sure he was all there would ever be.

The phone began to vibrate again, and Damien slipped out the door, padding barefoot down the hallway and then ducking into an empty bedroom to take the call.

"You're up early."

"So are you. I thought I'd have to call at least five or six more times to get your ass out of bed."

Drake sounded like he always did, gruff and in a

hurry. Nothing seemed amiss...except for the dread that rolled through Damien the moment his employer began to speak. Which was nonsense. He'd known a new job would come in. He would simply tuck Ariane into his life, and go on about his business. Nothing had really changed.

Except that apparently, everything had changed. He rubbed at his mark, barely aware he was doing it.

"What do you have for me?" Damien asked.

Drake chuckled. "No small talk? You must really want out of there. I wouldn't have left you hanging for so long, but there was always the off chance the Grigori would come back to the table. It didn't seem right to pull you out until I was sure."

"Meaning they came to collect their diamonds?"

Drake sighed. Money was the only thing he ever got wistful about.

"They came to collect their diamonds. We won't be seeing anything like those again. Doesn't it figure that you'd find the damned missing Grigori anyway? Bastards."

Damien remembered the diamond that should have been his, the feeling of peace and contentment that had flowed through him when he'd held it. It seemed like ages ago. It was a shock to realize that he felt no sense of loss. He hadn't even thought about the thing in over a week.

"Damien? Did you fall back asleep?"

"No...no, I'm here," he stammered, trying to shake it off. His life until now had been an organized thing, perfectly compartmentalized. He needed to fit Ariane into the appropriate compartment, or he was going to have problems. Because as it was, his obsession with her seemed to be spilling over into...well, everywhere.

Maybe a brief trip to clear his head and get his priorities in order wouldn't be such a bad thing after all.

"Pack your bag, Damien. There's no diamond in this job, but you'll make some good coin."

His lips felt numb when he spoke. "Lovely. Am I stealing, stabbing, or both?"

"Stealing, possibly with a side of stabbing. Quick job, important client. No muss, no fuss, and it's payday for you. A car will be there for you in twenty minutes."

"That's awfully short notice."

"And this client is awfully impatient." Drake's voice took on a hint of annoyance. "I figured you'd want to leave as soon as you could. There's nothing there, no cash, no glory. Except…is this still about the Grigori woman? Because if it is, I advise you to get your head out of your ass immediately. You're back on my time, Tremaine."

"Understood," Damien said flatly, and then listened with half an ear as Drake filled him in on the specifics. He mumbled something appropriate once Drake was done, and hung up. Afterward, he simply stood in the dark, empty bedroom. He didn't want to go. For the first blasted time that he could remember, he had exactly no interest in a job he normally would have considered an easy, lucrative bit of fun. He wanted to stay here. Or drag her off with him, which was absolutely out of the question.

He'd had quite enough of Ariane nearly being killed, thank you.

You could run, whispered a voice inside of him, one that had guided quite a few of his actions in his life. *You could run now and not look back. She'll manage.*

But *he* wouldn't manage. And that was the problem. She made him feel…

Well that was it, wasn't it? She'd made him *feel*. It wasn't something that occurred very often anymore. Or, if he was being honest, at all.

He was no fool. He'd spent centuries watching people fall in and out of what they called love. He didn't believe in love. He believed in want and need, which he and Ariane had in spades. And he believed in the power of the tangible. That was what held people together or tore them apart.

The marks they'd blended, those were real. The things he could provide for her were real as well. He took care of his treasures. He would take care of her. It didn't need to be any more complicated than that.

The thought soothed him, and the tension in his shoulders eased. If there was one thing he was capable of, it was spoiling Ariane. It might not work forever. But it would damn well work until he could figure out some other way to keep her with him.

Damien left the room, new purpose in his step.

He might not have a heart to give Ariane.

But everything else was hers.

Ariane listened to the low thrum of Damien's voice down the hall. She lay comfortably curled in the blankets, her body deliciously loose and warm. She didn't think she'd ever felt this good. No amount of imagining what joining with another vampire, biting and being bitten, would be like had done the experience justice.

But then she couldn't have imagined a man like Damien either.

She shifted gently, her fingertips grazing the mark that she knew was changed now, permanently. Interesting, to break the final tie with the Grigori this way. They would never accept her back now no matter what changed. Somehow, knowing that didn't hurt her at all. They had never really accepted her anyway. None but Sam...

She purposely turned her thoughts away from her sire. He wouldn't approve of this. Still, she was certain he'd eventually see that Damien was a good man. Not the best man, she thought with a smile, but a good one.

One of the many reasons she'd fallen in love with him.

Her smile faded as she turned that over in her mind. *In love with him.* She didn't question it. His presence had become as necessary to her as breathing. But what about Damien? She doubted he'd done this lightly. Whatever else he was, Damien wasn't reckless. What their bond signified to him, though, was a mystery.

He cared for her. She didn't question that. But more than that might take some time...possibly a lot of time. Which she would have, if she could just get through the next few days.

Ariane sighed and rolled over onto her back, waking up only because she couldn't shut her brain back off. Words drifted to her from Damien's conversation somewhere down the hall. Hmm...stabbing...car...twenty minutes...

She opened her eyes, hoping she'd misheard.

He was leaving? Already?

Damien slipped back into the room, shutting the door behind him. Rather than head back to bed, he went for his suitcase, pulling several pieces of clothing out and arranging them in a pile on the floor.

She pushed up onto her elbows to watch him. He looked distant, distracted. Not a good sign, when he'd been perfectly fine before the phone call. When she realized he was utterly lost in his own thoughts, she finally broke the silence.

"I take it you're not coming back to bed."

Damien snapped his head up to look at her, and for a split second she could see the tension etched onto his face. But it vanished almost as quickly as it appeared, replaced by a casual smile.

"Ah, you're awake. Yes, I've been called in. It's just for a few days, kitten." He straightened, reaching up to rub the back of his neck. "Nothing important. I'll be back before you know it. Mind if I use your bag? I hate to admit it, but mine's a bit large for this."

"No, go ahead," she said, marveling at how quickly he could shift from worried to devil-may-care. The latter, though, was a well-practiced act. She knew it now. He didn't like to share what was going on in that head of his. Sometimes that was probably a good thing, actually, but right now it was just frustrating.

She watched him take her things out of her duffel and stuff his in, then pull on a short-sleeved polo. His movements were as graceful as ever, but quick, efficient. She supposed he was always like this when he was heading out.

Her heart sank a little when she realized this wouldn't be the last time. Not when he was dashing off so easily and leaving her here. She didn't know what she'd thought... that maybe he'd want to take her with him when Drake's call finally came? She felt foolish, and deflated.

"You are coming back," she said, a half question that had him turning eyes on her that were very blue, even in the dark.

"Of course I'm coming back." He zipped up the bag, tossed it to land by the door, and surprised her by leaping on top of her. She laughed helplessly as he pinned her hands on either side of her head and grinned down at her.

"Just try and keep me away. You can't escape me now, you know. I've put my mark on you." He brushed his fingers over her mark with a look of possession that made her shiver. "Be thankful I'm a busy man. I'm going to wear you out terribly when I'm around."

Her smile remained, but faded. She was willing to accept that this was going to take some work, but "when I'm around" didn't sound very promising.

"I can't stay here forever, Damien. I mean, I'm sure everyone is very nice, but—"

"Ah, but that's the fun," Damien said, his eyes twinkling. "You can stay here, if you like. Though Chicago would be acceptable too. Vlad is careful about his territory, and you'll need to be somewhere protected in case the Grigori send someone after you again."

"Ah," she said, beginning to get a picture of how he envisioned their relationship. "I suppose you'll buy me a house," she said, keeping her tone carefully neutral.

"I hope you'll look while I'm away, kitten. Anything you like. I mean that. You've never really had a place of your own. Not one you chose. I want you to have a home you love."

It was sweet. Misguided, but so sweet she didn't know quite what to say. She knew immediately that he would spoil her incredibly if she let him, buying her a house, clothes, baubles, even a rack full of enormous and impractical swords if that's what she really wanted. It was pure Damien. He would happily fill her life with everything she'd ever wanted . . . while denying her the only thing she really wanted.

Him.

Ariane looked up at him, so very handsome . . . and so hopeful. She wouldn't crush him by saying no outright. He wouldn't understand. She would have to show him what she wanted. What she cared about.

Except that right now, there wasn't any time.

"What's the matter, kitten?" he asked, touching her nose with his finger. "You're not unhappy, are you?"

"No," Ariane replied. "I just wish you weren't leaving so quickly. That's all." With the hand he'd released, she reached up and pulled aside his collar, tracing the outline of the wings that now curved around his trio of cats. Protecting them. Not an interpretation Damien would probably accept right now, but she liked it. She didn't think anyone had ever protected Damien.

She was happy to be the first. The only.

"Oh, you'll be busy nursing your very large and forbidding friend, I'm sure," Damien said, his voice softening. "The other one hasn't even awakened yet. I wonder whether he will?"

"Sam thinks he might not," Ariane said. She hesitated, knowing before the words left her mouth that Damien wasn't going to react the way she'd been hoping. But she wouldn't hide it from him. He wasn't the only one with duties.

"Even if Lucan does wake up, he won't be well enough to travel for a few days," she said. "That's why Sam has asked for my help."

Damien went very still. "Define *help*."

Briefly, Ariane explained what needed to be done,

watching his expression darken with every word. When she'd finished, it took him a moment to collect himself.

"So you're going to risk your life. Again. For these miserable bastards who didn't want a thing to do with you for most of your existence."

Ariane sighed. "It's bigger than that. If we don't do something, a lot more than just the Grigori are at risk. This is important."

"Then someone else will do it."

She frowned at him. "No. I will."

"Why?" Damien said, a bite in his voice. "Out of some misguided sense of honor? Honor doesn't mean a damned thing if you're dead, Ariane. You shouldn't be involved in this. And if Sam cared all that much about you, he wouldn't be throwing you to the wolves!"

Damien sat up, his glare scorching. Ariane tried to ignore it, though she felt herself beginning to bristle. She'd been trapped in the desert for centuries, and yet somehow, she still had better relationship skills than Damien did. He made it hard to appreciate his concern for her when he was being a complete ass about it.

"Sam asked me because he trusts me," Ariane said flatly. "Because I'm capable. I'm not sure whether to be insulted or amazed that you don't seem to agree, given that you've seen me fight."

Damien gave an exasperated growl. "This has nothing to do with that."

Ariane rose to a sitting position, gathering the sheets protectively around her. If this was going to work between them, he was going to have to give up this archaic notion of becoming her protector. She didn't want a protector; she wanted a partner.

And she could already see that he wasn't in the mood to listen. Still, she was compelled to try.

"Damien, it has *everything* to do with that."

"How the hell are you getting that? Just because you can fight doesn't mean you should have to! You've done your bit. Let it go!"

Her jaw tightened. "Just because you can get paid for stealing and killing doesn't mean you ought to. But you don't hear me shouting at you not to go."

"That's not the same thing," he snapped.

Ariane felt her long-suffering patience fraying. "Why, because there's nothing in it for me? All my life, I've wanted to prove myself, and I've never been given the chance. I worked twice as hard as anyone else, and no one bothered to notice. I don't care what the Grigori think of me anymore, Damien, but I do care about using what I have to make a difference where I can. This matters. It matters to me." She paused. "Actually, I'd hoped you'd come with me."

Damien cursed and stood, throwing up his hands. "Are you mad? Of all the bloody hills to die on, you choose this one. A potentially insane Grigori harboring a soul-eating demon. And you'd like to go up against him together, as though there's much *anybody* can do about Sariel if he decides to fight. He's huge. He's ancient. He's at least ten times as competent as that bastard who tried to take you out in Charlotte." He shoved a hand through his hair, making it stand up in odd spikes. "Ariane, this is madness!"

She drew in a breath, barely keeping herself from shouting even though her throat hurt with the need to. That was what Damien wanted: a fight. It was easier for him that way. It was what he was used to. And it would give him an excellent excuse to storm off before he'd heard her out. That wasn't going to happen. Even if this ruined everything she'd hoped for, he was going to listen to the truth.

"You went up against Arsinöe and freed an entire bloodline. That qualifies as madness, I think, but here you stand."

His eyes flashed. "I was coerced. I didn't run off to risk my life voluntarily. And I wasn't alone."

"I won't be either."

"Damn it, Ariane! I thought last night meant that you were done with this nonsense, that we could move on to just enjoying one another!"

"At your leisure," Ariane said. "When you aren't risking your own life for profit. I don't expect you to change for me, Damien, and I realize that you have obligations because of what you are. But if this is going to work at all, you need to understand that I have obligations too. To what I am, who I am."

"Bull," Damien shot back. "This isn't an obligation, it's a choice, and a bloody stupid one. If you were so keen to run off and kill yourself, why did you even bother last night? Why take my mark if you were just going to throw it away?"

Ariane looked at him helplessly, knowing she was losing him. This was a rift she didn't have time to repair. All she could do was hope that the truth was enough to keep him.

"Because I love you," she said, and though her voice was quiet, the words seemed to fill the room.

Damien stared at her. "You..."

"I love you," Ariane said again, relieved that she'd

finally said the words even as she watched Damien shrinking back behind the shield he'd carried for so long. She knew then that he was going to walk away. Her throat constricted.

No, damn it. I will not cry.

"You can't possibly love me," Damien said, his voice hoarse.

"I can, and I do," Ariane replied, her eyes never leaving his, willing him to let her back in, just a little.

"But I'm wretched."

"Sometimes. But you're also warm, and funny, and sweet. You're honorable in your own twisted way. And even when you're awful, you're interesting about it." Her voice gentled. "I know you want me here, safe and tucked away and completely separate from the parts of your life you don't want me to see. But I'm not one of your prizes, tucked into that apartment you never visit. I can't be happy that way. I want to see things. I want to *live*. I'm not interested in being left behind anymore."

Standing there, in the middle of the room, he looked both beautiful and desolate. She'd hit him with a lot at once, Ariane knew. But he hadn't given her much of a choice. And maybe... maybe it was better this way. Better to lay it all out and let the chips fall where they may.

Even if the end result was painful for them both.

"I'm giving you what I can, Ariane. It's more than I've given anyone else. Try and understand that. There are parts of me, of my life, that—" He stopped, scrubbed a hand over his face, and tried again. "I don't know that I can give you what you're asking."

She knew he wasn't going to say the words she'd hoped for. He wasn't ready. Maybe he would never be.

But Ariane refused to let him go without the full knowledge of what he was walking away from. Maybe, in time, it would be strong enough to bring him back. If she was here to come back to.

"I don't need you to be perfect, Damien," she said. "I just need you."

Ariane saw his defenses waver, just for an instant. Then a car horn sounded outside, and all her hopes crumbled into dust.

Damien closed his eyes. Took a breath. And turned to pick up the duffel bag.

"I have to go, kitten," he said. The anger was gone from his voice, but so was everything else. He sounded tired.

"Damien..."

He turned and looked at her, his eyes so full of longing that it made her ache. And still, she couldn't hold him.

"I can't, darling. Not now. I just...I have to go. Take care of yourself, then, and..."

He stopped, shook his head, turned. And in seconds, he was gone, slipping out the door and out of her life as though he'd been nothing more than a shadow. Ariane sat very still as she listened to the car idling outside. As she heard the door slam and the sound of the car move away from the house.

Only then did she let herself break, the tears falling silently in the dark.

Things had changed so much, and yet she felt as though she were right back where she'd begun.

Alone.

chapter TWENTY-TWO

THE SKY WAS beginning to turn gray by the time she'd passed the guards to knock at the door.

Vlad answered, looking charmingly rumpled. He'd probably had his nose stuck in a book and forgotten the time. He was prone to doing that. He also appeared to be wearing a smoking jacket, a thing that struck her as funny and nearly sent her into hysterical giggles. She swallowed them back, sensing that they would quickly turn to tears, and she'd had enough of those on the way here.

She'd been holding it together. Somehow, she'd made it through last night, feigning indifference to Damien's sudden departure even though she'd seen Lyra shooting her sympathetic glances all evening. Everything was fine; everything was normal. She'd been good at pretending that once, able to smile and look serene even during her darkest moments among the Grigori. But Damien had ripped a hole in her, leaving a wound she had no idea how to heal. She'd waited centuries to be able to really give her heart to someone...and he'd rejected it.

If she got through the next forty-eight hours in one piece, Ariane supposed she would find a way to live with it. If she hadn't broken after all these years, she wouldn't now. But this kind of hurt, this raw, endless pain, was new to her.

He was gone. Damien had gone, and she doubted he was coming back. He'd turned himself into a fortress even she couldn't breach, and there was nothing to be done for it. She'd tried.

"Ariane!" Vlad said, his pleasure at seeing her obvious. "I wasn't sure when to expect you." He peered up at the sky. "You're cutting it a bit close. I would have sent the jet for you, but when I spoke with Jaden, he insisted—"

"I wanted to fly myself," Ariane said, attempting a smile. "I love the night air. And it's good to stretch my wings."

Mainly, she had just wanted to be alone. Unfortunately, though she'd stretched her wings, she hadn't cleared her head.

Vlad was eyeing her with interest. She knew he wanted to prod her about her wings, having only caught a glimpse of them the night Oren had attacked her. Normally, she would have been amused. He was too polite to come right out and ask her to unfurl them, but she knew he desperately wanted to. And at some point, she would show him. He'd been too kind to deny him something so simple, and considering all that was happening, she doubted that any of her kind's secrets would be staying that way for long. But right now, she felt only a bone-deep weariness that had leeched all the enjoyment out of everything. She couldn't even bring herself to be nervous about all that lay ahead tomorrow night at the meeting, though that would likely change.

"Well, come in, please," Vlad said after studying her face closely. "I know it's only been a few days, but it's been so much quieter since you and Damien left." He stepped aside as Ariane walked in past him, and she could feel his eyes on her, searching. She looked away. He was a very perceptive man . . . and she was a poor liar.

"How is . . . everything? I assume Sammael is on his way as well?"

"He is," Ariane said. "We left at the same time, just going different directions. He seemed to think he would make it tonight, but . . ." She trailed off and shrugged. Sam, it had become increasingly clear, had abilities far beyond anything she'd suspected. She had hated to see him go, when neither of them was sure what he would be walking back into.

He hadn't asked about Damien, seeming satisfied only that the Shade had gone. Ariane had kept her mark covered and said nothing. Despite their bond, she knew Sam had very clear limitations when it came to understanding or even picking up on feelings. And there was no way he would understand this.

"And how is Damien?" Vlad pressed, shutting the door behind them. "I half expected to see him walking in behind you."

Ariane looked at Vlad, at the sympathy in his eyes, and saw that he knew. Without saying a word, he'd figured out that Damien had left her. He'd probably even expected it. No one appeared to have been surprised . . . except her.

She'd expected more of him. And she'd been bitterly disappointed.

"He...he had a job. Somewhere. I'm not sure. It all happened very fast."

"Ah, I see. That's fairly typical," Vlad said, his voice gentle. He tilted his head down, just a little, those crystal-line eyes missing nothing. "Are you all right, Ariane?"

"I'm...yes. No. I don't know."

The whole sorry mess began to tumble out of her mouth, and whether it was fatigue or simply hitting her breaking point emotionally, Ariane was powerless to stop it. When she finally stopped for breath, it occurred to her that she had just unloaded all of her problems, in an opu-lent foyer, on the leader of one of the most powerful vam-pire dynasties in the world. It didn't make her feel much better, but Vlad, to his credit, did not run away.

"Well," he said. "So. You two...erm...bit one another."

"Yes."

"And then Drake called, and you had an argument."

"Yes."

"And then he told you he can't love you, although he would like to buy you a house."

"Basically."

Vlad rubbed the back of his neck, looking distinctly uncomfortable. "This really isn't my area, though you've certainly got my sympathy. He is a difficult creature, Ariane."

She sighed, feeling her eyes begin to water again. "I know."

Vlad put a comforting arm around her shoulders, a rare show of physical affection from a man who seemed almost ruthlessly self-contained. "Here, let's get you upstairs. We've a great deal to do tomorrow night, and at this point, rest is the most important thing for you." He ushered her quickly upstairs, to a room that was neat as a pin and blissfully devoid of any of Damien's things. She stepped inside, knowing she was just going to collapse on the bed and pass out without undressing.

She turned back to look at Vlad as he bid her good day, feeling absurdly grateful to him simply for existing.

"Thank you," she said. Vlad's smile was affectionate.

"For what it's worth, Ariane, I'm sorry. Damien has many fine qualities, none of which he will admit to…but that you could see them says a great deal for you. I have to think he'll come to his senses, but this will be hard for him."

Her shoulders slumped. "I don't know. I really don't. But I couldn't stay. It may not matter, after tomorrow…"

"Nonsense. I've spoken to Mormo and even had a quick word with Arsinöe, though you can never be certain which side she'll come down on. She could decide to defend Sariel just to be contrary. But I don't think so."

Ariane sighed, shaking her head. "I'm just worried that he's too strong. That trying to break his hold on the Grigori is only going to lead to something worse, something even you can't handle."

He shook his head and offered her a tired smile. "Ariane, whatever he may be able to do, Sariel is still just a vampire. He can't stand against the rest of us. Believe that. Now, get some sleep. We'll talk when you awaken," he said, and shut the door.

Ariane felt lethargy stealing through her as the sun rose outside, making her limbs feel leaden. She just made it to the bed, sprawling across it and unfolding her wings so that they covered her like a blanket. And she sank gratefully into deep, numb, dreamless sleep.

She woke early, just as the sun sank below the edge of the horizon.

At the very least, the sleep had refreshed her, though it had done nothing to ease her mind. And the nerves, though late, had arrived in full force. Tonight she was going to expose the ancients of her bloodline for what they had done. If she succeeded in her part, she would change the course of her dynasty. Or...what had been her dynasty. She was just a lowblood now.

But then, the lowbloods of the world had been the ones to bring about the greatest changes lately.

Ariane rose, showered, and dressed in a tank top and a pair of skinny white jeans. Then she went to the phone on the nightstand, pressed the number for an outside line, and called Elena. She hadn't been able to talk to her friend about all that had happened. But she owed Elena a call before she walked into whatever was going to happen tonight.

"Hey, Ari. I was about to get in trouble and call the mighty Dracul to give him an earful. Where have you *been*?"

"I'm in Chicago. Well, back in Chicago. I should have called before this, but it's been kind of...interesting. I wanted you to know I was all right."

Elena's relief was palpable, and she didn't seem at all angry, though Ariane felt plenty of guilt for her silence since Sam's discovery. Damien wasn't the only one who needed to get better at tending his relationships.

She took a few minutes to explain what had happened, keeping it brief, glossing over the Grigori's demon problem... and keeping any mention of Damien out of it. When she was finished, Elena was quiet for a moment.

"I need wings," she finally said with a soft laugh. "You've gotten some pretty good mileage these last couple of weeks."

"I only flew here on my own," Ariane said. "A plane works just as well most of the time."

"Yeah, it sort of lacks the coolness of being able to manifest an enormous pair of wings of your own, though," Elena replied. Then her tone turned serious. "So, Sariel is going down. Wow. Are you going to be all right? I mean, know you're surrounded by the leading badasses of the vampire world tonight, but still... this doesn't sound all that safe to me."

"It isn't, but I think it'll be okay," Ariane said, and then blew out a breath. "Hopefully."

"I wish you'd called yesterday. I would have ditched work and gotten myself up there somehow. You shouldn't be doing this without backup you know you can trust. Speaking of, is that Shade still hanging around?"

Ariane didn't know what to say. Finally, she settled on the simplest thing.

"No."

A sigh. "Damn it. I didn't want to be right about that. You two seemed like you might actually have a good thing going. Do I need to find him and kick his ass or something? I will, you know."

Ariane laughed, and it helped ease the ache in her chest, just a little. "No. I'll tell you all about it... after this. With wine. I'll come visit."

"You've got it. Stay awhile. I left the apartment empty, just in case."

"Maybe I will." These things were hard to think about...but she would have to. She still had a life to figure out. That hadn't changed. And at least she had a friend in Charlotte, though she would also have plenty of memories there that involved Damien. She would see.

And it was time to wrap this up. Her role in this was to be very simple, but she still needed to speak to Vlad and Lily before everyone arrived.

"Look, I have to go. I'll give you a call after this is all over."

Elena groaned. "You realize I'm going to worry until that phone call. Like, insane amounts of worry. Don't leave me hanging, okay?"

"I won't."

"Be safe, Ari. And don't worry about the Shade. He seemed pretty attached. Maybe you two will work it out."

Ariane lifted her hand to rub at her mark, a permanent reminder of the cat who had broken her heart. "I don't know," was all she said. And then, in case she didn't manage to see her friend again, she added, "Love you."

Elena's voice went to mush. "Oh. Damn it, Ari. I love you too. Now go be amazing with that sword of yours so I don't have to avenge you or anything. I have to go hurt some people at work now." There was the distinct sound of a sniffle before Elena hung up the phone.

It wasn't the same as it would have been if Damien had said it, but she was glad that someone found her love worthy of returning.

Ariane hung up the phone, feeling a little better. Drained, hollow...but talking to a friend had helped. And it was time to do what she'd come here for.

* * *

The foyer was alive with activity. Dracul courtiers and staff hurried back and forth, chattering excitedly. Ariane saw people cleaning, fresh flowers being put out, furniture being moved.

Ludo, the tall gypsy who Vlad seemed to keep as a jack-of-all-trades, spotted her and headed up the stairs to say hello. "Heard you were back," he said with a grin. "Flying solo this time?"

"You could say that," she said. "Are people here already?"

"Not yet. Just getting ready. Whenever we host the Council, it's always kind of a production. Especially this time." He looked at her closely. "You ready?"

"As ready as I'm going to be," Ariane said.

Ludo nodded, his teeth flashing white against his dusky skin when he gifted her with a brief smile. "Don't worry. Vlad always knows what he's doing, and there will be a lot of power on our side. Come on. I'll show you to where he is."

He brought her downstairs, past the library, to a cozy little sitting room she hadn't spent any time in when she'd been here before. The walls and furniture were done in dark colors and rich fabrics. Oil paintings of people she didn't recognize, all wearing odd clothing and posing with hounds or the trappings of ancient academia, hung on the walls. None of them looked nearly as friendly as the three faces that turned toward Ariane as she entered.

"There you are," Vlad said warmly.

He looked confident and just a little dangerous. She tried to take comfort in that.

"Come in and meet Lily and Ty, otherwise known as the ruler of the Lilim and her consort."

The man and woman rose, and Ariane walked forward to meet them, slightly self-conscious. This seemed to be what she did now: sleep with assassins and make nice with vampire nobility.

The man, tall, dark, and rangy with beautiful silver eyes, shook her hand first. When he spoke, his voice was a rich and musical brogue.

"Ariane, it's nice to finally meet you. I can already tell you're nicer than your blood brother, Sammael. Though even he admitted you were."

She smiled. "Nice to meet you too. I'm not sure if you're nicer than Jaden, though. He says not."

Ty laughed. "He's right."

Then the woman took her hand, and Ariane could feel the power she carried sizzle up her arm. Lily's smile, though, was anything but intimidating. She was a stunning woman, with big, glittering blue eyes and a wavy fall of auburn hair that was pulled away from her face.

"Hi. I'm Lily. And this has to be said—you're gorgeous."

Ariane's brows winged up, but she laughed, flattered. "Um, thank you. Everyone seemed to think I would look more like, well . . . a man."

"Fortunately for all of us, that's not the—Oh."

Lily stopped short when Ariane, flustered by the attention, had brushed her hair back over her shoulder. Lily's eyes dropped immediately to her mark. And then Ariane remembered. Tank top. Wings. Cat. She flushed and pulled her hair back over her shoulder to cover it. It didn't matter. Lily had seen it, and so had Ty. Neither, however, seemed inclined to mention it.

"Anyway," Lily said, her smile overly bright, "I'm glad to meet you." The smile faded and turned serious quickly.

"It's lucky you were with Vlad when everything happened. Do you know if Sammael made it to the desert?"

"I'm not sure," Ariane replied. "But he's incredibly strong, and fully healed. I can't imagine he didn't."

Vlad motioned for everyone to sit, and she moved to the couch where he was. Ariane knew these problems were the ones she ought to be focusing on. It was a relief, not to have to think about her foolish heart.

"I think everything is in place. Once Mormo performs the ritual, we should all have a better idea of what we're dealing with. I understand that Sammael was reluctant to be more specific about the exact location of this... thing... before he spoke to the other ancients, but I'm hopeful that the divination will tell us what we need to know regardless."

"He doesn't want anyone rushing into our territory without the permission of his brothers," Ariane said. "He seemed to think it would go badly for whoever tried." She thought of his wings, so beautiful and strange, and of the way he spoke about mortals as though he had never been one. "I'm inclined to agree."

Vlad sighed. "I wish he had more faith in the other leaders, but... he is Grigori."

Lily gave Ariane a sidelong glance. "I... hate to ask this. But is your, um, changed mark going to cause an issue with the ceremony?"

Ariane went cold. That was something she hadn't even considered. She'd been so consumed with Damien's leaving that it hadn't occurred to her that she was no longer quite a pureblood. She looked quickly at Vlad, but his smile was understanding.

"I've already consulted with Mormo. The changes

Damien's blood will effect in you will take time to manifest, if they do at all. And they may not. Your sire is incredibly strong. She seemed to think your blood would suffice."

Ariane slumped a little with relief. "Sam told you, then. That he's my sire."

"I would have suspected it anyway, but yes. That he cares for you is obvious. And, unusual."

Lily wrinkled her nose. "And he doesn't have to deal with Mormo. Lucky him."

Ariane tilted her head, surprised by the bitter edge to Lily's voice. "Do you know her?"

"I don't need to know her. She and Arsinöe keep finding reasons to delay the creation of a territory for my people. Arsinöe sticks to New York, and the Empusa is nowhere I'm even interested in being. There's plenty of New England that's technically Arsinöe's but functionally no one's, but *nooo*. Can't let the demon queen and her gutter cats get on with their lives." She looked wearily at Vlad. "I'm tired of fighting the battle, but I'm going to win this war, Vlad, I swear."

Vlad sighed and shifted, recrossing his legs. "I know. I waited until I could bully my way in, effectively. We couldn't do that for you. But we'll get there. You are at least a full member of the Council now, and that's something. Mormo is old and afraid, with a waning line and health that is fragile at best—and everyone knows it. I supported her dynasty because their stability benefits us all, not to mention that she can be a handy ally. But no, she won't cross Arsinöe. Mainly because she knows the Ptolemy will be first in line to move in when Mormo falls. She's trying to delay the inevitable. But we'll get there, Lily. She can't stop you."

Lily shook her head ruefully. "Right now, that's only because I have you standing behind me."

Ty grinned and planted a kiss on her cheek. "But it's such a nice view from back there."

She smacked him and laughed, and the tension lifted, if only briefly.

"I'm curious to see these women," Ariane admitted.

"Soon," Vlad said with a small smile that held little humor. "The trap is laid. Only wait for it to be sprung before you show yourself."

Ariane looked at Lily, whose expression was full of understanding.

"I was curious about them once too. I got my fill pretty quickly."

Ludo returned to the room then, carrying with him an air of importance that told Ariane the night was about to begin in earnest.

"They're arriving, my lord."

They all rose, Lily heading to Vlad's side, while Ty tugged playfully at Ariane's arm.

"I get to hide you," he said, "since the less Arsinöe and I see of one another, the better."

"Damien told me you were her hunter," Ariane said. She'd heard the story, which had even been murmured among the Grigori, of how the Ptolemy queen's prized hunter had freed the Cait Sith, prevented a war with the Dracul, and married the mortal heiress of the Lilim bloodline. She'd been awed that one vampire could do so much, and even the ancients had seemed to approve of the Lilim's awakening.

"I was her slave," Ty said, his eyes as bright as the moon. "She hasn't forgotten. And neither have I. Let's go."

chapter TWENTY-THREE

DAMIEN HAD NEVER had so little interest in work.

Of course, he'd never spent so many consecutive hours wondering where he'd fucked up so badly, either. So it was a new and fabulous experience all around.

He was only half paying attention as he picked the lock on yet another shabby apartment in one of the seedier parts of Atlanta, quickly and quietly slipping inside and shutting the door. This was his last stop on his tour of the homes of one very careless Empusa's very worthless servant, all of whom had been merrily raiding the treasure room while their mistress was on an extended holiday. No one was home this time, which made his life easier. He wasn't in the mood to fight. In fact, he wasn't in the mood to do much but sit and brood, which was disconcerting all in itself.

The search for the contracted items was halfhearted at best. The sort of vampire who left bloodstains on the carpet and dirty underthings in a pile in the bathroom was not likely to be one who came up with an original hiding spot for stolen jewelry.

Damien pawed through an overflowing dresser drawer, frowning. Cheap porn, stolen wallets...no and no. With an irritated sigh, he turned and scanned the bedroom with well-trained eyes. The carpet was flapped up against the far wall, revealing a hint of old hardwood beneath.

Yes, this thief was an idiot.

It took Damien all of five minutes to pull back the carpet, lift the loose board beneath, and retrieve a couple million dollars' worth of jewelry that would have made a museum curator's eyes bug out. He lifted it, watching the way the light reflected off a delicate diamond necklace. It made him think of the way the moonlight shone on Ariane's hair.

Gods, he was getting disgusting again.

He stood, not even bothering to put the board back. He refused to waste the time on someone who wasn't even a proper thief. The Empusa in question was an easily distractible know-nothing with a rotating stable of young men and a vile temper, and he had no doubt she paid her servants next to nothing. A shame that they hadn't been smarter about it. They were just lucky their mistress was too bloody lazy to do much but put them out of a job.

Damien's lip curled as he headed for the door. He'd keep the damned jewels if he didn't think Drake would send a legion of Shades after him just out of spite. His employer didn't seem keen on his prized Shade's mood the last couple of days. Nor the rather obvious reason for it.

Just wait until the tirade he'll deliver when he sees my mark. That should be a joy.

The door swung open just before he reached it, revealing a confounded-looking vampire who reeked of smoke and booze. Celebrating, Damien thought, his lips thinning as the thief began hissing at him. He might have considered taking a bath or ten first. *Bloody amateurish, gutterblooded...*

"I'll kill you!" the vampire shrieked.

"Oh, piss off," Damien growled, and took care of the problem with a single roundhouse kick to the head. The vamp went down like a ton of bricks, and Damien stepped over him, sparing him a single, disgusted glance before heading for the elevator. The jewelry was heavy in the pocket of the light trench coat he wore.

Diamonds. The less I see of these, the better, he thought. He'd had quite enough of diamonds. The Stars of Atlantis had vanished, but he had scads of less mystical diamonds in his apartment, kept under lock and key. Not a damned one of them had made him happy. Even the Grigori's magic diamond had given him a peace that had been no more than an illusion. Everything he'd collected, all the pretty, shiny things he'd hidden away like the magpie Ariane had jokingly compared him to meant nothing. All he had were objects, cold, dead, lifeless things. Much like himself.

Until he'd met Ariane.

Damien clenched his jaw and glared at the floor as the rickety old elevator descended to the first level. He was Damien Tremaine, master of his own destiny, expert thief, cold-blooded killer, and...no one gave a shit. He was as alone as he ever had been. As alone as he'd always thought he preferred.

Shockingly, his entire existence now seemed to suck.

Small wonder, since Ariane had been the only thing good in it.

Damien closed his eyes and groaned softly. What was he *doing*?

When the elevator door opened, it took him several seconds to register that there was an enormous white-haired giant glaring at him.

By the time it did, Lucan had him by the throat.

"You are not easy to find, Shade."

Damien gagged and managed to gasp out an answer as his feet dangled above the floor. "That's...the point... put me down!"

Lucan simply looked at him impassively. "If you run, I will break your legs."

He lowered Damien to the ground and allowed him a moment to cough while his windpipe recovered. At length, Damien finally looked up from where he was bent over, hands on his thighs.

Lucan loomed before him, watching him steadily and without an ounce of compassion. Damien couldn't fathom how he had gotten in here without causing a stir. He looked like a creature out of a fairy tale...or bloody Revelations. Lucan wore only simple leather pants and a pair of well-worn boots. His hair, as white as the snow, was pulled back in a simple leather thong. Lucan's chest was bare, and on either side of him were folded the most incredible wings he'd ever seen. Jaden had mentioned how amazing he'd thought them, but Damien hadn't bothered to look in on either Lucan or Sammael before he'd left. Now he understood. The wings were enormous, glorious things, covered in feathers that were the deep blue of a sky nearly faded to darkness and edged in a rich blue black.

Ariane's wings were beautiful, but diaphanous, fairy-like despite their strength. These were the wings of an avenging angel. It took him a moment to speak, though it was hard to keep from staring.

"I see you did finally wake up. What do you *want*, Lucan?"

Lucan's violet stare was disconcerting. It seemed to see a great deal. Far more than it should have. Damien fought the urge to squirm. Finally, Lucan spoke, in a voice that was both resonant and cool.

"Something is wrong. Sammael has been taken, and Ariane is in danger."

Damien stopped breathing at the words.

I should have been there. She asked me to come with her. I should have gone, damn it...I'm a fool, a bloody fool...

"What's going on? What's happened?" Damien's words came out in a rush as he straightened and stepped closer to Lucan, his wariness of the Grigori vanishing in the face of the terrible knowledge that this had to be bad for Lucan to have sought him out.

These were not beings who overreacted.

"Shortly after I wakened, I felt my brother cry out to me." For the first time, Lucan's face changed, his expression shifting subtly. It was an unpleasant shock to see that the man was capable of fear after all.

"He has been taken below. I can no longer hear him. Whether he lives yet..." He trailed off, then shook his head. "The demon has truly wormed his way into Sariel's mind. I fear Chaos has been allowed to waken. His sight reaches far. He will have seen what the Council members have waiting for Sariel, and warned him." His eyes were burning, piercing things. "Ariane will not stand a chance. None of them will. They do not understand what he is."

The words sent a sliver of ice directly through Damien's heart. "Gods above and below...is he loose?" Damien rasped. "Has Sariel already set him loose?"

Lucan shook his head. "No. But it's only a matter of time. We underestimated Chaos's strength. Even half asleep, he has broken the one closest to him. Perhaps he would have managed it with any of us, had we chosen another to lead." He sighed softly. "It's too late to know."

Damien tried to take it all in, all the implications. For the first time in memory, saving his own skin wasn't the first thing he thought of. All he could see in his mind's eye was Ariane, falling to a nightmare creature with raven wings. Terrified fury welled in his chest, so fast and powerful he felt as though it might tear a hole right through him.

"You bastard! You ignorant, pigheaded bastard! That *thing* is one of yours, isn't it? Your brother! You kept him chained up and fed him people's souls rather than do what you ought to have! This is your bloody fault, and now you've inflicted this mess on the rest of us!" He was shouting now, standing toe-to-toe with Lucan, his face turned up to the impassive giant.

"If anything happens to her, I swear I'll find a way to destroy you. I'll make sure your entire dynasty crumbles into dust. None of you will be safe. *None* of you."

Lucan stared at him, his face contorting with momentary fury. Then, incredibly, he looked away.

"As unimpressed as I am with you, Shade, you speak the truth."

Damien blinked. "What?"

"You speak the truth." Lucan's deep, melodious voice was strained. "When Chaos fell, he did it of his own free will. The destruction he caused was immense before we caught him, and by then he had found others to follow him. Dark things. Ones who fell so long ago that everything good had been consumed. In the beginning, we might have destroyed him, as we did the demons who didn't go to ground quickly enough. But…he had been our brother. We thought perhaps, one day, he would return to us." He closed his eyes. "That weakness may cost us everything."

Damien bared his teeth. "You, and everyone else. You lot aren't even human, are you? You never were. Not the ancients. Brother to a demon, all this about falling…you were never mortal."

Lucan opened his eyes and looked at him, and Damien saw the truth.

"No wonder you can be so bloody formidable and still understand so little," Damien spat, disgusted. He didn't know where the Grigori had come from, and he wasn't sure he wanted to. Every dynasty had been kissed by the gods, some of them very dark. A dynasty of creatures who were uncomfortably close to *being* gods had implications that he didn't even want to consider right now. He had to stop what had been set in motion.

All that mattered was saving Ariane.

"What do we need to do?" Damien asked. "Get me to Ariane, right now. I don't give a damn about Sammael—he's the one who got her into this mess. But I won't have her die."

Even just saying the words out loud forced something to give way inside of him, the walls he'd built crumbling where they'd already cracked. He thought of his life before she had come, how it had often seemed as though all the music and color had leeched out of his existence. How nothing could fill him up, no matter how hard he tried. And then he had met Ariane, and everything had begun to change.

You offered her what you could, the self-interested voice deep within him hissed. *You offered, and she rejected you. Get out of here, before you do something you can't take back.*

But he hadn't offered what he could. He'd offered only that which he wasn't afraid to, in return for the gift Ariane had offered: everything.

And in return, all she'd wanted, all she'd ever really wanted, was him. Such a simple and terrifying request, to share all the broken pieces of himself with another. But in that moment, Damien realized he wanted nothing more than that. He could think of no one he would rather entrust his heart to...the heart she alone had been able to remind him he had.

"I won't have her die," Damien said again, his voice breaking. "She's mine."

I love her.

But those last words remained unspoken. Those were for her.

Lucan looked at him, and Damien saw a flicker of what might have been some ancient and fathomless longing before it vanished, leaving the taciturn Grigori to give a curt nod.

"That is why I came. I was not impressed with Ariane's choice, but...you share a bond now. You share blood. And you have a great deal of ability. The wolf and the cat are admirable, but they can't reach the Council in time."

"Can we?" Damien asked.

"I fear we may have to go on to the desert," Lucan said. "The strength of the Council, and of Ariane, will be irresistible to Chaos. We have kept him weak. His Rising will require many souls, the more powerful, the better. That process, I fear, has already begun."

"Hell," Damien said. "He'll take them all."

Lucan's eyes turned bleak. "If he rises, there are others he will wake—"

"No," Damien snapped. Everything in him, every fiber of his being, was screaming at him to get to Ariane *now*. "We stop this, end of story."

"Then come," Lucan said. "I will carry you. We've wasted enough time."

Damien followed Lucan toward the stairs, knowing they were heading for the roof. He tried to take comfort in his skill, in the weight of the daggers sitting at his hips. Neither had ever truly failed him. But he had never tried to stop a demon that might be impossible to kill.

For the first time, he fully embraced the bond he'd forged with Ariane, not just physical, but mental. Those vampires who shared a mark could communicate without words. And in all the world, he and Ariane were the only two who wore both the Grigori wings and the Cait Sith cats. They had shared blood. She wasn't just his... he was hers.

Ariane, he thought, shouting the silent message to her with all the ability he had. *I'm coming. Be careful. I'm sorry... and I'm on my way.*

* * *

Ariane huddled in the small, hidden alcove behind one of the many tapestries lining the circular stone room beneath Vlad's mansion. It wasn't comfortable, and she was terrified someone was going to turn around and point accusingly right at where she was hiding, but so far so good.

The room was lit by what looked to be a very old, very large iron chandelier hung from the ceiling. Beyond that, the room contained only the tapestries on the wall and five long, curved benches with crimson velvet cushions arranged in a broken circle around the middle of the room.

Upon the cushioned benches sat the leaders of the American-based vampire dynasties, with the exception of Sariel.

He was late. And as the hour grew later, the tension in the room had increased. Sariel had been a constant presence at the Council, never shirking his duties. He had assured Vlad he would come tonight, aware as any of them how important the future of the Empusae was. And yet...nothing.

Ariane shifted uneasily. She'd been warned not to emerge until Sariel had been contained, but she was becoming increasingly uncomfortable. To stop herself from going over all the things that could go wrong again, she moved the heavy fabric just enough so that she could look out again.

She saw Lily and Ty talking quietly to one another. Across from them, giving the pair the most openly poisonous glare Ariane had ever seen, was a beautiful, exotic woman with kohl-rimmed eyes and jet-black hair cut in a sleek bob. She wore a sleeveless low-cut top of red silk and skinny black pants...and a great deal of gold jewelry that managed to set off her dark beauty instead of overpowering it. Arsinöe, as intimidating in real life as she was whispered to be in legend. On either side of her were people Ariane assumed were favored courtiers, a man and woman, sleek and beautiful and silent, each wearing black with a splash of red. Beside them were three women, including Diana, who wore diaphanous chitons, short togas of pure white that fastened over one shoulder with a golden clip. They whispered nervously among themselves, and Ariane didn't think any of the three were Mormo. And finally there was Vlad, leonine in a dark charcoal suit and a tie that matched his eyes, standing and speaking to Ludo, who nodded at whatever he had said and vanished through the arched doorway to the left.

Arsinöe appeared to have had enough.

"Vlad," she purred, and Ariane could hear the venom running just beneath the surface of her words, "we've all taken time out of our schedules for this with very little notice. Sariel has either found something better to do, or he suspects what will happen to him if he shows himself. Either way, the result is the same. There are enough of us here to do what must be done. If Sariel wishes to be hunted, he shall have it. So if the Empusa hasn't *died*, do you think we could get on with it?"

Vlad looked at his watch and narrowed his eyes. "I have to agree with you, Arsinöe. He isn't coming. Which makes our task even more urgent."

Arsinöe seemed satisfied, and Ariane wondered how Vlad could stand to be cordial to a woman who'd openly tried to destroy him not long ago. Politics, she guessed. But it was no wonder Lily looked edgy and Ty was so tense. The undercurrents in this room were pure poison.

"Perhaps we should discuss the Empusa's urgent matter first," Arsinöe suggested, looking hungrily at the small contingent of Empusae. "I would hate to deprive her of any counsel she might wish regarding her...decision... should the divination tire her."

Diana lifted her chin and leveled a glare at Arsinöe. "My mistress feels the matter of the Grigori is more important this evening. She says she'll address this *matter* you're so interested in at a later date."

Ariane watched as Arsinöe's lip began to curl, wondering whether they would even make it to the divination before a fight broke out.

"Let Ariane come out, then," Lily interjected, drawing everyone's attention. She looked directly at the tapestry. "It's all right. I think it's clear you're going to be the only Grigori here."

Ariane took a deep breath and pushed the tapestry aside, stepping out with every eye on her. She tried to focus on the encouraging smiles, rather than the heated glares she was getting from the Ptolemy contingent.

"Foolishness," she heard Arsinöe mutter. "This is a waste of time."

Vlad indicated the empty bench. "Please."

Ariane moved quickly to settle herself, feeling awkward about sitting alone. That was quickly forgotten, however, when Vlad looked toward the doorway and relief relaxed his features.

"Ah. We're ready to begin."

The lights flickered in the chandelier and went out, plunging the room into darkness. But a vampire's eyes could see well in the dark, and Ariane had no trouble watching the woman in the white robe walk in.

She seemed to glow with a light of her own, and Ariane

watched her, fascinated. She had never seen a vampire like this, one who seemed both old and not old at the same time. Her hair was snow white, far whiter, even, than Ariane's. It spilled over the shoulders of a robe made of white silk. The woman's skin was pale, but not the shade that denoted health for a vampire. It was sickly, almost ashen. Her face was beautiful…or it had been once. There was something ruined about it, something *off*, as though it were a mask that was concealing some terrible decay beneath it and was about to slip.

And yet there was power here. Ariane could feel it in the air, with every breath she took. It fairly radiated off this woman, Mormo, Empusa, leader of the Empusae, daughter of Hecate. Ariane smelled incense and oils and the faint, sweet scent of leaves long dead.

As Ariane watched, Mormo came to stand in the center of the room, lifted hands that looked more like old, hooked claws, and extended them out to her sides. Her eyes, milky white, glowed nonetheless. With a jolt, Ariane realized the woman was blind.

She cried out in Greek, a musical torrent of words that Ariane could barely decipher. She heard fragments, understood "Grant me wisdom" and "Grant me sight."

The glow from Mormo grew brighter, and her attendants rose, chanting in Greek. One came to stand before her, one on either side of her. Diana carried a simple golden chalice, which she handed to Mormo. The attendants then dropped to their knees in unison, and Ariane saw the flash of small knives that must have been tucked into the folds of their chitons. One after another, the women made a single cut on the underside of her wrist and let the blood fall to the ground. The instant the drops hit the floor, an intricate pattern, like a spiderweb, began to glow beneath all of their feet. In the center was a circle. And completely inside the circle was Mormo.

One by one, Arsinöe, Vlad, and Lily rose, moving to surround the leader of the Empusae, who extended the chalice to each in turn. Each gave a few drops of blood, crimson spattering against gold. Lily extended a claw. Arsinöe used a dagger. Vlad drew his wrist across his fangs. Ariane stood quickly, nearly forgetting her part. Her blood would play the most important role in this ritual, from what she had been told.

The cup pulsed with the power that had collected inside of it, lifeblood of the strongest vampires. Mormo held it out to Ariane, seeing her, Ariane was sure, with her strange blind eyes. Ariane fumbled a moment with her dagger but got it unsheathed quickly enough. She held her wrist over the chalice, slicing a thin, shallow line in her skin. Her blood, so dark as to be nearly black, dripped slowly out to mingle with the crimson.

Ariane stepped back quickly when it was done, feeling interested eyes watching her. She knew they had seen the dark blood, so different from their own. Still, she managed to look at everything and nothing, lifting her chin and moving quickly back to her place.

"Grigori," Mormo said, drawing out the word. It seemed to echo, filling the chamber.

Then she began to chant.

A haze grew around the Empusa, a swirling cloud that was at first bright white, then faded to dusky gray. Within, she continued her chanting, though that sound began to be drowned out by others. Screams. Hooves hitting the hard earth. The flutter of wings.

Ariane blinked, suddenly disoriented. The world around her began to go dark, and images started to flicker through her mind, disjointed at first, then more cohesive.

Beautiful beings falling from a war-torn sky, some with wings of ebony, others with wings the gray of the sky at morning. *Sammael's wings*, she thought. Some of these beings vanished as they hit the earth, crying out in pain to an indifferent moon. Others crawled into caves, fleeing underground from the burning sun. Still others stayed above, creating a fortress in the sand, hiding from the light and feeding by moonlight. Ariane saw the white hair, the burning violet eyes, and knew them... even Sam. He was one of nine, and Ariane knew all the faces, even Lucan's. All, save one.

For a time, the men Ariane knew as ancient ones did nothing but hunt their black-winged brethren, those even more cursed than they. The fortress in the sand grew, and in time, most of the dark wings either vanished or were killed. All but the strongest, whose torment of humankind became the sole focus of those who could sense them. Watchers. Grigori. One by one, the dark fallen were destroyed. But while the Grigori studied books, watched the sky, and tried to maintain some tenuous connection to wherever they had fallen from, one of their own had wings turning pitch-black.

The images flickered faster through Ariane's mind. A village of broken human bodies. And another. And another. A beautiful, masculine face with eyes full of hatred and madness, screaming in pain and fury. A pit so deep it seemed to go to the center of the world, and at the bottom, chained to the wall, weakened but dangerous yet, was the beautiful creature who had become something other, something twisted and violent.

A demon, Ariane thought. A fallen angel gone mad. And when he sank his teeth into the offerings his brothers gave him, he drank more than blood. He drank the soul.

There was the briefest flash of Sariel standing before the demon, hands extended as though for an embrace, before Ariane felt herself plunged into blackness so ice-cold that she thought she would never be warm again. Faintly, she heard Damien calling to her.

Be careful...I'm on my way...

Her eyes flew open and she gasped in a breath, utterly disoriented for a moment until she remembered where she was. She'd slumped down on the bench, barely upright.

With hazy vision, she looked around to see the others rising from their places. Someone shouted as they gathered around a figure curled into a fetal position, motionless, on the floor. Ariane forced herself to her feet, starting toward the knot of people, when Vlad looked up at her, his eyes still hazed with shock. "Ariane. Get Ludo. Get *someone*. She's not breathing."

Ariane nodded and rushed to the door. She ran down the damp, quiet corridor on her way to the stairs, still reeling from all she had seen. Sam wasn't truly a vampire. None of the ancients were. And their brother in chains... what he had done... what he *could* do...

He still whispered through her mind, in a voice dark and seductive.

I am Angel-No-More. I am Nothing. I am Everything. I am Chaos.

And I am Rising.

She didn't see Ludo until she reached the bottom of the stairs. He lay sprawled across the bottom steps, unconscious. Above, all was silent.

The single breath she drew in was sharp and eerily loud in the utter absence of noise. Then she was grabbed from behind and dragged backward, one hand covering her mouth, another wrapped around her waist. All the air left her lungs in a rush, far too quickly to scream. A voice filled her head, so loud that it shot a sliver of bright pain right above her right eye.

Do not struggle, Ariane.

A strange, sweet smell wafted into her nostrils, drugging her, taking her down into a dark place where she could rest, forget. She tried to keep her head above water, but the currents were too strong, too deep.

You will help him rise.

From far away, she thought she heard a feline roar, the rustle of wings.

Then everything went black.

chapter TWENTY-FOUR

WHEN SHE OPENED HER EYES, at first all she saw was shining silver.

The she realized she'd been sleeping with her hair in her face. Still, it took a moment for Ariane to move. She felt groggy, a little sick, and stiff from sleeping on the cold, hard floor of wherever she was.

She had a bad feeling that she knew the answer to that.

With a soft groan, she pushed herself up, despite the shooting pain that went through her head. With a tentative hand, she pushed her hair out of her face and blinked slowly, looking around the small cell she'd been placed in. Ariane breathed in and smelled sand and spice, desert wind and...something wonderfully familiar.

It was only then that she realized what had wakened her.

A big, sleek black cat watched her steadily from the other side of her cage.

At first she thought she was hallucinating. But no

matter how many times she blinked, the cat remained, its blue eyes fixed on her face. Damien's eyes. Somehow, he had come for her.

She opened her mouth to whisper his name, but his voice, clear as a bell, filled her head.

Don't speak, darling. I'm going to get you out of here. Can you walk?

His voice was full of emotion she hadn't dared hope for. However he'd gotten here, whatever it meant, the relief Ariane felt at his presence was overwhelming. It was then that she understood the sound of his voice as she'd blacked out at Vlad's. He'd used the blood bond between them to touch her thoughts . . . to let her know he was coming.

I think so.

She crawled to the big, beautiful cat and slid her fingers into the soft black fur, feeling the heart slowly beating beneath, the slow, even breaths. Then the fur beneath her hands became fabric and it was just Damien, looking slightly rumpled and blessedly real.

"You came," she whispered.

He held a finger to his lips with a hint of the wicked smile she'd fallen in love with.

Not here, kitten. We won't be alone for long, and we'll need more than just you and me to put up a fight. Lucan's checking on the rest.

Ariane found it impossible to take her hands away from the place on Damien's chest where she could feel his beating heart. *What are you doing here? How did you know?*

Damien pulled away, extracting a small, tied roll of fabric from the inside pocket of his coat. When he unrolled it, a set of picks was revealed, neatly organized.

He eyed the lock on the outside of the cage, selected two of the picks, and got to work, his hands sure.

We're lucky. These aren't exactly modern. I knew because Lucan found me. And he knew because he got some sort of mental warning from Sammael. You've been had, kitten. Sariel never left here. He had the lot of you delivered to him on a silver platter instead. Did you know that Lucan was the demon's keeper for over a thousand years? No wonder he's so bloody miserable to deal with.

Damien's chatter inside her head, warm and seemingly unconcerned, allowed Ariane to relax enough to stand and get her bearings. Her weapons had been taken, but she seemed little worse for wear. She didn't want to know how she'd been kept unconscious for so long. She imagined Sariel was much further gone and more deeply involved with Chaos than even Sam had imagined.

Is Sam down here? Is everyone else alive?

Damien glanced up at her, and she saw immediately that the light tone of his conversation had been a ruse. The worry and care in his eyes took her breath away.

I honestly don't know. The only one I gave a damn about was you.

The lock opened with a soft click, and Ariane saw only a blur of movement before she was in Damien's arms, gathered so tightly against him she could hardly breathe. He pressed his face into her hair, his breathing harsh. And then he did speak, whispering against her ear.

"I thought I'd lost you."

She melted into him, savoring the feel of him, solid and strong. All of her doubts about his feelings evaporated with a simple touch. Whether or not he ever said the words, his actions told her all she needed to know.

"I would have found a way back to you," she whispered.

His laugh was a single, ragged breath. "All the same, I'd rather be here to make sure of it." He moved to touch his forehead to hers, a gentle, tender gesture that surprised her.

"I love you," he said.

Words failed her. All she could manage for a response was to press her lips against his, trying to tell him everything she wanted to say without words. His arms came around her back, crushing her to him briefly before he stepped back, though he caught her hand in his tightly.

Let's go find the others.

They stepped out into a low-ceilinged corridor constructed of large, weathered blocks of stone. The air was cool and bone-dry, the air of the desert. Ariane could see numerous cells just like her own set along one side of the wall. How many had the ancients kept down here to feed their brother's hunger? All this time, she and the others had lived above this dungeon, completely unaware of what their dynasty was doing... and of what they truly were.

Lucan walked toward them, his wings visible, their tips nearly touching the floor. His voice echoed loudly in Ariane's mind.

I see the drugs have worn off. Good. The others have not all fared as well.

He beckoned to Damien, who quickly set to work unlocking each cell. In the silence of the corridor, Ariane began to have the oddest sensation of being watched, a feeling that had the hair at the back of her neck prickling. But each time she turned, there was nothing. Though Damien's efforts barely made a sound, they began to sound incredibly loud to her.

In each cell slumped one of the leaders of the dynasties: Vlad, Lily, Arsinöe, and finally Mormo, whose skin was almost translucent, her breath so faint it was easy to miss altogether. She hadn't recovered from the divination. Ariane wondered whether they had even bothered to drug her. None of the attendants had been taken, nor had Ty. Ariane hoped they hadn't been killed.

Damien avoided the unconscious Arsinöe, instead trying to rouse first Vlad, then Lily. Of the two, only Lily tried to get to her feet, but she couldn't seem to get her legs under her well enough. Vlad simply looked at all of them blearily, a strange haze fogging his eyes.

Damien bared his teeth. "They've been given enough of whatever this was to take down an army of vampires," he hissed. He looked at Ariane. "Didn't they inject you with it as well?"

"She carries Sammael's blood in its purest form," Lucan said quietly. "It will not affect her the same way it does the others."

"You were angels," Ariane murmured, her eyes skimming the beauty of Lucan's wings. "How can that be possible?"

Lucan surprised her with a small, sad smile that managed to transform his face into one of impossible beauty. "It simply *is*. We are like the vampire in some ways, and those we sire are barely different at all... but my brothers and I are endless. As is our curse, given as punishment for our fascination with mortals. No amount of distance between us and that which we once coveted has been enough to return us to what we were, so we are simply Grigori, serving neither darkness nor light. I do not expect you to understand."

She didn't, not really ... but she wanted to. Maybe after this, there would be time to try.

"So your isolation hasn't done *anyone* a bit of good," Damien muttered. He looked around. "Look, maybe each of us can get one of them. Lucan, you're big enough that you may even be able to get two. It may be a better idea to try saving who we can. Sammael's not here."

Then his head jerked up, his pupils dilating so that for just an instant he was the cat again, a hunter scenting another predator. Ariane didn't even want to turn. She already knew what she would see.

"He is here," Lucan said softly. "As are my brothers." He looked at Ariane. "This is not the time to fight. Do as they say."

Damien looked aghast. "Are you mad?" he hissed. "Then what did we—"

"Listen to Lucan. He still has a bit of sense left, it seems."

Ariane had to look then, compelled by the smooth, deadly sound of Sariel's voice. When she did, what she saw made her heart sink. Sariel and three of the other ancients stood in the corridor, blocking the way out. Their swords, all well suited to their owners' immense size, were drawn.

Sariel looked at each of them in turn, his eyes at last settling on Ariane. What she saw in them was so ancient and cold she wanted to scream.

"I did not give you enough credit, Ariane. Still, this ends the way it was always going to." He smirked. "What is it these vampires like to say? Blood is destiny? So it is with you. Such strong blood. Like my brother. He still fights, but not for much longer."

She felt Damien brush up against her, fingers brushing against her hand. Small comfort, but she was so glad he was there.

"You've gone insane," Ariane said. "You'd sacrifice everything for a demon who does nothing but destroy?"

Sariel made a low, ominous sound that was eerily close to a growl. "My *brother*," he said, "always saw what I could not. We've wasted so much time, denying ourselves. Watching over the worthless."

"Then we start again," Lucan said. "Build what we can for ourselves. Join the world we so hastily chose for ourselves, instead of waiting for a grace that will never come. This is not the answer, brothers."

"It's the only answer," Sariel spat. "Chaos saw the truth when I was blind to it. I am ready to leave this half-life and truly live. Look at us, Lucan!" He spread out his arms, the embodiment of beauty and power. "We try to purge the world of our brethren when we should be ruling it! We've been at odds too long. It's time to reconcile with the Dark Fallen. Consider yourself a reconciliation gift . . . brother."

Sariel looked at the ancients to his left. "Armaros, lock the rest back up. Baraqel, behind them in case they try to run."

Damien had his daggers out in an instant, sliding in front of Ariane to shield her before she realized what he was doing. She wished desperately for a sword, a dagger, anything so that they might at least be a match for Sariel and the others.

"Touch her and I'll kill you," Damien growled.

Sariel only looked at him, bemused. "No, you won't."

She felt a cold hand grip her upper arm, felt the bite

of steel in the small of her back, and knew that all of the ancients but Lucan and Sam had joined with Sariel...and with Chaos. Damien whipped his head around, his face falling when he saw the ancient called Ezekeel holding on to her.

"Come," Sariel said. "I'll escort you."

When he turned, Ariane saw that his wings, and the wings of his brothers, had all gone pitch-black.

There was a turn at the end of the corridor, leading to the most massive door Ariane had ever seen. It was made of some sort of metal, and despite its obvious age, it still had a sheen to it. The air felt heavier here, weighted with power that hissed and sizzled over her skin. It was uncomfortable, and it got worse the closer they got to the door. Still, she had no choice. The tip of Ezekeel's dagger bit into her back every time she slowed. And despite Damien's repeated glances back to check on her, he could do nothing.

They moved single file, Lucan first, then Damien, then her. Sariel led them, his brother Azazel at his side. They stopped at the doors, and Sariel looked calmly at Lucan.

"Do your duty one last time, brother."

Lucan stepped forward, and Ariane thought of what Sammael had told her, of how Lucan had been Chaos's keeper for centuries, making sure he was fed just enough to stay in the twilit state between waking and sleep. Lucan had had a wretched existence...and yet he still had more compassion than most of his brothers.

Lucan placed his hand on the doors, and a glowing seam appeared to split it in two. The two halves swung slowly open, revealing a pitch-dark chamber. Not even the light from the corridor penetrated the thick curtain of blackness that seemed to hang at the entrance. The air here felt thick, almost soupy, and Ariane began to find it hard to breathe.

Sariel stepped aside and looked at the three of them expectantly. For the first time, Ariane could see his excitement. It left a sick feeling in the pit of her stomach.

"In. All of you. I've fed him enough to waken him. He's waiting."

Ariane walked past Sariel, and as soon as she crossed the threshold, the prick of the blade left her back.

At first she could see nothing. She drank in what little air she could, feeling that strange pressure squeezing her. A hand grabbed hers. *Damien.* She squeezed it.

Whatever this is, kitten, we go down swinging together.

She didn't have the heart to respond, didn't want to acknowledge that this was probably it. All this struggling, all she'd done, and still she'd ended up given to this creature in the end. She thought of the illustration in her book, recoiled from it.

The darkness began to lift as they moved forward, subtly at first, then turning the room a sort of washed out gray. Ariane could see the stone floor, the high, domed ceiling. And then came the sight that made her stumble over her own feet.

"Ah, Sariel. I began to wonder if you had lied to me."

The voice, as silken and irresistible as it was sinister, came from the being chained to the floor in the center of the room.

Chaos.

Ariane had expected a monster. What she saw was a man who was undoubtedly kin to the other ancients, white hair hanging limp and filthy around a face that could have been painted on the ceiling of the Sistine Chapel. He was as beautiful as he was broken, his tattered ebony wings stretched at odd angles from his back, as though they'd been broken many times. Though his frame was tall and large, he was emaciated, skin stretched over bone.

Ariane felt a moment of pity. Then Chaos looked directly at her, and she saw the fire dancing at the center of eyes that were full black. There was more than madness there, more than pain and death. He was evil, distilled down to its very essence.

"The time for lies between us is past," Sariel said. "Look at the feast I've brought you."

Chaos leaned forward to peer hungrily at them, and despite his wasted form, covered only by a dirty loincloth, Ariane sensed that the only thing keeping Chaos from lunging at them was the chains.

"Ah, *Lucan*. My benevolent captor. I wondered where you'd gone."

Lucan said nothing, staring impassively ahead. Chaos swung his gaze to Damien and curled his lip in a sneer. "And a cat-thing. Adequate." Then he looked at Ariane, and his eyes lit. She tried to look away, into the distance, anywhere but into those two pits.

"Sammael's blood. Very nice. I've been promised your sire as well, *d'akara*." His gaze swung to Sariel. "Bring Sammael. Bring the rest of them."

His voice had a razor-sharp edge, and Ariane wondered whether Chaos was even completely sane. He sounded right on the verge of screaming.

Sariel motioned behind them at someone, then regarded his brother with the first hint of wariness Ariane had seen.

"The others are still drugged, Chaos. And you said they were for the—"

"He wants them all for himself, you stupid git," Damien snapped. "He'll probably suck your soul out, too, just for entertainment!"

Ariane's blood went cold when she saw Chaos's black gaze swing to Damien.

"Perhaps I'll take your tongue before I take you soul, cat."

Ariane heard footsteps behind her then and turned to see Sam, stoic as always, walking out of the darkness that surrounded them, ahead of Baraqel. He didn't look as though he'd been harmed, Ariane saw, relieved.

Sam's eyes met hers, just for an instant, and she could see he wasn't finished fighting quite yet. Hope, irrational but no less real for it, bloomed in her chest. Surely the four of them, even against a demon, could do some damage.

Sam glared defiantly at Chaos, then looked to Sariel. "Chaos betrayed us all, and yet you choose *him*? You are a fool, brother. I thought better of you. Better of you all."

Sariel was unmoved. "What have we gotten for all these years? Power that is not power, life that is not life. We've denied ourselves and looked to the skies, hoping, waiting to be forgiven. We are *pathetic*," he hissed. "At least the Dark Fallen have tasted this place. I want to *feel*." A shadow of something, some ancient pain, moved over his face. "I would feel before I am dust. I tire of watching over petulant children!"

"Then run," Lucan said quietly. "I spent years down here, guarding this monster. Since I left this barren place, I've lived more than I did in thousands of years. Run, and leave him chained."

"No!" Sariel snarled.

"You don't understand, Lucan," Chaos hissed. "You're still cold. My blood runs hot. I can give that to him. To all who follow me." He slanted a look at Sariel, and Ariane felt a sick twist in her stomach. Damien gave her hand a final squeeze.

"Forget the others, then. I am ready. Unchain me. Let me feed. Let me rise."

Sariel never hesitated. He pulled a key from his pocket, made of the same bright metal as Chaos's manacles, and with an ominous series of four clicks, freed the demon. Ariane shrank back as Chaos straightened, rubbing at his wrists and looking around as though he were seeing his prison for the first time. Slowly, painfully, he tried to stretch his mangled wings.

He turned to Sariel, a smile lighting the wasted beauty of his face so that just for an instant, he was an angel once more.

Then he drew back one hand, extended long black claws, and sent Sariel crashing to the floor with a single, brutal stroke. Dark blood flowed quickly into the dust, leaking from multiple wounds from the corner of Sariel's mouth.

He looked up at his brother, violet eyes wide. "Why... why..."

"Because I can."

Somewhere in the thick darkness beyond them, the doors crashed shut.

Ariane went cold when Chaos's eyes pegged her in the darkness.

"You, I think, little angel. You first."

He lunged at her with surprising strength and swiftness, his jaw opening and elongating until he was no

longer beautiful but some twisted monster. All she could
do was throw up her hands, a useless defense. There was
no time to do more, nothing she *could* do. She didn't see
Damien move, had no idea what he'd done until she heard
the furious roar and saw Chaos arch back with a tortured
scream.

Damien was attached to the demon's back, claws tearing and ripping at his already tattered wings. The weak
point, just as Ariane had told him. He hadn't forgotten.

Sam gave a battle cry that had dust and chunks of rock
raining from the ceiling, and she felt a silent brush of
wings beside her: Lucan.

The room erupted into pandemonium as Chaos sprang
into the air, thrashing to try detaching Damien. What light
there was began to fade, and the dust and debris began to
rain harder from the ceiling with the furious cries of fallen
angels. She whirled, looking for Chaos. She saw Sam ripping Baraqel's sword from his grasp, Lucan fending off
Ezekeel and Azazel. Time seemed to slow as she spun and
unfurled her wings from her back, thinking only of finding
Damien. There had to be something she could do, even if it
was only clawing at Chaos with her bare hands.

There was a tremendous thundering in the distance
as someone began to pummel the door. *Armaros*, she
thought. He'd stayed behind to relock the cages and was
one less ancient to deal with.

She caught a glimpse of wildly flapping black wings
and sprang into the air, only to be yanked back by her
hair. She cried out, more in surprise than pain, as she
crashed to the ground.

Then Sariel brought his boot down on her wing, and
she screamed, arching in pain. For an instant she could

see nothing, just a bright burst of white light to accompany the agony in her wing.

"No," Sariel said, his eyes wild. Then he looked above him, drawing his sword from the sheath between his wings. "Chaos! Here! Take her and rise, brother!"

As her bones began to knit, Sariel stomped his foot again, rebreaking fragile bone. This time Ariane roared, rolling onto her side and curling into herself. Chaos crashed to the ground in front of her, Damien nowhere to be seen. Blood as black as his wings poured from his wounds, but he moved quickly, coming to crouch beside her, baring a mouthful of razor-sharp teeth. In that moment, he was every bit the nightmarish creature she had envisioned.

She imagined Damien's body, broken and torn, hurled against one of the far walls, and reached out to him as Chaos leaned over her.

Damien... love you...

Chaos jerked backward suddenly, midnight eyes going wide as the tip of a sword erupted from his chest. He gagged, staggering, as the sword was withdrawn. And behind him was Damien, bloodied, unsteady, and covered in dust... but alive. In his hands was one of the ancients' swords.

As she watched, he swung the sword high over his head, aiming for Sariel.

A sound filled the room then, a shout so full of pain and fury that it seemed to encompass all the suffering of the world in a single sound. Damien froze. Ariane felt a single drop of blood trickle from her nose as the room was plunged into darkness. A sonic boom shook the floor, crumbling sections of wall. She could hear the stones falling as everything moved, and she pulled her wounded wings into herself, waiting for the final strike.

But none came.

The rumbling quieted quickly as the terrible, inhuman sound faded. Ariane opened her eyes to see that the world had turned a soft shade of gray from falling dust and rock, and the room was full of dim, dingy light.

Gingerly, she sat up, peering around, looking for any sign of life. Several enormous chunks of the ceiling had crashed to the floor, one not far from her. Then she saw Damien, sprawled on the floor where he'd been knocked off his feet.

That got her to her feet, stumbling over to him and kneeling down.

"Damien," she pleaded, her voice sounding harsh and strange. She shook him. "Damien, please..."

He groaned softly, but the smile he gave her when he rolled over and saw her was the most beautiful thing she'd ever seen. He sat up slowly, and Ariane threw her arms around him, holding him as tightly as she could.

"We're alive," he said, sounding amazed. "Did I kill him, then?"

"You did not. But you fought well, cat."

Ariane looked to see Sam slowly making his way toward them. He was bloodied and battered, but very much alive...as was Lucan, not far behind him. Damien stood, helping Ariane to her feet, and the four of them came together to look at what had once been Chaos's prison. The piles of ash that had once been fallen angels still smoldered, and the room smelled faintly of incense.

"Come," Lucan said, looking wearier than Ariane had ever seen an ancient look. The four of them picked their way out of the rubble, saying nothing. Though the suffocating feeling of the place had lifted, Ariane couldn't shake the sense that they were walking through a tomb.

At the threshold, they found the withered husk of what might once have been a man, but for the luxuriant black wings. It looked mummified, and the mouth was open in a silent scream.

"Sariel," Ariane said. She had never felt so numb.

Not far away lay the remains of Armaros. He had run, Ariane guessed, seeing too late all that his brother had truly become. He hadn't made it far.

Chaos was nowhere to be seen.

Damien pulled her back against him, wrapping his arms around her and holding her close. Though his skin was cool, he was the only thing that prevented her from feeling like ice.

"We lost," she said softly. "Chaos has risen."

Sam turned his head to look at Ariane, both pride and sorrow reflected in his eyes.

"No, *d'akara*. Living to fight another day is no loss. It's as I feared. Chaos will not be so easily destroyed." Then Sam looked at Damien, and what she saw there surprised her. "You have my gratitude, Damien Tremaine."

"And mine," Lucan said. "When the next battle comes, I will gladly fight at your side."

She felt him incline his head, accepting without a word the enormous compliment that had just been paid him... which, Ariane later thought, was probably best.

Together, the four of them started down the corridor to where they could hear the trapped and weakened vampires beginning to shout for them. Sam looked at Ariane, and in his eyes she saw every one of his thousands of years.

"This is only the beginning."

chapter TWENTY-FIVE

For weeks after Chaos had risen, Ariane had nightmares.

They were terrible things, images of burning eyes mixed with the sounds of screams, some of which sounded eerily like the family she had lost so long ago. When she woke at dusk every evening, though, it was with Damien's arms around her, dulling the pain of the monsters that stalked her mind and memory until slowly, they began to recede.

Finally, when the air had begun its subtle change from the warmth of summer to the earthy nip of fall, Ariane awoke one evening to find that she had slept the day through in complete peace.

They had been staying with Vlad, at his insistence, and Ariane didn't mind, though she was beginning to feel like she needed some space. The Dracul might be a book-worm, but he was a powerful man, and there was a constant flow of visitors. At first, they'd all been waiting for

Chaos to show himself quickly, girding themselves for a fight. Instead, there had been nothing but silence. Mormo had been revived, though for how long was anyone's guess. Sammael had assumed leadership of the Grigori with the unanimous support of the dynasty, with Lucan preferring to remain only as advisor, and the secrets beneath the dust and sand were exposed to every member. They would not be taken unaware.

Still, whatever Chaos planned, an immediate frontal attack on the dynasties did not seem to be it.

And Ariane wanted to start to move on with her life.

She opened her eyes and stretched, smiling when she heard the sound of Damien's voice. He was on the phone already—not an uncommon occurrence lately. She lifted her head to look at him, sitting in a chair by the dresser and looking adorably disheveled in his pajama pants. His eyes connected with hers, and he grinned.

That smile, lovely and just a little wicked, melted her every time.

"Yeah. Mmm-hmm. Well, I'm not going to fight about it. No, you keep your bloody paperwork. I know. All right, look, Drake, I've got something to do. Yes, I'll tell her. I'm hanging up now."

He held the phone way from his face for a moment, looking at it as though it were a foreign object. Ariane could hear Drake's deep voice still chattering away on the other end. Damien hung it up and put the phone on the dresser.

"Honestly, I think I liked him better when he was throwing files at me and telling me to get the hell out of his office."

She sat up, and he came to sit beside her on the bed,

tucking a lock of hair behind her ear. Ariane leaned into his touch. There had been a huge change in him since that night in the desert. He was still very much the irreverent, irritating assassin she'd fallen in love with, but he seemed...content. Happy. And not at all reserved about his love for her.

Ariane was fairly sure their friends found it obnoxious, but when one was in love with a man like Damien Tremaine, that was a way of life. She wouldn't trade a second of it.

"What did he want this time?" Ariane asked, bemused by Damien's disgruntled expression.

"You, I think, on a hot buttered roll and slathered in cream. He's asked me to thank you for agreeing to all this. Again."

She laughed. Alistair Drake's obvious fascination with her had become a running joke among their friends. It was flattering, she supposed. And Drake was an interesting man. But she suspected his interest had more to do with finally getting to have a Grigori, mixed blood though she now was, under the auspices of the House of Shadows.

"What *else* did he want?" she asked.

Damien blinked. "Hmm? Sorry, was thinking about the slathered in cream thing. Anyway, he would like... if we wouldn't be too terribly put out about it...for us to come home."

She raised her eyebrows. "Seattle, you mean?"

Damien hadn't breathed a word about returning to Washington, though she knew that eventually he was going to want to do something about the apartment of stuff she still hadn't seen. It was time, though...time to start living again. Drake had been wonderful about giving both of them the time to recuperate after all that had happened, but his calls to Damien had been more frequent lately, his interest in how he could adjust his operation to accommodate all that had happened obvious.

Especially since Damien had informed him that he and Ariane were now a package deal. The possibilities immediately had Drake salivating.

Damien slid the rest of the way onto the bed and relaxed against the headboard.

"Yes, well, we'll be traveling plenty, considering he wants us gathering information about whatever it is that demon's gone off to stir up. This is what happens when you make too many friends in high places. Less skulking and stabbing, more wandering around creepy little bookshops run by . . . well, I don't know, but I swear he was part troll. Oh, and we'll have to schmooze. Nothing like being PR for the Shades."

Ariane rubbed her hand against his. All of it sounded fascinating to her, but she wanted to be sure it wouldn't put Damien to sleep. He'd been slinking around in shadows for a long time.

"Will you miss it? The skulking and stabbing?"

His smile was slow and sweet. "No. I think it stopped being entertaining a long time ago, honestly. I was just too busy not giving a damn about anything to notice. This will be interesting, I think. The House of Shadows does all sorts of things, not just the basic nefarious services. It was high time I branched out. We'll travel the world. I can show you everything you've missed without worrying quite so much about having my head cut off."

She loved imagining it. She desperately wanted to see the world, and Damien was the perfect man to show it to her. Even if she didn't remotely believe he wouldn't ever find trouble for them to get into.

"Anyway," Damien said, "travel aside, we've got to have a home somewhere, and Drake would like us as close to his towering stack of paperwork as possible."

"Ah." She laughed. "I'd like to see Seattle. And the actual House of Shadows. And that apartment you never talk about."

"I don't want you to see that," Damien said.

Ariane lifted her eyebrows, surprised at the sting of the words. She'd thought he was finished holding back from her. Since that awful night in the desert, he'd given her everything she could have hoped for, finally letting go, letting her in. That he would want to hide his little dragon horde from her was an unhappy surprise—it seemed like such a small thing now.

But when he continued, she understood.

"I mean, I suppose you can see it, but I don't want to live in it. That was just a place to keep things. It was never really mine. Nowhere was." He stroked a finger down her arm, making her shiver. "I want our own magpie nest, as you called it once," Damien said, his eyes lighting. "I want a house, and I want us both to fill it with ridiculously expensive and shiny things we bring back from our travels. I want to make a home, Ariane. With you."

He couldn't have said anything that would have pleased her more.

"Really?" she asked, and giggled when he pushed her onto her back to rub noses with her, purring.

"Yes. We'll go house shopping. I'll drive you mad. And then we'll make love in every room in the place before we move anything in, for luck."

"You're a bad influence," she told him, then dragged him down for a kiss. He made a low, yummy sound, and the sound of purring grew louder. He grinned against her mouth, surprising her.

"What?" she asked.

"That's not me anymore, kitten, that's you. I've made you purr. It's incredibly sexy."

"Purring," she laughed, delighted that she'd gained something like that from their bond. "It'll be fur next." The prospect didn't seem to bother Damien.

"I hope so. We could go prowling together at night, you and I."

She smirked. "Or maybe you'll develop wings, and we can go flying."

His complexion went green immediately. "If they're there, I don't want to know. I have no interest in flying when I've got perfectly good ground to stand on."

"Drake would love you."

"Drake can shove it. The only one whose love I'm interested in is you."

Ariane tangled her fingers in his hair, thinking she had never seen such a perfectly imperfect man in all her life ... and that she wouldn't trade him for anything.

"I love you. Every bit of you," she said.

Damien covered her body with his own, a wicked smile turning his eyes the glowing blue of the evening sky.

"I love you, too, Ariane. But surely you must love some bits more than others. Let's see if we can find out which ..."

And in the darkness, the angel and the shadow twined together and were one.

Acknowledgments

As always, this book wouldn't have become the best version of what I had in mind without the tireless efforts and imagination of my editor, Selina McLemore, who continues to deserve the Official Seal of Awesomeness I once gave her. Thank you for *everything*!

Many thanks are owed, as always, to my buddies Cheryl Brooks, Marie Force, Loucinda McGary, and Linda Wisdom, who can make me laugh when I most need it and whose support has carried me through good times and bad. Long live the Lair!

And of course, I could never finish any book without my Brian, who is better than any imaginary hero could ever be. Thanks for all the love and support. At the end of every book, when I'm wretched and muttering in front of the computer (and probably in pajamas for the third day straight), you always manage to do something to remind me that I got one of the good ones.

Bailey "Bay" Harper's pleasantly boring
existence has been turned upside down ever
since her best friend, Lily, learned she was
a vampire queen. Now, when a mysterious
stranger shows up at Bay's door, inciting a
passion she's never before experienced, Bay
will have to decide once and for all just how
deeply into the world of night she wants to go.

Turn the page for a sneak peek
at the next book in the
Dark Dynasties series

Immortal Craving

chapter ONE

Somewhere in the Sasan Gir, Gujarat, India

HE AWAKENED to darkness.

When sensation began to return to him, he hardly understood what it was. The weight of his body settled on him like an ill-fitting cloak at first, uncomfortable, unfamiliar. The muscles in his face contracted. A frown. Why was he cold? Why was he...anything?

Scattered bits of memory swam tantalizingly close to the surface, shadows in the murk. But when he reached for them, they vanished. Frustrated, he inhaled, then stopped, startled, as air rushed into lungs that had long been still. Tasmin's eyes fluttered open.

Arre, kyaa?

He felt the cool damp on his skin, saw rough stone above him in the dark. He could feel the same stone beneath him, though smoother. His chest was bare, as were his feet. Words tangled together in his mind, some in a language he had never heard—yet somehow, he understood how to use them.

Where... am I?

Tentatively, he moved fingers, toes. Another indrawn breath, such a strange sensation. The air was damp, yet strangely sweet. It tasted of life. And with that simple taste came the hunger, and he remembered what he was.

Warrior. Magic weaver. Vampire.

Rakshasa.

Tasmin heard the word from somewhere deep inside himself, whispered in a voice not his own. With that, the fog that covered his mind began to clear, and images from his past began to emerge from shadow. So many faces he had known, their voices rising and falling in the music of their native tongues.

Now... silence.

He sat up slowly, instinctively testing his movement, his muscles, and looked around. Though the darkness was absolute, he could see that he was in a small cave, only barely high enough for a man to stand upright in. There was nothing inside. Nothing but him.

He was alone.

And yet he felt something, some energy that lingered in the space like a dark and malignant visitor. Perhaps someone had been here to check on him. Perhaps it was the lingering feel of whoever had put him here. Again, Tasmin wondered what had happened that he should have been torn from his brothers and placed in a hand-hewn cave alone. Had he died?

We have slept, whispered that odd voice inside his head. *Long enough to have the world change many times over. But we breathe again, and all the rest have gone.*

He gave his head a hard, decisive shake to silence the odd voice. These thoughts, bubbling up from the depths of his mind, did not feel like his own. Echoes, he hoped, only echoes of whatever had been done to him here. He would find his brothers, and all would be well. How long had he slept? Months? A year?

It took him a moment to get his balance, with his feet now unused to supporting him. But when he did, his movement was as fluid and natural as it ever had been. There was only one direction to go in. This cave seemed shallow, only really large enough to hold himself. A hiding place.

Or a grave.

Unnerved by the thought, Tasmin moved away from the back wall, the fabric of his simple *dhoti* brushing against his legs. The stone was rough but not uncomfortable beneath his feet, beneath his hand as he trailed it along the wall. His senses were keen with newly awakened hunger. He felt wonderfully, deliciously alive as his heart resumed its slow and steady rhythm in his chest.

Tonight, he would celebrate. He and his brothers would hunt and feast. He would drink until he was gorged with life-giving blood. And after, they would hunt down those who had done this to him. An image flickered through his mind, of a brutal queen whose hatred of his kind was surpassed only by her love for herself. It was almost certain that the Ptolemy had bound him in that dark sleep, perhaps aided by some of the darkest of his bloodline, those who hid in shadow alone. He would avenge himself... soon.

But not yet.

The mouth of the cave was small, the ceiling grown so low at that point that Tasmin had to go to his knees to push at the thick vegetation covering the entrance. Light, soft and faded as it always was at the end of day, began to filter through as the layers of vine parted. He heard the song of a bird, the whisper of the forest that had been his home for many years. Familiar sounds of the Gir, comforting.

When the first rays of dim light touched his skin, Tasmin drew his hand back with a startled hiss. Bright pain sent a shock up his arm, and he clutched his hand to his chest, confused.

Arre!

He had built up his tolerance well over the century he had lived, able to withstand even the brightest rays of the sun for extended periods of time if he wished. It was a gift of his line, one of many. He hadn't been burned since he was a fledgling, young and untried. Even if he had slept for a year, it should not feel like this.

A laugh, like a soft rustle of cloth in the darkest depths of his soul.

Suspicion, rife with horror, bloomed slowly as he held his hand before him in the darkness, saw skin so ashen it was as though he had been drained of blood and covered in dust. A corpse. Smoke coiled lazily from the place where the light had touched.

And he knew. To sleep so long, to become this dead and wraithlike thing...

It had not been a year.

It had been centuries.

Tasmin began to shake with rage and fear and hunger, lost in this strange place, lost in whatever it was he had become. He opened his mouth, pulling back his parched lips to reveal long and gleaming fangs.

And in the voice of a lion, he roared.

chapter TWO

D<small>ON'T LOOK AT ME THAT WAY</small>, Grimm. We're getting there."

The big black Newfoundland gave her another lingering, mournful look before heaving a long-suffering sigh and facing forward again. Bay Harper smirked as she continued trimming his forelegs. Grimm might be put out now, but once they were back home, the big baby would be looking for cookies and affection in short order.

Thankfully, he was not a grudge holder. She had a few clients that were . . . but she didn't have to live with them.

Bay worked, humming along with the music she played in the shop, glad she'd cleared her schedule for the afternoon so she could take it easy and work on her own dog. She hadn't realized quite how much she'd needed a break, however small. To say her life was full these days didn't even begin to cover it.

She guessed that was what happened when your best friend turned into a super-powerful vampire and needed you for moral support. Not that she had anyone with similar experiences to compare with.

"Crap," Bay murmured as her last conversation with Lily flitted through her mind. "I need to vacuum again. Lily's coming over for a movie night tomorrow."

Grimm gave a slight wag of his bushy tail at the mention of Lily's name, despite the indignities he was currently suffering, and Bay smiled. The Newf might not be sure about everyone—and everything—currently residing at the Bonner mansion, but the owner was one of his favorite people.

That made two of them.

Lily MacGillivray, once Lily Quinn, had changed in some ways since discovering she was the sole heiress of an ancient vampire bloodline. The fangs, for starters. The permanent inability to sunbathe too. But the crazy supernatural stuff notwithstanding, Lily was still Lily. Kind, loyal, funny, and with a spine of steel. And she still loved a good action-adventure flick featuring superheroes in spandex.

Bay brushed absently at a big glob of black fur that attached itself to the front of her Scooby-Doo scrubs and blew a curly lock of blond hair that had escaped her ponytail out of her face. She worked quickly, focused as she drew sections of fur through her fingers and snipped with the shears. Grimm was, for the moment, incredibly soft, smelling faintly of the sugar-cookie-scented conditioner she'd used.

"Good boy," she praised quietly. For a dog that had

been largely neglected for his first year before he'd come into rescue, Grimm had given her his trust quickly and completely. She figured spoiling the crap out of him probably had something to do with it. He made Bay wonder why she'd waited so long to get a dog of her own. He was a hell of a lot more rewarding than any of her boyfriends had been.

In the front of the shop, the bell above the front door jingled merrily as someone wandered in. Bay barely registered the sound, knowing it was either someone stopping by to make an appointment or to pick up something from the small selection of grooming supplies she carried. Shelby, the college student she had working the front desk part-time, could handle it.

Grimm turned his head again, but this time his deepset eyes were focused on the doorway. An odd sound blended with the music, making Bay pause and tilt her head. It took her a minute to figure out what it was...and when she did, it surprised her.

She'd never heard Grimm growl before, not once in the six months she'd had him.

But he was sure doing it now.

"It's okay, big guy," she said, stroking a soothing hand down his side. His eyes never left the empty doorway. It was as though she wasn't even there.

There was a crash, a high-pitched yelp from the front. Bay's heart leaped into her throat as she clenched her fist around the grooming shears, a million terrible images flickering through her mind at once.

It's the middle of the damned day nobody robs a store in the middle of the day it has to be a psycho oh God what if he has a gun oh God oh God oh God...

Grimm threw back his head and bayed, then launched himself off the table.

"Grimm, no!" she shouted, but he'd hit the ground running, vanishing quickly out the door. Bay chased after him, terrified that if someone had come in armed, they would absolutely shoot a dog that looked like a bear. If she just got robbed, Bay didn't care...she would rather lose the money than lose the dog.

Bay sprinted out the doorway and around the corner, then skidded to a halt in the small waiting area. Grimm had stopped barking but moved quickly to place himself between her and the man on the floor, using his big, warm body as a barricade.

"Bay," Shelby breathed as she hurried around the counter to join her, the pink streaks in her dark hair matching the shade staining her cheeks. "He just stumbled in here and passed out! Do you think he's a druggie or something?"

Bay was silent for a moment, staring at the figure of a man lying spread-eagle in a wild scatter of shampoo bottles in the middle of the room. He'd taken out her new display in his fall. Even the quickest glance told her he was likely way too young for a heart attack, but then again, weirder things had happened.

The thought of him dying on her floor while she gawked lit a fire under her.

"Maybe we should call nine-one-one," Bay said. She pushed around Grimm with effort, rushing to the man's side and crouching down. He was on his stomach, and only his profile was visible. She knew instantly she'd never seen him before.

Grimm joined her, pressing against her shoulder as he

leaned down to give the man a wary sniff. His tail, always an indicator of his mood, was a stiff flag behind him. The dog gave a low, unhappy moan.

Bay leaned closer, inhaling. No booze—all she caught was an intriguing hint of spice that was very...male. Good cologne, she guessed, then pushed the thought away. Seeing his chest rise and fall slowly, the unmistakable rhythm of breathing, sent relief coursing through her along with a whole lot of adrenaline. He wasn't dead. A junkie, maybe, though he didn't have that look about him.

Or maybe he's just sick.

Her eyes flickered over his face again, just quickly enough for her to register that he was far from sickly looking. Actually, he was gorgeous.

"Sir?" she asked loudly, shaking him by the shoulder. "Sir, can you hear me?"

A soft groan indicated he was coming to...she hoped.

"Sir, if you can hear me, I'm calling an ambulance right now. We'll get you some help."

She gestured to Shelby, who headed for the phone on the counter. Bay had only begun to turn her head back toward the man when he shot to his feet in a scatter of shampoo bottles, moving so quickly she barely knew what was happening. There was a whisper of air against her cheek, and then he was on his feet, backing away from where she crouched. His hand was at his temple, and he winced as though his head hurt.

Bay rose quickly to her feet, a protective hand on her dog as he once again put himself between her and the stranger with a volley of deep, threatening barks.

The man's eyes moved quickly from the dog to the mess, and then to the two women staring at him wide-eyed.

He spat a word in a language Bay didn't understand, then held out one hand as the other fell away from his temple.

"Please...a moment. I'm not going to hurt you."

His voice was silken, a warm tenor no less commanding for its softness. His accent was a blend, faintly British but with an exotic lilt.

"You need to leave," Shelby said, her voice shaking.

"Shelby," Bay said softly, a gentle reproach. Whatever was wrong here, freaking out on their part was not going to help it. When she looked at her friend, however, she could see something was very wrong. Shelby had gone sheet white, her dark eyes huge as she stared at the man's face.

"*Shelby*," she said more sharply, hoping to draw her attention away. The look on her friend's face wasn't one she'd ever seen before...or ever wanted to see again.

"His...*eyes*...," Shelby whispered.

Bay looked sharply at him, and when his eyes locked with hers, she finally understood.

The guy who'd just wrecked her shampoo display wasn't human. Not even close.

His eyes were a bright, burning gold, more akin to molten metal than the more muted shades she'd seen among the werewolves who stayed among Lily's dynasty. They were intense, mesmerizing. He stared at her for an instant that felt much longer than it truly was, and in her head, she heard his voice as clearly as if he'd been speaking in her ear. It was far too intimate, and still it made her shiver.

Be still. I would speak with you.

His gaze returned to Shelby, who was fumbling now with the phone. Bay heard Shelby's terrified, sobbing breaths even out instantly, heard the phone being clicked off, and then the gentle creak of the stool behind the counter as the girl settled herself on it. She said nothing.

"So you're a vampire," Bay said quietly, adrenaline still pumping hard and fast through her veins. Only Grimm's reassuring presence kept her from running out the door, the urge to flee an instinct that her rational mind knew would make no difference. If he wanted to catch her, he would. She should have known what he was as soon as he'd gotten up—no human could move so fast.

"I don't know how you're out in the middle of the afternoon, but whatever you came in here for, I can't help you."

Bay was glad her voice sounded so steady, considering her legs felt like Jell-O.

The man said nothing, his expression guarded. And despite herself, despite knowing she was in the presence of a creature who had just thralled her employee into a happy stupor, a creature who was out during the day when there was no earthly way he should be, Bay felt the vampire's physical appeal slam into her like a fist.

They're all beautiful. You're used to it, she told herself, furious at the way her heartbeat quickened. And a treacherous little voice in the back of her mind responded, *They may all be beautiful . . . but not like this.*

Those remarkable eyes, deep-set and almond shaped, watched her steadily from beneath a pair of dark, slashing brows. His nose was strong, his lips tantalizingly full, and his square jaw was covered in a light growth of stubble. The vampire's hair, wavy and black as sin, was cut short enough not to fall into his eyes but long enough to tousle, and Bay had to tear her eyes away when her fingers curled reflexively into her palm, itching to run her fingers through it, over every inch of this stranger's tanned and gold-dusted skin.

It was Grimm's soft growl that finally sliced through her haze. She blinked rapidly and shook her head, making sure not to meet the vampire's eyes again. Lily had been very clear about how to protect herself from the less well-behaved members of the species, and Bay was glad for it. Poor Shelby was going to be in her own little world until this guy left, and then, Bay knew, the girl wouldn't remember any of this. A heavy thrall could really do a number on a person.

She didn't want her own brain messed with to boot.

Finally, he spoke. "You're close friends with the ruler of the Lilim, aren't you?" he asked. "Lily MacGillivray. And you're Bailey Harper. This is the information I was given."

"Given by who?" Bay asked, fighting back the fresh sliver of fear working its way down her spine. He'd said he had no intention of hurting them, but still . . . vampires didn't come looking for her. Especially not daywalking vampires with wild eyes and problems staying conscious.

He moved to pick up a pair of sunglasses on the floor, and she was struck again by his natural grace. It shouldn't have surprised her. The majority of the vampires now in Tipton had started as Cait Sith, cat-shifters, before joining Lily's dynasty. The lot of them had grace and beauty in spades. But there was something different here, something more. And she hated herself a little as her eyes crawled over the lithe, muscular frame that even his light jacket and loose jeans couldn't disguise.

Bay gritted her teeth and inhaled, trying to center herself.

The vampire slid his sunglasses on. It was a small

relief, but she'd take it, even though knowing he was watching her from behind them was still unnerving. He regarded her silently for a moment, studying her so intently that Bay felt a hot flush creeping into her cheeks. Finally, he spoke, and managed to surprise her.

"I...apologize," he said, his brows drawing together slightly as he looked down at the mess he'd made by falling. "We'll start over. My name is Tasmin Singh. I can walk in the light because it is a gift of my line. And I'm looking for your friend because..." He trailed off for a moment, then looked away. "It is a long story."

"Something to do with you passing out in the middle of my store?" Bay asked.

His features tightened for an instant before his expression cleared again. "Perhaps. I slept far longer than is natural, and I still seem to be...adjusting. That should pass in time. I came here because I seek answers. The Queen of the Lilim will know those who can find them. Of this I am certain."

Bay's eyebrows rose at the cryptic response. There was something *off* about him, something she couldn't put her finger on that went beyond the obvious weirdness. Sadly, it didn't make him any less fascinating to her.

"Okay," she said, drawing the word out. "Well, Tasmin, you, um, would have done better just waiting until nightfall and knocking on Lily's door. Whoever told you where to find me could have told you where to find her." She tilted her head at him. "Why *didn't* you just go there? You can see I'm no vamp. I'm just a dog groomer."

She thought she caught the faintest hint of a smile, if only for a moment. It turned his lips soft, sultry, and she felt a knot of pleasure coil deep in her belly.

No. No no no. She liked things that were quirky, odd, and even weird. Things. Not guys. Because every time she was drawn to one of those qualities in a guy, it ended up biting her in the ass. And this particular guy looked about as safe as a wounded tiger.

"I see. You've attracted quite a noble beast as a guardian."

She stroked her hand over Grimm's back, unsure if Tasmin was giving her a compliment or just being sarcastic. Grimm leaned into her harder and growled at the vampire again. The sound was soft, but it was a clear warning.

"He is noble," Bay said flatly. "More than most people manage to be. And he's an excellent judge of character."

Tasmin inclined his head slightly, any trace of a smile gone. "Of that I have no doubt. Beasts often are. That he has chosen you speaks well of you."

She blinked. "Oh. I…thanks." She tried to shrug off the pleasure she felt at the simple praise. It didn't matter what this strange, gorgeous vampire thought of her.

"That still doesn't explain why you came in here."

"The sun is still high. I had some time. And I wondered what sort of mortal would be considered such a friend to a powerful queen. I'm still not sure whether your relationship means I should expect to find her wise or a reckless fool." He considered her. "In any case, you're not what I expected."

Bay's eyes narrowed. She knew she was considered a curiosity among the vampires here, a mortal with no apparent interest in anything Lily could offer her except friendship. But she didn't appreciate being gawked at like a sideshow freak by some outsider.

"Well," she said stiffly, "what you see is what you get. I'm not that interesting. Now if you don't mind, I've got some things to do before I close up for the day, and I need my help back."

She turned her head to look at Shelby, who was thumbing idly through a magazine, a dreamy expression on her face. It unsettled her to see that the thrall was still so deep.

"Shouldn't that have worn off by now?" Bay asked.

"It will wear off when I decide it does."

Bay looked sharply at him. "That's not how it works."

"It is how *I* work."

The matter-of-fact arrogance in his statement finally sparked her temper. She pushed aside any lingering fear and walked quickly around Grimm, striding right up to Tasmin. Despite the sunglasses, she saw his surprise and had to fight back a thin smile. No doubt he'd expected the puny mortal to cower and grovel. But that wasn't how *she* worked.

Bay came to a stop only a foot away from him and glared up into his impassive face. Being so close, and this time with him aware and looking down at her, left her momentarily off-balance. He was just the right height—maybe five-ten—to fit herself against, tall enough to wind herself around, short enough to reach if she rose up on her toes to press her mouth to his . . .

The scent of him was stronger now, intoxicating. And fending off another hot punch of desire only made her angrier. She never let men make her uncomfortable. It was a point of pride with her. So why couldn't she find her footing with this one?

"Listen," she snapped, "I don't know what you are or what's wrong with you, but if you want to find out what the Lilim are like, I suggest you head in that direction. I'm sure you'll get an answer to your questions one way or another . . . if you can make it through the wolves to ask. Now if you'll excuse me, I've got better things to do than satisfy your curiosity."

She started to turn and felt his hand clamp on her wrist, not hard, but with a controlled strength that she knew could shatter bones if he wanted. Her fury was a dull roar in her ears as she whipped her head around.

"What—"

But the words died in her throat at his expression, the lips pulled back to reveal gleaming fangs. It was the snarl of a creature not remotely human, a killer. And the voice that came from his throat was nothing like the sensual purr of before.

"You dare chastise me, human?" The words sounded like they'd been dragged through gravel and oil, oozing up from deep in his chest.

Then he cried out, his head snapping back, his body arching as though an electric current had just passed through his body. The sunglasses clattered to the floor again, and Grimm barked just behind her, though it sounded oddly far off. Tasmin's eyes met hers again, and the amount of pain and fear she saw in that instant left her reeling. His hand tightened on her wrist before going lax.

"Help me," he breathed.

She just managed to get her arms around him to break his fall, sinking slowly to the floor with Tasmin in her arms. Whatever this man needed, she knew, it was more than just answers.

But right this second he needed help. He needed *her.*

Even though she cursed herself for it, even though

she'd declared vampire problems off-limits to herself, Bay knew she was in big trouble. Her compassion had always been as much her strength as it had been her Achilles heel.

And this time, whichever it turned out to be, she wasn't going to be able to just walk away.

THE DISH

Where authors give you the inside scoop!

♥ ♥ ♥ ♥ ♥ ♥ ♥ ♥ ♥ ♥ ♥ ♥ ♥ ♥ ♥ ♥ ♥ ♥ ♥

From the desk of Kendra Leigh Castle

Dear Reader,

I admit it: I love a bad boy.

From the Sheriff of Nottingham to Severus Snape, Spike to Jack Sparrow, it's always the men who seem beyond saving that throw my imagination into overdrive. So it's no wonder that this sort of character arrived in my very first Dark Dynasties book and has stuck around since, despite the fact that most of the other characters either (a)wonder why he hasn't been killed or (b)would like to kill him themselves. Or both, depending on the day. His name is Damien Tremaine. He's a vampire, thief, assassin, and as deadly as they come. In fact, he spent much of *Dark Awakening* trying to kill the hero and heroine. He positively revels in the fact that he has few redeeming qualities. And I just. Couldn't. Resist.

Writing SHADOW RISING, the third installment in the Dark Dynasties series, proved an interesting challenge. The true bad boy takes a special kind of woman to turn him around, and I knew it would take a lot to pierce the substantial (and very stylish) armor that Damien had built up over the centuries. Enter Ariane, a vampire who is formidable in her own right but really remarkable because of her innocence, despite being hundreds of years old. As a member of the reclusive and mysterious Grigori dynasty, Ariane remembers nothing of her life before being turned. All she knows is the hidden desert compound of her kind, a place she has never been allowed to leave. She's long been restless...but when her closest friend goes missing and she's forbidden to search for him, Ariane takes matters into her own untried but very capable hands. Little does she know that her dynasty's leader has hired an outside vampire who specializes in finding those who don't want to be found—and that once she crosses paths with him, he'll make very sure that their paths keep crossing, whether she likes it or not.

All of the couples I write about have their differences, but Damien and Ariane are polar opposites. She's sheltered, he's jaded. She longs to feel everything, while Damien's spent years burying every emotion. And she is, of course, exactly what he needs, which is the first thing to have actually frightened Damien in...well, ever. Damien's slow and terrifying realization that he's finally in over his head was both a lot of fun to write, and exactly what he deserved. After all, redemption is satisfying, but it's not supposed to be *easy*.

Between Damien's sharp tongue and sharper killer instincts, Ariane has her hands full from the get-go. Fortunately, she finds him just as irresistible as I do. Like so many dark and delicious bad boys, there's more to Damien than meets the eye. If you're interested in finding out whether this particular assassin has the heart of a hero, I hope you'll check out SHADOW RISING. I'll be honest: Damien never really turns into a traditional knight in shining armor. But if you're anything like me...you won't want him to anyway.

Enjoy!

Kendra Leigh Castle

Kendra Leigh Castle

♥ ♥ ♥ ♥ ♥ ♥ ♥ ♥ ♥ ♥ ♥ ♥ ♥ ♥ ♥

From the desk of Jennifer Haymore

Dear Reader,

When Meg Donovan, the heroine of PLEASURES OF A TEMPTED LADY (on sale now), entered my office for the first time, I mistook her for her twin sister, Serena.

"Serena!" I exclaimed. "How are you? Please, take a seat."

She slowly shook her head. "Not Serena," she said quietly. "Meg."

I stared at her. I couldn't do anything else, because my throat had closed up tight. For, dear reader, Meg was dead! Lost at sea and long gone, and I'd written two complete novels and a novella under that assumption.

Finally, I found my scrambled wits and gathered them tight around me.

"Um," I said hopefully, "Serena…that's not a funny joke. My income relies on my journalistic credibility. You know that, right?"

She just looked at me. Then she shrugged. "Sorry. I am Meg Donovan. And though the world might like to pretend that I am Serena, I know who I am."

"But...but...you're dead." Now I sounded like a petulant child. A rather warped and quite possibly disturbed petulant child.

She finally took the seat I'd offered Serena, and, settling in, she leaned forward. "No, Mrs. Haymore. I'm not dead. I'm very much alive, and I'd like you to write my story."

Oh, Lord.

I looked down to rub the bridge of my nose between my thumb and forefinger, fighting off a sudden headache. If this really was Meg, I was in big, big trouble.

Finally I looked up at her. "All right," I said slowly. "So you're Meg. Back from the dead."

"That's correct," she said.

I studied her closely. Her twin Serena and I have become good friends since I wrote her story for her, and now that I really looked at this woman, the subtle differences between her and her twin grew clearer. This woman was about ten pounds thinner than Serena. And though her eyes were the same shade of blue, something about them seemed harder and wary, as though she'd gone through a difficult time and come out of it barely intact.

"So who was it that rescued you, then?" I asked. "Pirates? Slavers?"

Her expression grew tight. Shuttered. "I'd like to skip that part, if you don't mind."

I raised a brow. This wasn't going to work out between us if she demanded I skip all the good stuff. But I'd play along. For now. "All right, then. Where would you like to start?"

"With my escape."

"Ah, so it *was* pirates, then."

She gave a firm shake of her head. "No. I meant my escape from England."

"That doesn't make sense," I said. "You'll be wanting to stay in England. Your family is there." I didn't say it, but I was pretty sure the man who loved her was there, too.

"I can't stay in England. You must help me."

I clasped my hands on top of my desk. "Look, Meg. I really like your family, so I'm sitting here listening to what you have to say. But I'm a writer who writes happy, satisfying stories about finding true love and living happily ever after. Is that what you're looking for?"

"No!"

I sighed. I'd thought not.

She leaned forward again, her palms flat on the desk. "I need you to write me out of England, because I need to protect my family, and..."

"And...?" I prompted when she looked away, seemingly unwilling to continue.

"And...Captain Langley. You see, as long as I stay in England, they're all in danger."

I fought the twitch that my lips wanted to make to form a smile. So she did know about Captain William Langley...and she obviously cared for him. Whatever danger she was worried about facing meant nothing in the face of the depth of love that might someday belong to William Langley and Meg Donovan.

"I see." I looked into her eyes. "I might be able to make an exception this time. I will do whatever I can to help you protect your family."

Note that I didn't tell her I'd help her to escape. Or to get out of England.

A frantic, wonderful plan was forming rapidly in my mind. Yeah, I'd write her story. I'd "help" her keep Langley and her family safe. But once I did that, once I gained her trust, I'd find a way to make them happy, to boot. Because I'm a romance writer, and that's what I do.

"Thank you," she murmured, glassy tears forming in her eyes. "Thank you so much."

I raised a warning finger. "Realize that in order for this to work, you need to tell me everything."

She hesitated, her lips pressed hard together. Then she finally nodded.

I flipped up my laptop and opened a new document. "Tell me your story, Miss Donovan. From the moment of your rescue."

And that was how I began to write the love story of Meg Donovan, the long-lost Donovan sister.

I truly hope you enjoy reading Meg's story! Please come visit me at my website, www.jenniferhaymore.com, where you can share your thoughts about my books, sign up for some fun freebies and contests, and read more about the characters from PLEASURES OF A TEMPTED LADY.

Sincerely,

Jennifer Haymore

♥ ♥ ♥ ♥ ♥ ♥ ♥ ♥ ♥ ♥ ♥ ♥ ♥ ♥ ♥

From the desk of Jill Shalvis

Dear Reader,

Ever feel like you're drowning? In FOREVER AND A DAY, my hero, Dr. Josh Scott, is most definitely drowning. He's overloaded, overworked, and on the edge of burnout. He's got his practice, his young son, his wheelchair-bound sister, and a crazy puppy. Not to mention the weight of the world on his shoulders from taking care of everyone in his life. He's in so deep, saving everyone around him all the time, that he doesn't even realize that *he's* the one in need of saving. It would never occur to him.

Enter Grace Brooks. She's a smart smartass and, thanks to some bad luck, pretty much starting her life over from scratch. Losing everything has landed her in Lucky Harbor working as Josh's dog walker. And then as his nanny. And then before he even realizes it, as his everything. In truth, she's saved him, in more ways than one.

Oh, how I loved watching the sure, steady rock that is Josh crumble, only to be slowly but surely helped back together again by the sexy yet sweet Grace.

And don't forget to pick up the other "Chocaholic" books, *Lucky in Love* and *At Last*, both available wherever books and ebooks are sold.

Happy Reading!

Jill Shalvis

Jill Shalvis

♥ ♥ ♥ ♥ ♥ ♥ ♥ ♥ ♥ ♥ ♥ ♥ ♥ ♥ ♥

From the desk of Kristen Callihan

Dear Reader,

I'm half Norwegian—on my mother's side. If there is one thing you need to know about Norwegians, it's that they are very egalitarian. This sense of equality defines them in a number of ways, but one of the more interesting aspects is that Norwegian men treat women as equal partners.

Take my grandfather. He was a man's man in the truest sense of the term. A rugged fisherman and farmer who hung out with the fellas, rebuilt old cars, smoked a pipe, and made furniture on the side. Yet he always picked up his own plate after dinner. He never hesitated to go to the market if my grandmother needed something, nor did he complain if he had to cook his own meals when she was busy. My grandfather was one of the most admirable men I've known. Thus when I began to write about heroes, I gravitated toward men who share some of the same qualities as my Norwegian ancestors.

Ian Ranulf, the hero of MOONGLOW, started out as a bit of an unsavory character in *Firelight*. All right, he was a total ass, doing everything he could to keep Miranda and Archer apart. So much so that, early on, my editor once asked me if I was sure Ian wasn't the real villain. While Ian did not act on his best behavior, I always knew that he was not a bad man. In fact, I rather liked him. Why? Because Ian loves and respects women in a way that not many of his peers do. While he feels inclined to protect a woman from physical harm, he'd never patronize her. For that, I could forgive a lot of him.

In MOONGLOW, Ian is a man living a half-life. He has sunk into apathy because life has not been particularly kind to him. And so he's done what most people do: He's retreated into a protective shell. Yet when he meets Daisy, a woman who will not be ignored, he finds himself wanting to live for her. But what I found interesting about Ian is that when he begins to fall for Daisy, he does not think, "No, I've been burned before; I'm not going to try again." Ian does the opposite: He reaches for what he wants, even if it terrifies him, even with a high possibility of failure.

While Ian certainly faces his share of physical battles in MOONGLOW, it is his dogged pursuit of happiness and his willingness to love Daisy as an equal that made him one of my favorite characters to write.

Happy Reading,

Kristen Callihan